编 委 会

当代科学技术基础理论与前沿问题研究丛书

中国科学技术大学
校友文库

Micro-scale
Plasticity Mechanics

微尺度塑性力学

By

Shaohua Chen

Tzuchiang Wang

编著

陈少华 王自强

University of Science and
Technology of China Press

中国科学技术大学出版社

内 容 简 介

本书系统地介绍了材料微尺度力学行为的尺寸效应实验现象,重点介绍了几种具有代表性的微尺度应变梯度塑性理论及对微尺度实验现象的解释,以及对裂纹尖端微尺度范围内解理断裂的应用。此外,还融会贯通地介绍了国内外学者的原创性工作和创新性学术思想。

全书共8章。第1章介绍了应变梯度塑性理论的应用背景及经典微极理论;第2章介绍了金属材料典型的微尺度力学实验现象;第3至7章介绍了几种典型的应变梯度理论及其应用;第8章介绍了应变梯度理论在微观断裂力学中的应用。

本书适合从事固体微尺度力学、先进材料的微结构设计与力学性能优化、微机电和微电子元件力学行为研究的科技工作者及工程师使用和参考,也可供力学专业及材料专业的高年级本科生和研究生阅读参考。

Micro-scale Plasticity Mechanics

Shaohua Chen & Tzuchiang Wang

Copyright © 2009 University of Science and Technology of China Press

All rights reserved.

Published by University of Science and Technology of China Press

96 Jinzhai Road, Hefei 230026, P. R. China

图书在版编目(CIP)数据

微尺度塑性力学 = Micro-scale Plasticity Mechanics：英文/陈少华,王自强编著. 一合肥：中国科学技术大学出版社,2009.4

(当代科学技术基础理论与前沿问题研究丛书：中国科学技术大学校友文库)

"十一五"国家重点图书

ISBN 978 - 7 - 312 - 02268 - 5

Ⅰ.微… Ⅱ.①陈…②王… Ⅲ.塑性力学—英文 Ⅳ.O344

中国版本图书馆 CIP 数据核字(2009)第 046780 号

中国科学技术大学出版社出版发行

地址：安徽省合肥市金寨路 96 号,230026

网址：http://press.ustc.edu.cn

合肥晓星印刷有限责任公司印刷

全国新华书店经销

开本：710×1000 1/16 印张：18.25 字数：290 千

2009 年 5 月第 1 版 2009 年 5 月第 1 次印刷

印数：1—1 500 册

定价：58.00 元

总　序

侯建国

（中国科学技术大学校长、中国科学院院士、第三世界科学院院士）

　　大学最重要的功能是向社会输送人才。大学对于一个国家、民族乃至世界的重要性和贡献度，很大程度上是通过毕业生在社会各领域所取得的成就来体现的。

　　中国科学技术大学建校只有短短的 50 年，之所以迅速成为享有较高国际声誉的著名大学之一，主要就是因为她培养出了一大批德才兼备的优秀毕业生。他们志向高远、基础扎实、综合素质高、创新能力强，在国内外科技、经济、教育等领域做出了杰出的贡献，为中国科大赢得了"科技英才的摇篮"的美誉。

　　2008 年 9 月，胡锦涛总书记为中国科大建校五十周年发来贺信，信中称赞说：半个世纪以来，中国科学技术大学依托中国科学院，按照全院办校、所系结合的方针，弘扬红专并进、理实交融的校风，努力推进教学和科研工作的改革创新，为党和国家培养了一大批科技人才，取得了一系列具有世界先进水平的原创性科技成果，为推动我国科教事业发展和社会主义现代化建设做出了重要贡献。

　　据统计，中国科大迄今已毕业的 5 万人中，已有 42 人当选中国科学院和中国工程院院士，是同期（自 1963 年以来）毕业生中当选院士数最多的高校之一。其中，本科毕业生中平均每 1,000 人就产生 1 名院士和 700 多名硕士、博士，比例位居全国高校之首。还有众多的中青年才俊成为我国科技、企业、教育等领域的领军人物和骨干。在历年评选的"中国青年五四奖章"获得者中，作为科技界、科技创新型企业界青年才俊代表，科大毕业生已连续多年榜上有名，获奖总人数位居全国高校前列。鲜为人知的是，有数千名优秀毕业生踏上国防战线，为科技强军做出了重要贡献,涌现出 20 多名科技将军和一大批国防科技中坚。

为反映中国科大五十年来人才培养成果,展示毕业生在科学研究中的最新进展,学校决定在建校五十周年之际,编辑出版《中国科学技术大学校友文库》,于 2008 年 9 月起陆续出书,校庆年内集中出版 50 种。该《文库》选题经过多轮严格的评审和论证,入选书稿学术水平高,已列为国家"十一五"重点图书出版规划。

入选作者中,有北京初创时期的毕业生,也有意气风发的少年班毕业生;有"两院"院士,也有 IEEE Fellow;有海内外科研院所、大专院校的教授,也有金融、IT 行业的英才;有默默奉献、矢志报国的科技将军,也有在国际前沿奋力拼搏的科研将才;有"文革"后留美学者中第一位担任美国大学系主任的青年教授,也有首批获得新中国博士学位的中年学者;……在母校五十周年华诞之际,他们通过著书立说的独特方式,向母校献礼,其深情厚意,令人感佩!

近年来,学校组织了一系列关于中国科大办学成就、经验、理念和优良传统的总结与讨论。通过总结与讨论,使我们更清醒地认识到,中国科大这所新中国亲手创办的新型理工科大学所肩负的历史使命和责任。我想,中国科大的创办与发展,首要的目标就是围绕国家战略需求,培养造就世界一流科学家和科技领军人才。五十年来,我们一直遵循这一目标定位,有效地探索了科教紧密结合、培养创新人才的成功之路,取得了令人瞩目的成就,也受到社会各界的广泛赞誉。

成绩属于过去,辉煌须待开创。在未来的发展中,我们依然要牢牢把握"育人是大学第一要务"的宗旨,在坚守优良传统的基础上,不断改革创新,提高教育教学质量,早日实现胡锦涛总书记对中国科大的期待:瞄准世界科技前沿,服务国家发展战略,创造性地做好教学和科研工作,努力办成世界一流的研究型大学,培养造就更多更好的创新人才,为夺取全面建设小康社会新胜利、开创中国特色社会主义事业新局面贡献更大力量。

是为序。

2008 年 9 月

Preface

Micro-scale plasticity mechanics was developed in 1990s due to the developments in micro-design, micro-manufacturing and microelectronic packaging. It is a new field that attracts many researchers' interests in the world.

Many experiments have found that materials display strong size effects when the characteristic length scale associated with non-uniform plastic deformation is on the order of microns. The classical plasticity theories can not predict the size effects of material behavior at the micron scale since there is no length scales including in their constitutive relations. Apparently, some microscopic understanding of plasticity is necessary in order to accurately describe deformation at small scales. These considerations have motivated Fleck and Hutchinson to develop a phenomenological theory of strain gradient plasticity intended for applications to materials and structures whose dimension controlling plastic deformation falls roughly within a range from a tenth of a micron to ten microns. After that, a lot of scholars make further contributions to this area with the considerations to propose theories with more clearly physical backgrounds and more simple frameworks.

In this book, we introduce the experimental backgrounds of the micro-scale mechanics with the help of many typical micro-scale experiments. After that, we systematically introduce several typical micro-scale plasticity theories and their applications in explaining the experimental results. Lastly, micro-scale plasticity theories are applied in the fracture mechanics field to explain the cleavage fracture in the scope of micro-meters near the crack tip. This book includes not only the achievements of many foreign scholars, but also those of the authors themselves.

Many scientists in China contribute to this area, such as Prof. K. C. Hwang of Tsinghua University, Prof. G. K. Hu of Beijing Institute of Technology, etc. Due to the limitations of the length of this book, we did not focus on their achievements. The readers can consult them face to face if it is necessary.

Chapters 1～5 and 8 are written by Shaohua Chen; Chapters 6～7 are written by Tzuchiang Wang.

SC would give his gratitude to his wife, Miss Wen-Ling, for her collections and scanning of the electronic photos in Chapters 1～5 and 8.

The work of the two authors is supported by NSFC.

Shaohua Chen & Tzuchiang Wang

March 29, 2009 in Beijing

Contents

1 Introduction

1.1 Brief introduction of experimental observations

Many experiments have found that materials display strong size effects when the characteristic length scale associated with non-uniform plastic deformation is on the order of microns. For example, Fleck et al. (1994) did torsion experiments of thin copper wires with different micrometer diameters and found that the non-dimensional torque increases by a factor of 3 as the wire diameter decreases from 170 to 12 microns, while no increase of work-hardening in simple tension is observed. In ultra thin beams bending experiments, Stolken and Evans (1998) observed a significant increase in the non-dimensional bending hardening moments when the beam thickness decreases from 100 to 12.5 microns, while the results for simple tension experiments display no size effects. For an aluminum-silicon matrix reinforced by silicon carbide particles, Lloyd (1994) observed that the flow strength increases when the particle diameter was reduced from 16 to 7.5 microns with the volume fraction of particles fixed at 15%. More convincing experimental evidence of the size dependence of material behavior at the micro level is from the micro or nano-indentation hardness tests. The measured indentation hardness of metallic materials increases by a factor of two when the depth of indentation decreases from 10 microns to 1 micron (Nix, 1989; Stelmeshenko et al. , 1993; Ma and Clarke, 1995; Poole et al. , 1996; McElhaney et al. , 1998).

The classical plasticity theories can not predict the size effects of material behavior at the micron scale since there is no length scales including in their constitutive relations. The predictions based on the classical plasticity theories for non-uniform deformation do not show a size effect after normalization. However, there is an impending need to deal with design and manufacturing issues at the micron level, such as in thin films whose thickness is on the order of 1 micron or less, actuators and micro-electro-mechanical systems (MEMS) where the entire system size is less than 10 microns; microelectronic packaging where features are smaller than 10 microns; advanced composites where particle or fiber size is on the order of 10 microns; as well as in micromachining. The current design tools, such as finite element method (FEM) and computer aided design (CAD), are based on classical continuum theories, which may not be suitable at such a small length scale. On the other hand, it is still not possible to perform quantum and atomistic simulations on realistic time and length scales required for the micro level structures. A continuum theory for micro level applications is thus needed to bridge the gap between conventional continuum theories and atomistic simulations.

Another objective that needs the development of a micron level continuum theory is to link macroscopic fracture behavior to atomistic fracture processes in ductile materials. In a remarkable series of experiments, Elssner et al. (1994) measured both the macroscopic fracture toughness and atomic work of separation of an interface between a single crystal of niobium and a sapphire single crystal. The macroscopic work of fracture was measured using a four-point bend specimen designed for the determination of interfacial toughness, while the atomic value was inferred from the equilibrium shapes of microscopic pores on the interface. The interface between the two materials remained atomistically sharp, i.e., the crack tip was not blunted even though niobium is ductile and has a large number of dislocations. The stress level needed to produce atomic decohesion of a lattice or a strong interface is typically on the order of 0.03 times Young's modulus, or 10 times the tensile yield stress. Hutchinson (1997) pointed out that the maximum stress level that can be achieved near a crack tip is not larger than 4 or 5 times the tensile yield stress of metals, according to models based on conventional plasticity theories. This clearly falls short of triggering the atomic decohesion observed in Elssner et al.'s (1994) experiments. Attempts to link macroscopic cracking to atomic fracture are frustrated by the inability of conventional plasticity theories to model stress-strain behavior adequately at the small scales involved in crack tip deformation.

Apparently, some microscopic understanding of plasticity is necessary in order to accurately describe deformation at small scales.

1.2　An overview of strain gradient plasticity theory

When a material is deformed, dislocations are generated, moved, and stored, and the storage causes the material to work harden. Dislocations become stored for one of two reasons: they accumulate by trapping each other in a random way, or they are required for compatible deformation of various parts of the material. In the former case the dislocations are referred to as statistically stored dislocations (Ashby, 1970), while in the latter case they are called geometrically necessary dislocations and are related to the gradients of plastic shear in a material

(Nye, 1953; Cottrell, 1964; Ashby, 1970). Plastic strain gradients appear either because of the geometry of loading or because of inhomogeneous deformation in the material, as in the aforementioned experiments. As examples: in the plastic twisting of a cylinder or bending of a beam, the strain is finite at the surface but zero along the axis of twist or of bending (Figures 1.1(a) and 1.1(b)); in the hardness test the strain is large immediately beneath the indenter but zero far from it; and in the plastic zone at the tip of a crack in an otherwise elastic medium steep gradients of plastic strain appear (Figures 1.1(c) and 1.1(d)); in the deformation of plastic crystals containing hard, non-deforming particles, local strain gradients are generated between particles; and in the plastic deformation of polycrystals, the mismatch of slip at the boundaries of the grains can induce gradients of plastic strain there (Figures 1.1(e) and 1.1(f)).

These considerations have motivated Fleck and Hutchinson (1993, 1997) and Fleck et al. (1994) to develop a phenomenological theory of strain gradient plasticity intended for applications to materials and structures whose dimension controlling plastic deformation falls roughly within a range from a tenth of a micron to ten microns. This theory has been applied to many problems where strain gradient effects are expected to be important, including analyses of crack tip fields (Huang et al., 1995, 1997; Xia and Hutchinson, 1996). The Fleck-Hutchinson theory fits the mathematical framework of higher order continuum theories of elasticity (Toupin, 1962; Koiter, 1964; Mindlin, 1963, 1964), with the strain gradients represented either in terms of the gradients of rotation in the couple-stress theory of strain gradient plasticity (Fleck and Hutchinson, 1993; Fleck et al., 1994) or in terms of both rotation and stretch gradients in a more general isotropic-hardening theory based on all the quadratic invariants of the strain gradient tensor (Fleck and Hutchinson, 1997). The couple stress theory used by Fleck and Hutchinson (1993) also bears some resemblance to the early work of

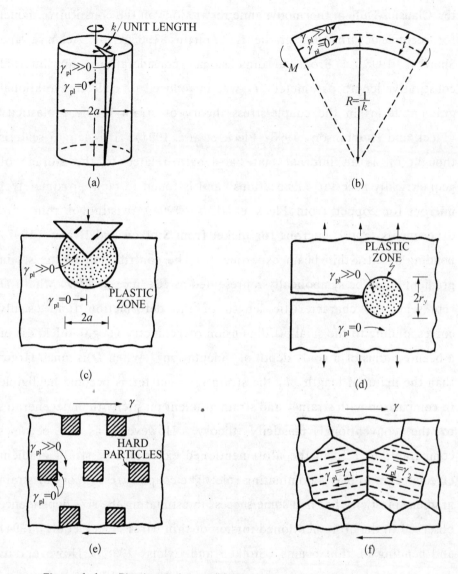

Figure 1.1   Plastic strain gradient are caused by the geometry of deformation (a, b), by local boundary conditions (c, d) or by the microstructure itself (e, f). (Fleck et al., 1994)

Kroener (1962) who studied the connection between lattice curvature associated with dislocations and couple stresses and developed a non-local continuum theory based on that connection. The work-conjugate of the rotation and/or stretch gradient of deformation defines the higher order stress which is required for this class of strain gradient theory to satisfy the Clausius-Duhem thermodynamic restrictions on the constitutive model for second deformation gradients (Gurtin, 1965a, b; Acharya and Shawki, 1995). From a dimensional consideration, an internal constitutive length parameter, l, was introduced to scale the rotational gradient terms in the couple-stress theory of strain gradient plasticity (Fleck and Hutchinson, 1993; Fleck et al. , 1994). This length scale is thought of as an internal material length related to the storage of geometrically necessary dislocations, and is found to be approximately 4 microns for copper from Fleck et al. 's (1994) twisting of thin wire experiments, and 6 microns for nickel from Stolken and Evans' (1997) bending of ultra-thin beam experiments. The contribution of the strain gradient could be symbolically represented as $l\mathrm{d}\varepsilon/\mathrm{d}x \sim \varepsilon(l/D)$ where D represents the characteristic length of the deformation field usually corresponding to the smallest dimension of geometry (e. g. , thickness of a beam, radius of a void, depth of indentation). When D is much larger than the material length, l, the strain gradient terms become negligible in comparison with strains, and strain gradient plasticity then degenerates to the conventional plasticity theory. However, as D becomes comparable to l as in the aforementioned experiments, strain gradient effects begin to play a dominating role. The couple-stress theory of strain gradient plasticity has had some success in estimating the size dependence observed in the aforementioned torsion of thin wires (Fleck et al. , 1994) and bending of thin beams (Stolken and Evans, 1998). However, its prediction of indentation hardness (Shu and Fleck, 1998) falls short of agreement with the significant increase of 200% or even 300% observed in micro-indentation or nano-indentation tests (Nix, 1989; De Huzman et al. , 1993; Stelmashenko et al. , 1993; Ma and Clarke, 1995; Poole et al. , 1996; McElhaney et al., 1998). For this reason, Fleck and Hutchinson (1997) proposed an extended theory of strain gradient plasticity theory which includes both rotation gradient and stretch gradient of the deformation in the constitutive model. The work-conjugates of rotation and stretch gradients of deformation are couple stress and higher order stress, respectively. Accordingly, two more internal material lengths are introduced in addition to l.

Fleck and Hutchinson (1993, 1997) used the dislocation theory to motivate their formulation of strain gradient plasticity. However, the actual theory was formulated by replacing effective stresses and strains in conventional plasticity with higher order effective stresses and strains which contain strain gradient terms scaled by a phenomenological material length to be determined from experiments. In other words, the Fleck-Hutchinson theory is developed primarily based on the macroscopically measured uniaxial stress-strain behavior. Micromechanical experiments such as micro-indentation, micro-torsion and micro-bending were not used at the stage of theory construction, but rather were used to fit the material length l. The remarkable agreement between the strain gradient law proposed by Nix and Gao (1998) and the micro-indentation data for various materials indicates that the linear relation between the square of indentation hardness and the inverse of indent depth represents a fundamental, intrinsic nature of deformation at the microscale. This provides a strong motivation to develop an alterative formulation in which the strain gradient law in Nix and Gao (1998) is incorporated as a fundamental postulate. Gao et al. (1999) proposed a multiscale, hierarchical framework to facilitate such a marriage between plasticity and dislocation theory. A mesoscale cell with linear variation of strain field is considered. Each point within the cell is considered as a microscale sub-cell within which dislocation interaction is assumed to (approximately) obey the Taylor relation so that the strain gradient law proposed by Nix and Gao (1998) applies. On the microscale, the effective strain gradient η is to be treated as a measure of the density of geometrically necessary dislocations whose accumulation increases the flow stress strictly following the Taylor model. In the other words, microscale plastic law is assumed to occur as slip of statistically stored dislocation in a background of geometrically necessary dislocations and the microscale plastic deformation is assumed to obey the Taylor work hardening relation and the associative law of conventional plasticity. The notion of geometrically necessary dislocation is connected to the gradient of the strain field on the level of the mesoscale cell. Higher order stresses are introduced as thermodynamic conjugates of the strain gradients at the mesoscale level on which the plasticity theory is formulated. This ensures that the theory obeys the Clausius-Duhem thermodynamic restrictions of a continuum constitutive model. This hierarchical structure provided a systematic approach for constructing the mesoscale constitutive law by averaging microscale plasticity laws over the representative cell. This theory differs from the other phenomenological theories in its mechanism-based guiding principles, although it fits nicely within the mathematical frame of the phenomenological theory by Fleck and Hutchinson (1997).

In comparison, no work conjugates of strain gradients have been defined in alternative gradient theories (Aifantis, 1984; Zbib and Aifantis, 1989; Muhlhaus and Aifantis, 1991) which represent the strain gradient effects as the first and second Laplacian of effective strain. Acharya and Bassani (1995) have considered possible formulations of strain gradient plasticity which retains the essential structures of conventional plasticity and obeys thermodynamic restrictions; they conclude that the only possible formulation is a flow theory with strain gradient effects represented as an internal variable which acts to increase the current tangent-hardening modulus. However, there has not been a systematic way of constructing the tangent modulus so as to validate this framework. Chen and Wang (2000) proposed a detail method to increase the tangential-hardening modulus using the strain gradient terms according to Acharya and Bassani (1995). Then Chen and Wang (2001, 2002) proposed a new strain gradient theory. In contrast to the existing strain gradient theories, it preserves the essential structure of the incremental version of conventional couple stress deformation theory and no extra boundary value conditions beyond the conventional ones, are required. No higher-order stress or higher-order strain rates are introduced either. The key features of the new theory are that the rotation gradient influences the material character through the interaction between the Cauchy stresses and the couple stresses; the stretch gradient measures explicitly enter the constitutive relations only through the instantaneous tangent modulus and the boundary value problem of incremental equilibrium is the same as that in the conventional theories. The tangent hardening modulus is influenced by not only the generalized effective strain but also the effective stretch gradient.

In 2004, Huang et al. thought that the MSG plasticity theory is a higher-order continuum theory that involves higher order governing equations and requires additional boundary conditions. It is therefore more complex than conventional plasticity theories, and the finite element method (FEM) for the higher-order continuum theory is also more complex than the standard FEM (Shu and Fleck, 1999; Huang et al., 2000). Shi et al. (2001) recently used the singular perturbation method to investigate a solid subject to a constant body force, and showed that the effect of higher-order stress is significant only within a thin layer near the boundary of the material. The thickness of boundary layer is on the order of 10 nm, which is much smaller than the characteristic length scale (e.g., microns) the strain gradient plasticity theories are intended for. Therefore, for material properties that represent an average over the micron scale and above, such as the micro-indentation hardness, the higher-order stress has little or essentially no effect (Huang et al., 2000; Saha et al., 2001). However, it is important to separate the effect of higher-order stress from the strain gradient effect; the former is within a thin boundary layer (thickness on the order of 10 nm) and the latter comes from the Taylor dislocation model and is important at the micron scale. Since the effect of higher-order stress is negligible away from the thin boundary layer, is it possible to develop a strain gradient plasticity theory based on the dislocation model to incorporate the strain gradient effect without the higher-order stress? The governing equations in such a theory (Huang et al., 2004) are essentially the same as the conventional plasticity theories, and therefore require no additional boundary conditions. Its difference with the corresponding higher-order MSG plasticity theory is significant only within the thin boundary layer.

Many other researchers have contributed substantially to the gradient plasticity theory also, such as Aifantis (1984), Naghdi and Srinivasa (1993), Shizawa and Zbib (1999), Hwang et al. (2003), Liu and Hu (2005), Xun et al. (2004) Abu Al-Rub and Voyiadjis (2006), Swaddiwudhipong et al. (2006).

The gradient-dependent theory abandons the assumption that the stress at a given point is uniquely determined by the history of strain at this point only. It takes into account possible interactions with other material points in the vicinity of that point.

1.3 Micro-polar theory

Since most of the strain gradient theories are in fact a particular case of generalized continua, such as micromorphic continua (Eringen, 1968), or continua with microstructure (Mindlin, 1964), which were all inspired by the pioneering work of the Cosserat brothers (Cosserat and Cosserat, 1909), we introduce the micro-polar theory in this section. The Cosserat continuum (or micro-polar continuum) enhances the kinematic description of deformation by an additional field of local rotation.

In the general couple stress theory, the work-conjugated rotation, ω, is treated as an independent kinematic quantity with no direct dependence upon u and distinct from the associated rotation $\theta \equiv (1/2)\,\mathrm{curl}\ u$. ω is called micro-rotation which can be schemed in Figure 1.2. σ denotes the symmetric part of Cauchy stress and τ denotes the anti-symmetric part of Cauchy stress, m denotes the overall couple stress tensor.

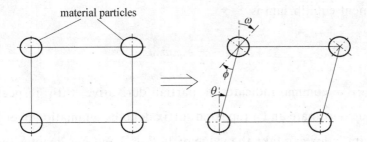

material particles

Figure 1.2　Definition of the micro-rotation ω.

Neglecting the body forces and body couples, the principle of virtual work for the general couple stress theory is

$$\int_V [(\sigma_{ij} + \tau_{ij})\,\delta\gamma_{ij} + m_{ij}\delta\chi_{ij}]\mathrm{d}V = \int_S [T_i\delta u_i + q_i\delta\omega_i]\mathrm{d}S \quad (1.1)$$

where $\chi_{ij} = \omega_{i,j}$ is the work-conjugated curvature tensor and $\gamma_{ij} = u_{i,j} + e_{ijk}\omega_k$ is called the relative displacement gradient tensor. V is the volume of the body and S is the surface of it.

The above virtual work statement can be rearranged to the form

$$\int_V (\sigma_{ij}\delta\varepsilon_{ij} + \tau_{ij}\delta\alpha_{ij} + m_{ij}\delta\chi_{ij})\mathrm{d}V = \int_S [T_i\delta u_i + q_i\delta\omega_i]\mathrm{d}S \quad (1.2)$$

where the symmetric tensor ε_{ij} is the usual strain tensor,

$$\varepsilon_{ij} = (u_{i,j} + u_{j,i})/2 \quad (1.3)$$

and the anti-symmetric tensor α_{ij} is the relative rotation tensor

$$\alpha_{ij} = e_{ijk}\omega_k - (u_{j,i} - u_{i,j})/2 = e_{ijk}(\omega_k - \theta_k) \quad (1.4)$$

Via the divergence theorem, the left in Eq.(1.2) can be written

$$\int_V (\sigma_{ij}\delta\varepsilon_{ij} + \tau_{ij}\delta\alpha_{ij} + m_{ij}\delta\chi_{ij})\mathrm{d}V$$

$$= \int_S (\sigma_{ij} + \tau_{ij})\,n_j\delta u_i\,\mathrm{d}S - \int_V (\sigma_{ij} + \tau_{ij})_{,j}\delta u_i\,\mathrm{d}V$$

$$+ \int_S m_{ij} n_j \delta\omega_i \, dS + \int_V \tau_{jk} e_{ijk} \delta\omega_i \, dV - \int_V m_{ij,\,j} \delta\omega_i \, dV \qquad (1.5)$$

then, the equilibrium relation of force in V is

$$t_{ij,\,j} = \sigma_{ij,\,j} + \tau_{ij,\,j} = 0 \qquad (1.6)$$

and moment equilibrium is

$$\tau_{jk} = \frac{1}{2} e_{ijk} m_{ip,\,p} \qquad (1.7)$$

Here, a comma indicates a partial derivative with respect to a Cartesian coordinate and a repeated suffix denotes summation over 1 to 3. A subscript index can take the value of 1, 2 or 3 and e_{ijk} denotes the usual permutation symbol.

Traction equilibrium on the surface S of the body is

$$T_i = (\sigma_{ij} + \tau_{ij}) n_j, \quad q_i = m_{ij} n_j \qquad (1.8)$$

The strain energy density function w in the general couple stress theory depends upon the strain tensor $\boldsymbol{\varepsilon}$, the curvature tensor $\boldsymbol{\chi}$ and the relative rotation $\boldsymbol{\alpha}$ as following

$$w(\boldsymbol{\varepsilon}, \boldsymbol{\chi}, \boldsymbol{\alpha}) = \int_0^{\varepsilon_{ij}} \sigma_{ij} \, d\varepsilon_{ij} + \int_0^{\chi_{ij}} m_{ij} \, d\chi_{ij} + \int_0^{\alpha_{ij}} \tau_{ij} \, d\alpha_{ij} \qquad (1.9)$$

then, the constitutive relations are

$$\sigma_{ij} = \frac{\partial w}{\partial \varepsilon_{ij}}, \quad m_{ij} = \frac{\partial w}{\partial \chi_{ij}}, \quad \tau_{ij} = \frac{\partial w}{\partial \alpha_{ij}} \qquad (1.10)$$

References

Abu Al-Rub, R. K., Voyiadjis, G. Z., 2006. A physical based gradient plasticity theory. Int. J. Plasticity 22, 654 – 684.

Acharya, A. and Bassani, J. L., 1995. On non-local flow theories that preserve the classical structure of incremental boundary value problems. In Micromechanics of Plasticity and Damage of Multiphase Materials, IUTAM Symposium, Paris, Aug 29 – Sept 1.

Acharya, A. and Shawki, T. G., 1995. Thermodynamic restrictions on constitutive equations for second-deformation-gradient inelastic behavior. J. Mech. Phys. Solids 43, 1751 – 1772.

Aifantis, E. C., 1984. On the microstructural origin of certain inelastic models. Trans. ASME J. Eng. Mater. Technol. 106, 326 – 330.

Ashby, M. F., 1970. The deformation of plasticity non-homogeneous alloys. Phil. Mag. 21, 399 – 424.

Chen, S. H. and Wang, T. C., 2000. A new hardening law for strain gradient plasticity. Acta Mater., 48(16), 3997 – 4005.

Chen, S. H. and Wang, T. C., 2001. Strain gradient theory with couple stress for crystalline solids. European J. Mech. A/Solids 20, 739 – 756.

Chen, S. H. and Wang, T. C., 2002. A new deformation theory for strain gradient effects. Int. J. Plasticity 18, 971 – 995.

Cosserat, E., Cosserat, F., 1909. Theorie des Corps Deformables (Herman et fils, Paris).

Cottrell, A. H., 1964. In "The mechanical properties of matter", p. 277, Wiley, New York.

De Guzman, M. s., Neubauer, G., Flinn, P. and Nix, W. D., 1993. The role of indentation depth on the measured hardness of materials. Materials Research Symposium Proceedings 308, 613 – 618.

Elssner, G., Korn, D. and Ruehle, M., 1994. The influence of interface impurities on fracture energy of UHV diffusion bonded metal-ceramic bicrystals. Scripta Metall. Mater. 31, 1037 – 1042.

Eringen, A. C., 1968. Theory of micropolar elasticity, in: H. Leibowitz, ed., Fracture. An Advanced Treatise (Academic Press, New York), 621 – 729.

Fleck, N. A. and Hutchinson, J. W., 1993. A phenomenological theory for strain gradient effects in plasticity. J. Mech. Phys. Solids 41, 1825 – 1857.

Fleck, N. A. and Hutchinson, J. W., 1997. Strain Gradient Plasticity. Advances in Applied Mechanics ed. J. W. Hutchinson and T. Y. Wu, 33, 295 – 361 Academic Press, New York.

Fleck, N. A., Muller, G. M., Ashby, M. F. and Hutchinson, J. W., 1994. Strain gradient plasticity: theory and experiment. Acta Metal. et Mater. 42, 475 – 487.

Gao, H., Huang, Y., Nix, W. D. and Hutchinson, J. W., 1999. Mechanism-based strain gradient plasticity-I. theory. J. Mech. Phys. Solids 47, 1239 – 1263.

Gurtin, M. E., 1965a. Thermodynamics and the possibility of spatial interaction in rigid heat conductors. Arch. Ration. Mech. Anal. 18, 335 – 342.

Gurtin, M. E. , 1965b. Thermodynamics and the possibility of spatial interaction in elastic materials. Arch. Ration. Mech. Anal. 19, 339 – 352.

Huang, Y. , Zhang, L. , Guo, T. F. and Hwang, K. C. , 1995. Near-tip fields for cracks in materials with strain gradient effects. In Proceedings of IUTAM Symposium on Nonlinear Analysis of Fracture, ed. Willis, J. R. , 231 – 242, Kluwer Academic Publishers, Cambridge, England.

Huang, Y. , Zhang, L. , Guo T. F. and Hwang, K. C. , 1997. Mixed mode near-tip fields for cracks in materials with strain gradient effects. J. Mech. Phys. Solids 45, 439 – 465.

Huang, Y. , Xue, Z. , Gao, H. , Nix, W. D. , Xia, Z. C. , 2000. A study of micro-indentation hardness tests by mechanism-based strain gradient plasticity. J. Mater. Res. 15, 1786 – 1796.

Huang, Y. , Qu, S. , Hwang, K.C. , Li, M. , Gao, H. , 2004. A conventional theory of mechanism-based strain gradient plasticity. Int. J. Plasticity 20, 753 – 782.

Hutchinson, J. W. , 1997. Linking scales in mechanics. In: Karihaloo, B. L. , Mai, Y. W. , Ripley, M. I. , Ritchie, R. O. (Eds). Advances in fracture research. Pergamon Press, Amsterdam, 1 – 14.

Hwang, K.C. , Jiang, H. , Huang, Y. , Gao, H. , 2003. Finite deformation analysis of mechanism-based strain gradient plasticity: torsion and crack tip field. Int. J. Plasticity 19, 235 – 251.

Koiter, W. T. , 1964. Couple-stresses in the theory of elasticity, I and II , Proc. Roy. Netherlands Acad. Sci. B67, 17 – 64.

Kroener, E. , 1962. Dislocations and continuum mechanics. Appl. Mech. Rev. 15, 599 – 606.

Liu, X. , Hu. G. , 2005. A continuum micromechanical theory of overall plasticity for particulate composites including particle size effect. Int. J. Plasticity 21, 777 – 799.

Lloyd, D. J. , 1994. Particle reinforced aluminum and magnesium matrix composites. Int. Mater. Rev. 39, 1 – 23.

Ma, Q. , Clarke, D. R. , 1995. Size dependent hardness in silver single crystals. J. Mater. Res. 10, 853 – 863.

McElhaney, K. W. , Vlassak, J. J. , Nix, W. D. , 1998. Determination of indenter tip geometry and indentation contact area for depth-sensing indentation experiments. J. Mater. Res. 13, 1300 – 1306.

Mindlin, R. D. , 1963. Influence of couple-stress on stress concentrations. Exp. Mech. 3,

1 – 7.

Mindlin, R. D., 1964. Microstructure in linear elasticity, Arch. Rational Mech. Abal. 16, 51 – 78.

Muhlhaus, H. B. And Aifantis, E. C., 1991. The influence of microstructure-induced gradients on the localization of deformation in viscoplastic materials. Acta Mech., 89, 217 – 231.

Naghdi, P. M. and Srinivasa, A. R., 1993. A dynamical theory of structured solids. Ⅱ special constitutive equations and special cases of the theory, Phil. Trans. R. Soc. Lond. A, 345, 459 – 476.

Nix, W. D., 1989. Mechanical properties of tin films. Metall. Trans. 20A, 2217 – 2245.

Nix, W. D., Gao, H., 1998. Indentation size effects in crystalline materials: a law for strain gradient plasticity. J. Mech. Phys. Solids 46, 411 – 425.

Nye, J. F., 1953. Some geometrical relations in dislocated crystal. Acta Metall. 1, 153 – 162.

Poole, W. J., Ashby, M. F. And Fleck, N. A., 1996. Microhardness of annealed and work-hardened copper polycrystals. Scripta Metall. Mater. 34, 559 – 564.

Saha, R., Xue, Z., Huang, Y., Nix, W.D., 2001. Indentation of a soft metal film on a hard substrate: strain gradient hardening effects. J. Mech. Phys. Solids 49, 1997 – 2014.

Shi, M., Huang, Y., Jiang, H., Hwang, K. C., Li, M., 2001. The boundary-layer effect on the crack tip field in mechanism-based strain gradient plasticity. Int. J. Fracture 112, 23 – 41.

Shizawa, K. and Zbib, H. M., 1999. A thermodynamical theory of gradient elastoplasticity with dislocation density tensor I: Fundamentals. Int. J. Plasticity, 15, 899 – 938.

Shu, J. Y., Fleck, N. A., 1998. The prediction of a size effect in microindentation. Int. J. Solids Struct. 35, 1363 – 1383.

Stelmashenko, N. A., Walls, M. G., Brown, L. M., Milman, Y. V., 1993. Microindentation on W and Mo oriented single crystals: an STM study. Acta Metall. Mater. 41, 2855 – 2865.

Stolken, J. S. And Evans, A. G., 1998. A microbend test method for measuring the plasticity length scale. Acta Mater. 46, 5109 – 1515.

Swaddiwudhipong, S., Tho, K.K., Hua, J., Liu, Z.S., 2006. Mechanism-based strain gradient plasticity in C^0 axisymmetric elemet. Int. J. Solids Struct. 43, 1117 – 1130.

Toupin, R., 1962. Elastic materials with couple-stresses, Arch. Rational Mech. Anal. 11, 385 – 414.

Xia, Z. C. and Hutchinson, J. W. , 1996. Crack tip fields in strain gradient plasticity. J. Mech. Phys. Solids 44, 1621 – 1648.

Xun, F. , Hu, G. and Huang, Z. , 2004. Size-dependence of overall in-plane plasticity for fiber composites. Int. J. Solids Structures 41, 4713 – 4730.

Zbib, H. and Aifantis, E. C. , 1989. On the localization and postlocalization behavior of plastic deformation. Part I . On the initiation of shear bands; Part II . On the evolution and thickness of shear bands; Part III . On the structure and velocity of Portevin-Le Chatelier bands. Res. Mech, 261 – 277, 279 – 292, and 293 – 305.

2   Micro-scale experiments

2.1   Torsion experiments on copper wires

In Fleck et al. (1994), the tensile and torsional responses were measured for polycrystalline copper wires (99.99% purity) ranging in diameters from 12 to 170 micrometers. In uniaxial tension strain gradients are negligible and hardening is due to the accumulation of statistically stored dislocations. In torsion of a circular wire the shear strain γ varies with radius r from the axis of twist, such that $\gamma = \kappa r$, where κ is the twist per unit length of the wire. The strain gradient $d\gamma/dr = \kappa$ induces a density ρ_G of geometrically necessary dislocations of order κ/b, where b is the Burger's vector. Thus the wire is hardened by both statistically stored and geometrically necessary dislocations. For a given shear strain at the surface of the wire (or, equivalently, for a given average strain across the section) the thinner wire has the greater strain gradient $d\gamma/dr$ and the higher density of geometrically necessary dislocations. Faster work hardening in the thinner wire is expected. The experiments below done by Fleck et al. (1994) confirm this expectation.

2.1.1   Test method

In the torsion experiments of thin copper wires with different diameters done by Fleck et al. (1994), the tension tests were performed on a 50 mm gauge length of copper wire, using a conventional screw driven test machine and a specially designed sensitive load cell. The load cell consisted of a 0.5 mm thick cantilever beam of rectangular section; it was loaded transversely at its free end by the copper wire. Strain gauges were placed near the built-in end of the beam and were used to detect the load on the copper wire.

The torsion tests were performed using a specially designed screw driven torsion machine sketched in Figure 2.1. The bottom end of the copper wire specimen (of gauge length 2 mm) was glued to a lower grip, and the top end to a 60 mm long glass filament; the glass filament acted as a torsional load cell. The free end of the glass filament was twisted using a gear drive train and electric motor. The twist along the length of the glass filament was measured by two needle pointers and protractors, and gave a measure of the torque. Calibration of the glass filament load cell was carried out separately using a dead weight and pulley

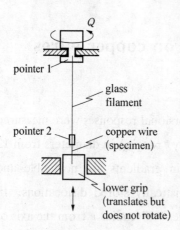

Figure 2.1   Schematic of torsion test. (Fleck et al., 1994)

arrangement. The torsional strength of the copper wires roughly scales with diameter to the third power; to maximize sensitivity of the torsional load cell glass filaments were used of diameter in the range 55 – 250 micrometers.

The relative twist of the two ends of the copper wire was measured by the needle pointer attached to the top end of the wire (the other end was fixed to the lower grip of the test machine which could translate but not rotate). During a test the wire was elongated by a few percent, causing the glass filament to bow. This was corrected for by translating the lower grip of the test machine via a gear drive.

Fleck et al. (1994) did the tension and torsion test, which were performed on commercially pure, cold drawn copper wires of diameter in the range 12 to 170 micrometers. All the wires were annealed, giving grain sizes between 5 and 25 micrometers, the larger diameter wires having the larger grain sizes. The tension tests were performed at a strain rate of 10^{-3} s^{-1}, and the torsion tests were performed such that the shear strain rate at the surface of the wire was also 10^{-3} s^{-1}.

2.1.2 Experimental results

The uniaxial tension data for the copper wires done by Fleck et al. (1994) are shown in Figure 2.2 and the torsion response is given in Figure 2.3. Typical responses are given for each wire diameter $2a$; generally, they performed at least four tests of each type for each diameter of wire. From Figure 2.2, it can conclude that there is only a minor influence of wire diameter on tensile behavior. No systematic trend between tensile stress-strain curve and diameter emerges for diameters in the range 12 to 30 micrometers. The data for $2a = 170\,\mu$m is approximately 10% below that of the other curves, perhaps because the grain size was significantly larger here than in the other wires.

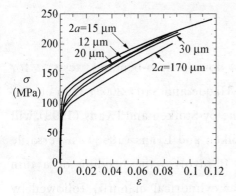

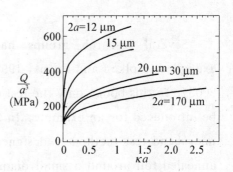

Figure 2.2 True stress σ vs strain ε tension data for copper wires of diameters $2a$ in the range 12 − 170 μm. (Fleck et al., 1994)

Figure 2.3 Torsional response of copper wires of diameter $2a$ in the range 12 − 170 μm. (Fleck et al., 1994)

The torsion data in Figure 2.3 have been displayed in the form Q/a^3 vs κa, where Q is the torque, a the wire radius and κ the twist per unit length. The non-dimensional group κa may be interpreted as the magnitude of the shear strain at the surface of the wire. The group Q/a^3 gives a measure of the shear stress across the section of the wire in some averaged sense. Dimensional analysis establishes the fact that Q/a^3 is a function of κa but is otherwise independent of a for any constitutive law which does not contain a length scale. Thus, if the local shear stress at any point in the wire were to depend only upon shear strain and not strain gradient, the curves of Q/a^3 vs κa would superpose. Plainly they do not. There is a systematic increase in torsional hardening with decreasing wire diameter. For example, at $\kappa a = 0.3$, the value of Q/a^3 for $2a = 12\ \mu\mathrm{m}$ is approximately three times the value of Q/a^3 for $2a = 170\ \mu\mathrm{m}$. This supports the notion that strain gradient strengthening plays an increasingly dominant role with decreasing wire diameter.

2.2　Micro-meter thin-beam bending

Several research groups have done micro-bending tests (for examples, Stolken and Evans, 1998; Haque and Saif, 2003; Guo et al., 2005). In this book, only the test done by Stolken and Evans (1998) will be introduced for an example. In Stolken and Evans (1998), a versatile microbend test method is designed. It involves the bending of a thin annealed foil around a small diameter cylindrical mandril, followed by measurement of the unloaded and loaded radii of curvature. This test fully characterizes the moment-curvature relation, subject to independent knowledge of the elastic modulus of the foil material.

2.2.1　Experimental design

Foils are used in the microbending tests. In microbending, measurements of loads and bending moments are difficult to control strain levels in a precise manner. To obviate both of these difficulties, Stolken and Evans (1998) devised a procedure as shown in Figure 2.4. It relies only on the measurement of curvature, by means of a confocal optical microscope. The foil is plastically bent around a small cylindrical mandril by means of loads applied through a profiled die. This loading causes the foil to acquire a strain state dictated by the radius of curvature of the mandril R_0, present over the length, πR_0. The load is removed, causing the foil to

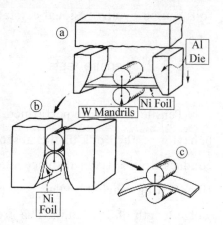

Figure 2.4　A schematic of the microbend test. (Stolken & Evans, 1998)

elastically unload, such that the new radius of curvature over the length πR_0 increases to R_f. Since the unloading is strictly elastic and the Young's modulus of the foil material is known, the difference in the radii of curvature, $\Delta R = R_f - R_0$, enables determination of the moment that existed when the load was present. Moreover, the surface strain ε_b of the foil in the loaded state is simply related to the radius of curvature by

$$\varepsilon_b = h/2R_0 \qquad (2.1)$$

where h is the foil thickness. By choosing mandrils with different radii, R_0, a range of strains may be accessed, with corresponding moments governed by the stress-strain behavior of the material.

The foils used in Stolken and Evans' (1998) experiment comprised cold-rolled high purity (99.994%) Ni, having thicknesses $h = 12.5, 25,$

50 μm. Each foil was cut into eight strips 2.5 mm wide and 24 mm long, parallel to the original rolling direction. Four of these served as tensile specimens, the remaining four were cut into quarters to produce 16 microbend coupons, 2.5 mm wide and 6 mm long. This ensured that the tensile and bend axes of all samples were parallel to the original rolling direction. These procedures minimized systematic differences between foils caused by any residual crystallographic texture.

2.2.2   Tensile tests

Tensile tests were performed in order to characterize the stress-strain behavior of the foils in the absence of strain gradients. The tests were conducted at a fixed displacement rate by using an electro-mechanical fiber testing machine. The specimens were clamped between grips at a gauge length of 12.7 mm. The cross-head displacement was measured by using an LVT, while a 100N load cell measured the applied force: both recorded digitally. The cross-head speed coincided with a strain rate of $10^{-3}/$s. The strains were determined from the initial gage length and the cross-head displacement.

Representative stress-strain curves are summarized in Figure 2.5.

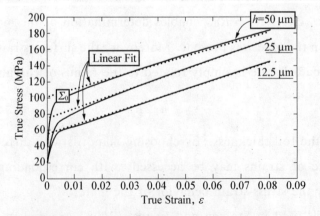

Figure 2.5   Tensile stress-strain curves measured for the three foil thicknesses. (Stolken & Evans, 1998)

There are two key features: (i) The strain hardening is essentially linear and about the same for all foil thicknesses; (ii) The yield strength increases as the foil thickness increases.

Accordingly, the plastic response can be expressed by

$$\sigma = \Sigma_0 + \varepsilon_{pl} E_p \qquad (2.2)$$

where Σ_0 is an effective yield strength, ε_{pl} the plastic strain and E_p the hardening coefficient. The data for all three foil thicknesses can be fit to a single tensile stress-strain law when the yield strength is re-expressed as

$$\Sigma_0 = \Sigma_0^* (d/h) \qquad (2.3)$$

where d is the grain size and $\Sigma_0^* = 144$ MPa. Note that this trend is opposite to that found by others on deposited metal film (Emery and Povirk, 2003). However, results for these films have only been reported in the as-deposited (unannealed) state. The reason for the decrease in yield strength in the thinnest foil is not understood.

2.2.3 Microbend tests

The measured bend radii, ΔR, are converted into bending moments M by using

$$M/bh^2 = \overline{E}h/12\Delta R \qquad (2.4)$$

Where b is the foil width and $\overline{E}$ the plane strain Young's modulus for Ni ($\overline{E} = 220$ GPa).

Note that the moments needed to induce these surface strains, when normalized by h^2, are substantially larger for the 12.5 μm foil than for the two thicker foils. When plotted in this manner, the results for all three foil thicknesses should superpose in the absence of a plasticity length scale and when the tensile yield strengths are the same. Accordingly, this difference is attributed to the length scale. Moreover, upon normalizing with the tensile yield strength, using $M/\Sigma_0 bh^2$ (Figure 2.6), this difference is exacerbated, since the thinnest foils have the lowest tensile yield strength.

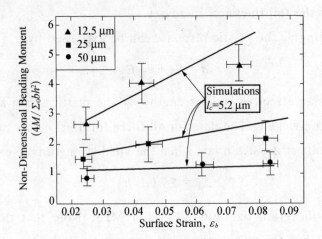

Figure 2. 6   Bending moment vs the surface strain
for all three foil thicknesses. (Stolken & Evans, 1998)

2.3 Micro-meter particle reinforced metal matrix composite

The particulate aspect ratio and the volume fraction, as well as the strain hardening exponent of the matrix material had important influences on the composite properties, and some quantitative relations were developed by using cell models (Christman et al. , 1989; Bao et al. , 1991). The predicted results are consistent with experimental results. In addition, a self-consistent analysis model has been used successfully to predict the behavior of the PMMC (Corbin and Wilkinson, 1994). More recently, a systematic experimental research for the metallic fiber reinforced Al-alloy matrix for a series of the volume fraction of fiber was carried out (Boland et al. , 1998). The results showed that the high material strengthening was obtained. On the researches of the particle size effect, the experimental results showed that the strength of the PMMC was sensitive to the particle size. The conclusion was that the smaller the particle, the higher the composite strength. An example is given to illustrate the test process and the experimental results.

2.3.1 Mechanical tests

The materials used by Ling (2000) are 2124Al alloy and 2124Al reinforced with 17% volume fraction of 3, 13 and 37 micrometers SiC particles.

The dynamic compression testing was performed on a Split Hopkinson Pressure Bar (SHPB). A lot of descriptions of SHPB apparatus have been presented so the illustration is omitted here. To keep one dimensional stress in the specimen during loading, compressive specimen is cylindrical with 5 mm diameter and 5 mm high, the rolling direction parallel to the compression axis. Strain rate of 2100/s is chosen for all the tests so that mechanical responses under the same strain rate would be obtained. Data including stress-strain relation curve of each specimen could be obtained by wave profiles recorded.

2.3.2 Experimental results

Stress-strain curves of the materials, subjected to dynamic compression (strain rate about 2100/s), are given in Figure 2.7. One of the prominent features in these curves is that, under the same loading condition, the flow stress of the materials depends on

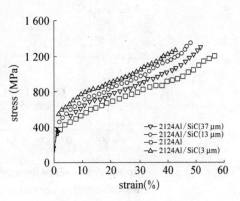

Figure 2.7 Stress-strain curves of 2124 Al and its composites under dynamic compression. (Ling, 2000)

the size of the SiC particles. The smaller the SiC particle, the higher the flow stress of the composites. Among them, the composite containing $3\,\mu m$ SiC particles has the highest flow stress and the matrix material, 2124 Al alloy is of the lowest flow stress under the same loading condition.

Another representative experimental results done by Lloyd (1994) is given in Figure 2.8, in which the volume fraction of particles, SiC, is 15% and the diameters of the particles are 16 and $7.5\,\mu m$, respectively. From Figure 2.8, one can see that the curve predicted for the smaller particle reinforcement composite is much higher than that for the larger one. Figure 2.8 also shows the stress-strain curves predicted by the unit cell model based on classical plasticity for two cell aspect ratios $h/R = 1$ and $h/R = 2$ (Xue et al., 2002). The differences between these two curves are relatively insensitive to the cell aspect ratio and it is clearly observed that the classical plasticity significantly underestimates the effect of reinforcements and can not predict the particle size effect.

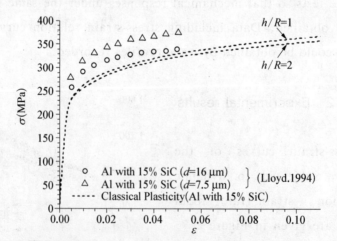

Figure 2.8   Experimental stress-strain data for an aluminum matrix reinforced by silicon carbide particles with different diameters and the curves predicted by classical plasticity are also shown for the cell aspect ratio $h/R = 1$ and 2. (Xue et al., 2002)

2.4　Micro and nano-indentation

A variety of techniques have been developed to measure mechanical properties with ultra-low load indentation which can be classified broadly according to the type of indenter used in the measurement. In general, sharp, geometrically-similar indenters such as the Berkovich triangular pyramid are useful when one wishes to probe properties at the smallest possible scale. Among the properties routinely measured with the Berkovich indenter are the hardness and elastic modulus (Oliver and Pharr, 1992). For testing systems in which the specimen temperature can be controlled, it is also possible to determine parameters characteristic of thermally-activated plastic flow, such as the activation energy and stress exponent for creep. With special indenters, it is also possible to make indentations in brittle materials with radial cracks extending from the edges of the contact which allows one to explore fracture behavior at the micron scale and measure fracture toughness in volumes of material a few microns or less in diameter (Pharr et al. , 1993). Sharp indenters are also potentially useful in the study of residual stresses in thin surface regions and layers, although residual stress influences on indentation behavior are usually small and difficult to detect (Tsui et al. , 1996; Bolshakov et al. , 1996).

Spherical indenters are also frequently employed in the measurement of mechanical properties by ultra-low load indentation methods (Field and Swain, 1993, 1995). The primary advantage of the spherical indenter is that indentation contact begins elastically as the load is first applied, but then changes to elastic-plastic at higher loads, thereby allowing one to explore yielding and associated phenomena. Although the point of initial yielding is sometimes difficult to identify experimentally because plasticity commences well below the surface (Tabor, 1986), one can in principle use a spherical indenter to determine the elastic modulus, yield stress, and strain-hardening behavior of a material all in one simple test. Moreover, it is sometimes possible to deduce much of the uniaxial stress-strain curve from spherical indentation data (Tabor, 1951).

Another reason for interest in spherical indenters is that even the sharpest Berkovich diamonds are rounded at some small scale; effective tip radii are usually on the order of 10 – 100 nm (Tsui et al., 1996). Thus, the indentation behavior of very small Berkovich indentations requires that the influence of the spherical tip geometry on the contact mechanics be considered.

The two mechanical properties measured most frequently using indentation techniques are the hardness, H, and the elastic modulus, E. As the indenter is pressed into the sample, both elastic and plastic deformation occurs, which results in the formation of a hardness impression conforming to the shape of the indenter. During indenter withdrawal, only the elastic portion of the displacement is recovered, which facilitates the use of an elastic solution in modeling the contact process (Oliver and Pharr, 1992). Figure 2.9 shows a typical load-displacement curve and the deformation pattern of an elastic-plastic sample during and after indentation. In Figure 2.9, h_{max} represents the displacement at the peak load, P_{max}. h_c is the contact depth and is defined as the depth of the indenter in contact with the sample under load. h_f is the final displacement after complete unloading. S is the initial unloading contact stiffness, $S = dP/dh \mid_{h = h_{max}}$.

Nanoindentation hardness is defined as the indentation load divided by the projected contact area of the indentation. It is the mean pressure that a material can support under load. From the load-displacement curve, hardness can be obtained at the peak load.

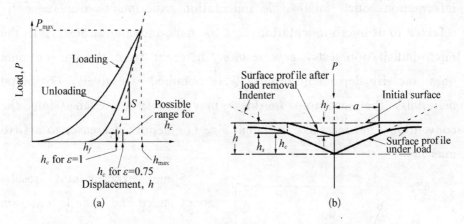

Figure 2.9　　Schematic of load-displacement curve of micro or nanoindentation (a) and the deformation pattern of an elastic-plastic sample during and after indentation (b).

$$H = \frac{P_{\max}}{A} \qquad (2.5)$$

where A is the projected contact area of the hardness impression and is estimated by evaluating an empirical formulae. For a perfect Berkovich indenter, the area function can be obtained as

$$A = 24.56\,h_c^2. \qquad (2.6)$$

The contact depth can be estimated from the load-displacement data as

$$h_c = h_{\max} - \varepsilon\,\frac{P_{\max}}{S} \qquad (2.7)$$

where ε is a constant that depends on the indenter geometry ($\varepsilon = 0.75$ for a Berkovich indenter).

The process of indentation test can be found in lots of references, which is neglected in this book.

Recently, with the advancement of experimental technique and measuring precision, it is possible to carry out the indentation tests at the scale of one micron or sub-micron for obtaining more detailed material information. Such small scale indentation experiments are frequently referred to as micro-indentation tests (or nano-indentation tests). In the micro-indentation tests, new results, different from the conventional ones, the size dependent results, were obtained extensively. For metal materials, the measured hardness may double or even triple the conventional hardness as the indent size (or depth) decreases to a fifth micron.

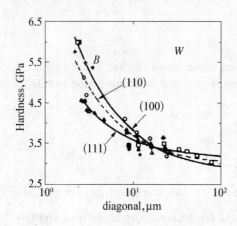

Figure 2.10　Effect of indent size upon indentation hardness for tungsten single crystals. (taken from Fleck & Hutchinson, 1997)

Some experimental results about micro and nano-indentation are given as examples to illustrate the size effects found in indentation tests. The measured indentation hardness of metals and ceramics increases by a factor of about two as the width of the indent decreases from about 10 micrometers to 1 micrometer. Figure 2.10 is the experimental results done by Stelmashenko et al. (1993) for tungsten single crystals. The indent size is characterized by the diagonal of the indent from a Vickers micro-indent. A minor effect of crystal orientation on hardness is evident. The depth dependence of the hardness of copper is shown in Figure 2.11 for both (111) single crystal copper and for a cold worked sample of polycrystalline copper. These measurements were made by McElhaney et al. (1998). Special care has been taken by the authors to account for the effects of pile-up and sink-in which occur during indentation. Thus the depth dependence of the hardness shown in the figure arises from real material behavior and is not associated with errors in the contact area.

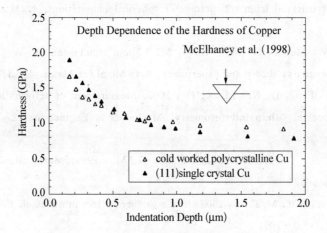

Figure 2. 11 Depth dependence of the hardness of (111) single crystal copper and cold worked polycrystalline copper. (taken from Gao, et al. , 1999)

References

Bao, G. , Hutchinson J. W. , McMeeking, R. M. , 1991. Particle reinforcement of ductile matrices against plastic flow and creep. Acta Metall. Mater. 39, 1871 – 1882.

Boland, F. , Colin, C. , Salmon, C. , et al. , 1998. Tensile flow properties of Al-based matrix composites reinforced with a random planar network of continuous metallic fibers. Acta Mater. 46, 6311 – 6323.

Bolshakov, A. , Oliver, W. C. and Pharr, G. M. , 1996. Influences of stress on the measurement of mechanical properties using nanoindentation: Part $\mathbb{II}$ Finite element simulations. J. Mater. Res. , 11, 760 – 768.

Christman T. , Needleman A. , Suresh, S. , 1989. An experimental and numerical study of deformation in metal ceramic composites. Acta Metall. Mater. 37, 3029 – 3050.

Corbin S. F. , Wilkinson, D. S. , 1994. The influence of particle distribution on the mechanical response of a particulate metal-matrix composite. Acta Metall. Mater. 42, 1311 – 1318.

Emery, R. D. , Povirk, G. L. , 2003. Tensile behavior of free-standing gold films. Part I. Coarse-grained films. Acta Mater. 51, 2067 – 2078.

Field, J. S. and Swain, M V. , 1993. A simple predictive model for spherical indentation J. Mater. Res. 8, 297 – 306.

Field, J. S. and Swain, M V. , 1995. Determining the mechanical-properties of small volumes of material from submicrometer spherical indentations. J. Mater. Res. 10, 101 – 112.

Fleck, N. A. , Muller, G. M. , Ashby, M. F. and Hutchinson, J. W. , 1994. Strain gradient plasticity: theory and experiment. Acta Metal. et Mater. 42, 475 – 487.

Guo, X. H. , Fang, D. N. , Li, X. D. , 2005. Measurement of deformation of pure Ni foils by speckle pattern interferometry. Mechanics in Engineering, 27, 22 – 25 (in Chinese).

Harding, D. S. , Oliver, W. C. and Pharr, G. M. , 1995. Mater. Res. Soc. Symp. Proc. 356, 663.

Haque, M. A. , Saif, M. T. A. , 2003. Strain gradient effect in nanoscale thin films. Acta Mater. 51, 3053 – 3061.

Ling, Z. , 2000. Deformation behavior and microstructure effect in 2124Al/SuCp composite. J. Comp. Mater. 34, 101 – 115.

Lloyd, D. J. , 1994. Particle reinforced aluminum and magnesium matrix composites. Int. Mater. Rev. 39, 1 – 23.

McElhaney, K. W. , Vlassak, J. J. , Nix, W. D. , 1998. Determination of indenter tip geometry and indentation contact area for depth-sensing indentation experiments. J. Mater. Res. 13, 1300 – 1306.

Oliver, W. C. and Pharr, G. M. , 1992. An improved technique for determining hardness and elastic-modulus using load and displacement sensing indentation experiments. J. Mater. Res. 17, 1564 – 1583.

Pharr, G. M. , Harding, D. S. , Oliver, G. M. , 1993. In: Nastasi, M. , Parkin, D. M. , Gleiter, H. (Eds.). Mechanical properties and deformation behavior of materials having ultra-fine microstructures, Kluwer Academic Publishers, Netherlands, 449.

Stelmashenko, N. A. , Walls, M. G. , Brown, L. M. , Milman, Y. V. , 1993. Microindentation on W and Mo oriented single crystals: an STM study. Acta Metall. Mater. 41, 2855 – 2865.

Stolken, J. S. And Evans, A. G. , 1998. A microbend test method for measuring the plasticity length scale. Acta Mater. 46, 5109 – 1515.

Tabor, D. , 1986. In: Blau, P. J. , Lawn, B. R. (Eds.). Microindentation techniques in materials sciences and engineering. American Society for testing and materials, Philadelphia, 129.

Tabor, D. , 1951. The hardness of metals, Oxford University press, London.

Tsui, T. Y. , Oliver, W. C. and Pharr, G. M. , 1996. Influences of stress on the measurement of mechanical properties using nanoindentation. 1. Experimental studies in an aluminum alloy. J. Mater. Res. 11, 752 – 759.

Xue, Z. , Huang, Y. and Li, M. , 2002. Particle size effect in metallic materials: a study by the theory of mechanism-based strain gradient plasticity. Acta Mater. 50, 149 – 160.

3 Theories proposed by Fleck and Hutchinson

The constitutive models of conventional plasticity theories possess no intrinsic material lengths, therefore cannot explain the size-dependent material behavior at the micron and sub-micron scales in Chapter 2. There are however many dislocations at the micron scale such that their collective behavior on plastic work hardening of materials should be characterized by a continuum (but not conventional) plasticity theory. For this reason, strain gradient plasticity theories have been developed from the notion of geometrically necessary dislocations.

There are two frameworks of strain gradient plasticity theories. The first one is Mindlin's (1963, 1964) framework of higher-order continuum theories, and it involves the higher-order stress as the work conjugate of strain gradient. The order of equilibrium equations are higher than that in the conventional continuum theories, therefore additional boundary conditions are required. Examples in this class include Fleck and Hutchinson (1993, 1997, 2001), Fleck et al. (1994), Gao et al. (1999a, b), Huang et al. (2000a, b), Qiu et al. (2001, 2003), Gurtin (2002, 2003), Hwang et al. (2002, 2003), Wang et al. (2003). The other framework of strain gradient plasticity theories does not involve the higher-order stress, and requires no additional boundary conditions. The plastic strain gradient (or inverse elastic strain gradient) comes into play through the incremental plastic modulus. Examples in this class include Acharya and Bassani (1995), Acharya and Beaudoin (2000), Chen and Wang (2000, 2001, 2002), Bassani (2001), Beaudoin and Acharya (2001), Evers et al. (2004), Huang et al. (2004) and Abu Al-Rub and Voyiadjis (2004, 2006).

In this chapter, we will introduce the phenomenological strain gradient plasticity theories proposed by Fleck and Hutchinson in 1993 and 1997. The theory proposed by Fleck and Hutchinson in 1993 is called CS theory due to the basis of general couple stress theory and only rotation gradient considered. The theory proposed in 1997 by them is called usually SG theory because the stretch gradient has been introduced in contrast to the CS one.

3.1　Couple stress theory (CS)

In 1993, Fleck and Hutchinson proposed a kind of strain gradient theory in order to explain the size effects found in the micro-scale experiments, which we call couple stress theory. In couple stress theory it is assumed that a surface element dS of a body can transmit both a force vector TdS (where T is the force traction vector) and a torque qdS (where q is the couple stress traction vector). The surface forces are in equilibrium with the unsymmetric Cauchy stress, which is decomposed into symmetric part σ and an anti-symmetric part τ. Now introduce the Cartesian coordinates x_i. Then $(\sigma_{ij} + \tau_{ij})$ denote the components of T_i on a plane with unit normal n_i such that

$$T_i = (\sigma_{ij} + \tau_{ij})n_j \tag{3.1}$$

Similarly let μ_{ij} denote the components of q_i on a plane with normal n_i

$$q_i = \mu_{ij} n_j \qquad (3.2)$$

$\boldsymbol{\mu}$ is the couple stress tensor, it can be decomposed into a hydrostatic part $\boldsymbol{\mu I}$ (where $\boldsymbol{I}$ is the second order unit tensor) and a deviatoric component $\boldsymbol{m}$. Koiter (1964) had shown that the hydrostatic part of $\boldsymbol{\mu}$ does not enter the field equations and can legitimately be assumed to vanish; thus $\boldsymbol{\mu} \equiv \boldsymbol{m}$.

Equilibrium of force within the body gives

$$\sigma_{ij,\,j} + \tau_{ij,\,j} = 0 \qquad (3.3)$$

and equilibrium of moments gives

$$\tau_{jk} = \frac{e_{ijk} m_{ip,\,p}}{2} \qquad (3.4)$$

where we have neglected the presence of body forces and body couples. Thus $\boldsymbol{\tau}$ is specified once the distribution of $\boldsymbol{m}$ is known.

The principle of virtual work is conveniently formulated in terms of a virtual velocity field $\dot{u}_i$. The angular velocity vector $\dot{\theta}_i$ has the components

$$\dot{\theta}_i = \frac{e_{ijk} \dot{u}_{j,\,k}}{2} \qquad (3.5)$$

Denoting the rate at which work is absorbed internally per unit volume by $\dot{U}$, the equation of virtual work reads

$$\int_V \dot{U} dV = \int_S [T_i \dot{u}_i + q_i \dot{\theta}_i] dS \qquad (3.6)$$

Where the volume V is contained within the closed surface S. With the aid of the divergence theorem and the equilibrium relations (3.4) and (3.5), the right-hand side of the above equation may be rearranged to the form

$$\int_S [T_i \dot{u}_i + q_i \dot{\theta}_i] dS = \int_V [\sigma_{ij} \dot{\varepsilon}_{ij} + m_{ij} \dot{\chi}_{ij}] dV \qquad (3.7)$$

Where the infinitesimal strain tensor is ε_{ij} and the infinitesimal curvature tensor is χ_{ij}, which can be obtained as

$$\varepsilon_{ij} = \frac{(u_{i,j} + u_{j,i})}{2} \qquad \chi_{ij} = \theta_{i,j} \qquad (3.8)$$

Note that the curvature tensor can be expressed in terms of the strain gradients as $\chi_{ij} = e_{ikl}\varepsilon_{jl,k}$. For the case of an incompressible solid, $\sigma_{ij}\dot{\varepsilon}_{ij} = s_{ij}\dot{\varepsilon}_{ij}$ where s is the deviatoric part of $\boldsymbol{\sigma}$.

Fleck et al. (1993) assumed that the strain energy density w of a homogeneous isotropic solid depends on the scalar invariants of the strain tensor $\boldsymbol{\varepsilon}$ and the curvature tensor $\boldsymbol{\chi}$. Since the rotation is defined as $\theta_i \equiv e_{ijk}u_{k,j}/2$, we have $\chi_{ii} = 0$. Thus $\boldsymbol{\chi}$ is an unsymmetric deviatoric tensor. Further, they assumed that the solid was incompressible, so the symmetric tensor $\boldsymbol{\varepsilon}$ is also deviatoric. The von Mises strain invariant $\varepsilon_e = \sqrt{2\varepsilon_{ij}\varepsilon_{ij}/3}$ is used to represent the contribution to w from statistically stored dislocations and the invariant $\chi_e = \sqrt{2\chi_{ij}\chi_{ij}/3}$ is used to represent the contribution to w from geometrically necessary dislocations. Any contribution to w from the invariant $\chi_{ij}\chi_{ji}$ is neglected for the sake of simplicity. It is mathematically convenient to assume that w depends only on the single scalar measure E_e where

$$E_e^2 = \varepsilon_e^2 + l_{cs}^2\chi_e^2 \qquad (3.9)$$

Here, l_{cs} is the material length scale introduced into the constitutive law, required on dimensional grounds.

Next define an overall stress measure Σ_e as the work conjugate of E_e with

$$\Sigma_e = \frac{dw(E_e)}{dE_e} \qquad (3.10)$$

And note that the overall stress Σ_e is a unique function of the overall strain measure E_e. The work done on the solid per unit volume equals the increment in strain energy,

$$\delta w = s_{ij}\delta\varepsilon_{ij} + m_{ij}\delta\chi_{ij} \tag{3.11}$$

Which enables one to determine s and m in terms of the strain state of the solid as

$$s_{ij} = \frac{2\Sigma_e}{3E_e}\varepsilon_{ij} \qquad m_{ij} = \frac{2l_{cs}^2\Sigma_e}{3E_e}\chi_{ij} \tag{3.12}$$

Substitution of the above equations into the expressions of $\varepsilon_e^2 = 2\varepsilon_{ij}\varepsilon_{ij}/3$ and $\chi_e^2 = 2\chi_{ij}\chi_{ij}/3$ gives, via equation (3.10),

$$\Sigma_e^2 = \sigma_e^2 + l_{cs}^{-2}m_e^2 \tag{3.13}$$

Where $\sigma_e = \sqrt{3s_{ij}s_{ij}/2}$ is the usual von Mises effective stress and $m_e = \sqrt{3m_{ij}m_{ij}/2}$ is the analogous effective couple stress. The measures σ_e and m_e are the work conjugates of ε_e and χ_e, respectively, such that $dw = \sigma_e d\varepsilon_e + m_e d\chi_e$. Indeed, this work relation may be used as the defining equation for σ_e and m_e. The deformation theory is fully prescribed once a function form is assumed for Σ_e in terms of E_e.

Assuming the relation between the generalized effective stress and strain is an exponent hardening one,

$$\frac{\Sigma_e}{\Sigma_0} = \left(\frac{E_e}{E_0}\right)^n \tag{3.14}$$

Then the strain energy density can be written as

$$w = \frac{\Sigma_0 E_0}{n+1}\left(\frac{E_e}{E_0}\right)^{n+1} \tag{3.15}$$

Substituting equation (3.4) into (3.3), we can obtain the governing equation, from which the anti-symmetric part of Cauchy stress can be obtained,

$$\sigma_{ij,j} + \frac{1}{2}e_{ijk}m_{kl,lj} = 0 \tag{3.16}$$

However, from the above equation, one can see that the fourth order derivation of displacement emerges which leads to a very complex boundary conditions.

3.2 Strain gradient (SG) theory proposed by Fleck and Hutchinson (1997)

In the above sub-section, the couple stress strain gradient theory (CS) proposed by Fleck et al. (1993) has been introduced, in which only the rotation gradient is considered. Using the CS theory, they found that it cannot explain the size effects in the indentation experiments. Based on the CS theory, Fleck and Hutchinson suggested another version of strain gradient theory, which is commonly called SG theory. Not only the rotation gradient but also the stretching gradient is involved. Here, we briefly introduce the SG deformation theory in order to give the readers a simple knowledge.

With u_i as the displacements, $\varepsilon_{ij} = \dfrac{(u_{i,j} + u_{j,i})}{2}$ is the strain tensor and $\eta_{ijk} = \eta_{jik} = u_{k,ij}$ is the tensor of second gradient of displacements. The latter can be expressed in terms of the gradients of strains as $\eta_{ijk} = \varepsilon_{jk,i} + \varepsilon_{ik,j} - \varepsilon_{ij,k}$. An incompressible solid has $\varepsilon_{kk} = 0$ and $\eta_{ikk} = 0$. Let $\varepsilon'_{ij} = \varepsilon_{ij} - \delta_{ij}\varepsilon_{kk}/3$ be the strain deviator. Let $\eta^H_{ijk} = \dfrac{1}{4}(\delta_{ik}\eta_{jpp} + \delta_{jk}\eta_{ipp})$ be the "hydrostatic" part of η, which vanishes for incompressible deformations, and let $\eta'_{ijk} = \eta_{ijk} - \eta^H_{ijk}$ be the deviator. Smyshlyaev and Fleck (1996) have proved that the deviator of the strain gradient tensor has three invariants

$$\eta'_{iik}\eta'_{jjk} \qquad \eta'_{ijk}\eta'_{ijk} \qquad \eta'_{ijk}\eta'_{kji} \tag{3.17}$$

For a more general case of an incompressible isotropic non-linear deformation theory solid, Fleck and Hutchinson (1997) combined the invariants of the strain and strain gradient to a generalized effective strain

E_e, which is defined as

$$E_e^2 = \frac{2}{3}\varepsilon'_{ij}\varepsilon'_{ij} + c_1\,\eta'_{iik}\eta'_{jjk} + c_2\,\eta'_{ijk}\eta'_{ijk} + c_3\,\eta'_{ijk}\eta'_{kji} \qquad (3.18)$$

Under uniform strain, E_e is the von Mises strain invariant. The coefficients c_i have the dimension of length^2. For incompressible deformations of isotropic, centro-symmetric solids (3.18) is the general combination of quadratic invariants of the strains and strain gradients (Toupin, 1962; Mindlin, 1964).

The deformation theory is based on the measure E_e. Through this measure, the strain gradients as well as the strains contribute to the energy of deformation and, therefore, to the level of stress. It is convenient at this stage to re-express $\boldsymbol{\eta}'$ in terms of a unique orthogonal decomposition introduced by Smyshlyaev-Fleck (1996). They have shown that $\boldsymbol{\eta}'$ may be written as

$$\boldsymbol{\eta}' = \boldsymbol{\eta}'^{(1)} + \boldsymbol{\eta}'^{(2)} + \boldsymbol{\eta}'^{(3)} \qquad (3.19)$$

Where $\boldsymbol{\eta}'^{(i)} \cdot \boldsymbol{\eta}'^{(j)} = 0$ for $i \neq j$. The three parts $\boldsymbol{\eta}'^{(i)}$ are defined as follows. First, introduce the fully symmetric tensor $\boldsymbol{\eta}'^s$ where

$$\eta'^s_{ijk} = \frac{1}{3}\left[\,\eta'_{ijk} + \eta'_{jki} + \eta'_{kij}\,\right] \qquad (3.20)$$

Note that $\boldsymbol{\eta}'^s$ has the symmetries $\eta'^s_{ijk} = \eta'^s_{jki} = \eta'^s_{kij}$ in addition to the symmetry in the first two indices $\eta'^s_{ijk} = \eta'^s_{jik}$. The symmetric triad η'^s has ten independent components. The eight components of the remainder $\boldsymbol{\eta}'^A \equiv \boldsymbol{\eta}' - \boldsymbol{\eta}'^s$ can be specified in terms of the deviatoric part of the curvature tensor $\chi'_{ij} = \theta_{i,j} = \frac{1}{2}e_{iqr}\eta'_{jqr}$ as follows:

$$\eta'^A_{ijk} = \eta'_{ijk} - \eta'^s_{ijk} = \frac{2}{3}e_{ikp}\chi'_{pj} + \frac{2}{3}e_{jkp}\chi'_{pi} \qquad (3.21)$$

Note that the decomposition of $\boldsymbol{\eta}'$ into the parts $\boldsymbol{\eta}'^s$ and $\boldsymbol{\eta}'^A$ is an orthogonal decomposition, i.e., $\eta'^s_{ijk}\eta'^A_{ijk} = 0$.

The orthogonal decomposition of $\boldsymbol{\eta}'$ into the three tensors $\boldsymbol{\eta}'^{(i)}$ is given by

$$\eta'^{(1)}_{ijk} = \eta'^s_{ijk} - \frac{1}{5} [\delta_{ij} \eta'^s_{kpp} + \delta_{jk} \eta'^s_{ipp} + \delta_{ki} \eta'^s_{jpp}] \tag{3.22}$$

$$\eta'^{(2)}_{ijk} = \frac{1}{6} [e_{ikp} e_{jlm} \eta'_{lpm} + e_{jkp} e_{ilm} \eta'_{lpm} + 2\eta'_{ijk} - \eta'_{jki} - \eta'_{kij}] \tag{3.23}$$

$$\eta'^{(3)}_{ijk} = \frac{1}{6} [- e_{ikp} e_{jlm} \eta'_{lpm} - e_{jkp} e_{ilm} \eta'_{lpm} + 2\eta'_{ijk} - \eta'_{jki} - \eta'_{kij}]$$

$$+ \frac{1}{5} [\delta_{ij} \eta'^s_{kpp} + \delta_{jk} \eta'^s_{ipp} + \delta_{ki} \eta'^s_{jpp}] \tag{3.24}$$

Note that each of the three quantities $\boldsymbol{\eta}'^{(i)}$ possess the symmetry $\eta'^{(n)}_{ijk} = \eta'^{(n)}_{jik}$ and satisfies the incompressibility constraint that $\eta'^{(n)}_{ijj}$ vanishes.

The combined strain quantity E_e can be written in terms of ε' and $\eta'^{(i)}$ by making use of (3.22 – 3.24) to get, after somewhat lengthy manipulation,

$$E_e^2 = \frac{2}{3} \varepsilon'_{ij} \varepsilon'_{ij} + l_1^2 \eta'^{(1)}_{ijk} \eta'^{(1)}_{ijk} + l_2^2 \eta'^{(2)}_{ijk} \eta'^{(2)}_{ijk} + l_3^2 \eta'^{(3)}_{ijk} \eta'^{(3)}_{ijk} \tag{3.25}$$

where the length parameters l_i are related to the c_i's by

$$l_1^2 = c_2 + c_3, \; l_2^2 = c_2 - \frac{1}{2} c_3, \; l_3^2 = \frac{5}{2} c_1 + c_2 - \frac{1}{4} c_3 \tag{3.26}$$

In the form (3.25), it is obvious that the measure is positive definite if all the l_i are nonzero.

To obtain the third form, it is noted that for incompressible deformations the last two invariants in (3.25) can be expressed in terms of the invariants of the gradient of rotation. With rotation as $\theta_i = \frac{1}{2} e_{ijk}$ $u_{k,j}$, e_{ijk} as the permutation symbol, and $\chi'_{ij} = \theta_{i,j} = e_{ipk} \varepsilon'_{kj,p}$ as the rotation gradients,

$$\eta'^{(2)}_{ijk} \eta'^{(2)}_{ijk} = \frac{4}{3} \chi'_{ij} \chi'_{ij} + \frac{4}{3} \chi'_{ij} \chi'_{ji} \quad \eta'^{(3)}_{ijk} \eta'^{(3)}_{ijk} = \frac{8}{5} \chi'_{ij} \chi'_{ij} - \frac{8}{5} \chi'_{ij} \chi'_{ji}$$

$$\tag{3.27}$$

Thus, an equivalent alternative expression to (3.18) or (3.25) is

$$E_e^2 = \frac{2}{3}\varepsilon'_{ij}\varepsilon'_{ij} + l_1^2\,\eta'^{(1)}_{ijk}\,\eta'^{(1)}_{ijk} + \left(\frac{4}{3}l_2^2 + \frac{8}{5}l_3^2\right)\chi'_{ij}\chi'_{ij} + \left(\frac{4}{3}l_2^2 - \frac{8}{5}l_3^2\right)\chi'_{ij}\chi'_{ji}$$

$$(3.28)$$

The following two combinations of the length parameters were designated as being a couple stress solid (CS) and a strain gradient solid (SG) by Fleck and Hutchinson (1997)

$$\text{CS}: \quad l_1 = 0 \quad l_2 = \frac{1}{2}l \quad l_3 = \sqrt{\frac{5}{24}}\,l \tag{3.29}$$

$$\text{SG}: \quad l_1 = l \quad l_2 = \frac{1}{2}l \quad l_3 = \sqrt{\frac{5}{24}}\,l \tag{3.30}$$

For simplicity, a power law dependence of the strain energy density w on the effective strain E_e will be assumed of the form

$$w = \frac{n}{n+1}\Sigma_0 E_0 \left(\frac{E_e}{E_0}\right)^{\frac{n+1}{n}} \tag{3.31}$$

Where Σ_0, $E_0 = \Sigma_0/(3\mu)$ and the strain-hardening exponent n are taken to be material constants, μ is the shear modulus. For the case of uniaxial tension, the uniaxial stress σ is related to the axial strain ε by the familiar expression

$$\sigma = \Sigma_0 \left(\frac{\varepsilon}{E_0}\right)^{1/n} \tag{3.32}$$

Here, the deformation theory of Fleck and Hutchinson (1997) are introduced. The effective stress Σ_e is the work conjugate of E_e, with

$$\Sigma_e = \frac{dw(E_e)}{dE_e} \tag{3.33}$$

With the particular choice for $w(E_e)$ given by (3.31), note that Σ_e is a power law function of E_e:

$$\Sigma_e = \Sigma_0 \left(\frac{E_e}{E_0}\right)^{1/n} \tag{3.34}$$

Let σ_{ij} be the symmetric second order stress tensor and $\tau_{ijk} = \tau_{jik}$ the higher order stress tensor. Assume the solid is incompressible and can support Cauchy stress, couple stresses and double stresses. Then the work done per unit volume equals the increment in strain energy

$$\delta w = \sigma_{ij}\delta\varepsilon_{ij} + \tau'_{ijk}\delta\eta'_{ijk} \tag{3.35}$$

Where the primes denote deviatoric measures. The work relation above and the definition (3.25) enable use to write the deviatoric stress $(\boldsymbol{\sigma}', \boldsymbol{\tau}')$ in terms of the strain state of the solid as

$$\sigma'_{ij} = \frac{\partial w(\varepsilon'_{ij}, \eta'_{ijk})}{\partial\varepsilon'_{ij}} = \Sigma_e \frac{\partial E_e}{\partial\varepsilon'_{ij}} = \frac{2}{3}\frac{\Sigma_e}{E_e}\varepsilon'_{ij} \tag{3.36}$$

$$\tau_{ijk} = \frac{\partial w(\varepsilon'_{ij}, \eta'_{ijk})}{\partial\eta'_{ijk}} = \Sigma_e \frac{\partial E_e}{\partial\eta'_{ijk}} = \sum_{I=1}^{3} \tau'^{(I)}_{ijk} \tag{3.37}$$

Where

$$\tau'^{(I)}_{ijk} = \frac{\Sigma_e}{E_e}l_I^2\eta'^{(I)}_{ijk} \quad \text{(no sum on } I) \tag{3.38}$$

Note that the three stress measures $\tau'^{(I)}_{ijk}$ are the unique orthogonal decomposition of τ'_{ijk}, and they are the work conjugates to the three-strain gradient measures $\eta'^{(I)}_{ijk}$, giving

$$\delta w = \sigma'_{ij}\delta\varepsilon'_{ij} + \sum_{I=1}^{3} [\tau'^{(I)}_{ijk}\delta\eta'^{(I)}_{ijk}] \tag{3.39}$$

An explicit formula for the overall effective stress measure Σ_e is derived by substituting (3.36 – 3.38) into (3.25),

$$\Sigma_e^2 = \frac{3}{2}\sigma'_{ij}\sigma'_{ij} + \sum_{I=1}^{3} [l_I^{-2}\tau'^{(I)}_{ijk}\tau'^{(I)}_{ijk}] \tag{3.40}$$

The equilibrium equation in the incompressible limit can be obtained from the principle of virtual work as

$$f_k + \sigma'_{ik, i} - \tau'_{ijk, ij} + H_{, k} = 0 \tag{3.41}$$

Where f_k is the body force and $H = \dfrac{1}{3}\,\sigma_{kk} - \dfrac{1}{2}\,\tau_{jpp,\,j}$ is the hydrostatic stress.

The three independent surface tractions $\hat{t}_k$ on the surface S of the incompressible body are

$$\hat{t}_k = n_i(\sigma'_{ij} - \tau'_{ijk,\,j}) + D_k(n_i n_j n_p \tau'_{ijp}) - D_j(n_i \tau'_{ijk})$$
$$+ [n_i n_j \tau'_{ijk} - n_k(n_i n_j n_p \tau'_{ijp})](D_q n_q) \tag{3.42}$$

And the two independent double-stress-tractions $\hat{r}_k$ tangential to S are

$$\hat{r}_k = n_i n_j \tau'_{ijk} - n_i n_j n_k n_p \tau'_{ijp} \tag{3.43}$$

Where $D_k()$ is the surface gradient operator,

$$D_k() = ()_{,\,k} - n_k \frac{\partial()}{\partial n} \tag{3.44}$$

A reformulation of strain gradient theory is given by Fleck and Hutchinson in 2001, in which the theory proposed by themselves in 1997 has been improved in a manner that elastic and plastic strains are decomposed. Both the flow and deformation versions of the new formulation employ the displacement components and plastic strain amplitude as the primary variables in the variational statement of boundary value problems. This aspect accounts for the advantages of this class of formulations in framing finite element representations for numerical solutions. Only the primary variable and their first gradients enter the variational statement of the problems. For most higher-order theories, such as that of Fleck and Hutchinson (1997), the primary variables are the displacement components, but both their first and second gradients enter the variational statement, significantly increasing the difficulty of developing an accurate finite element representation. The coefficients in the new reformulation depending on the three material length parameters can be evaluated in the current state or at the current state of a sequence of iterations in the case of the deformation theory, and therefore do not require the introduction of higher-order elements for the solution variables in the incremental or iterative problem.

In the theory proposed by Fleck and Hutchinson (1997), the length parameters are also present in the elastic range. While the theory reformulated by Fleck and Hutchinson (2001) use the plastic strains as primary variables, which leads to a formulation with conventional behavior in the elastic range.

3.3   Torsion of thin wires

Fleck et al. in 1994 consider torsion of a circular cyilndrical bar as an example of the application of the strain gradient theory proposed by Fleck and Hutchinson (1993) and compare the analysis results to the experimental ones on the thin copper wires.

Taking the x_3 axis of a Cartesian coordinate system (x_1, x_2, x_3) to lie along the axis of the bar and a cylinrical polar coordinate system (r, θ, x_3) for later convenience, as shown in Figure 3.1. The radius of the bar is a and κ is the twist per unit length of the bar. They assume the same displacement field as in classical torsion as

$$u_1 = -\kappa x_2 x_3, \quad u_2 = \kappa x_1 x_3, \quad u_3 = 0$$

(3. 45)

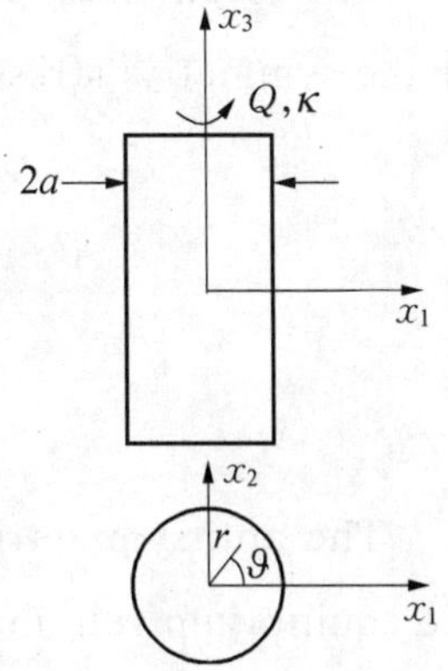

Figure 3. 1   Plots of two coordinate systems on a thin wire.

The associated non-vanishing components of strain are

$$\varepsilon'_{13} = \varepsilon'_{31} = -\frac{1}{2}\kappa x_2, \quad \varepsilon'_{23} = \varepsilon'_{32} = \frac{1}{2}\kappa x_1, \quad \varepsilon_e = \frac{1}{\sqrt{3}}\kappa r \qquad (3.46)$$

and the non-vanishing deviatoric components of curvature tensor are

$$\chi'_{11} = \chi'_{22} = -\frac{1}{2}\kappa, \quad \chi'_{33} = \kappa, \ \chi_e = \kappa \tag{3.47}$$

Then, the effective strain E_e can be obtained as

$$E_e = \sqrt{\epsilon_e^2 + l_{cs}^2 \chi_e^2} = \kappa\sqrt{\frac{1}{3}r^2 + l_{cs}^2} \tag{3.48}$$

The relation between the effective stress and effective strain is assumed as

$$\Sigma_e = \Sigma_0 E_e^N \tag{3.49}$$

The non-vanishing components of the deviatoric couple stress tensor are

$$m_{11} = m_{22} = -\frac{1}{3}\Sigma_0 E_e^{N-1} l_{cs}^2 \kappa, \quad m_{33} = \frac{2}{3}\Sigma_0 E_e^{N-1} l_{cs}^2 \kappa \tag{3.50}$$

The mean stress $\sigma_{kk}/3$ vanishes, and the non-vanishing components of the symmetric stress tensor are

$$\sigma_{13} = \sigma_{31} = -\frac{1}{3}\Sigma_0 E_e^{N-1} \kappa x_2 \tag{3.51}$$

$$\sigma_{23} = \sigma_{32} = \frac{1}{3}\Sigma_0 E_e^{N-1} \kappa x_1 \tag{3.52}$$

The anti-symmetric components τ_{ij} of the stress tensor follow from the equilibrium relation

$$\tau_{23} = -\frac{1}{2}m_{11,1} = -\frac{(1-N)}{18}\Sigma_0 l_{cs}^2 \kappa^3 E_e^{N-3} x_1 \tag{3.53}$$

and

$$\tau_{13} = \frac{1}{2}m_{22,2} = \frac{(1-N)}{18}\Sigma_0 l_{cs}^2 \kappa^3 E_e^{N-3} x_2 \tag{3.54}$$

The fundamental equations of equilibrium are satisfied by the above solution. The boundary tractions $\overline{T}_i$ and $\overline{q}_i$ also vanish on the cylindrical surface of the bar. Hence the displacement field satisfies all requirements.

The relation between the torque Q and the twist per unit length κ is deduced most simply by noting that the strain energy for a unit length of the bar is given by

$$\int_V w(E_e)\mathrm{d}V = \int_V \left(\int_0^\kappa \Sigma_e(E_e)\right)\mathrm{d}V = \int_0^\kappa Q(\kappa)\mathrm{d}\kappa \qquad (3.55)$$

Since Σ_e and Q are homogeneous and of degree N in E_e and κ, respectively, the above equation can be re-write as

$$\int_V w(E_e)\mathrm{d}V = \int_V \frac{\Sigma_e E_e}{N+1}\mathrm{d}V = \frac{Q\kappa}{N+1} \qquad (3.56)$$

Substituting Eqs. (3.48) and (3.49) into (3.56) and integrate over the volume to get

$$Q = \frac{6\pi\Sigma_0 \kappa^N}{N+3}\left[\left(\frac{a^2}{3} + l_{cs}^2\right)^{\frac{N+3}{2}} - l_{cs}^{N+3}\right] \qquad (3.57)$$

Then

$$\frac{Q}{a^3} = \Sigma_0(\kappa a)^N \frac{6\pi}{N+3}\left\{\left[\frac{1}{3} + \left(\frac{l_{cs}}{a}\right)^2\right]^{(N+3)/2} - \left(\frac{l_{cs}}{a}\right)^{N+3}\right\} \qquad (3.58)$$

From simulating the tensile curves of experiment we take $N = 0.22$. If we choose torsional response curve of $2a = 30$ μm as a calibration one, we get $l = 3.75$ μm (Chen and Wang, 2000). The comparisons of predicted results with the experiment results are shown in Figure 3.2. The theoretical predictions given by the theory of Fleck and Hutchinson (1993) agree very well with experiment results. Comparison to the experiments clearly demonstrates an influence of wire diameter on torsional hardening, an effect not observed in the tensile tests. Fleck et al. (1994) attributed this to an added, geometrically necessary component of the dislocation density stored during deformation.

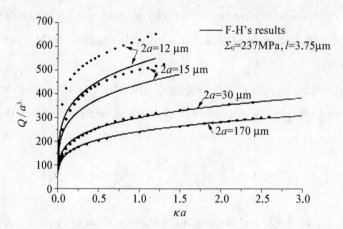

Figure 3. 2   Plots of torque against the surface strain for copper wires with different diameters and various symbols denote the experimental results of Fleck et al. (1994)

3.4 Bending of thin beams

In 1998, Stolken and Evans did the bending experiment and observed a strong size effect whereby thin beams display much stronger plastic work hardening than thick ones and no size dependence is observed in the tension test.

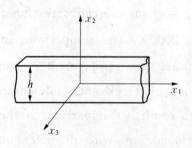

Figure 3. 3   Coordinate system on the ultra-thin beam and h is the thickness of the beam.

Due to small deformation considered, in bending, subject to plane strain deformation, Cartesian (x_1, x_2, x_3) coordinates are adopted as shown in Figure 3. 3. κ is the curvature and h is the beam's thickness. The displacement field is

$$u_1 = \kappa x_1 x_2, \quad u_2 = -\kappa(x_1^2 + x_2^2)/2, \quad u_3 = 0$$

$$(3.59)$$

The velocity field is,

$$v_1 = \dot{\kappa} x_1 x_2, \quad v_2 = -\dot{\kappa}(x_1^2 + x_2^2)/2, \quad v_3 = 0 \qquad (3.60)$$

The non-vanishing strain rates are

$$\dot{\varepsilon}_{11} = -\dot{\varepsilon}_{22} = \dot{\kappa} x_2 \qquad (3.61)$$

The non-vanishing strain components are

$$\varepsilon_{11} = -\varepsilon_{22} = \kappa x_2 \qquad (3.62)$$

The non-vanishing components of curvature tensors are

$$\chi_{31} = -\kappa \qquad (3.63)$$

The effective strain and the effective curvature tensor are

$$\varepsilon_e = \frac{2}{\sqrt{3}} \kappa |x_2|, \quad \chi_e = \sqrt{\frac{2}{3}} \kappa \qquad (3.64)$$

The stretch gradient is given by

$$\eta_{ijk}^{(1)} \eta_{ijk}^{(1)} = \frac{76}{75} \kappa^2 \qquad (3.65)$$

In Begley and Hutchinson (1998), we know that

$$E_e^2 = \varepsilon_e^2 + l_1^2 \eta_{ijk}^{(1)} \eta_{ijk}^{(1)} + l_{cs}^2 \chi_e^2, \qquad (3.66)$$

where $l_{cs}^2 = 2 l_2^2 + 12 l_3^2/5$, $\varepsilon_e = \sqrt{\dfrac{2}{3} \varepsilon'_{ij} \varepsilon'_{ij}}$, $\chi_{ij} = \theta_{i,j}$, $\chi_e = \sqrt{\dfrac{2}{3} \chi_{ij} \chi_{ij}}$ and

$l_2 = \sqrt{\dfrac{6}{5}} l_3$.

Eq. (3.66) can be represented in the following form

$$\begin{cases} E_e^2 = \varepsilon_e^2 + l^2 \eta^2 \\ \eta = \sqrt{c_1 \eta_{ijk}^{(1)} \eta_{ijk}^{(1)} + \chi_e^2} \end{cases} \qquad (3.67)$$

where η is called the effective strain gradient and $l = l_{cs}$, $c_1 = \left(\dfrac{l_1}{l_{cs}}\right)^2$.

We know that the length scale l_1 for the stretch gradient is very small and l_{cs} that corresponds to the rotation gradient is larger (Stolken and Evans, 1998), then from Eq. (3.67), we can find that $c_1 = \left(\dfrac{l_1}{l_{cs}}\right)^2$ is very small and $\eta_{ijk}^{(1)}\eta_{ijk}^{(1)}$ has the same order as χ_e^2. In order to be consistent with the theory in analyzing the torsion experiment, we can omit the term of $\eta_{ijk}^{(1)}\eta_{ijk}^{(1)}$ in Eq. (3.67) and adopt $\eta = \chi_e$, that is only the rotation gradient is considered while investigating the bending experiment.

From simulating the tensile test results of thin beams, the relation between the stress and plastic strain can be expressed as (Stolken and Evans, 1998)

$$\sigma = \Sigma_0 + \varepsilon_{pl}E_p \tag{3.68}$$

where Σ_0 is the yield strength, ε_{pl} is the plastic strain and E_p the hardening coefficient. Then the relation between the effective stress and effective strain can be obtained

$$\sigma_e = \frac{\sqrt{3}}{2}\Sigma_0 + \frac{3}{4}E_p\varepsilon_{ep} \tag{3.69}$$

where ε_{ep} is the effective plastic strain.

Stolken and Evans (1998) have analyzed this problem based on the strain gradient theory given by Fleck and Hutchinson (1997). The hardening relation including the effect of strain gradient plasticity is

$$\Sigma_e = \frac{\sqrt{3}}{2}\Sigma_0 + \frac{3}{4}E_pE_e, \quad E_e = \sqrt{\varepsilon_e^2 + l^2\eta^2}, \quad \eta = \chi_e = \sqrt{\frac{2}{3}\chi_{ij}\chi_{ij}} \tag{3.70}$$

The strain energy density takes the form

$$w = \frac{E_e}{8}(3E_pE_e + 4\sqrt{3}\Sigma_0) \tag{3.71}$$

and the total energy per unit length is

$$W = \int_{-h/2}^{h/2} wb\,dx_2 \tag{3.72}$$

where b is the width of the beam.

Then the bending moment M can be obtained

$$M = \frac{dW}{d\kappa} \tag{3.73}$$

Combining Eqs. (3.64), (3.70)–(3.73), we obtain

$$M = \Sigma_0 b \left[\frac{h}{4} \sqrt{h^2 + 2l^2} + \frac{1}{2} l^2 \ln \left(\frac{\sqrt{h^2/2 + l^2} + \sqrt{2}\,h/2}{l} \right) \right]$$

$$+ \frac{1}{12} E_p \kappa b (h^3 + 6l^2 h) \tag{3.74}$$

The non-dimensional moment is

$$\frac{4M}{\Sigma_0 bh^2} = \sqrt{1 + 2\left(\frac{l}{h}\right)^2} + 2\left(\frac{l}{h}\right)^2 \ln \left[\frac{\sqrt{h^2/2 + l^2} + \sqrt{2}\,h/2}{l} \right]$$

$$+ \frac{1}{3\Sigma_0} E_p \kappa \left(h + 6\frac{l^2}{h} \right) \tag{3.75}$$

The length scale l is determined as $l = 6.12\ \mu$m by fitting Eq. (3.75) to all of the bending moment measurements (Chen and Wang, 2000) as shown in Figure 5.5 in Chapter 5.

3.5 Micro-indentation hardness

Indentation tests have been used extensively to characterize the plastic properties of solids. Historically, one of the primary goals of indentation testing has been to estimate the yield stress by measuring the hardness, defined as the load on the indenter divided by the area of the resulting impression. Recently, hardness has been shown to be size-dependent when the width of the impression is below about fifty microns.

Such small-scale experiments are often referred as micro-indentation tests. The measured hardness may be double or even triple as the size of indent decreases from about fifty microns to one micron. In effect, the smaller the scale the stronger the solid will be. This is a large effect which almost certainly has significant implications for other applications of metal plasticity at the micron scale. A size-dependence of indentation hardness is not encompassed by conventional plasticity. Simple arguments based on dimensional analysis, reveal that any plasticity theory which does not contain a constitutive length parameter will predict size-independent indentation hardness.

Begley and Hutchinson (1998) used the Fleck and Hutchinson strain gradient plasticity theory (1997) to determine the effect of the material length scale on predicted hardness for small indents. Prior to this work, Shu and Fleck (1998) applied the eariler version of the plasticity theory that accounts for contributions of rotation gradients to hardening but not of stretch gradients. They found that a version of the theory based on rotation gradients alone cannot account for the strong size-dependence observed experimentally. The two primary goals in Begley and Hutchinson (1998)'s work are: (i) to assess the effectiveness of strain gradient plasticity theory accounting for the strong size-dependence observed in indentation tests; and (ii) to infer values of the constitutive length parameters via correlation of the predicted results with experimental data available in the literature.

a) Length scale

The effective strain measure used to define the deformation theory in Fleck and Hutchinson (1997) is taken to be an isotropic invariant

$$E_e^2 = \frac{2}{3}\varepsilon'_{ij}\varepsilon'_{ij} + l_1^2 \eta'^{(1)}_{ijk} \eta'^{(1)}_{ijk} + \left(\frac{4}{3}l_2^2 + \frac{8}{5}l_3^2\right)\chi'_{ij}\chi'_{ij} + \left(\frac{4}{3}l_2^2 - \frac{8}{5}l_3^2\right)\chi'_{ij}\chi'_{ji}$$

$$(3.76)$$

Begley and Hutchinson (1998) rewrote the above equation as

$$E_e^2 = \frac{2}{3}\varepsilon'_{ij}\varepsilon'_{ij} + l_1^2 \eta'^{(1)}_{ijk} \eta'^{(1)}_{ijk} + \frac{2}{3}l_{cs}^2 \chi'_{ij}\chi'_{ij} + \left(\frac{4}{3}l_2^2 - \frac{8}{5}l_3^2\right)\chi'_{ij}\chi'_{ji}$$

(3.77)

where $l_{cs}^2 = (2l_2^3 + 12l_3^2/5)$. The invariant $\eta'^{(1)}_{ijk} \eta'^{(1)}_{ijk}$ depends on both stretch and rotation gradients. For deformation which are irrotational $\chi_{ij} = 0$, only the first of the length parameters, l_1, has any influence. It is through $l_1^2 \eta'^{(1)}_{ijk} \eta'^{(1)}_{ijk}$ that stretch gradients make their presence felt.

To reduce the set of length parameters from three to two, Begley and Hutchinson (1998) exclude any dependence on $\chi_{ij}\chi_{ji}$ in the above equation by taking $l_2 = \sqrt{6/5}\, l_3$ such that the above equation becomes

$$E_e^2 = \frac{2}{3}\varepsilon'_{ij}\varepsilon'_{ij} + l_1^2 \eta'^{(1)}_{ijk} \eta'^{(1)}_{ijk} + \frac{2}{3}l_{cs}^2 \chi'_{ij}\chi'_{ij}$$

(3.78)

From (3.77), it can be noted that this combination is positive if both l_1 and l_{cs} are non-zero. As mentioned above, l_{cs} controls the size effect in wire torsion, while the outcome of micro-indentation will be that l_1 is by far the more important of the two parameters. Thus, it seems likely that both length parameters, l_1 and l_{cs}, must be retained for general application of the theory. Moreover, unless it turns out that these two length parameters have fixed proportion for all metals, it would appear that experimental data from at least two different types of small scale tests will be required to separately determine l_1 and l_{cs}.

A strain energy density function is assumed in the form

$$W(E_e) = w(E_e) + \frac{E}{6(1-2\nu)}\varepsilon_{ii}^2$$

(3.79)

where E is Young's modulus and ν is Poisson's ratio. The dependence on deviatoric quantities $w(E_e)$ is chosen such that in uniaxial tension the stress-strain behavior derived from (3.79) reproduces the Ramberg-Osgood tensile relation

$$\varepsilon = \frac{\sigma}{E} + \frac{3}{7}\frac{\sigma_y}{E}\left(\frac{\sigma}{\sigma_y}\right)^n$$

(3.80)

The work increment per unit volume associated with an arbitrary variation of the displacements is

$$\delta W = \sigma_{ij}\delta\varepsilon_{ij} + \tau_{ijk}\delta\eta_{ijk} \tag{3.81}$$

b) Finite element formulation and indentation model

The finite element model is illustrated in Figure 3.4. The contact radius is defined as a, the depth of penetration of the indenter is δ. The half-angle of the indenter, β, is taken to be $72°$, which corresponds to a Vickers indenter. The indenter is assumed to be rigid. Contact between the indenter and the substrate is assumed to be frictionless. Studies on conventional elastic-plastic solids indicate little difference between the hardness predicted for a frictionless indenter and that for an indenter-substrate system permitting no sliding. The material is modeled as being a semi-infinite half plane; the size of the mesh was chosen by decreasing the size relative to the contact radius until there was a negligible change in the calculated hardness.

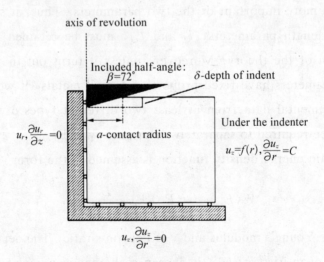

Figure 3.4   Geometry of the axisymmetric indentation model and boundary condition. (Begley & Hutchinson, 1998)

It is important to note that admissibility requirements of the second gradient terms require C_1 continuity in displacements. Previous strain gradient modeling efforts have explored a variety of types of elements (Xia and Hutchinson, 1996) and have shown that element performance is strongly dependent on the constitutive behavior. Based on this earlier work, an element similar to one initially derived for plate applications was chosen by Begley and Hutchinson (1998). The element is a three noded triangle with eighteen degrees of freedom. For each node, the nodal variables are u_r, $\partial u_r/\partial r$, $\partial u_r/\partial z$, u_z, $\partial u_z/\partial r$, $\partial u_z/\partial z$. Thus, the elements produce C_1 continuity at the nodes.

Axisymmetry dictates that u_r and $\partial u_r/\partial z$ are zero along the axis of symmetry. The vertical displacement along the bottom of the mesh was constrained to be zero, while the radial quantities were unconstrained. Derivatives of displacements must be specified in addition to displacements, as they are additional nodal degrees of freedom.

For a frictionless indenter, the proper boundary condition underneath the indenter is a constraint between the radial and vertical displacements, the nodes in the contact region are constrained to fall on the indenter, with freedom to slide up and down the face of the indenter. For small strain theory and the shallow indenters considered there, this can be approximated by specifying the downward displacement and allowing the radial displacement to be free. The more shallow the indenter is, the more accurate are these linearized boundary conditions. Thus, the following modified boundary conditions under the indenter were imposed

$$\text{(i)} \ u_z(r) = -\delta + \frac{r}{\tan\beta} \quad \frac{\partial u_z}{\partial r} = \frac{1}{\tan\beta} \tag{3.82}$$

$$\text{(ii) no restriction on } u_r, \ \frac{\partial u_r}{\partial r}, \ \frac{\partial u_r}{\partial z}, \ \frac{\partial u_z}{\partial z} \tag{3.83}$$

In addition to approximating zero shear traction under the indenter, (3.83) results in a zero double stress traction, enforced by the variational principle.

The contact between the indenter and the substrate was simulated by assuming a contact radius, a, and iterating to find the proper indentation depth, δ, for that size of indent. The proper indentation depth is defined as the depth at which the normal pressure between the indenter and material goes to zero at the edge of contact, i.e., at $r = a$. Using small strain theory for shallow indenters, the pressure is given by the traction in the vertical direction, given by

$$t_k = \sigma_{2k} - \tau_{2jk,j} - \tau_{2lk,l} \tag{3.84}$$

The pressure under the indenter simplifies to

$$t_z = \sigma_{zz} - 2\frac{\partial \tau_{zrz}}{\partial r} - \frac{\partial \tau_{zzz}}{\partial z} \tag{3.85}$$

For the strain gradient solid, evaluating the traction under the indenter using (3.85) and the finite element solution proved unreliable, due to the difficulty in evaluating the derivatives of the higher order stress quantities. To avoid this, the correct depth was assumed to be that at which the nodal forces went to zero at the edge of contact. Since the nodal force represent the integrated average of the tractions over the element faces, this is consistent with the zero-traction criterion.

c) Numerical results

Begley and Hutchinson (1998) take $l_1 = l_{cs} = l$ in their numerical calculations, but they argue that in their study, identification of l by fitting the solutions for the SG solid to experimental indentation data should be regarded as an approximate determination of l_1 with no implication for l_{cs}.

The experimental data from McElhaney et al. (1998) for copper single crystals are plotted in Figure 3.5, in which Nix's (1998) result for the size-dependent hardness

$$\left(\frac{H}{H_0}\right)^2 = 1 + \frac{h^*}{h} \tag{3.86}$$

is included in the figure. H_0 is the hardness predicted by the conventional plasticity theory and H is the one from strain gradient plasticity theory. The linear dependence of $(H/H_0)^2$ with $1/h$ displayed by the data over

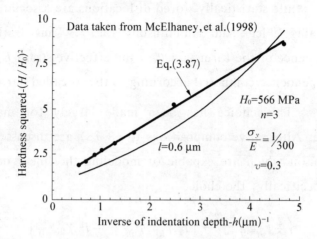

Figure 3.5　Comparison of the experimental results of McElhaney et al. (1998) with the theoretical predictions of Nix (Eq. 3.86) and the predictions of Fleck & Hutchinson SG theory. (Begley & Hutchinson, 1998)

the range from $h = 1/5 - 2\ \mu$m is striking. Nix extrapolated the unnormalized data to $1/h = 0$ to obtain $H_0 = 556$ MPa. The value, $h^* = 1.68\ \mu$m, in (3.86) gives the best fit to the data. Poole et al. (1996) also presented plots of H^2 vs $1/h$ for their micro-indentation data on two sets of copper polycrystals, one annealed and one work hardened. Their data indicates a value of h^* for the work hardened copper, which is roughly one quarter that for the annealed copper. Their data, however, is less convincing as to the linear dependence of $(H/H_0)^2$ on $1/h$.

　　The calculation results by Begley and Hutchinson (1998) are superimposed in Figure 3.5 for the case $n = 3$, using $H_0 = 556$ MPa and accounting for the difference between the pyramidal and conical indenters. The least squares fit outlined earlier results in the value $l = 0.6\ \mu$m. The results predicted by Begley and Hutchinson (1998) do not produce a linear dependence of $(H/H_0)^2$ on $1/h$ over the full range of $1/h$. The dependence of their results seen in Figure 3.5 is a consequence of the composition of the invariants employed in (3.78) in strain gradient plasticity, strain gradients are associated with geometric dislocations, while statistically stored dislocations are associated with the deviator strains (Fleck and Hutchinson, 1997). Thus, rather than a linear dependence of the form $\rho_s + \rho_G$, the effective strain E_e in (3.78) models a dependence composed according to the so-called harmonic mean as $\sqrt{\rho_s^2 + \rho_G^2}$. This choice has been made largely for mathematical convenience. Alternative compositions to (3.78) are discussed by Fleck and Hutchinson which are capable of modeling the linear dependence, $\rho_s + \rho_G$. Specifically, the choice

$$E_e = \left[\left(\frac{2}{3} \epsilon'_{ij} \epsilon'_{ij} \right)^{\lambda/2} + \left(l_1^2 \eta'^{(1)}_{ijk} \eta'^{(1)}_{ijk} + \frac{2}{3} l_{cs}^2 \chi'_{ij} \chi'_{ij} \right)^{\lambda/2} \right]^{1/\lambda} \qquad (3.87)$$

models the linear dependence for $\lambda = 1$ and reduces to (3.78) for $\lambda = 2$.

3.6 Size effects in particle reinforced metal matrix composites

Wei (2001) has used the F-H strain gradient plasticity theory to simulate the mechanical response of the PMMC. A detailed analysis of the particle size effects is carried out. Adopting the strain gradient plasticity theory, the composite stress-strain curves depend on the following parameters: the Young's modulus ratio of both particle and matrix; Poisson's ratio; particle volume fraction; particle aspect ratio; strain hardening exponent of matrix material; a normalized particle volume with the material length scale parameter. A series stress-strain relations depending on all the parameters mentioned above have been given by Wei (2001). In order to examine the F-H strain gradient plasticity theory, comparisons with experiments are analyzed and the material length scale parameter is predicted. In this section, we only give the comparison results to the experiments and the other details can be found in the paper by Wei (2001).

The first application is to the Al – 4wt% Mg alloy reinforced by the SiC particle. This experiment has been done by Yang et al. (1990). The dependence of compressive stress strain relations on the particle sizes for the higher particle volume fraction case (large value of f_p) in experiment and analysis is shown in Figure 3.6. $\kappa = A/B = R/H$ is the particle and cell aspect ratio as shown in Figure 3.7. The experimental result corresponds to the two particle sizes, i.e., when the particle radii are 13 micron and 165 micron. According to these particle sizes, Wei (2001) determined the particle volume V_p in the analytical results. Moreover, from Figure 3.6, when the composite length scale L is taken as 6.45 microns, both results are consistent qualitatively and quantitatively, when the strain value is smaller than 2%. When the strain value is larger than 2%, the analytical results for the small particle case will go up quickly and deviate from the experimental result. Wei (2001) regards this as the reason that a perfect model is used in the analysis and damages and particle cracking always exist in the real solid.

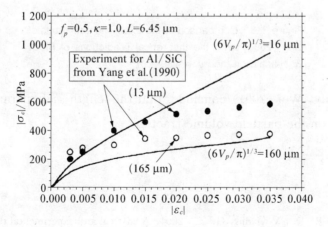

Figure 3.6   Comparison of the experimental results of Yang et al. (1990) with the theoretical predictions of Fleck & Hutchinson theory. (Wei, 2001)

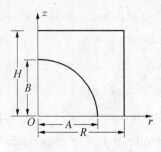

Figure 3. 7   Cell geometry. (Wei, 2001)

Another application is to the experiment of 2124Al reinforced by SiC particles done by Ling (2000). The dependence of the compressive stress strain curves on the particle sizes for the lower particle fraction from experimental results and analytical results is shown in Figure 3. 8. From Figure 3. 8, when the composite length scale parameter L is taken as 4. 25 microns, both results are consistent qualitatively and quantitatively.

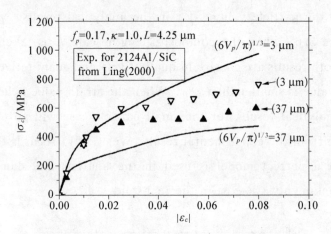

Figure 3. 8   Comparison of the experimental results of Ling (2000) with the theoretical predictions of Fleck & Hutchinson theory. (Wei, 2001)

Roughly, Wei (2001) concludes that the length scale parameter L is dependent on the particle volume fraction.

References

Abu Al-Rub, R. K., Voyiadjis, G. Z., 2004. Analytical and experimental determination of the material intrinsic length scale of strain gradient plasticity theory from micro- and nano-indentation experiments. Int. J. Plasticity 20, 1139 – 1182.

Abu Al-Rub, R. K., Voyiadjis, G. Z., 2006. A physical based gradient plasticity theory.

Int. J. Plasticity 22, 654 – 684.

Acharya, A. and Bassani, J. L., 1995. On non-local flow theories that preserve the classical structure of incremental boundary value problems. In Micromechanics of Plasticity and Damage of Multiphase Materials, IUTAM Symposium, Paris, Aug 29 – Sept 1.

Acharya, A., Beaudoin, A. J., 2000. Grain-size effect in viscoplastic polycrystals at moderate strains. J. Mech. Phys. Solids 48, 2213 – 2230.

Bassani, J. L., 2001. Incompatibility and a simple gradient theory of plasticity. J. Mech. Phys. Solid 49, 1983 – 1996.

Beaudoin, A. J., Acharya, A., 2001. A model for rate-dependent flow of metal polycrystals based on the slip plane lattice incompatibility. Mater. Sci. Eng. A 309 – 310, 411 – 415.

Begley, M. R. and Hutchinson, J. W., 1998. The mechanics of size-dependent indentation. J. Mech. Phys. Solids 46, 2049 – 2068.

Chen, S. H. and Wang, T. C., 2000. A new hardening law for strain gradient plasticity. Acta Mater., 48(16), 3997 – 4005.

Chen, S. H. and Wang, T. C., 2001. Strain gradient theory with couple stress for crystalline solids. European J. Mech. A/Solids 20, 739 – 756.

Chen, S. H. and Wang, T. C., 2002. A new deformation theory for strain gradient effects. Int. J. Plasticity 18, 971 – 995.

Evers, L. P., Brekelmans, W. A. M., Geers, M. G. D., 2004. Scale dependent crystal plasticity framework with dislocation density and grain boundary effects. Int. J. Solids Struct. 41, 5209 – 5230.

Fleck, N. A. and Hutchinson, J. W., 1993. A phenomenological theory for strain gradient effects in plasticity. J. Mech. Phys. Solids 41, 1825 – 1857.

Fleck, N. A. and Hutchinson, J. W., 1997. Strain Gradient Plasticity. Advances in Applied Mechanics ed. J. W. Hutchinson and T. Y. Wu, 33, 295 – 361 Academic Press, New York.

Fleck, N. A., Muller, G. M., Ashby, M. F. and Hutchinson, J. W., 1994. Strain gradient plasticity: theory and experiment. Acta Metal. et Mater. 42, 475 – 487.

Fleck and Hutchinson, 2001. A reformulation of strain gradient plasticity. J. Mech. Phys. Solids 49, 2245 – 2271.

Gao, H., Huang, Y., Nix, W. D. and Hutchinson, J. W., 1999a. Mechanism-based strain gradient plasticity-I. theory. J. Mech. Phys. Solids 47, 1239 – 1263.

Gao, H., Huang, Y., Nix, W. D., 1999b. Modeling plasticity at the micrometer scale. Naturwissenschaften 86, 507 – 515.

Gurtin, M.E. , 2002. A gradient theory of single-crystal viscoplasticity that accounts for geometrically necessary dislocations. J. Mech. Phys. Solids 50 (1), 5 – 32.

Gurtin, M.E. , 2003. On a framework for small-deformation viscoplasticity: free energy, microforces, strain gradients. Int. J. Plasticity 19, 47 – 90.

Hill, R. , 1950. Mathematical theory of plasticity. Oxford University Press, Oxford, England.

Huang, Y. , Gao, H. , Nix, W. D. and Hutchinson, J. W. , 2000a. Mechanism based strain gradient plasticity-II. Analysis. J. Mech. Phys. Solids 48, 99 – 128.

Huang, Y. , Xue, Z. , Gao, H. , Nix, W. D. , Xia, Z. C. , 2000b. A study of micro-indentation hardness tests by mechanism-based strain gradient plasticity. J. Mater. Res. 15, 1786 – 1796.

Huang, Y. , Qu, S. , Hwang, K.C. , Li, M. , Gao, H. , 2004. A conventional theory of mechanism-based strain gradient plasticity. Int. J. Plasticity. 20, 753 – 782.

Hwang, K.C. , Jiang, H. , Huang, Y. , Gao, H. , Hu, N. , 2002. A finite deformation theory of strain gradient plasticity. J. Mech. Phys. Solids 50, 81 – 99.

Hwang, K.C. , Jiang, H. , Huang, Y. , Gao, H. , 2003. Finite deformation analysis of mechanism-based strain gradient plasticity: torsion and crack tip field. Int. J. Plasticity 19, 235 – 251.

Koiter, W. T. , 1964. Couple-stresses in the theory of elasticity, I and II, Proc. Roy. Netherlands Acad. Sci. B67, 17 – 64.

Ling, Z. , 2000. Deformation behavior and microstructure effect in 2124Al/SuCp composite. J. Comp. Mater. 34, 101 – 115.

McElhaney, K. W. , Vlassak, J. J. , Nix, W. D. , 1998. Determination of indenter tip geometry and indentation contact area for depth-sensing indentation experiments. J. Mater. Res. 13, 1300 – 1306.

Mindlin, R. D. , 1963. Influence of couple-stress on stress concentrations, Exp. Mech. 3, 1 – 7.

Mindlin, R. D. , 1964. Microstructure in linear elasticity, Arch. Rational Mech. Abal. 16, 51 – 78.

Nix, W. D. , Gao, H. , 1998. Indentation size effects in crystalline materials: a law for strain gradient plasticity. J. Mech. Phys. Solids 46, 411 – 425.

Poole, W. J. , Ashby, M. F. And Fleck, N. A. , 1996. Microhardness of annealed and work-hardened copper polycrystals. Scripta Metall. Mater. 34, 559 – 564.

Qiu, X. , Huang, Y. , Nix, W.D. , Hwang, K.C. , Gao, H. , 2001. Effect of intrinsic lattice resistance in strain gradient plasticity. Acta Mater. 49, 3949 – 3958.

Qiu, X., Huang, Y., Wei, Y., Gao, H., Hwang, K. C., 2003. The flow theory of mechanism-based strain gradient plasticity. Mech. Mater. 35, 245 – 258.

Shu, J. Y., Fleck, N. A., 1998. The prediction of a size effect in microindentation. Int. J. Solids Struct. 35, 1363 – 1383.

Smyshlyaev, V. P. And Fleck, N. A., 1996. The role of strain gradients in the grain size effect for polycrystals. J. Mech. Phys. Solids 44, 465 – 495.

Stolken, J. S. And Evans, A. G., 1998. A microbend test method for measuring the plasticity length scale. Acta Mater. 46, 5109 – 1515.

Toupin, R., 1962. Elastic materials with couple-stresses, Arch. Rational Mech. Anal. 11, 385 – 414.

Wang, W., Huang, Y., Hsia, K. J., Hu, K. X., Chandra, A., 2003. A study of microbend test by strain gradient plasticity. Int. J. Plasticity. 19, 365 – 382.

Wei, Y., 2001. Particle size effects in the particle-reinforced metal-matrix composites. Acta Mech. Sinica 17, 45 – 58.

Xia, Z. C. and Hutchinson, J. W., 1996. Crack tip fields in strain gradient plasticity. J. Mech. Phys. Solids 44, 1621 – 1648.

Yang, J., Cady, C., Hu, M. S., et al., 1990. Effects of damage on the flow strength and ductility of a ductile Al-alloy reinforced with SiC particles. Acta Metall. Mater. 38, 2613 – 2619.

4　MSG and TNT theories

4.1　A law for strain gradient plasticity

Analysis of indentation experiments by Nix and Gao (1998) has shed some light on both the material l introduced by Fleck and Hutchinson (1993) and the experimental law needed to advance a mechanism-based theory of strain gradient plasticity. Nix and Gao (1998) started from the Taylor relation between the shear length and dislocation in a material,

$$\tau = \alpha \mu b \sqrt{\rho_T} = \alpha \mu b \sqrt{\rho_S + \rho_G} \qquad (4.1)$$

where ρ_T is the total dislocation density, ρ_S is the density of statistically stored dislocations, ρ_G is the density of geometrically necessary dislocations, μ is the shear modulus, b is the Burgers vector and α is an empirical constant usually ranging from 0.2 to 0.5. A gradient in the strain field is accommodated by geometrically necessary dislocations, so that an effective strain gradient η can be defined as

$$\eta = \rho_G b \qquad (4.2)$$

This expression allows η to be interpreted as the curvature of deformation under bending and twist per unit length under torsion.

If the von Mises rule is used, the tensile flow stress can be written as

(Nix and Gao, 1998)

$$\sigma = \sqrt{3}\,\tau = \sqrt{3}\,\alpha\mu b \sqrt{\rho_s + \eta/b} \qquad (4.3)$$

In the absence of the strain gradient term, Nix and Gao (1998) identify the uniaxial stress-strain law

$$\sigma = \sqrt{3}\,\alpha\mu b \sqrt{\rho_s} = \sigma_Y f(\varepsilon) \qquad (4.4)$$

as the hardening due to the statistically stored dislocations alone, where σ_Y is the yield stress. For convenience, they define the state of plastic yield as

$$\sigma = \sigma_Y \quad \varepsilon = \varepsilon_Y \quad f(\varepsilon_Y) = 1 \qquad (4.5)$$

where ε_Y is usually taken as 0.2% for ductile metals. Combining (4.3) and (4.4) leads to a law for strain gradient plasticity

$$\sigma = \sigma_Y \sqrt{f^2(\varepsilon) + l\eta} \qquad (4.6)$$

Where

$$l = 3\alpha^2 \left(\frac{\mu}{\sigma_Y}\right)^2 b \qquad (4.7)$$

is identified as the material length introduced by Fleck and Hutchinson (1993, 1997). In terms of macroscopic properties of structural metals, the ratio between μ and σ_Y is typically on the order of 100, suggesting that l is on the order of $10^4 b$, which is indeed on the order of microns.

4.2   Deformation theory of MSG

Gao et al. (1999) proposed a mechanism-based strain gradient plasticity theory (MSG). Here we briefly introduce the deformation theory of MSG.

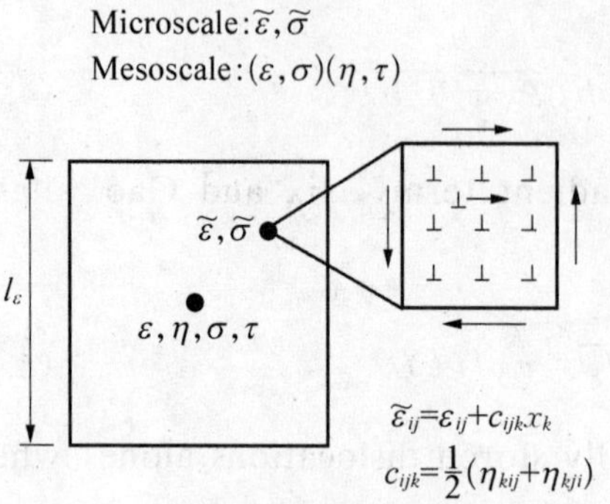

Microscale: $\widetilde{\varepsilon}, \widetilde{\sigma}$
Mesoscale: $(\varepsilon, \sigma)(\eta, \tau)$

l_ε

$\widetilde{\varepsilon}, \widetilde{\sigma}$

$\varepsilon, \eta, \sigma, \tau$

$\widetilde{\varepsilon}_{ij} = \varepsilon_{ij} + c_{ijk} x_k$
$c_{ijk} = \frac{1}{2}(\eta_{kij} + \eta_{kji})$

Figure 4. 1　The multiscale framework for MSG and l_ε is the size of the mesoscale representative cell.

Consider a unit cell on the mesoscale with the length of all edges equal to l_ε (Figure 4. 1). The mesoscale cell size l_ε is much smaller than the intrinsic material l in (4. 6) associated with strain gradient plasticity. Within this cell, the displacement field is assumed to vary as

$$\widetilde{u}_k = \varepsilon_{ik} x_i + \frac{1}{2} \eta_{ijk} x_i x_j + o(x^3)$$

(4. 8)

where x_i denotes the local coordinates with origin at the center of the cell. ε_{ij} is the symmetric strain, $\varepsilon_{ij} = \frac{1}{2}(u_{i,j} + u_{j,i})$ and η_{ijk} is second gradient of the displacement field, $\eta_{ijk} = u_{kij}$. For simplicity, MSG theory does not consider the elastic deformation and compressibility of materials.

The condition of incompressibility can be stated as

$$\varepsilon_{ii} = 0 \quad \eta_{ijk}^H = \frac{1}{4}(\delta_{ik} \eta_{jpp} + \delta_{jk} \eta_{ipp}) = 0$$

(4. 9)

where η_{ijk}^H denotes the hydrostatic part of η_{ijk}, following the notation of Fleck and Hutchinson (1997). Under these restrictions, the work increment per unit volume of solid due to an arbitrary variation of displacement u is

$$\delta w = \sigma'_{ij} \delta \varepsilon_{ij} + \tau'_{ijk} \delta \eta_{ijk}$$

(4. 10)

where σ'_{ij} denotes the deviatoric stress components, and τ'_{ijk} are the deviatoric components of the higher order stress tensor conjugated to the strain gradient tensor η_{ijk}.

When the cell is sufficiently small, higher order displacement gradients can be ignored and the strain field varies linearly as

$$\tilde{\varepsilon}_{ij} = \varepsilon_{ij} + \frac{1}{2}(\eta_{kij} + \eta_{kji})x_k \qquad (4.11)$$

The microscale strain $\tilde{\varepsilon}_{ij}$ is thus related to the mesoscale strain ε_{ij} and strain gradient η_{ijk}.

Following classical plasticity theory (Hill, 1950), the microscale effective strain can be defined as

$$\tilde{\varepsilon}_e^2 = \frac{2}{3}\tilde{\varepsilon}_{ij}\tilde{\varepsilon}_{ij} \qquad (4.12)$$

$$\tilde{\varepsilon}_e \delta \tilde{\varepsilon}_e = \frac{2}{3}\tilde{\varepsilon}_{ij}\delta \tilde{\varepsilon}_{ij} \qquad (4.13)$$

The incremental plastic work can be expressed as $\tilde{\sigma}'_{ij}\delta\tilde{\varepsilon}_{ij}$.

In MSG theory, it is assumed that the essential structure of conventional plasticity is preserved on the microscale, thus the associated rule of plastic normality holds

$$\frac{d\tilde{\varepsilon}_{ij}}{d\tilde{\varepsilon}_e} = \frac{3}{2}\frac{\tilde{\sigma}'_{ij}}{\tilde{\sigma}_e} \qquad (4.14)$$

where $\tilde{\sigma}_e = \sqrt{3\tilde{\sigma}'_{ij}\tilde{\sigma}'_{ij}/2}$ is the effective stress and $\tilde{\varepsilon}_e = \sqrt{2\tilde{\varepsilon}_{ij}\tilde{\varepsilon}_{ij}/3}$.

Combining equations (4.13) and (4.14) yields

$$\tilde{\sigma}'_{ij} = \frac{2}{3}\frac{\tilde{\sigma}_e}{\tilde{\varepsilon}_e}\tilde{\varepsilon}_{ij} \qquad (4.15)$$

where

$$\tilde{\sigma}_e = \sigma_Y \sqrt{f^2(\tilde{\varepsilon}_e) + l\eta} \qquad (4.16)$$

The microscale and mesoscale are linked by the plastic work equality,

$$\int_{V_{\text{cell}}} \tilde{\sigma}'_{ij}\delta\tilde{\varepsilon}_{ij}\,dV = (\sigma'_{ij}\delta\varepsilon_{ij} + \tau'_{ijk}\delta\eta_{ijk})V_{\text{cell}} \qquad (4.17)$$

Inserting the kinematic assumption

$$\delta\tilde{\varepsilon}_{ij} = \delta\varepsilon_{ij} + \frac{1}{2}(\delta\eta_{kij} + \delta\eta_{kji})x_k \qquad (4.18)$$

into equation (4.17) and equating the corresponding coefficients of $\delta\varepsilon_{ij}$ and $\delta\eta_{kij}$ lead to the constitutive equations for the deformation theory of MSG.

The mesoscale constitutive equations are summarized as

$$\sigma'_{ij} = 2\varepsilon_{ij}\sigma_e/3\varepsilon_e \tag{4.19}$$

$$\tau'_{ijk} = l_\varepsilon^2[\sigma_e(\Lambda_{ijk} - \Pi_{ijk})/\varepsilon_e + n\sigma_{ref}^2\varepsilon_e^{2n-1}\Pi_{ijk}/\sigma_e] \tag{4.20}$$

where

$$\sigma_e = \sigma_Y\sqrt{f^2(\varepsilon_e) + l\eta} \tag{4.21}$$

$$\Lambda_{ijk} = \frac{1}{72}[2\eta_{ijk} + \eta_{kji} + \eta_{kij} - (\delta_{ik}\eta_{ppj} + \delta_{jk}\eta_{ppi})/4] \tag{4.22}$$

$$\Pi_{ijk} = \frac{\varepsilon_{mn}}{54\varepsilon_e^2}[\varepsilon_{ik}\eta_{jmn} + \varepsilon_{jk}\eta_{imn} - (\delta_{ik}\varepsilon_{jp} + \delta_{jk}\varepsilon_{ip})\eta_{pmn}/4] \tag{4.23}$$

The effective strain gradient in MSG theory has the same definition as that in Fleck and Hutchinson (1997),

$$\eta^2 = c_1\eta'_{iik}\eta'_{jjk} + c_2\eta'_{ijk}\eta'_{ijk} + c_3\eta'_{ijk}\eta'_{kji} \tag{4.24}$$

which measures the density of geometrically necessary dislocations. The three constants c_1, c_2, c_3 are determined by Gao et al. (1999) using a series of distinct dislocation models consisting of plane strain bending, pure torsion and two dimensional axisymmetric void growth and finally they obtained

$$\eta = \sqrt{\eta'_{ijk}\eta'_{ijk}/4} \tag{4.25}$$

An important question is whether the MSG constitutive law could be written in the form

$$\sigma'_{ij} = \frac{\partial W}{\partial\varepsilon_{ij}} \qquad \tau'_{ijk} = \frac{\partial W}{\partial\eta_{ijk}} \tag{4.26}$$

where $W = W(\boldsymbol{\varepsilon}, \boldsymbol{\eta})$ is a strain energy density function. This is clearly impossible because the MSG constitutive equations do not satisfy the reciprocity relation, i.e.

$$\frac{\partial \sigma'_{ij}}{\partial \eta_{kmn}} \neq \frac{\partial \tau'_{kmn}}{\partial \varepsilon_{ij}} \tag{4.27}$$

required for the existence of a strain energy function.

Discussion

The MSG constitutive equations will be analyzed in next section and will be further studied with a detailed investigation of micro-indentation. Here we give the discussion by Gao et al. (1999) on a few issues of MSG theory.

  a) Taylor hardening model

Some discussion of the Taylor hardening model might be helpful to gain a deeper understanding of the connection between MSG and the dislocation interaction processes. Dislocation theory indicates that the Peach-Koehler force due to interaction of a pair of dislocations is proportional to

$$\sigma_{\text{pair}} \sim \frac{\mu b}{2\pi(1-\nu)L} \tag{4.28}$$

This stress sets a critical value for the applied stress to break or untangle the interactive pair so that slip can occur even if one of the dislocation is pinned by an obstacle. In the Taylor model this picture is generalized to the interaction of a group of statistically stored dislocation which trap each other in a random way. If the mean dislocation spacing is L, the critical stress required to untangle the interaction dislocation and to induce significant plastic deformation is defined as the Taylor flow stress

$$\sigma = \frac{\alpha \mu b}{L} = \alpha \mu b \sqrt{\rho} \tag{4.29}$$

where $\rho = 1/L^2$ is the dislocation density. Alternatively, the Taylor flow stress can also be viewed as the "passing stress" for a moving dislocation to glide through a forest of tangled dislocations without being pinned. The similarity between the Taylor model and the interaction of a pair of dislocations indicates the potential of using (4.29) as a fundamental measure of dislocation interaction at length scales close to those of discrete dislocations.

b) *Strain gradient length scale l*

The material length l corresponds to the scale at which the effects of strain gradient become comparable to those of strain. In the presence of a strong strain gradient, the total dislocation density ρ is considered to be the sum of statistically stored dislocations $\rho_s = 1/L_s^2$ and geometrically necessary dislocations $\rho_G = \eta/b$. The strain gradient effects become significant when ρ_s and ρ_G are of the same order of magnitude. Equating

$$\rho_s = \rho_G \qquad\qquad (4.30)$$

immediately suggests that

$$\eta^{-1} = L_s^2/b \qquad\qquad (4.31)$$

is a fundamental length scale signifying the strain gradient effects. Nix and Gao (1998) have shown that L_s^2/b is a fundamental length scale which is related to the material length l and the uniaxial stress strain behavior $\sigma_0 = \sigma_Y f(\varepsilon)$ by the following relations

$$\hat{l} = \frac{L_s^2}{b}, \ L_s \simeq \frac{\mu b}{\sigma_0}, \ l \simeq \hat{l}_{\text{yield}} \qquad\qquad (4.32)$$

where $\hat{l}_{\text{yield}}$ is the value of $\hat{l}$ at yielding. Therefore, the material length l is a fundamental length scale related to Burgers vector and dislocation spacing at yielding, and is a fundamental measure of the deformation length at which geometrically necessary dislocations constitute a significant fraction of the total dislocation population.

c) *Mesoscale cell size l_ε*

The theory of strain gradient plasticity is intended for applications with deformation length scales in the range of 0.1 to 10 micron (Fleck and Hutchinson, 1997). Since plasticity theories describe the collective behavior of a large number of dislocations, the range of validity of MSG should be larger than the mean dislocation spacing. A dislocation spacing of 0. 1 micron corresponds to a dislocation density on the order of 10^{10} cm^{-2}, which is typical for a deformed crystal. The cell size l_ε in the MSG theory is a resolution parameter which controls the accuracy with which the strain gradient is calculated in each cell. This parameter needs to be sufficiently small to ensure accuracy of the strain gradient. However, since the Taylor hardening model is assumed to govern, this cell also needs to be large enough to contain a sufficient number of dislocations to ensure the accuracy of the flow stress. In other words, there is a fundamental inconsistency in trying to capture both the strain gradient and the flow stress accurately. A compromise between these two conflicting requirements dictates a suitable choice of l_ε. Gao et al. (1999) propose to define

$$l_\varepsilon = \beta L_{\text{yield}} = \beta \frac{\mu b}{\sigma_Y} \qquad (4.33)$$

where l_{yield} is the mean spacing between statistically stored dislocations at yielding and β is a constant coefficient to be determined from experiments. Dislocation spacing provides a fundamental measures of the "discreteness" limit for continuum plasticity, similar to atomic spacing as a measure of the discreteness limit for continuum elasticity. For stress levels below the yield point, plastic deformation is negligible and elasticity theory is usually used to analyze the deformation. For stresses above the yield point, the mean dislocation spacing becomes smaller than l_{yield} so that l_ε is always larger than the dislocation spacing for the intended application range. The condition $\beta > 1$ ensures that there are multiple dislocations within the mesoscale cell.

For typical structural metals, Gao et al. (1999) take the following numbers as representative estimates of the relevant length scales:

$$\mu/\sigma_Y = 100, \ b = 0.1 \text{ nm}, \ L_{\text{yield}} = 10 \text{ nm} \qquad (4.34)$$

$$l_\varepsilon \sim 10 - 100 \text{ nm} \quad l \sim 1 - 10 \text{ nm} \qquad (4.35)$$

where the cell size parameter β is taken to be from 1 to 10.

With the exception of single crystal materials, there is usually more than one microstructural length scale in an engineering material. Examples of such length scales include grain size, particle spacing, layer thickness, etc. Dislocations are usually not uniformly distributed. These complications make it difficult to calculate the strain gradient length l directly from microstructure. MSG theory is convenient to relate the material length, $l = 3\alpha^2 (\mu/\sigma_Y)^2 b$, to macroscopically measurable quantities such as the yield stress σ_Y, which account for, in an average sense, the effects of various microstructural features. For example, the Hall-Petch relation indicates that the uniaxial flow stress increases with the reduction in grain size,

$$\sigma_Y = c_0 + c_1 d^{-1/2} \tag{4.36}$$

where d is the mean grain diameter. The grain size thus affects the strain gradient plasticity indirectly through its influence on σ_Y and on the constitutive length l.

4.3   Bending of thin beams

Huang et al. (2000) used the MSG theory to analyze several phenomena that are influenced by plastic strain gradients. In this section, MSG plasticity theory is used to investigate bending of ultra-thin beams. For simplicity, the beam is assumed to be under plane-strain bending.

The Cartesian reference frame is set such that the x_1 axis coincides with the neutral axis of the beam, and bending is applied in the (x_1, x_2) plane. A unit beam width is taken in the out-of-plane (x_3) direction. The curvature is designated κ and the beam thickness is designated h. Strains in the Cartesian reference frame and the effective strain ε are given by

$$\varepsilon_{11} = -\varepsilon_{22} = \kappa x_2, \quad \varepsilon_{12} = 0, \quad \varepsilon_e = \frac{2}{\sqrt{3}} \kappa |x_2| \qquad (4.37)$$

where ε_{22} is obtained from the assumptions of plane strain deformation ($\varepsilon_{33} = 0$) and incompressibility ($\varepsilon_{kk} = 0$). The corresponding displacement field is $u_1 = \kappa x_1 x_2$, $u_2 = -\frac{1}{2}\kappa(x_1^2 + x_2^2)$. The non-vanishing strain gradients in the Cartesian reference frame and the effective strain gradient η are given by

$$\eta_{112} = \eta_{222} = -\kappa, \quad \eta_{121} = \eta_{211} = \kappa, \quad \eta = \kappa \qquad (4.38)$$

The constitutive equations give non-vanishing deviatoric stresses and higher-order stresses as

$$\sigma'_{11} = -2\sigma'_{22} = \text{sign}(x_2)\frac{\sigma_e}{\sqrt{3}} \qquad (4.39)$$

$$\frac{6}{5}\tau'_{121} = \frac{6}{5}\tau'_{211} = -\tau'_{222} = 6\tau'_{233} = 6\tau'_{323} = \frac{\kappa l_\varepsilon^2 \sigma_Y^2 f(\varepsilon_e)f'(\varepsilon_e)}{24} \cdot \frac{1}{\sigma_e} \qquad (4.40)$$

where $\text{sign}(x_2)$ stands for the sign of x_2, σ_e is the flow stress and l_ε is the mesoscale cell size.

The equilibrium equation and traction-free boundary conditions on the top and bottom surfaces of the beam ($x_2 = \pm h/2$) give the hydrostatic stress $x_2 = \pm h/2$

$$H = -\sigma'_{22} + \frac{d\tau'_{222}}{dx_2} \qquad (4.41)$$

The double-stress traction $\hat{r}_k$ at the cross section of the beam is zero, while the non-vanishing stress traction is $\hat{t}_1 = H + \sigma'_{11} - 2\frac{d\tau'_{211}}{dx_2}$. There is a line traction at the edge between the cross section and top surface ($x_2 = h/2$) of the beam, given by $\hat{p}_1 = (2\tau'_{211} - \tau'_{222})_{x_2 = h/2}$. The line traction at the edge between the cross section and bottom surface ($x_2 = -h/2$) is just the negative of the above expression. These stress and line tractions give a pure bending moment M, i. e. , there are no net forces or torques in the cross section. The bending moment M can be obtained from the integration over the cross section of moments induced by these traction as

$$M = \int_{-h/2}^{h/2} \left[\frac{2}{\sqrt{3}} | x_2 | \sigma_e + \frac{\kappa l_\varepsilon^2}{9} \frac{\sigma_Y^2 f(\varepsilon_e) f'(\varepsilon_e)}{\sigma_e} \right] dx_2 \qquad (4.42)$$

This moment-curvature relation can also be obtained from the principle of virtual work by enforcing the equality of interval virtual work done by stresses and higher-order stresses in the beam and external virtual work done by the moment, similar to the method used by Fleck and Hutchinson (1997) for torsion.

The bending moment M, normalized by its counterpart $M_0(\kappa h)$ for classical plasticity, versus the normalized curvature κh is shown in Figure 4. 2 for several ratios of intrinsic material length to beam thickness l/h, where the ratio of mesoscale cell size to dislocation spacing at plastic yielding is $\beta = 10$, and M_0 can be obtained from (4. 42) by taking $l = 0$ and $l_\varepsilon = 0$. The horizontal lines in Figure 4. 2 correspond to the bending moment estimated by Fleck and Hutchinson's (1997) phenomenological

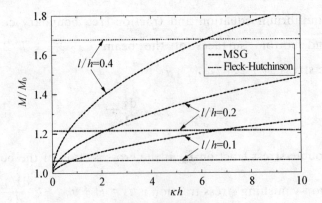

Figure 4. 2   The normalized bending moment vs the normalized curvature for several ratios of intrinsic material length to beam thickness. (Huang et al. , 2000)

strain gradient plasticity since both M and M_0 are proportional to κ^N. The intrinsic material lengths in phenomenological strain gradient plasticity are $l_1 = l/8$, $l_2 = l/2$, and $l_3 = l\sqrt{5/24}$, as suggested by Begley and Hutchinson (1998), where l'_is are defined in Gao et al. (1999). This combination of material lengths for phenomenological strain gradient plasticity and $\beta = 10$ for MSG plasticity are also used in the following comparisons between two strain gradient plasticity theories for torsion of thin wires. As far as bending is concerned, it appears that the MSG representation significantly underestimates the plastic work hardening reported by Stolken and Evans (1998) at small curvatures κ, which displays relatively large moment increases due to strain gradients in the range of small κ. However, this is reversed at large curvatures, i.e., MSG plasticity gives a larger bending moment than phenomenological strain gradient plasticity when the curvature is large.

4.4　Torsion of thin wires

MSG theory is also used to investigate torsion of thin wires by Huang et al. (2000). Details are as follows.

The Cartesian reference frame is set such that the x_1 and x_2 axes are within the cross section of the wire, while the x_3 axis coincides with the central axis of the wire. The twist per unit length is designated κ and the radius of the wire is designated a. The displacement field is $u_1 = -\kappa x_2 x_3$, $u_2 = \kappa x_1 x_3$, $u_3 = 0$. The non-vanishing strains and strain gradients in the Cartesian reference frame and the effective strain ε and effective strain gradient η are given by

$$\varepsilon_{13} = \varepsilon_{31} = -\frac{\kappa}{2}x_2, \ \varepsilon_{23} = \varepsilon_{32} = \frac{\kappa}{2}x_1, \ \varepsilon_e = \frac{1}{\sqrt{3}}\kappa r \qquad (4.43)$$

$$\eta_{231} = \eta_{321} = -\kappa, \quad \eta_{132} = \eta_{312} = \kappa, \quad \eta = \kappa \qquad (4.44)$$

where $r = \sqrt{x_1^2 + x_2^2}$ is the radius in polar coordinates (r, θ).

From the constitutive equations, Huang et al. (2000) give the non-vanishing deviatoric stresses and higher-order stresses as

$$\sigma'_{13} = \sigma'_{31} = \frac{2\varepsilon_{13}}{3\varepsilon_e}\sigma_e, \quad \sigma'_{23} = \sigma'_{32} = \frac{2\varepsilon_{23}}{3\varepsilon_e}\sigma_e \qquad (4.45)$$

$$-\tau'_{113} = \tau'_{223} = -2\tau'_{311} = -2\tau'_{131} = 2\tau'_{322} = 2\tau'_{232}$$
$$= \frac{\kappa l_\varepsilon^2}{36}\frac{x_1 x_2}{r^2}\left[\frac{\sigma_Y^2 f(\varepsilon_e) f'(\varepsilon_e)}{\sigma_e} - \frac{\sigma_e}{\varepsilon_e}\right] \qquad (4.46)$$

$$\tau'_{123} = \tau'_{213} = \frac{\kappa l_\varepsilon^2}{72}\frac{x_1^2 - x_2^2}{r^2}\left[\frac{\sigma_Y^2 f(\varepsilon_e) f'(\varepsilon_e)}{\sigma_e} - \frac{\sigma_e}{\varepsilon_e}\right] \qquad (4.47)$$

$$\tau'_{132} = \tau'_{312} = \frac{\kappa l_\varepsilon^2}{72}\left[\frac{x_1^2}{r^2}\frac{\sigma_Y^2 f(\varepsilon_e) f'(\varepsilon_e)}{\sigma_e} + \frac{x_2^2}{r^2}\frac{\sigma_e}{\varepsilon_e}\right] \qquad (4.48)$$

$$\tau'_{231} = \tau'_{321} = -\frac{\kappa l_\varepsilon^2}{72}\left[\frac{x_2^2}{r^2}\frac{\sigma_Y^2 f(\varepsilon_e) f'(\varepsilon_e)}{\sigma_e} + \frac{x_1^2}{r^2}\frac{\sigma_e}{\varepsilon_e}\right] \qquad (4.49)$$

where σ_e is the flow stress and l_ε is the mesoscale cell size.

The equilibrium equation and traction-free boundary condition on the lateral surface of the wire $(r = a)$ give a vanishing hydrostatic stress, i.e.,

$$H = 0 \qquad (4.50)$$

The double-stress traction $\hat{r}_k$ in the cross section of the wire is zero, while the non-vanishing stress tractions are $\hat{t}_1 = \sigma'_{31} - 2\dfrac{d\tau'_{311}}{dx_1} - 2\dfrac{d\tau'_{321}}{dx_2}$,

$\hat{t}_2 = \sigma'_{32} - 2\dfrac{d\tau'_{312}}{dx_1} - 2\dfrac{d\tau'_{322}}{dx_2}$. There is a line traction along the circumferential (θ) direction at the edge between the cross section and lateral surface $(r = a)$ of the wire, given by $\hat{p}_\theta = \dfrac{\kappa l_\varepsilon^2}{36}\dfrac{\sigma_Y^2 f(\varepsilon_e) f'(\varepsilon_e)}{\sigma_e}$.

These stress and line tractions give a pure torque T, i.e., there are no net forces or bending moments in the cross section. The torque T can be obtained from the integration over the cross section of torque induced by theses tractions as

$$T = \frac{2}{3}\pi\kappa \int_0^a r \left[\left(r^2 + \frac{l_\varepsilon^2}{12} \right) \frac{\sigma_e}{\varepsilon_e} + \frac{l_\varepsilon^2}{12} \frac{\sigma_Y^2 f(\varepsilon_e) f'(\varepsilon_e)}{\sigma_e} \right] dr \qquad (4.51)$$

This torque vs. twist-per-unit-length relation can also be obtained from the principle of virtual work by enforcing the equality of interval virtual work done by stresses and higher-order stresses in the wire and external virtual work done by the torque, as detailed in Fleck and Hutchinson (1997).

The torque T, normalized by its counterpart T_0 (κa) for classical plasticity, versus the normalized twist per unit length κa is plotted in Figure 4.3 for several ratios of intrinsic material length to wire radius, l/a, where T_0 can be obtained from (4.51) by taking $l = 0$ and $l_\varepsilon = 0$. The horizontal lines in Figure 4.3 correspond to the torque estimated by Fleck and Hutchinson's (1997) phenomenological strain gradient plasticity since both T and T_0 are proportional to κ^N. It is observed that phenomenological strain gradient plasticity gives a larger torque than MSG plasticity at small twists per unit length, but this is reversed when the twist per unit length becomes large.

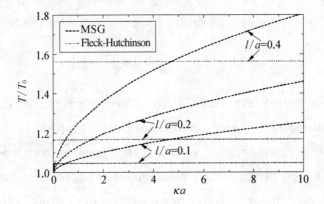

Figure 4.3   The normalized torque vs the normalized twist per unit length for several ratios of material length to wire radius. (Huang et al., 2000)

4.5 Micro-indentation hardness

Gao et al. (1999) have developed the finite element method for the theory of MSG plasticity. The indentation hardness has been calculated by the numerical method and compared with the experimental data given by McElhaney et al. (1998) for polycrystalline and single crystal copper.

In MSG plasticity the density of geometrically necessary dislocations is related to η_{ijk} through its invariants as

$$\rho_G b = \sqrt{c_1 \, \eta_{iik} \eta_{jjk} + c_2 \, \eta_{ijk} \eta_{ijk} + c_3 \, \eta_{ijk} \eta_{kji}} \qquad (4.52)$$

The three constants c_1, c_2 and c_3 scale the three quadratic invariants for the incompressible third order tensor η_{ijk} and are determined from three distinct dislocation models consisting of plane strain bending, pure torsion and two-dimensional axisymmetric void growth (Gao et al., 1999).

$$c_1 = 0, \; c_2 = 1/4, \; c_3 = 0 \qquad (4.53)$$

which suggests that the density of geometrically necessary dislocations consistent with the notion of most efficient dislocation configuration is

$$\rho_G = \frac{1}{2b} \sqrt{\eta_{ijk} \eta_{ijk}} \qquad (4.54)$$

Arsenlis and Parks (1999) considered density of geometrically necessary dislocations based on the integrated properties of dislocation lines within a representative volume. They studied both open periodic networks of dislocations, which have long-range geometric consequences, and closed three-dimensional dislocation structures, which self-terminate, having no geometric consequence. Based on the implications of these structures on the presence of geometrically necessary dislocations in a polycrystalline material, they introduced the so-called Nye factor $\bar{r}$ to relate geometrically necessary dislocation density to plastic strain gradients. For bending and torsion of FCC polycrystals Arsenlis and Parks have found the Nye factor to be $\bar{r} = 1.85$ and $\bar{r} = 1.93$, respectively. The Nye factor modifies Eq. (4.54) to

$$\rho_G = \frac{\bar{r}}{2b}\sqrt{\eta_{ijk}\eta_{ijk}} \tag{4.55}$$

Then the length scale in equation (4.7) can be re-written as

$$l = \overline{M}^2 \alpha^2 (\mu/\sigma_{ref})^2 \, \bar{r}b \tag{4.56}$$

where $\overline{M} = 3.06$ is called the Taylor factor (Bishop and Hill, 1951a and 1951b; Taylor, 1938). It is the ratio of tensile flow stress to shear flow stress in FCC polycrystalline materials.

In the micro-indentation, when the depth of indentation, h, is significantly larger than tens of micrometers, the strain gradients effects become negligible and the corresponding hardness degenerates to the hardness H_0 in classical plasticity. The plastic work hardening exponent is determined as $n = 0.3$ from the uniaxial stress-strain data for copper documented by McLean (1962), which is consistent with the findings of Fleck et al. (1994) for polycrystalline copper. The reference stress in uniaxial tension is $\sigma_{ref} = 408$ MPa. This leads to a prediction of the indentation hardness $H_0 = 834$ MPa for a large depth of indentation ($\gg$ micrometers), which is in excellent agreement with the experimentally measured hardness for polycrystalline copper (McElhaney et al., 1998). For single crystal copper, the reference stress is taken as $\sigma_{ref} = 283$ MPa and the predicted hardness is $H_0 = 581$ MPa, consistent with the experimentally measured hardness for single crystal copper (McElhaney et al., 1998).

The Taylor factor is fixed at $\overline{M} = 3.06$ for FCC materials, as suggested by Bishop and Hill (1951a and 1951b). The Nye factor is taken as $\bar{r} = 2$ for polycrystalline copper and $\bar{r} = 3$ for single crystal copper

(Arsenlis and Parks, 1999). Burger's vector for copper is $b = 0.255$ nm. The micro-indentation hardness calculated by the mesoscale cell size parameter β. This is consistent with the study of Huang et al. (2000), who have shown that the effect of β is rather small in micro-bending, micro-torsion, growth of micro-voids, and cavitation instabilities.

The microindentation hardness data, however, depend strongly on the empirical coefficient α in the Taylor model, which is on the order of 1 (Nix and Giebling, 1985). Based on the numerical simulation of microindentation hardness experiments Gao et al. (1999) have determined the coefficient α by fitting microindentation hardness data for polycrystalline and (111) single crystal copper. Figure 4.4 presents the microindentation hardness predicted by MSG plasticity, $(H/H_0)^2$, versus the inverse of indentation depth, $1/h$, where H is the microindentation hardness, H_0 is the indentation hardness without the strain gradient effects, and h is the depth of indentation. The experimental data discussed by Nix and Gao (1998) are also plotted in Figure 4.4 for comparison.

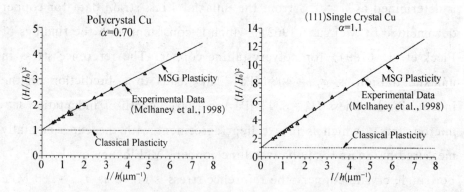

Figure 4.4 Depth dependence of the hardness of polycrystalline and (111) single crystal copper and H_0 is the indentation hardness without strain gradient effects (i.e., for large depth of indentation). (Gao et al., 1999)

For polycrystalline Cu, Gao et al. (1999) take $H_0 = 834$ MPa, $\overline{M} = 3.06$, $\overline{r} = 2$, and $\alpha = 0.7$. It is clearly observed that the numerically predicted hardness based on MSG plasticity agree remarkably well with the experimentally measured microindentation hardness data over a wide range of indentation depth, from $0.1\ \mu$m to several micrometers. The parameter α (= 0.70) estimated from the experimental data has the correct order of magnitude. Moreover, the numerical results based on MSG plasticity do give a straight line in Figure 4.4, consistent with the estimate based on dislocation models (Nix and Gao, 1998). It notes that there is an intrinsic incompatibility between such linear dependence and the phenomenological theories of strain gradient plasticity (Begley and Hutchinson, 1998).

For (111) single crystal copper, Gao et al. (1999) take H_0 = 581 MPa, $\overline{M} = 3.06$, $\overline{r} = 3$, and $\alpha = 1.1$. Once again excellent agreements are observed between the numerically predicted microindentation hardness based on MSG plasticity and the experimental data. MSG plasticity again gives a straight line in Figure 4.4, consistent with the estimate based on dislocation models (Nix and Gao, 1998).

4.6 Size effects in the particle-reinforced metal matrix composites

Many experiments for particle-reinforced metal matrix composites (PMMC) have found scale effects for different particle sizes. Xue et al. (2002) has used MSG theory to investigate the size effects in PMMC. They adopt a unit cell model shown in Figure 4.5. The particle is elastic, while the matrix is elastic-plastic and is characterized by MSG plasticity. The same unit cell model was also used by Bao et al. (1991) to investigate the effect of particle volume fraction and shape on the plastic work hardening behavior of metal-matrix composites except that the matrix material was characterized by classical plasticity and no size effect could be predicted.

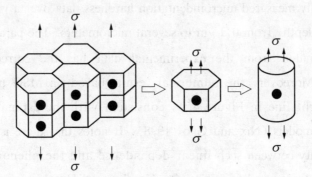

Figure 4.5 A schematic diagram of the unit cell
model for a finite metallic matrix containing a single
second phase particle. (Xue et al., 2002)

Figure 4.5 shows a uniform distribution of second phase particles. Such a periodic distribution can be characterized by a unit cell model, as shown in the hexagonal matrix cell containing a single particle. In order to further simplify the analysis, Xue et al. (2002) approximate the hexagonal cell by a cylinder as shown in Figure 4.5. The height and diameter of the cylinder are $2h$ and $2R$, respectively. The diameter of the spherical particle is d, and is related to h and R through the particle volume fraction V_f,

$$V_f = \frac{\frac{\pi}{6}d^3}{2\pi R^2 h} = \frac{d^3}{12R^2 h}. \tag{4.57}$$

The material properties are taken from Lloyd's experiments for an aluminum matrix reinforced by silicon carbide particles. The SiC particles are linear elastic and isotropic, with Young's modulus $E_{SiC} = 427$ GPa and Poisson's ratio $\nu_{SiC} = 0.17$. The Al matrix is elastic-plastic, and its uniaxial stress-strain relation is well represented by a power law, $\sigma = 464\varepsilon^{0.136}$ MPa, as shown in Figure 4.6. Xue et al. (2002), adopt the following piecewise elastic-power law hardening relation also shown in Figure 4.6 in order to incorporate the elastic deformation of aluminum,

$$\sigma = \begin{cases} E_{Al}\varepsilon & \varepsilon \leqslant \sigma_Y / E_{Al} \\ 464\varepsilon^{0.136} \text{ MPa} & \varepsilon > \sigma_Y / E_{Al} \end{cases} \tag{4.58}$$

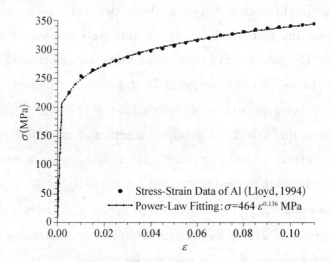

Figure 4.6   The experimental stress-strain data of aluminum (Lloyd, 1994) and the power-law fitting $\sigma = 464\varepsilon^{0.136}$ MPa. (Xue et al., 2002)

where $E_{Al} = 76$ GPa is the aluminum Young's modulus reported by Lloyd, and σ_Y is the yield stress which can be determined by the continuity of elastic and power-law relation in the above equations at the plastic yielding point. $\sigma_Y = 208$ MPa, which is in excellent agreement with the aluminum yield stress of 207 MPa reported by Lloyd (1994). The Poisson ratio of aluminum is $\nu_{Al} = 0.33$.

Finite element method has been used by Xue et al. (2002) to analyze the axisymmetric unit cell model in Figure 4.5. The lateral surface remains traction-free, and the top surface is subjected to a uniform axial displacement u_0. The symmetry condition is imposed at the middle section of the unit cell. The nominal axial strain in the cell is evaluated by the ratio of the uniform displacement u_0 on the top surface to the half cell height h. The nominal axial stress in the cell is determined by the total axial force divided by the cell cross section area πR^2, where the total axial force is obtained from the nodal forces of all nodes on the top surface.

Figure 4.7 shows the stress-strain curves predicted by the unit cell model based on classical plasticity for two cell aspect ratios $h/R = 1$ and

h/R = 2. The difference between these two curves are very small, indicating that the numerical results are relatively insensitive to the cell aspect ratio. The stress-strain data for an aluminum matrix reinforced by 15% SiC particles (V_f = 15%) with 16 and 7.5 μm diameters are also shown. It is clearly observed that classical plasticity significantly underestimates the effect of reinforcements and can not predict the particle size effect. The significant differences between the classical plasticity theory and the experimental data for relatively small (e.g. 7.5 μm) and large particles (e.g. 16 μm) shown in Figure 4.7 can be attributed to the strain gradient effect associated with the geometrically necessary dislocations, as discussed in the next paragraph.

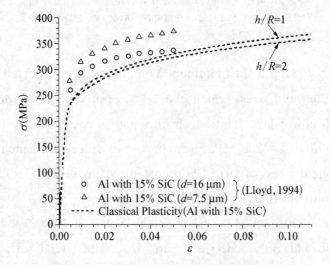

Figure 4.7　The experimental stress-strain data for an aluminum matrix reinforce by 16 μm diameter and by 7.5 μm diameter silicon carbide particles at 15% particle volume fracture and the curves are predicted by the classical plasticity for the cell aspect ratio h/R = 1 and 2. (Xue et al., 2002)

Figure 4.7 also shows that the differences between the experimental data for 16 μm diameter particles and the classical plasticity theory decrease with the increasing strain, and these differences seem to vanish at a strain level of 5% as shown by the interception of experimental and class plasticity curves. This is because the second phase particles fracture as the strain increases and the cracked particles gradually lose their reinforcing effect. Therefore, even though the reinforced particles improve plastic work hardening of metal-matrix composites, fracture of these particles at relatively large strains may lead to significant degradation of the composite behavior.

MSG theory is used by Xue et al. (2002) to predict the size effect in this kind of composite and the shear modulus of aluminum μ_{Al} = 28.6 GPa, Burgers vector b = 0.283 nm, the empirical material constant α in the Taylor dislocation model are needed additionally. They do not account for the effect of particle cracking and debonding.

Figure 4.8 shows the strong size effect of the overall stress-strain curve predicted by MSG plasticity for SiC/Al material system with different sizes of SiC particles. The particle volume fraction is the same as that in Lloyd's (1994) experiments, V_f = 15%, while the empirical material constant in the Taylor dislocation model α = 0.3. The prediction based on classical plasticity is also shown for comparison. The plastic work hardening predicted by MSG plasticity increases with the decrease in particle diameter, which is consistent with the experiment (Lloyd,

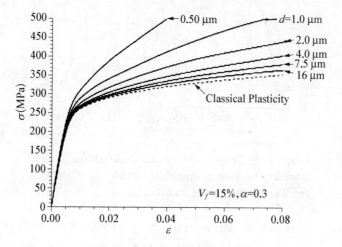

Figure 4.8　The stress-strain curves predicted by MSG plasticity for various particle diameters d. (Xue et al., 2002)

1994). The curve for 7.5 μm diameter particles already shows the size effect since it is clearly above those for 16 μm diameter particles and for classical plasticity. The particle size effect becomes much more drastic as the particle diameter decreases to the order of 1 μm or smaller, consistent with Nan and Clarke's (1996) study.

Figure 4.9 shows the stress-strain curve predicted by MSG plasticity for different empirical material constants in the Taylor dislocation model, $\alpha = 0.3, 0.4$ and 0.5. the particle volume fraction $V_f = 15\%$, while the particle diameter $d = 7.5 \, \mu m$ is same as that in Lloyd's (1994) experiments. The curve for classical plasticity is also shown for comparison. It is observed that the curve for $\alpha = 0.5$ is significantly higher than that for $\alpha = 0.3$, and both are much higher than the curve for classical plasticity. The intrinsic material length associated with strain gradient plasticity almost triples as α increases from 0.3 to 0.5 such that the strain gradient effect becomes more significant.

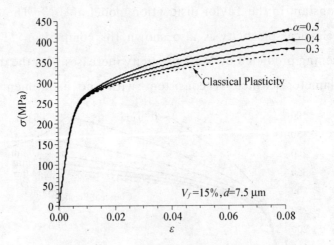

Figure 4.9 The stress-strain curves predicted by MSG plasticity for various empirical material constant α in the Taylor dislocation model. (Xue et al., 2002)

Figure 4.10 shows the stress-strain curve predicted by MSG plasticity for different particle volume fractions, ranging from μm (aluminum volume only) to 35%. Two particle diameters in Lloyd's (1994) experiments are taken, $d =$

16 and 7.5 μm, and the empirical material constant in the Taylor dislocation model $\alpha = 0.3$. At particle volume fraction $V_f = 5\%$, the difference between two curves for $d = 16$ and 7.5 μm is still rather small. However, as the particle volume fraction increases, there is a strong coupling effect between the particle volume fraction and particle size, and the particle size effect becomes much more significant.

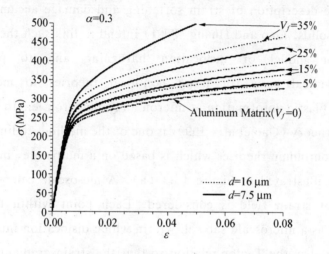

Figure 4.10   The stress-strain curves predicted by MSG plasticity for various particle volume fracture V_f.
(Xue et al. , 2002)

4.7   Taylor-based non-local theory of plasticity (TNT)

In 2001, Gao and Huang explore the possibility of modeling size dependent plasticity within the framework of non-local continuum theories. It is known that the basic balance laws in a non-local continuum theory are identical to classical local theories, i. e. , the order of governing equations remains the same as that of a classical theory. In comparison with a high order theory, a non-local theory does not require additional boundary conditions and the length scale is introduced into the constitutive equations via non-local variables which are expressed as an integral of local variables over all the material points in the body. Various non-local plasticity theories (e.g., Bazant et al., 1984; Bazant and Lin, 1988; Chen, 1999) have already been used in the past to provide a length scale in the description of strain softening and damage accumulation in deformed solids. Gao and Huang (2001) intend to link such theories with the Taylor model of dislocation hardening and to provide a micromechanical basis for using non-local theories to model size-dependent plastic deformation at micron and submicron length scales.

MSG theory (Gao et al., 1999) is one of the methods to link Taylor's model to continuum theories which is based on a multiscale, hierarchical framework illustrated in Figure 4.11 (a). A mesoscale cell with linear variation of strain field is considered. Each point within the cell is considered as a microscale sub-cell within which dislocation interaction is assumed to obey the Taylor relation so that the strain gradient law $\sigma_e = \sigma_{ref}\sqrt{f^2(\varepsilon_e) + l\eta}$ applies. On the microscale, the η term is simply viewed as a measure of the density of geometrically necessary dislocations whose accumulation increases the flow stress. In other words, microscale plastic flow is assumed to occur as slip of statistically stored dislocations in a background of geometrically necessary dislocations and the microscale plastic deformation is assumed to obey the Taylor work hardening relation and the associative laws of conventional plasticity. The notion of geometrically necessary dislocations is connected to the gradient of the strain field on the level of the mesoscale cell. Higher-order stresses are introduced as thermodynamic conjugates of the strain gradients at the mesoscale level on which the MSG plasticity is formulated. This hierarchical structure provides a systematic approach for constructing the mesoscale constitutive laws by averaging microscale plasticity laws over the representative cell.

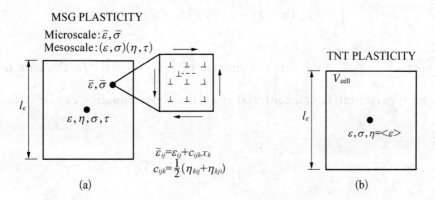

Figure 4. 11   The multiscale frameworks of MSG and TNT.
(Gao & Huang, 2001)

The density of geometrically necessary dislocations ρ_G has been expressed in terms of the gradient of plastic strain, leading to theories of strain gradient plasticity with higher-order stresses and strains. In TNT theory, Gao and Huang (2001) express ρ_G in terms of plastic strain only, they write the strain gradients as a non-local integral of strains such that ρ_G can be calculated from strains without having to resort to the mesoscale, the framework is shown in Figure 4. 11 (b). Consider the Taylor expansion of a strain component ε_{ij} in the neighborhood of point x

$$\varepsilon_{ij}(x+\xi) = \varepsilon_{ij}(x) + \varepsilon_{ij,m}\xi_m + O(|\xi|^2) \tag{4.59}$$

where ξ denotes local coordinates centered at x. Integrating this equation with ξ_k over a small representative volume V_{cell} containing x (Figure 4. 11 (b)), we find

$$\int_{V_{cell}} \varepsilon_{ij}(x+\xi)\xi_k \, dV = \varepsilon_{ij}(x)\int_{V_{cell}} \xi_k \, dV + \varepsilon_{ij,m}\int_{V_{cell}} \xi_k\xi_m \, dV$$

$$\tag{4.60}$$

where the characteristic size l_ε of V_{cell} is assumed to be sufficiently small such that terms of higher order in l_ε are negligible. Therefore, the gradient term $\varepsilon_{ij,k}$ can be expressed in terms of an integral of strain ε,

$$\varepsilon_{ij,k} = \int_{V_{\text{cell}}} \left[\varepsilon_{ij}(\boldsymbol{x}+\boldsymbol{\xi}) - \varepsilon_{ij}(\boldsymbol{x}) \right] \xi_m \,\mathrm{d}V \left(\int_{V_{\text{cell}}} \xi_k \xi_m \,\mathrm{d}V \right)^{-1} \quad (4.61)$$

where $\left(\int_{V_{\text{cell}}} \xi_k \xi_m \,\mathrm{d}V \right)^{-1}$ is the inverse of $\int_{V_{\text{cell}}} \xi_k \xi_m \,\mathrm{d}V$. In the case of a cubic representative cell centered at $\boldsymbol{x}$, the above equation can be reduced to

$$\varepsilon_{ij,k} = \frac{1}{I_\varepsilon} \int_{V_{\text{cell}}} \varepsilon_{ij} \xi_k \,\mathrm{d}V \quad (4.62)$$

where I_ε is the moment of inertia of the representative cell and is related to the edge length l_ε of the cube by

$$I_\varepsilon = \int_{V_{\text{cell}}} \xi_1^2 \,\mathrm{d}V = \frac{1}{12} l_\varepsilon^5 \quad (4.63)$$

The above example is the key idea of TNT theory. By representing strain gradients as a non-local integral of strains, the density of geometrically necessary dislocations as a non-local variable in the constitutive equations can be calculated, which involves no higher-order stresses nor strain gradients.

The deviatoric strain gradients η'_{ijk} will be treated as non-local variables,

$$\eta'_{ijk} = \frac{1}{I_\varepsilon} \int_{V_{\text{cell}}} \left[\varepsilon_{ik}\xi_j + \varepsilon_{jk}\xi_i - \varepsilon_{ij}\xi_k - \frac{1}{4}(\delta_{ik}\xi_j + \delta_{jk}\xi_i)\varepsilon_{pp} \right] \mathrm{d}V$$

$$(4.64)$$

$$\eta = \sqrt{\eta'_{ijk}\eta'_{ijk}/4} \quad (4.65)$$

where a cubic representative cell centered at $\boldsymbol{x}$ is assumed for simplicity. In the limit of $l_\varepsilon \to 0$, the right-hand side of the above equation naturally converges to the strain gradient form of η'_{ijk}. The general averaging procedure described in equation (4.61) should be used for cells of other shapes and for points near the boundary.

4.7.1 Deformation theory of TNT

The deformation theory of Taylor-based non-local theory（TNT）of plasticity assumes the same structure as the classical plasticity theories（Hill，1950）. The strain can be expressed as

$$\varepsilon_{ij} = \varepsilon'_{ij} + \frac{1}{3}\varepsilon_{kk}\delta_{ij} \tag{4.66}$$

where $\varepsilon_{kk} = \sigma_{kk}/3K$ and $K = E/[3(1-2\nu)]$ is the elastic bulk modulus.

The deviatoric strains ε'_{ij} are proportional to the deviatoric stress σ'_{ij}, such that

$$\varepsilon'_{ij} = \frac{3\varepsilon_e}{2\sigma_e}\sigma'_{ij} \tag{4.67}$$

where $\varepsilon_e = \sqrt{2\varepsilon'_{ij}\varepsilon'_{ij}/3}$ is the effective strain and $\sigma_e = \sqrt{3\sigma'_{ij}\sigma'_{ij}/2}$ the effective stress.

The yield criterion is

$$\sigma_e = \sigma = \sigma_{\text{ref}}\sqrt{f^2(\varepsilon_e) + l\eta} \tag{4.68}$$

where $l = 18\alpha^2(\mu/\sigma_{\text{ref}})^2 b$ can be found in MSG theory.

4.7.2 Flow theory of TNT

In the flow theory of TNT, the constitutive equations are expressed in rate form. The strain rate can be expressed as

$$\dot{\varepsilon}_{ij} = \dot{\varepsilon}'_{ij} + \frac{1}{3}\dot{\varepsilon}_{kk}\delta_{ij} \tag{4.69}$$

where $\dot{\varepsilon}_{kk} = \dot{\sigma}_{kk}/3K$.

The deviatoric strain rate consists of an elastic part and a plastic part,

$$\dot{\varepsilon}'_{ij} = \dot{\varepsilon}^{e'}_{ij} + \dot{\varepsilon}^{P}_{ij} \tag{4.70}$$

where the elastic strain rate $\dot{\varepsilon}^{e'}_{ij} = \dot{\sigma}'_{ij}/2\mu$, μ is the shear modulus. The plastic strain rate $\dot{\varepsilon}^{P}_{ij}$ is proportional to the deviatoric stress rate, such that

$$\dot{\varepsilon}^{P}_{ij} = \frac{3}{2}\frac{\dot{\varepsilon}^{P}_{e}}{\sigma_{e}}\sigma'_{ij} \tag{4.71}$$

where $\dot{\varepsilon}^{P}_{e} = \sqrt{2\,\dot{\varepsilon}^{P}_{ij}\dot{\varepsilon}^{P}_{ij}/3}$ is the effective plastic strain rate.

The constitutive relation can be written as

$$\dot{\sigma}_{kk} = 3K\dot{\varepsilon}_{kk} \tag{4.72}$$

$$\dot{\sigma}'_{ij} = \begin{cases} 2\mu\left[\dot{\varepsilon}'_{ij} - \dfrac{3\sigma'_{ij}}{4\sigma_{e}}\dfrac{6\mu\sigma'_{kl}\dot{\varepsilon}'_{kl} - \sigma^2_{\mathrm{ref}}\,l\dot{\eta}}{3\mu\sigma_{e} + \sigma^2_{\mathrm{ref}}\,f_{p}f'_{p}}\right], & \sigma_{e} = \sigma \quad \text{or} \quad \dot{\sigma}_{e} \geqslant 0 \\[2mm] 2\mu\dot{\varepsilon}'_{ij}, & \sigma_{e} < \sigma \quad \text{or} \quad \dot{\sigma}_{e} < 0 \end{cases}$$

$$\tag{4.73}$$

where $\sigma = \sigma_{\mathrm{ref}}\sqrt{f^2_{p}(\varepsilon^{P}_{e}) + l\eta}$, f_{p} is a function of plastic strain, and it is related to the elastic-plastic uniaxial stress strain relation $\sigma_{e} = \sigma_{\mathrm{ref}}f(\varepsilon_{e})$. The strain gradient can be expressed as

$$\dot{\eta} = \frac{1}{4\eta}\eta'_{ijk}\dot{\eta}'_{ijk} \tag{4.74}$$

$$\dot{\eta}'_{ijk} = \frac{1}{I_{\varepsilon}}\int_{V_{\mathrm{cell}}}\left[\dot{\varepsilon}_{ik}\xi_{j} + \dot{\varepsilon}_{jk}\xi_{i} - \dot{\varepsilon}_{ij}\xi_{k} - \frac{1}{4}(\delta_{ik}\xi_{j} + \delta_{jk}\xi_{i})\dot{\varepsilon}_{pp}\right]\mathrm{d}V$$

$$\tag{4.75}$$

Under proportional deformation, it can be shown that the flow theory of TNT coincides with the deformation theory of TNT.

Gao and Huang (2001) has analyzed several phenomena that are related to plasticity at the micron scale, such as bending of thin beam, torsion of thin wire, growth of microvoids, particle reinforced composites. They find that the difference between the TNT and MSG theories results from a negligible term of order l^2_{ε}, so that the analysis are omitted in this book. The reader can find the details in Gao and Huang (2001).

References

Arsenlis, A. and Parks, D. M., 1999. Crystallographic aspects of geometrically necessary and statically stored dislocation density. Acta Mater. 47, 1597 – 1611.

Bao, G., Hutchinson J. W., McMeeking, R. M., 1991. Particle reinforcement of ductile matrices against plastic flow and creep. Acta Metall. Mater. 39, 1871 – 1882.

Bazant, Z. P., Belytschko, T. B., Chang, T. B., 1984. Continuum theory for strain softening. ASME J. Engng. Mech. 110, 1666 – 1691.

Bazant, Z. P. and Lin, F. B., 1988. Non-local yield limit degradation. Int. J. Numer. Mech. Engng. 26, 1805 – 1823.

Bishop, J. F. W. and Hill, R., 1951a. A theory of plastic distortion of a polycrystalline aggregate under combined stresses. Philos. Magazine, 42, 414 – 427.

Bishop, J. F. W. and Hill, R., 1951b. A theoretical derivation of the plastic properties of a polycrystalline face-centered metal. Philos. Magazine, 42, 1298 – 1307.

Begley, M. R. and Hutchinson, J. W., 1998. The mechanics of size-dependent indentation. J. Mech. Phys. Solids 46, 2049 – 2068.

Chen E. P., 1999. Non-local effects on dynamic damage accumulation in brittle solids. Int. J. Num. Meth. Geomech. 23, 1 – 22.

Fleck, N. A. and Hutchinson, J. W., 1993. A phenomenological theory for strain gradient effects in plasticity. J. Mech. Phys. Solids 41, 1825 – 1857.

Fleck, N. A. and Hutchinson, J. W., 1997. Strain Gradient Plasticity. Advances in Applied Mechanics ed. J. W. Hutchinson and T. Y. Wu, 33, 295 – 361 Academic Press, New York.

Fleck, N. A., Muller, G. M., Ashby, M. F. and Hutchinson, J. W., 1994. Strain gradient plasticity: theory and experiment. Acta Metal. et Mater. 42, 475 – 487.

Gao, H., Huang, Y., Nix, W. D. and Hutchinson, J. W., 1999. Mechanism-based strain gradient plasticity- I . theory. J. Mech. Phys. Solids 47, 1239 – 1263.

Gao, H. and Huang, Y., 2001. Taylor based non-local theory of plasticity. Int. J. Solids Struct., 38, 2615 – 2637.

Hill, R., 1950. Mathematical theory of plasticity. Oxford University Press, Oxford, England.

Huang, Y., Gao, H., Nix, W. D. and Hutchinson, J. W., 2000. Mechanism based strain gradient plasticity- II . Analysis. J. Mech. Phys. Solids 48, 99 – 128.

Lloyd, D. J., 1994. Particle reinforced aluminum and magnesium matrix composites. Int. Mater. Rev. 39, 1 – 23.

McElhaney, K. W., Vlassak, J. J., Nix, W. D., 1998. Determination of indenter tip geometry and indentation contact area for depth-sensing indentation experiments. J. Mater. Res. 13, 1300 – 1306.

McLean, D. , 1962. Mechanical properties of metals. Wiley, New York.

Nan, C. W. , Clarke, D. R. , 1996. The influence of particle size and particle fracture on the elastic/plastic deformation of metal matrix composites. Acta Mater. 44, 3801 – 3811.

Nix, W. D. , Gao, H. , 1998. Indentation size effects in crystalline materials: a law for strain gradient plasticity. J. Mech. Phys. Solids 46, 411 – 425.

Nix, W. D. and Gibeling, J. C. , 1985. Mechanism of time-dependent flow and fracture of metals. Metals/materials technology Series 8313 – 004. ASM, Metals Park.

Stolken, J. S. And Evans, A. G. , 1998. A microbend test method for measuring the plasticity length scale. Acta Mater. 46, 5109 – 1515.

Taylor, G. I. , 1938. Plastic strain in metals. J. Inst Metals 62, 307 – 324.

Xue, Z. , Huang, Y. and Li, M. , 2002. Particle size effect in metallic materials: a study by the theory of mechanism-based strain gradient plasticity. Acta Mater. 50, 149 – 160.

5 C-W strain gradient plasticity theory

5.1 A hardening law for strain gradient plasticity theory

Interest in the modeling of length-scale effects in plasticity has led to the development of non-local theories of inelastic response due to the availability of a preferred material length-scale in these theories. In the context of gradient type non-local flow-theories of plasticity, the two primary phenomenological proposals are the works of Aifantis (1984) and Fleck and Hutchinson (1993).

In the theory of Aifantis (1984), the flow stress is assumed to depend on the Laplacian of the effective plastic strain, γ, i.e., $\phi(\sigma, \gamma, \nabla^2 \gamma)$ can be taken to be a particular form of a yield function with such a dependence, with yielding represented by $\phi = 0$, where σ represent the Cauchy stress. All other constitutive specifications remain the same as in the conventional theory into which such a non-local term is introduced.

In the J_2 flow theory introduced by Fleck and Hutchinson (1993), the body is assumed to perform work due to couple-stresses and the plastic work-rate is assumed to arise out of the conventional Cauchy stress (asymmetric) working on the plastic strain rate plus the couple stresses working on the plastic curvature rate. Two separate constitutive equations, one for the plastic strain rate and the other for the plastic curvature rate are specified in terms of the stress, couple-stress and their time rates of stressing. Since the plastic strain rate field on the body and the plastic curvature rate field are not independent, it is clear that the theory dictates the necessary of the satisfaction of a compatibility condition, between the stress field, couple-stress field and their rate fields, in order for the theory to be consistent.

A distinguishing feature of the abovementioned theories from the conventional local theories of rate-independent plasticity is also the fact that they require additional boundary conditions, on appropriate variables, for the solution of the problem of incremental equilibrium.

A new non-local inelastic constitutive theory is proposed first by Acharya and Bassani (1995). The model retains the algebraic nature of the flow rules of conventional theories. This feature, which is in contrast to the existed higher order strain gradient theory, allows the problem of incremental equilibrium to be stated without extra boundary conditions or higher-order stresses. In this section we will introduce the theory framework of Acharya and Bassani (1995).

5.1.1 The framework of Acharya and Bassani's proposition

The proposal of Acharya and Bassani (1995) only modify conventional plasticity theories by means of incorporating gradients of strain into the instantaneous hardening functions, while preserving the linear relationship between rate quantities. In what follows, this is outlined explicitly for a J_2 flow theory.

For a phenomenological J_2 flow theory at small strains (the idea remains identical for finite kinematics) the constitutive specification, for the loading branch, reads

$$\tau_e = \sqrt{\frac{1}{2}\boldsymbol{\sigma}' \cdot \boldsymbol{\sigma}'} \tag{5.1}$$

$$\dot{\tau} = h(\gamma_e,\ G)\dot{\gamma}_e \tag{5.2}$$

$$\dot{\boldsymbol{\varepsilon}}_p = \left(\frac{\dot{\gamma}_e}{2\tau_e}\right)\boldsymbol{\sigma}' \tag{5.3}$$

$$\dot{\boldsymbol{\sigma}} = C(\dot{\boldsymbol{\varepsilon}} - \dot{\boldsymbol{\varepsilon}}_p) \tag{5.4}$$

Where $\boldsymbol{\sigma}$ is the Cauchy stress and $\boldsymbol{\sigma}'$ is its deviator, τ_e is the non-local flow-stress in shear, h is the non-local hardening moduli, γ_e is the effective plastic strain which is work conjugate to τ_e, G is a suitable gradient term, $\boldsymbol{\varepsilon}_p$ is the plastic strain, $\boldsymbol{\varepsilon}$ is the total strain and C is the tensor of elastic moduli. Again, the key feature of these flow equations is that gradients enter explicitly only in the hardening function, rather than in the yield function, and only the Cauchy stress enters the formulation, i.e., higher-order stresses are not present. A candidate for the gradient effect may be, following Aifantis (1984), $G = \nabla^2 \gamma$.

5.1.2 A hardening law for strain gradient plasticity

Most of the strain gradient plasticity theories introduce the higher order stress which is required for this class of strain gradient theories to satisfy the Clausius-Duhem thermodynamic restrictions on the constitutive model for second deformation gradients (Gurtin, 1965a, b; Acharya and Shawki, 1995; Fleck et al., 1993; Fleck and Hutchinson, 1997, 2001; Gao et al., 1999). In comparison, no work conjugate of strain gradient has been defined in the alternative gradient theories (Aifantis, 1984; Zbib and Aifantis, 1989, 1992; Muhlhaus and Aifantis, 1991) which represent the strain gradient effects as terms relative with Laplacian of effective strain. Retaining the essential structure of conventional plasticity and obeying thermodynamic restrictions, Acharya and Bassani (1995) conclude that the only possible formulation is a flow theory with strain gradient effects represented as an internal variable, which acts to increase the current tangent-hardening modulus. However, there has not been a systematic way of constructing the tangent modulus so as to validate this framework.

A hardening law for strain gradient plasticity is proposed by Chen and Wang (2000a), which retains the essential structure of the incremental version of conventional J_2 deformation theory and obeys thermodynamic restrictions. The key feature of the new proposal is that the term of strain gradient plasticity represents as an internal variable to increase the tangent modulus. This feature which is in contrast to several proposed theories, allows the problem of incremental equilibrium equations to be stated without higher-order stress, higher-order strain rates or extra boundary conditions. The general idea is presented and compared with the theory given by Fleck-Hutchinson (1997). The new hardening law is demonstrated by two experiment tests i. e. thin wire torsion and ultra-thin beam bending tests. The theoretical results agree well with the experiment results.

Assuming the displacement is u_i, the strain tensor is ε_{ij} and the strain gradient is defined as

$$\eta_{ijk} = u_{k, ij} \tag{5.5}$$

The deviatoric part of the strain gradient tensors could be decomposed into three unique, mutually orthogonal third orders deviatoric tensors (Smyshlyaev and Fleck, 1995)

$$\eta'_{ijk} = \eta_{ijk}^{(1)} + \eta_{ijk}^{(2)} + \eta_{ijk}^{(3)} \tag{5.6}$$

Fleck and Hutchinson (1997) introduced the generalized effective strain

$$E_e^2 = \frac{2}{3} \varepsilon'_{ij} \varepsilon'_{ij} + l_1^2 \eta_{ijk}^{(1)} \eta_{ijk}^{(1)} + l_2^2 \eta_{ijk}^{(2)} \eta_{ijk}^{(2)} + l_3^2 \eta_{ijk}^{(3)} \eta_{ijk}^{(3)} \tag{5.7}$$

In Begley and Hutchinson (1998), Eq. (5.7) becomes

$$E_e^2 = \varepsilon_e^2 + l_1^2 \eta_{ijk}^{(1)} \eta_{ijk}^{(1)} + l_{cs}^2 \chi_e^2 \qquad (5.8)$$

where $l_{cs}^2 = 2l_2^2 + 12l_3^2/5$, $\varepsilon_e = \sqrt{\dfrac{2}{3}\varepsilon'_{ij}\varepsilon'_{ij}}$, $\chi_{ij} = \theta_{i,j}$, $\chi_e = \sqrt{\dfrac{2}{3}\chi_{ij}\chi_{ij}}$ and

$l_2 = \sqrt{6/5}\,l_3$.

Eq. (5.8) can be represented in the following form

$$\begin{cases} E_e^2 = \varepsilon_e^2 + l^2 \eta^2 \\ \eta = \sqrt{c_1 \eta_{ijk}^{(1)} \eta_{ijk}^{(1)} + \chi_e^2} \end{cases} \qquad (5.9)$$

where η is called the effective strain gradient and $l = l_{cs}$, $c_1 = \left(\dfrac{l_1}{l_{cs}}\right)^2$.

The overall stress measure Σ_e as the work conjugate of E_e is

$$\Sigma_e = \frac{dW(E_e)}{dE_e} \qquad (5.10)$$

For the purpose of the following section we shall adopt a simple functional relationship between Σ_e and E_e

$$\Sigma_e = A(E_e) \qquad (5.11)$$

In the conventional plasticity theories, σ_e is the work conjugate of ε_e and defined by

$$\sigma_e = \frac{dW(\varepsilon_e)}{d\varepsilon_e} \qquad (5.12)$$

where $\sigma_e = \sqrt{\dfrac{3}{2}S_{ij}S_{ij}}$ is the usual Von Mises effective stress.

The work done on the solid per unit volume equals the increment in strain energy

$$\delta W = S_{ij}\delta\varepsilon'_{ij} + \sigma_m \delta\varepsilon_m \qquad (5.13)$$

The components S_{ij} of the deviatoric stress tensor can be obtained as

$$S_{ij} = \frac{2\sigma_e}{3\varepsilon_e}\varepsilon_{ij} \qquad (5.14)$$

From Eq. (5.14), we know that the normality is assumed to be met and there is a yield surface.

The hardening relationship of Eq. (5.12) can be expressed as following

$$\sigma_e = A(\varepsilon_e) \tag{5.15}$$

The incremental form of Eq. (5.14) can be expressed as

$$\dot{S}_{ij} = \frac{2\varepsilon_{ij}}{3\varepsilon_e}\dot{\sigma}_e + \frac{2\dot{\varepsilon}_{ij}}{3\varepsilon_e}\sigma_e - \frac{2\varepsilon_{ij}\sigma_e}{3\varepsilon_e^2}\dot{\varepsilon}_e \tag{5.16}$$

and the incremental form of Eq. (5.15) is

$$\dot{\sigma}_e = A'(\varepsilon_e)\dot{\varepsilon}_e \tag{5.17}$$

where $A'(\varepsilon_e)$ is the tangent hardening modulus in the incremental version of conventional J_2-deformation theory.

While the strain gradient is considered, the hardening strength is related with not only the density of statistically stored dislocation but also the density of geometrically necessary dislocation. The former is related with the homogeneous deformation ε, the latter with the non-homogeneous deformation and the strain gradient $l\eta$ in a material. We know that when the characteristic length of the deformation field L usually corresponding to the smallest dimension of geometry is much larger than the material length l, the strain gradient terms become negligible in comparison with strains, and strain gradient plasticity theory then degenerates to the conventional plasticity theory. However, while L becomes comparable to l, strain gradient effects begin to play a dominating role. Instructed by this idea, we propose a new incremental hardening relationship instead of Eq. (5.17),

$$\dot{\sigma}_e = A'(\varepsilon_e)\left(1 + \frac{l^2\eta^2}{\varepsilon_e^2}\right)^{\alpha}\dot{\varepsilon}_e = B(\varepsilon_e, l\eta)\dot{\varepsilon}_e \tag{5.18}$$

where η is the effective strain gradient defined in Eq. (5.9), $B(\varepsilon_e, l\eta)$ is the hardening function including the effect of strain gradient and α is the exponent, in this section, $\alpha = 1$ is taken.

On each incremental step, both the effective strain ε_e and the effective strain gradient η can be obtained from the updated displacement fields. Hence $l\eta$ is only a given parameter in Eq. (5.18) and it doesn't invoke higher-order stress or higher-order strain rates. The conventional incremental constitutive relation (5.16) is still adaptable in the present theory.

The difference between the present strain gradient theory and the incremental version of conventional J_2 deformation theory is shown as follows.

a) The conventional J_2 deformation theory (Hill, 1950; Kachanov, 1971) can be expressed as follows. The constitutive relations are

$$S_{ij} = \Lambda e_{ij}, \qquad \sigma_m = K\varepsilon_m \qquad (5.19)$$

where

$$\Lambda = \frac{2\sigma_e}{3\varepsilon_e} \qquad (5.20)$$

S_{ij} denotes the deviatoric stress, e_{ij} denotes the deviatoric strain, σ_m is the spherical part of stress and ε_m is the spherical part of strain.

The hardening relation between the effective stress and effective strain takes the form

$$\sigma_e = A(\varepsilon_e) \qquad (5.21)$$

Then

$$\Lambda = \frac{2\sigma_e}{3\varepsilon_e} = \frac{2}{3}\frac{A(\varepsilon_e)}{\varepsilon_e} \qquad (5.22)$$

From Eqs. (5.19), (5.21), the incremental version of conventional J_2 deformation theory can be obtained

$$\dot{S}_{ij} = \Lambda\dot{e}_{ij} + \dot{\Lambda}e_{ij}, \quad \dot{\sigma}_m = K\dot{\varepsilon}_m \qquad (5.23)$$

$$\dot{\sigma}_e = A'(\varepsilon_e)\dot{\varepsilon}_e \qquad (5.24)$$

where Λ can be obtained from the following equation

$$\dot{\Lambda} = \left[\frac{2}{3}A'(\varepsilon_e) - \Lambda\right]\dot{\varepsilon}_e/\varepsilon_e \tag{5.25}$$

b) In the present strain gradient theory, the constitutive relations are the same as that in the conventionally incremental J_2 deformation theory, i.e. Eq. (5.23). But the increment version of the hardening law between the effective stress and the effective strain is different from the conventional one (i.e. Eq. (5.24)) while considering the strain gradient effect. It means that Λ is different from the conventional one.

From Eq. (5.20), we have

$$\sigma_e = \frac{3}{2}\Lambda\varepsilon_e \tag{5.26}$$

Combining Eq. (5.26) and Eq. (5.18), we obtain the equation about Λ in the present strain gradient theory,

$$\dot{\sigma}_e = \frac{3}{2}[\Lambda\dot{\varepsilon}_e + \dot{\Lambda}\varepsilon_e] = B\dot{\varepsilon}_e \tag{5.27}$$

where $B = A'(\varepsilon_e)\left(1 + \dfrac{l^2\eta^2}{\varepsilon_e^2}\right)^\alpha$.

Then one can easily obtained the following equation

$$\dot{\Lambda} = \left[\frac{2}{3}B - \Lambda\right]\dot{\varepsilon}_e/\varepsilon_e \tag{5.28}$$

Comparing Eq. (5.25) and (5.28), we can find the difference between the incremental version of conventional J_2 deformation theory and the present strain gradient theory.

As for the flow theory, we can put out it conveniently as follows. The relation of the plastic strain rate and the deviatoric stress for the conventional J_2 flow theory is

$$\dot{\varepsilon}_{ij}^p = \lambda S_{ij} \tag{5.29}$$

where

$$\lambda = \frac{3}{2}\frac{\dot{\varepsilon}_e^p}{\sigma_e} \tag{5.30}$$

here $\dot{\varepsilon}_e^p$ is the rate of the effective plastic strain and $\dot{\varepsilon}_e^p = \sqrt{\frac{2}{3}\dot{\varepsilon}_{ij}^p\dot{\varepsilon}_{ij}^p}$.

The relation of the spherical strain rate and the spherical stress rate is

$$\dot{\varepsilon}_m = \dot{\sigma}_m / K \tag{5.31}$$

where $K = \dfrac{E}{1-2\nu}$, E is the Young's modulus and ν is the Poisson ratio.

Considering the elastic strain, the constitutive relation is

$$\begin{cases} \dot{e}_{ij} = \dfrac{1}{2\mu}\dot{S}_{ij} + \dfrac{3}{2}\dfrac{\dot{\varepsilon}_e^p}{\sigma_e}S_{ij} \\[2mm] \dot{\varepsilon}_m = \dfrac{1-2\nu}{E}\dot{\sigma}_m \end{cases} \tag{5.32}$$

then, we have

$$\begin{cases} \dot{S}_{ij} = 2\mu\left(\dot{e}_{ij} - \dfrac{3}{2}\dfrac{\dot{\varepsilon}_e^p}{\sigma_e}S_{ij}\right) \\[2mm] \dot{\sigma}_m = K\dot{\varepsilon}_m \end{cases} \tag{5.33}$$

The hardening relation in the conventional J_2 flow theory is

$$\dot{\sigma}_e = A'(\varepsilon_e^p)\dot{\varepsilon}_e^p \tag{5.34}$$

The strain gradient flow theory takes the same constitutive equation (5.33) as the constitutive equation.

While considering the strain gradient effect, the hardening relation, i.e. Eq. (5.18), should be used instead of Eq. (5.34),

$$\dot{\sigma}_e = B(\varepsilon_e, l\eta)\dot{\varepsilon}_e \tag{5.35}$$

Comparing the conventional flow theory and the strain gradient flow theory, we can find that the difference is only between Eq. (5.34) and Eq. (5.35).

5. 1. 3   Comparisons between the theoretical predictions and experiment results

5.1.3.1   Torsion of thin wires

A Cartesian coordinate system (x_1, x_2, x_3) and a cylindrical polar coordinate system (r, θ, x_3) are introduced as shown in Figure 5. 1 and x_3 axis is parallel to the axis of the wire. The radius of the wire is a. κ is the twist per unit length of the wire and taken to be positive without loss of generality. Take the displacement field as in classical torsion

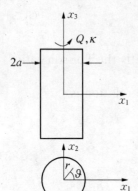

Figure   5. 1
Coordinate systems
for thin wires.

$$u_1 = -\kappa x_2 x_3, \qquad u_2 = \kappa x_1 x_3, \qquad u_3 = 0$$

$$(5. 36)$$

and the velocity field is as follows,

$$v_1 = -\dot{\kappa} x_2 x_3, \qquad v_2 = \dot{\kappa} x_1 x_3, \qquad v_3 = 0$$

$$(5. 37)$$

The associated non-vanishing components of strain rate and strain are

$$\begin{cases} \dot{\varepsilon}_{13} = \dot{\varepsilon}_{31} = -\dfrac{1}{2}\dot{\kappa} x_2, \ \dot{\varepsilon}_{23} = \dot{\varepsilon}_{32} = \dfrac{1}{2}\dot{\kappa} x_1 \\[2mm] \varepsilon_{13} = \varepsilon_{31} = -\dfrac{1}{2}\kappa x_2, \ \varepsilon_{23} = \varepsilon_{32} = \dfrac{1}{2}\kappa x_1 \end{cases}$$

$$(5. 38)$$

The non-vanishing components of the curvature tensor are

$$\chi_{11} = \chi_{22} = -\frac{1}{2}\kappa, \ \chi_{33} = \kappa \qquad (5. 39)$$

then, the effective strain and the effective strain gradient are

$$\varepsilon_e = \frac{1}{\sqrt{3}}\kappa r, \qquad \chi_e = \kappa \qquad (5. 40)$$

The stretch gradient in Eq. (5.7) can be calculated according to Smyshlyaev and Fleck (1996)

$$\eta_{ijk}^{(1)} \eta_{ijk}^{(1)} = 0 \tag{5.41}$$

The generalized effective strain takes the form

$$E_e = \sqrt{\varepsilon_e^2 + l^2 \chi_e^2} = \kappa \sqrt{\frac{1}{3} r^2 + l^2} \tag{5.42}$$

Now, the incremental version of the strain gradient J_2 deformation theory and the new hardening relationship, Eq. (5.18), will be used to investigate the torsion problem and here take $\alpha = 1$. According to Eq. (5.15), we have

$$A(\varepsilon_e) = \sigma_0 \varepsilon_e^N, \quad \sigma_0 = \Sigma_0 \tag{5.43}$$

so Eq. (5.18) becomes

$$\dot{\sigma}_e = N\sigma_0 \varepsilon_e^{N-1} \left(1 + \frac{l^2 \eta^2}{\varepsilon_e^2}\right) \dot{\varepsilon}_e = N\sigma_0 \varepsilon_e^{N-1} \left(1 + \frac{3l^2}{r^2}\right) \dot{\varepsilon}_e \tag{5.44}$$

From Eq. (5.44), we find that the term reflecting the effect of strain gradient has no relation with the deformation history, so for the problem of thin wire torsion, after integrating Eq. (5.44) one can obtain following equation,

$$\sigma_e = \sigma_0 \varepsilon_e^N \left(1 + \frac{3l^2}{r^2}\right) \tag{5.45}$$

Thus, it is reasonable and convenient to use Eq. (5.45) to solve the problem of thin wire torsion.

In this problem, $\eta = \chi_e$ and the non-vanishing components of stress can be obtained according to Eq. (5.14),

$$\tau_{13} = \tau_{31} = \frac{2\varepsilon_{13}}{3\varepsilon_e}\sigma_e, \quad \tau_{23} = \tau_{32} = \frac{2\varepsilon_{23}}{3\varepsilon_e}\sigma_e \tag{5.46}$$

then the non-vanishing components of stress in the cylindrical coordinate system can be expressed as

$$\tau_{\theta z} = \frac{1}{\sqrt{3}}\sigma_e \qquad (5.47)$$

Since there is no higher order stresses, the overall torque Q can be obtained from the integration over the cross section of torques produced by the stress components as follows

$$Q = \int_0^{2\pi}\int_0^a \tau_{\theta z} r^2 \mathrm{d}r\mathrm{d}\theta = \frac{2\pi a^3}{(N+3)(\sqrt{3})^{N+1}}\Sigma_0(\kappa a)^N\left[1+\frac{3(N+3)}{N+1}\left(\frac{l}{a}\right)^2\right]$$

$$(5.48)$$

The normalized torque can be written as

$$\frac{Q}{a^3} = \frac{2\pi\Sigma_0}{(N+3)(\sqrt{3})^{N+1}}(\kappa a)^N\left[1+\frac{3(N+3)}{N+1}\left(\frac{l}{a}\right)^2\right] \qquad (5.49)$$

The comparisons of Eq. (5.49) with test results for copper wires of different diameters are shown in Figure 5.2. From Figure 5.2 we can find that all curves predicted by Eq. (5.49) for different diameters are consistent well with the test results and here $l = 2.82\ \mu\mathrm{m}$.

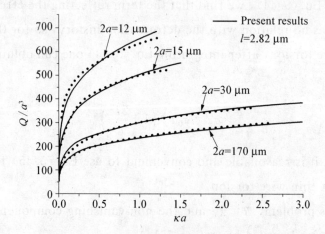

Figure 5.2   Comparisons between the experimental results (Fleck et al., 1994) and the predictions of the strain gradient theory with a new hardening law.

From Eq. (5.47) we know that $\tau_{\theta z}$ is the only non-vanishing component of the stresses and it depends only on r. It is easy to verify that all the equilibrium equations are met and the traction free conditions on the lateral boundary of the wire are also satisfied. Hence Eq. (5.36) provides a true displacement field for our theory.

5.1.3.2 Bending of thin beams

In 1998, Stolken and Evans did the bending experiment and observed a strong size effect whereby thin beams display much stronger plastic work hardening than thick ones and no size dependence is observed in the tension test.

Due to small deformation considered, in bending, subject to plane strain deformation, Cartesian (x_1, x_2, x_3) coordinates are adopted as shown in Figure 5.3. κ is the curvature and h is the beam's thickness. The displacement field is

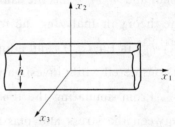

Figure 5.3 Coordinate system for ultra-thin beams.

$$u_1 = \kappa x_1 x_2, \ u_2 = -\kappa(x_1^2 + x_2^2)/2, \ u_3 = 0 \tag{5.50}$$

which yields the velocity field,

$$v_1 = \dot{\kappa} x_1 x_2, \ v_2 = -\dot{\kappa}(x_1^2 + x_2^2)/2, \ v_3 = 0 \tag{5.51}$$

The non-vanishing strain rates can be obtained from (5.51) as

$$\dot{\varepsilon}_{11} = -\dot{\varepsilon}_{22} = \dot{\kappa} x_2 \tag{5.52}$$

Then, the non-vanishing strain components are

$$\varepsilon_{11} = -\varepsilon_{22} = \kappa x_2 \tag{5.53}$$

The non-vanishing components of curvature tensors can be written as

$$\chi_{31} = -\kappa \tag{5.54}$$

Eq. (5.53) and (5.54) lead to the effective strain and the effective curvature tensor

$$\varepsilon_e = \frac{2}{\sqrt{3}}\kappa |x_2|, \ \chi_e = \sqrt{\frac{2}{3}}\kappa \tag{5.55}$$

The stretch gradient is given by

$$\eta_{ijk}^{(1)} \eta_{ijk}^{(1)} = \frac{76}{75} \kappa^2 \tag{5.56}$$

We know that the length scale l_1 for the stretch gradient is very small and l_{cr} that corresponds to the rotation gradient is larger (Stolken and Evans, 1998), then from Eq. (5.9), we can find that $c_1 = \left(\frac{l_1}{l_{cs}}\right)^2$ is very small and $\eta_{ijk}^{(1)} \eta_{ijk}^{(1)}$ has the same order as χ_e^2. In order to be consistent with the theory in analyzing the torsion experiment, we can omit the term of $\eta_{ijk}^{(1)} \eta_{ijk}^{(1)}$ in Eq. (5.9) and adopt $\eta = \chi_e$, that is only the rotation gradient is considered while investigating the bending experiment.

From simulating the tensile test results of thin beams, the relation between the stress and plastic strain can be expressed as (Stolken and Evans, 1998)

$$\sigma = \Sigma_0 + \varepsilon_{pl} E_p \tag{5.57}$$

where Σ_0 is the yield strength, ε_{pl} is the plastic strain and E_p the hardening coefficient. Then the relation between the effective stress and effective strain can be obtained

$$\sigma_e = \frac{\sqrt{3}}{2} \Sigma_0 + \frac{3}{4} E_p \varepsilon_{ep} \tag{5.58}$$

where ε_{ep} is the effective plastic strain.

Now, using the new hardening relationship, i. e. Eq. (5.18), we investigate the same problem. According to Eq. (5.58), the stress-strain curve in uniaxial tensile state can be expressed as

$$\sigma = \frac{\sqrt{3}}{2} \Sigma_0 + \frac{3}{4} E_p \varepsilon_{pl} \tag{5.59}$$

Actually, Eq. (5.59) should be represented as follows

$$\begin{cases} \sigma = \hat{\Sigma}_0 + \hat{E}_p \varepsilon, & \varepsilon \geqslant \varepsilon_0 \\ \sigma = E\varepsilon, & \varepsilon \leqslant \varepsilon_0 \end{cases} \tag{5.60}$$

where ε_0 is the yield strain, $\hat{\Sigma}_0 = \dfrac{2\sqrt{3}\Sigma_0 E}{4E + 3E_p}$ and $\hat{E}_p = \dfrac{3E_p E}{4E + 3E_p}$, $E = 220$ GPa is the Young's modulus for Ni.

So the relation of the effective stress and effective strain is

$$\begin{cases} \sigma_e = \hat{\Sigma}_0 + \hat{E}_p \varepsilon_e, & \varepsilon_e \geqslant \varepsilon_0 \\ \sigma_e = E\varepsilon_e, & \varepsilon_e \leqslant \varepsilon_0 \end{cases} \tag{5.61}$$

From Eq. (5.59), we can get the yield strength σ_0, which is corresponding to the yield strain ε_0,

$$\sigma_0 = \frac{\sqrt{3}}{2}\Sigma_0 \tag{5.62}$$

then

$$\varepsilon_0 = \frac{\sigma_0}{E} = \frac{\sqrt{3}\Sigma_0}{2E} \tag{5.63}$$

Substituting Eqs. (5.62) and (5.63) into (5.61), we find that Eq. (5.61) is a continuous function at the point of $\varepsilon_e = \varepsilon_0$ as shown in Figure 5.4.

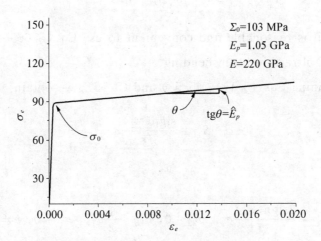

Figure 5.4   Relation between the effective stress and effective strain.

Considering the strain gradient plasticity, from Eqs. (5.61) and (5.18), we can get

$$\begin{cases} \dot{\sigma}_e = \hat{E}_p \dot{\varepsilon}_e \left(1 + \dfrac{l^2 \eta^2}{\varepsilon_e^2}\right), & \varepsilon_e \geqslant \varepsilon_0 \\[4mm] \dot{\sigma}_e = E \dot{\varepsilon}_e \left(1 + \dfrac{l^2 \eta^2}{\varepsilon_e^2}\right), & \varepsilon_e \leqslant \varepsilon_0 \end{cases} \tag{5.64}$$

Substituting Eq. (5.55) into (5.64) yieds

$$\begin{cases} \dot{\sigma}_e = \hat{E}_p \dot{\varepsilon}_e \left(1 + \dfrac{l^2}{2x_2^2}\right), & \varepsilon_e \geqslant \varepsilon_0 \\[4mm] \dot{\sigma}_e = E \dot{\varepsilon}_e \left(1 + \dfrac{l^2}{2x_2^2}\right), & \varepsilon_e \leqslant \varepsilon_0 \end{cases} \tag{5.65}$$

From Eq. (5.65), we find that the term describing the strain gradient effect has no direct relation with the deformation history, so for the problem of ultra-thin beam bending, we can rewrite Eq. (5.65) as following,

$$\begin{cases} \sigma_e = (\hat{\Sigma}_0 + \hat{E}_p \varepsilon_e) \left(1 + \dfrac{l^2}{2x_2^2}\right), & \varepsilon_e \geqslant \varepsilon_0 \\[4mm] \sigma_e = E \varepsilon_e \left(1 + \dfrac{l^2}{2x_2^2}\right), & \varepsilon_e \leqslant \varepsilon_0 \end{cases} \tag{5.66}$$

Then it is reasonable and convenient to use Eq. (5.66) to solve the problem of ultra-thin beam bending.

Combining Eqs. (5.14), (5.53) and (5.55), we obtain

$$S_{11} = \frac{\text{sign}(x_2)}{\sqrt{3}} \sigma_e \tag{5.67}$$

then

$$\sigma_{11} = \frac{2\text{sign}(x_2)}{\sqrt{3}} \sigma_e, \ \sigma_{22} = 0, \ \sigma_{33} = \frac{1}{2}\sigma_{11}, \ \sigma_{ij} = 0 \ (i \neq j) \tag{5.68}$$

The moment M can be obtained from the integration over the cross section by the components of stress as

$$M = 2 \int_0^{h/2} \sigma_{11} b x_2 \, \mathrm{d}x_2 \tag{5.69}$$

Substituting Eqs. (5.66), (5.68) into Eq. (5.69), the moment M can be expressed as

$$M = \frac{bE\varepsilon_0}{\sqrt{3}\,\kappa^2}(\varepsilon_0^2 + 2l^2\kappa^2) + \frac{b}{\sqrt{3}\,\kappa^2}\left[\frac{3}{2}\frac{\hat{\Sigma}_0}{}(\varepsilon_{max}^2 - \varepsilon_0^2) + \hat{E}_p(\varepsilon_{max}^3\right.$$

$$\left. - \varepsilon_0^3) + 2\hat{\Sigma}_0 l^2\kappa^2\ln\frac{\varepsilon_{max}}{\varepsilon_0} + 2\hat{E}_p l^2\kappa^2(\varepsilon_{max} - \varepsilon_0)\right]$$

(5.70)

where

$$\varepsilon_{max} = \frac{\kappa h}{\sqrt{3}}$$

(5.71)

Comparisons of the theoretical prediction of Eq. (5.70) with the bending test results of different thickness are shown in Figure 5.5. From Figure 5.5 we can find that the calculation results agree well with the test results and the length scale $l = 3.3\ \mu$m.

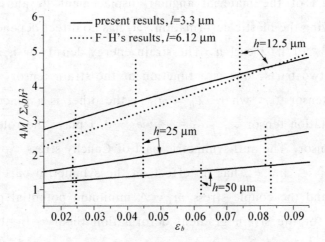

Figure 5.5   Comparisons between the experimental results (Stolken & Evans, 1998) and theoretical predictions of SG theory and the strain gradient theory with a new hardening law.

From Eq. (5.68), we know that σ_{11} and σ_{33} are the non-vanishing components of stresses and depend only on x_2. It is obvious that all the conventional equilibrium equations are met and the traction free conditions on the boundary of the beam are also satisfied. Hence, Eq. (5.50) is a true displacement field.

5.2 C-W couple-stress strain gradient plasticity theory

A new phenomenological strain gradient theory for crystalline solid is proposed by Chen and Wang (2001), which is called C-W couple stress-strain grdient plasticity theory. It fits within the framework of general couple stress theory and involves a single material length scale l_{cs}. In the C-W theory three rotational degrees of freedom ω_i are introduced, which denotes part of the material angular displacement θ_i and is induced accompanying the plastic deformation. ω_i has no direct dependence upon u_i while $\theta = (1/2) \cdot \mathrm{curl}\ \boldsymbol{u}$. The strain energy density w is assumed to consist of two parts: one is a function of the strain tensor ε_{ij} and the curvature tensor χ_{ij}, where $\chi_{ij} \equiv \omega_{i,j}$; the other is a function of the relative rotation tensor α_{ij}. $\alpha_{ij} = e_{ijk}(\omega_k - \theta_k)$ plays the role of elastic rotation tensor. The anti-symmetric part of Cauchy stress τ_{ij} is only the function of α_{ij} and α_{ij} has no effect on the symmetric part of Cauchy stress σ_{ij} and the couple stress m_{ij}. A minimum potential principle is developed for the strain gradient deformation theory. In the limit of vanishing l_{cs}, it reduces to the conventional counterparts: J_2 deformation theory. Equilibrium equations, constitutive relations and boundary conditions are given in details. For simplicity, the elastic relation between the anti-symmetric part of Cauchy stress, τ_{ij}, and α_{ij} is established and only one elastic constant exists between the two tensors. Combining the same hardening law as that used in Fleck et al. (1994), the present theory is used to investigate two typical examples, i.e. thin metallic wire torsion and ultra-thin metallic beam bend, the analytical results agree well with the experiment results. While considering the stretching gradient, the new hardening law (Chen and Wang, 2000) is used to analyze the two typical problems. The flow theory version of the present theory is given also.

As we know the gradient of displacement β_{ij} can be written as

$$\beta_{ij} = \partial_i u_j \qquad (5.72)$$

and it can be divided into two parts: strain tensor and rotation tensor,

$$\beta_{ij} = \varepsilon_{ij} - W_{ij} \qquad (5.73)$$

For crystalline solid, the rotation tensor W_{ij} can be decomposed into two parts,

$$W_{ij} = W_{ij}^e + W_{ij}^p \qquad (5.74)$$

where W_{ij}^e is the elastic rotation tensor and W_{ij}^p is the plastic rotation tensor.

The angular displacement accompanying the plastic deformation can be chosen as an independent rotation vector ω_i, which is directly related to the plastic rotation tensor W_{ij}^p according to the following formula,

$$W_{ij}^p = - e_{ijk} \omega_k \qquad (5.75)$$

The rotation vector θ_i corresponding to W_{ij} denotes the material angular displacement, $\theta \equiv (1/2) \operatorname{curl} u$. The relative curvature tensor is $\alpha_{ij} = e_{ijk} (\omega_k - \theta_k) = W_{ij}^e$, which is an anti-symmetric tensor and directly relates to the rotation vector accompanying elastic deformation. Since ω_i is independent and has no relation with the displacement vector u_i, α_{ij} does not vanish, which is different from the theory proposed by Fleck et al. (1994) and Fleck and Hutchinson (1993).

We define the symmetric part of Cauchy stress, σ_{ij}, as the work conjugate of the strain tensor ε_{ij}; the couple stress tensor m_{ij} as the work conjugate of the curvature tensor χ_{ij}, where $\chi_{ij} = \omega_{i,j}$. The anti-symmetric part of Cauchy stress, τ_{ij}, is the work conjugate of the relative curvature tensor α_{ij}. The deviatoric part s_{ij} of Cauchy stress and deviatoric part m'_{ij} of couple stress are defined as the work conjugates of ε'_{ij}, χ'_{ij} respectively; σ_m and m_m are defined as the work conjugates of ε_m and χ_m respectively, then one can obtain

$$\delta w = s_{ij}\delta\varepsilon'_{ij} + m'_{ij}\delta\chi'_{ij} + \sigma_m\delta\varepsilon_m + m_m\delta\chi_m + \tau_{ij}\delta\alpha_{ij} \tag{5.76}$$

where $s_{ij} \equiv \sigma_{ij} - (1/3)\delta_{ij}\sigma_{kk}$, $m'_{ij} \equiv m_{ij} - (1/3)\delta_{ij}m_{kk}$ and the term $\tau_{ij}\delta\alpha_{ij}$ plays the role of the work produced by elastic curvature tensor.

Eq. (5.76) enables one to determine s_{ij}, m'_{ij}, σ_m, m_m and τ_{ij} in terms of the strain and curvature tensor states of the solid as

$$s_{ij} = \frac{\partial w}{\partial \varepsilon'_{ij}}, \quad m'_{ij} = \frac{\partial w}{\partial \chi'_{ij}}, \quad \sigma_m = \frac{\partial w}{\partial \varepsilon_m}, \quad m_m = \frac{\partial w}{\partial \chi_m}, \quad \tau_{ij} = \frac{\partial w}{\partial \alpha_{ij}} \tag{5.77}$$

In the present paper, we assume that the strain energy density w can be expressed as

$$w(\varepsilon, \chi, \alpha) = w_0(\varepsilon, \chi) + w_1(\alpha) \tag{5.78}$$

It means that the anti-symmetric stress τ_{ij} depends only on the relative rotation tensor α_{ij}. In other words, τ_{ij} is only the function of elastic rotation vector. Meanwhile the relative rotation tensor α_{ij} has no effect on σ_{ij} and m_{ij}.

For isotropic material, w_1 should be the isotropic scalar function of the tensor α_{ij}. Since α_{ij} is an anti-symmetric tensor, according to Spencer (1971), α_{ij} has only one independent invariant, $\alpha_{ij}\alpha_{ji}$. Hence we have

$$w_1(\alpha_{ij}) = w_1(J_2) \tag{5.79}$$

where

$$J_2 = \alpha_{ij}\alpha_{ij} \tag{5.80}$$

Substituting Eq. (5.78) and Eq. (5.79) into Eq. (5.77), one can obtain

$$\sigma_{ij} = \frac{\partial w_0}{\partial \varepsilon_{ij}}, \quad m_{ij} = \frac{\partial w_0}{\partial \chi_{ij}}, \quad \tau_{ij} = \frac{\partial w_1}{\partial J_2} \cdot \frac{\partial J_2}{\partial \alpha_{ij}} = 2w'_1(J_2)\alpha_{ij} \quad (5.81)$$

According to the work by Fleck-Hutchinson (1993) and Fleck et al. (1994), it is mathematically convenient to assume that the strain energy density w_0 depends only upon the single scalar strain measure E_e, where

$$E_e^2 = \varepsilon_e^2 + l_{cs}^2 \chi_e^2 \quad (5.82)$$

The length scale l_{cs} is a material length scale related with rotation gradient and required on dimensional grounds, $\varepsilon_e^2 = \frac{2}{3}\varepsilon'_{ij}\varepsilon'_{ij}$, $\chi_e^2 = \frac{2}{3}\chi'_{ij}\chi'_{ij}$.

An effective stress measure Σ_e is defined as the work conjugate of E_e, which is proposed by Fleck and Hutchinson (1993) and the hardening relation between Σ_e and E_e is,

$$\Sigma_e = \frac{dw_0(E_e)}{dE_e} = f(E_e) \quad (5.83)$$

then

$$s_{ij} = \frac{2\Sigma_e}{3E_e}\varepsilon'_{ij}, \quad m'_{ij} = \frac{2}{3}l_{cs}^2\frac{\Sigma_e}{E_e}\chi'_{ij}, \quad \sigma_m = \frac{1}{3}\sigma_{kk}, \quad m_m = \frac{1}{3}m_{kk} \quad (5.84)$$

and

$$\Sigma_e = (\sigma_e^2 + l_{cs}^{-2}m_e^2)^{1/2} \quad (5.85)$$

where

$$\begin{cases} \sigma_e^2 = \frac{3}{2}s_{ij}s_{ij}, \quad m_e^2 = \frac{3}{2}m'_{ij}m'_{ij} \\ \\ \varepsilon_e^2 = \frac{2}{3}\varepsilon'_{ij}\varepsilon'_{ij}, \quad \chi_e^2 = \frac{2}{3}\chi'_{ij}\chi'_{ij} \end{cases} \quad (5.86)$$

Consider a body of volume V and surface S comprised of non-linear elastic solid; the solid satisfied the constitutive law Eq. (5.81). Stress traction T_i^0 acts on a portion S_T of the surface of the body, on the remaining portions S_u the displacement is prescribed as u_i^0 and couple stress traction q_i^0 acts on a portion S_q, on the remaining portions S_ω of the surface the rotation is prescribed as ω_i^0. Then the following principle of minimum potential energy may be stated:

Consider all admissible displacement fields u_i and rotation vector fields ω_i which satisfy $u_i = u_i^0$ and $\omega_i = \omega_i^0$ on the part of the boundaries S_u and S_ω respectively. The real displacement fields and the real rotation vector fields render the potential energy $P(u, \omega)$ to be minimum. The potential energy $P(u, \omega)$ is expressed as following,

$$P(u, \omega) = \int_V w(\varepsilon, \chi, \alpha) dV - (\int_{S_T} T_i^0 u_i dS + \int_{S_q} q_i^0 \omega_i dS)$$

(5.87)

The strain gradient theory proposed by Fleck and Hutchinson (1993) and Fleck et al. (1994) falls within the classification of reduced couple stress theory. The pertinent kinematic quantities in reduced couple stress theory are the displacement u and the overall rotation $\theta \equiv (1/2) \text{curl } u$. The relative rotation tensor α vanishes for the particular choice $\omega \equiv \theta$ and the curvature tensor $\chi_{ij} = \dot{\theta}_{i,j}$, $\chi_{ii} = 0$. The force equilibrium and moment equilibrium is the same as Eq. (1.6) and Eq. (1.7), respectively, but the moment m is only the deviatoric part and the spherical part m_m can not enter the equilibrium equations.

In this paper, the rotation vector ω is independent and has no relation with the displacement u. $\chi_{ij} = \omega_{i,j}$ and its work conjugate, the couple stress m_{ij}, includes the deviatoric part m'_{ij} and the spherical part m_m. The spherical part of couple stress is not zero in the present paper since the independent rotation vector ω is introduced and different from other theories. The spherical part of couple stress plays an important role in obtaining the boundary conditions. Details about the importance of the spherical part's existence can be found in the paper by Green et al. (1968).

5.3　Verification of C-W couple-stress strain gradient plasticity theory

5.3.1　Thin wire torsion

As a typical example, we assume that

$$w_1 = C_1 J_2 \tag{5.88}$$

where C_1 is a material constant.

From Eq. (5.81), it follows

$$\tau_{ij} = 2C_1 \alpha_{ij} \tag{5.89}$$

In this section torsion of thin copper wires with different diameters is analyzed using the present theory. A Cartesian coordinate system (x_1, x_2, x_3) and a cylindrical polar coordinate system (r, θ, x_3) are introduced as shown in Figure 5.1 and x_3 axis is parallel to the axis of the wire. The radius of the wire is a. κ is the twist per unit length of the wire and taken to be positive without loss of generality.

The equilibrium equations for stresses and couple stresses are

$$t_{ij,j} = \sigma_{ij,j} + \tau_{ij,j} = 0 \tag{5.90}$$

$$\tau_{jk} = \frac{1}{2} e_{ijk} m_{ip,p} \tag{5.91}$$

$$\tau_{ij} = 2C_1 \alpha_{ij} = 2C_1 e_{ijk} (\omega_k - \theta_k) \tag{5.92}$$

Now we introduce K_1, which is called the volumetric modulus of bend-torsion, then we have

$$m_m = K_1 l_{cs}^2 \chi_m \tag{5.93}$$

where $\chi_m = \dfrac{1}{3}\chi_{ii}$ and m_m denotes the spherical part of couple stress, i.e. $m_{ij} = m'_{ij} + m_m\delta_{ij}$.

In order to compare the results of the present theory and that proposed by Fleck and Hutchinson (1993) reasonably, the hardening relation, the traction boundary conditions and the displacement boundary conditions are taken to be the same as that used in Fleck et al. (1994). The solid is assumed to be incompressible for strain tensor. The boundary conditions for couple stresses on the lateral face can be expressed as follows (details in Fleck et al. (1994)),

$$m_{\theta r} = m_{zr} = 0 \quad \text{on} \quad r = a \tag{5.94}$$

$$\overline{q}_r = 0 \quad \text{on} \quad r = a \tag{5.95}$$

where the definition of $\overline{q}_r$ can be found in Fleck et al. (1994). An alternative boundary condition instead of Eq. (5.95) is

$$m_{rr} = 0 \quad \text{on} \quad r = a \tag{5.96}$$

On the end faces there are the following boundary conditions,

$$u_r = 0, \ u_\theta = 0, \ u_z = 0 \quad \text{on } z = 0 \tag{5.97}$$

$$u_r = 0, \ u_\theta = \kappa rL, \ u_z = 0 \quad \text{on } z = L \tag{5.98}$$

$$m_{rz} = m_{\theta z} = 0, \ m'_{zz} = \frac{2}{3}l_{cs}^2\Sigma_0\kappa^n\left(\frac{r^2}{3} + l_{cs}^2\right)^{\frac{n-1}{2}} \quad \text{on} \quad z = 0 \tag{5.99}$$

$$m_{rz} = m_{\theta z} = 0, \ m'_{zz} = \frac{2}{3}l_{cs}^2\Sigma_0\kappa^n\left(\frac{r^2}{3} + l_{cs}^2\right)^{\frac{n-1}{2}} \quad \text{on} \quad z = L \tag{5.100}$$

where L is the total length of the thin wire as shown in Figure 5.1.

(i) If the solid is assumed to be incompressible for bend-torsion, thus $K_1 \rightarrow \infty$, we can find that the corresponding solutions to the above boundary value problem is

$$u_1 = -\kappa x_2 x_3, \ u_2 = \kappa x_1 x_3, \ u_3 = 0 \tag{5.101}$$

$$\omega_r = -\frac{1}{2}\kappa r, \ \omega_\theta = 0, \ \omega_z = \kappa z \tag{5.102}$$

It is verified as following:

From the displacement field, we have the non-vanishing components of strain

$$\varepsilon'_{13} = \varepsilon'_{31} = -\frac{1}{2}\kappa x_2, \quad \varepsilon'_{23} = \varepsilon'_{32} = \frac{1}{2}\kappa x_1, \quad \varepsilon_e = \frac{1}{\sqrt{3}}\kappa r \tag{5.103}$$

and the non-vanishing deviatoric components of curvature tensor are

$$\chi'_{11} = \chi'_{22} = -\frac{1}{2}\kappa, \quad \chi'_{33} = \kappa, \quad \chi_e = \kappa \tag{5.104}$$

The spherical part of curvature tensor is

$$\chi_m = \frac{1}{3}\chi_{kk} = 0 \tag{5.105}$$

Here, the simple power law relationship between Σ_e and E_e using in Fleck et al. (1994) is adopted also

$$\Sigma_e = \Sigma_0 E_e^n \tag{5.106}$$

The non-vanishing component of Cauchy stress only is

$$\sigma_{\theta z} = s_{\theta z} = \frac{1}{3}\Sigma_0 \kappa E_e^{n-1} r \tag{5.107}$$

The non-vanishing deviatoric components of couple stress are

$$m'_{rr} = -\frac{1}{3}l_{cs}^2 \Sigma_0 \kappa E_e^{n-1}, \quad m'_{\theta\theta} = -\frac{1}{3}l_{cs}^2 \Sigma_0 \kappa E_e^{n-1}, \quad m'_{zz} = \frac{2}{3}l_{cs}^2 \Sigma_0 \kappa E_e^{n-1}$$

$$\tag{5.108}$$

where

$$E_e = \kappa \left(\frac{r^2}{3} + l_{cs}^2\right)^{\frac{1}{2}} \tag{5.109}$$

From Eq. (5.107), we find that the non-vanishing component of Cauchy stress is only related with r, the equilibrium equations of stress, i.e. Eqs. (5.90) are met.

Since the components of couple stress in Eq. (5.108) are only related with r, Eq. (5.91) can be reduced

$$\begin{cases} \dfrac{\partial m_{rr}}{\partial r} + \dfrac{m_{rr} - m_{\theta\theta}}{r} = 0 \\[3mm] \dfrac{1}{r}\dfrac{\partial m_m}{\partial \theta} = 0 \\[3mm] \dfrac{\partial m_m}{\partial z} = 0 \end{cases} \tag{5.110}$$

m_m can not be determined from Eq. (5.93) and becomes an independent unknown variable. Combining the boundary condition, Eq. (5.96), we obtain,

$$m_m = \frac{1}{3} l_{cs}^2 \kappa^n \Sigma_0 \left(\frac{1}{3} r^2 + l_{cs}^2 \right)^{\frac{n-1}{2}} \tag{5.111}$$

The torque produced by the spherical part of moment in the present theory is

$$Q_1 = \int_0^{2\pi}\int_0^a m_m r \, dr \, d\theta = \frac{2\pi l_{cs}^2 \Sigma_0 \kappa^n}{n+1}\left[\left(\frac{a^2}{3} + l_{cs}^2\right)^{\frac{n+1}{2}} - l_{cs}^{n+1}\right] \tag{5.112}$$

The overall torque produced by $\sigma_{\theta z}$, m'_{zz}, m_m on the end face is

$$Q = \frac{6\pi \Sigma_0 \kappa^n}{n+3}\left[\left(\frac{a^2}{3} + l_{cs}^2\right)^{\frac{n+3}{2}} - l_{cs}^{n+3}\right] \tag{5.113}$$

The above equation is the same as Eq. (6.9) in Fleck et al. (1994). From simulating the tensile curves of experiment we take $n = 0.22$. If we choose torsional response curve of $2a = 15 \ \mu\text{m}$ as a calibration curve, we get $l_{cs} = 4.5 \ \mu\text{m}$. Comparisons with the experiment results are shown in Figure 5.6.

From above we proved that $\omega_i = \theta_i$ is the corresponding solution to the special boundary conditions of Eqs. (5.94) – (5.100). If we take another set of boundary conditions, for example

$$u_r = 0, \ u_\theta = 0, \ u_z = 0 \quad \text{on } z = 0 \tag{5.114}$$

$$u_r = 0, \ u_\theta = \kappa r L, \ u_z = 0 \quad \text{on } z = L \tag{5.115}$$

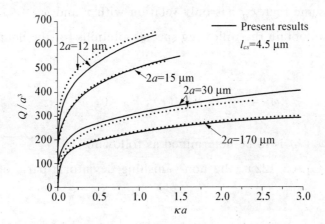

Figure 5.6 Comparisons between the experimental results (Fleck et al., 1994) and the predictions of C-W couple stress strain gradient theory.

$$m_{rz} = m_{\theta z} = 0, \quad \omega_z = 0 \quad \text{on} \quad z = 0 \tag{5.116}$$

$$m_{rz} = m_{\theta z} = 0, \quad \omega_z = 0 \quad \text{on} \quad z = L \tag{5.117}$$

$$m_{\theta r} = m_{zr} = 0 \quad \text{on} \quad r = a \tag{5.118}$$

$$m_{rr} = 0 \quad \text{on} \quad r = a \tag{5.119}$$

One can find another set of solution $\omega_i \neq \theta_i$ to the above set of boundary conditions and here it is omitted.

(ii) If K_1 has a limit value, one will know also that $\omega_i = \theta_i$ is no longer a solution to the boundary conditions of Eqs. (5.94)–(5.100) and $\alpha_{ij} \neq 0$. The anti-symmetric stress τ_{ij} will not vanish.

We can prove that the displacement field in Eq. (5.101) is the correct displacement solution. From the displacement field the material rotation field can be obtained,

$$\theta_r = -\frac{1}{2}\kappa r, \quad \theta_\theta = 0, \quad \theta_z = \kappa z \tag{5.120}$$

The non-vanishing components of strain tensor and the effective strain are

$$\varepsilon_{\theta z} = \varepsilon_{z\theta} = \frac{1}{2}\kappa r, \quad \varepsilon_e^2 = \frac{\kappa^2 r^2}{3} \tag{5.121}$$

We assume that χ_{ij} has only relation with r and $\omega_\theta = \theta_\theta$, $\omega_z = \theta_z$, then one can obtain the following special solutions for the boundary value problem,

$$\omega_r = -\frac{1}{2}\kappa r + \tilde{\omega}_r(r), \quad \omega_\theta = 0, \quad \omega_z = \kappa z \tag{5.122}$$

Now $\tilde{\omega}_r(r)$ is to be determined as following:

From Eq. (5.122), the non-vanishing deviatoric parts of curvature tensor are

$$\begin{cases} \chi'_{rr} = -\frac{1}{2}\kappa + \frac{2}{3}\tilde{\omega}'_r - \frac{1}{3}\frac{\tilde{\omega}_r}{r} \\[2mm] \chi'_{\theta\theta} = -\frac{1}{2}\kappa + \frac{2}{3}\frac{\tilde{\omega}_r}{r} - \frac{1}{3}\tilde{\omega}'_r \\[2mm] \chi'_{zz} = \kappa - \frac{1}{3}\frac{\tilde{\omega}_r}{r} - \frac{1}{3}\tilde{\omega}'_r \end{cases} \tag{5.123}$$

and the effective rotation gradient is

$$\chi_e^2 = \frac{2}{3}\left[(\chi'_{rr})^2 + (\chi'_{\theta\theta})^2 + (\chi'_{zz})^2\right] \tag{5.124}$$

then

$$E_e^2 = \frac{\kappa^2 r^2}{3} + \frac{2}{3}l_{cs}^2\left[\left(-\frac{\kappa}{2} + \frac{2}{3}\tilde{\omega}'_r - \frac{1}{3}\frac{\tilde{\omega}_r}{r}\right)^2 \right.$$
$$\left. + \left(-\frac{\kappa}{2} + \frac{2}{3}\frac{\tilde{\omega}_r}{r} - \frac{1}{3}\tilde{\omega}'_r\right)^2 + \left(\kappa - \frac{1}{3}\tilde{\omega}'_r - \frac{1}{3}\frac{\tilde{\omega}_r}{r}\right)^2\right] \tag{5.125}$$

The non-vanishing anti-symmetric stresses are

$$\tau_{\theta z} = -\tau_{z\theta} = 2C_1\tilde{\omega}_r \tag{5.126}$$

The non-vanishing components of Cauchy stress are

$$t_{\theta z} = \frac{\Sigma_0\kappa}{3}E_e^{n-1}r + 2C_1\tilde{\omega}_r, \quad t_{z\theta} = \frac{\Sigma_0\kappa}{3}E_e^{n-1}r - 2C_1\tilde{\omega}_r \tag{5.127}$$

The non-vanishing components of couple stress are

$$\begin{cases} m_{rr} = m'_{rr} + m_m = \dfrac{2}{3}\Sigma_0 E_e^{n-1}l_{cs}^2\left(-\dfrac{\kappa}{2} + \dfrac{2}{3}\tilde{\omega}'_r - \dfrac{1}{3}\dfrac{\tilde{\omega}_r}{r}\right) + \dfrac{K_1 l_{cs}^2}{3}\left(\tilde{\omega}'_r + \dfrac{\tilde{\omega}_r}{r}\right) \\[3mm] m_{\theta\theta} = m'_{\theta\theta} + m_m = \dfrac{2}{3}\Sigma_0 E_e^{n-1}l_{cs}^2\left(-\dfrac{\kappa}{2} + \dfrac{2}{3}\dfrac{\tilde{\omega}_r}{r} - \dfrac{1}{3}\tilde{\omega}'_r\right) + \dfrac{K_1 l_{cs}^2}{3}\left(\tilde{\omega}'_r + \dfrac{\tilde{\omega}_r}{r}\right) \\[3mm] m_{zz} = m'_{zz} + m_m = \dfrac{2}{3}\Sigma_0 E_e^{n-1}l_{cs}^2\left(\kappa - \dfrac{1}{3}\tilde{\omega}'_r - \dfrac{1}{3}\dfrac{\tilde{\omega}_r}{r}\right) + \dfrac{K_1 l_{cs}^2}{3}\left(\tilde{\omega}'_r + \dfrac{\tilde{\omega}_r}{r}\right) \end{cases}$$

$$(5.128)$$

Now, from Eq. (5.127) we can find that the non-vanishing components have only relation with r, so Eq. (5.90) is met.

Substituting Eq. (5.126) and Eq. (5.128) into Eq. (5.91), one can find that the second and third equations in Eq. (5.91) are met automatically and from the first equation in Eq. (5.91) we can obtain

$$2(n-1)E_e^{n-2}l_{cs}^2\Sigma_0\left(-\frac{\kappa}{2} + \frac{2}{3}\tilde{\omega}'_r - \frac{1}{3}\frac{\tilde{\omega}_r}{r}\right)E'_e + 2E_e^{n-1}l_{cs}^2\Sigma_0\left|\frac{2}{3}\tilde{\omega}''_r\right.$$

$$\left. - \frac{1}{3}\frac{\tilde{\omega}'_r}{r} + \frac{1}{3}\frac{\tilde{\omega}_r}{r^2}\right| + 2E_e^{n-1}l_{cs}^2\Sigma_0(\tilde{\omega}'_r r^{-1} - \tilde{\omega}_r r^{-2})$$

$$+ K_1 l_{cs}^2(\tilde{\omega}''_r + \tilde{\omega}'_r r^{-1} - \tilde{\omega}_r r^{-2}) = 12C_1\tilde{\omega}_r$$

$$(5.129)$$

and $\tilde{\omega}_r$ can be solved from the above equation through numerical calculation and it must meet following conditions,

$$\tilde{\omega}_r\big|_{r=0} = 0 \quad m_{rr}\big|_{r=a} = 0 \qquad (5.130)$$

The corresponding overall torque produced by $t_{\theta z}$ and m_{zz} can be expressed as

$$Q = \int_0^{2\pi}\int_0^a t_{\theta z}r^2\,\mathrm{d}r\,\mathrm{d}\theta + \int_0^{2\pi}\int_0^a m_{zz}r\,\mathrm{d}r\,\mathrm{d}\theta \qquad (5.131)$$

The numerical results are shown in Figure 5.7 and Figure 5.8 for a set of parameters, $\Sigma_0 = 237$ MPa, $n = 0.22$, $l_{cs} = 4.5$ μm, $2a = 15$ μm,

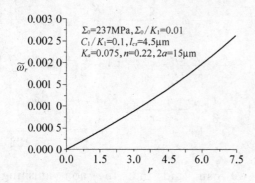

Figure 5.7   Relation curve of r and $\tilde{\omega}_r$.

$\kappa = \dfrac{1}{15}$, $\Sigma_0 / K_1 = 0.01$, C_1 / K_1 $= 0.1$. From Figure 5.7 and Figure 5.8 we find that the boundary conditions in Eq. (5.130) are met and for this kind of case one can find that $\omega_i \neq \theta_i$. The curve of κa versus Q / a^3 for $2a = 15 \ \mu$m is shown in

Figure 5.9. From Figure 5.9 one can find that the present results are consistent well with the experiments results. Comparing with the theoretical curve of $2a = 15 \ \mu$m in Figure 5.6, one can find that the finite value of K_1 has little influence on the overall torque. It means that if K_1 is large enough comparing with Σ_0, the predictions based on $K_1 \rightarrow \infty$ are correct.

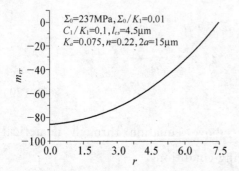

Figure 5.8   Relation curve of r and m_{rr}.

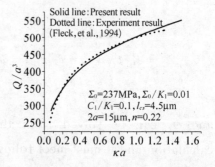

Figure 5.9   Plot of torque against surface strain for copper wire with diameter $2a = 15 \ \mu$m and K_1 is a finite value.

5.3.2   Ultra-thin beam bend

Ultra-thin beam bending with different thickness is analyzed using the present theory. Cartesian (x_1, x_2, x_3) coordinates are adopted as

shown in Figure 5. 10. κ is the curvature,
h is the beam's thickness and b is the
beam's width.

The classical displacement fields are

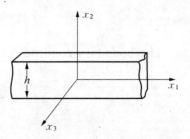

$$u_1 = \kappa x_1 x_2,$$

$$u_2 = -\kappa(x_1^2 + x_2^2)/2, \quad u_3 = 0$$

(5. 132)

Figure 5. 10 Coordinate systems of ultra-thin beams. (the same as Figure 5. 3)

The non-vanishing strain components are

$$\varepsilon_{11} = -\varepsilon_{22} = \kappa x_2 \tag{5.133}$$

The components of the overall rotation vector are

$$\theta_1 = 0, \ \theta_2 = 0, \ \theta_3 = -\kappa x_1 \tag{5.134}$$

From simulating the tensile test results of thin beams, the relation between the stress and plastic strain can be expressed as (Stolken and Evans, 1998)

$$\sigma = \Sigma_0 + \varepsilon_{pl} E_p \tag{5.135}$$

where Σ_0 is the yield strength, ε_{pl} is the plastic strain and E_p the hardening coefficient.

The hardening relation including the effect of strain gradient plasticity is

$$\Sigma_e = \frac{\sqrt{3}}{2}\Sigma_0 + \frac{3}{4}E_p E_e, \ E_e = \sqrt{\varepsilon_e^2 + l_{cs}^2 \chi_e^2} \tag{5.136}$$

The non-vanishing components of Cauchy stress and the moment in Stolken and Evans (1998) are

$$\sigma_{11} = \frac{4\Sigma_e}{3E_e}\kappa x_2, \ \sigma_{33} = \frac{2\Sigma_e}{3E_e}\kappa x_2, \ m_{31} = -\frac{2\Sigma_e}{3E_e}l_{cs}^2 \kappa \tag{5.137}$$

and

$$\tau_{ij} = 0, \ (i, \ j = 1, \ 2, \ 3) \tag{5.138}$$

The boundary conditions on the lateral faces are,

$$\sigma_{12} = \sigma_{22} = \sigma_{32} = 0, \ m_{12} = m_{22} = m_{32} = 0 \quad \text{on } x_2 = \pm h/2 \tag{5.139}$$

$$\sigma_{13} = \sigma_{23} = 0, \ m_{13} = m_{23} = m_{33} = 0 \quad \text{on } x_3 = \pm b/2 \tag{5.140}$$

$$\sigma_{33} = \frac{2\Sigma_e}{3E_e} \kappa x_2 \quad \text{on } x_3 = \pm b/2 \tag{5.141}$$

The boundary conditions on the end faces are

$$\sigma_{11} = \frac{4\Sigma_e}{3E_e} \kappa x_2, \ t_{21} = t_{31} = 0, \ \text{on } x_1 = \pm L/2 \tag{5.142}$$

$$m_{11} = m_{21} = 0, \ m_{31} = -\frac{2\Sigma_e}{3E_e} l_{cs}^2 \kappa \quad \text{on} \quad x_1 = \pm L/2 \tag{5.143}$$

where $E_e = \sqrt{\frac{4}{3}\kappa^2 x_2^2 + \frac{2}{3}\kappa^2}$.

Since τ_{ij} specially vanishes for the ultra-thin beam bend with the theory proposed by Fleck and Hutchinson (1993), we can find easily that while using the present strain gradient theory to investigate the same problem with the same boundary conditions and same hardening law in Stolken and Evans (1998), the solutions to this special boundary conditions are as following;

$$u_1 = \kappa x_1 x_2, \quad u_2 = -\kappa(x_1^2 + x_2^2)/2, \quad u_3 = 0 \tag{5.144}$$

$$\omega_1 = 0, \ \omega_2 = 0, \ \omega_3 = -\kappa x_1 \tag{5.145}$$

The equilibrium equations of Eqs. (5.90)–(5.92) are all met.

It must be noted that if the boundary conditions change the solution will change also, i.e., $\omega_i \neq \theta_i$.

5.4 C-W strain gradient plasticity theory

Combining the hardening law (Chen and Wang, 2000) and the C-W couple strees gradient theory, we proposed the C-W strain gradient plasticity theory, in which not only the rotation gradient but also the stretch gradient is considered. The hardening law is expressed as following

$$\dot{\Sigma}_e = f'(E_e)\left(1 + \frac{l_1 \eta_1}{E_e}\right)^{1/2} \dot{E}_e \tag{5.146}$$

η_1 in the above equation denotes the effective stretching gradient and can be expressed as

$$\eta_1 = \sqrt{\eta_{ijk}^{(1)} \eta_{ijk}^{(1)}} \tag{5.147}$$

where $\eta_{ijk}^{(1)}$ denotes the stretching gradient tensor and can be obtained from the second differential of the displacement vector, which can be found in Chen and Wang (2000). l_1 is the length scale related with the stretch gradient.

The corresponding constitutive relations are as follows,

$$\sigma_{ij} = \frac{2\Sigma_e}{3E_e}\varepsilon'_{ij} + K\varepsilon_m \delta_{ij} \qquad m_{ij} = \frac{2\Sigma_e}{3E_e}l_{cs}^2 \chi'_{ij} + K_1 l_{cs}^2 \chi_m \delta_{ij} \tag{5.148}$$

$$\begin{cases} E_e^2 = \varepsilon_e^2 + l_{cs}^2 \chi_e^2 \qquad \Sigma_e = (\sigma_e^2 + l_{cs}^{-2} m_e^2)^{1/2} \\ \sigma_e^2 = \frac{3}{2} s_{ij} s_{ij} \qquad m_e^2 = \frac{3}{2} m'_{ij} m'_{ij} \end{cases} \tag{5.149}$$

The incremental form can be written as

$$\begin{cases} \dot{s}_{ij} = \dfrac{2\dot{\Sigma}_e}{3E_e}\varepsilon'_{ij} - \dfrac{2\Sigma_e}{3E_e^2}\varepsilon'_{ij}\dot{E}_e + \dfrac{2\Sigma_e}{3E_e}\dot{\varepsilon}'_{ij} \\[3mm] \dot{m}'_{ij} = \dfrac{2}{3}l_{cs}^2\dfrac{\dot{\Sigma}_e}{E_e}\chi'_{ij} - \dfrac{2l_{cs}^2\Sigma_e}{3E_e^2}\chi'_{ij}\dot{E}_e + \dfrac{2l_{cs}^2\Sigma_e}{3E_e}\dot{\chi}'_{ij} \\[3mm] \dot{\sigma}_m = \dfrac{1}{3}\dot{\sigma}_{kk}, \quad \dot{m}_m = \dfrac{1}{3}\dot{m}_{kk} \end{cases} \tag{5.150}$$

The J_2 flow theory version of the present theory is given as follows.

The strain tensor consists of elastic and plastic parts. The curvature tensor also consists of the two corresponding parts. Thus the strain rate and the curvature tensor rate can be expressed

$$\dot{\varepsilon}_{ij} = \dot{\varepsilon}_{ij}^e + \dot{\varepsilon}_{ij}^p \quad \dot{\chi}_{ij}^p = \dot{\omega}_{i,j} \tag{5.151}$$

Assuming the existence of couple stresses in the elastic-plastic body. The elastic strain state ε_{ij}^e is obtained.

$$\varepsilon_{ij}^e = \mu_{ijkl}\sigma_{kl} \tag{5.152}$$

where μ_{ijkl} is the elastic compliance tensor.

Since the angular displacement ω_i is directly related to the plastic curvature tensor χ_{ij}^p, hence we only need to address the constitutive equation for χ_{ij}^p.

The yield surface Φ can be written as

$$\Phi = \Phi(\sigma_e, m_e, Y) \tag{5.153}$$

where $\sigma_e = \sqrt{\dfrac{3}{2}s_{ij}s_{ij}}$ is the Von Mises effective stress, $m_e = \sqrt{\dfrac{3}{2}m'_{ij}m'_{ij}}$ is the effective couple stress, and Y is the current flow stress.

Plastic flow is normal to the yield surface such that

$$\dot{\varepsilon}_{ij}^p = \dot{\lambda}\frac{\partial\Phi}{\partial\sigma_{ij}} \quad l_{cs}\dot{\chi}_{ij}^p = l_{cs}^{-1}\dot{\lambda}\frac{\partial\Phi}{\partial m_{ij}} \tag{5.154}$$

According to Fleck and Hutchinson (1993), Σ_e is called the overall effective stress denoted by Eq. (5.85) and the overall effective plastic strain rate is defined as $\dot{E}_e^p = \sqrt{(\dot{\varepsilon}_e^p)^2 + (l_{cs}\dot{\chi}_e^p)^2}$, where the effective strain rate is $\dot{\varepsilon}_e^p = \sqrt{\dfrac{2}{3} \dot{\varepsilon}_{ij}^p \dot{\varepsilon}_{ij}^p}$ and the effective curvature tensor rate is $\dot{\chi}_e^p =$

$\sqrt{\dfrac{2}{3} \dot{\chi}_{ij}^p \dot{\chi}_{ij}^p}$. Then the yield surface (5.153) generalizes to

$$\Phi(\Sigma_e, Y) = \Sigma_e - Y = 0 \tag{5.155}$$

The plastic strain rate and the plastic curvature tensor rate can be given

$$\dot{\varepsilon}_{ij}^p = \frac{3}{2h(\Sigma_e)} \frac{s_{ij}}{\Sigma_e} \dot{\Sigma}_e \qquad l_{cs} \dot{\chi}_{ij}^p = \frac{3}{2h(\Sigma_e)} \frac{l_{cs}^{-1} m'_{ij}}{\Sigma_e} \dot{\Sigma}_e \tag{5.156}$$

According to the hardening law proposed by Fleck et al. (1994) and Fleck and Hutchinson (1993),

$$\dot{\Sigma}_e = f'(E_e^p) \dot{E}_e^p = A(E_e^p) \dot{E}_e^p \tag{5.157}$$

$$\dot{\Sigma}_e = \frac{3}{2} \frac{s_{ij}}{\Sigma_e} \dot{s}_{ij} + \frac{3}{2} \frac{l_{cs}^{-1} m'_{ij}}{\Sigma_e} l_{cs}^{-1} \dot{m}'_{ij} \tag{5.158}$$

For this kind of hardening law, the tangent modulus h of the stress Σ_e versus plastic strain E_e^p curve in simple tension is $h = \dot{\Sigma}_e / \dot{E}_e^p = A(E_e^p)$. While considering the stretching gradient, only the tangent modulus h changes and $h = A(E_e^p) \left(1 + \dfrac{l_1 \eta_1}{E_e^p}\right)^{1/2}$.

The constitutive equation for the anti-symmetric stress rate is

$$\dot{\tau}_{ij} = 2C_1 \dot{\alpha}_{ij} = 2C_1 e_{ijk}(\dot{\omega}_k - \dot{\theta}_k) \tag{5.159}$$

5.5　Thin wire torsion and ultra-thin beam bend

C-W strain gradient theory is used to analyze the thin-wire torsion problem in this section. From above we know that Eqs. (5.101) and

(5. 102) are the true field for the special boundary conditions Eqs. (5. 94) −(5. 100). Here we take Eqs. (5. 101) and (5. 102) to check the overall torque produced by the new hardening law.

The anti-symmetric stress vanishes. The non-vanishing components of strain and the deviatoric components of curvature tensor are the same as Eqs. (5. 103)−(5. 104).

The displacement field yields the stretching gradient

$$\eta^{(1)}_{ijk} \eta^{(1)}_{ijk} = 0 \tag{5.160}$$

Then

$$\eta_1 = 0 \tag{5.161}$$

Substituting the effective strain, effective rotation gradient and the effective stretching gradient into the hardening law, Eq. (5. 146), then

$$\dot{\Sigma}_e = n\Sigma_0 E_e^{n-1} \dot{E}_e \tag{5.162}$$

After integrating Eq. (5. 162) one can obtain the following equation

$$\Sigma_e = \Sigma_0 E_e^n \tag{5.163}$$

Thus, it is reasonable and convenient to use Eq. (5. 163) to solve the problem of thin wire torsion and from section 5.3.1, we can easily obtain the overall torque.

The new hardening law, equation (5. 146), is adopted to analyze bending of ultra-thin beams with different thickness. From above, we know that Eqs. (5. 144) and (5. 145) are the true field for the special boundary conditions Eq. (5. 139)−(5. 143). Here we take Eqs. (5. 144) and (5. 145) to check the overall moment produced by the new hardening law.

The anti-symmetric stress vanishes. The non-vanishing components of strain are the same as equation (5. 133) and the deviatoric components of curvature tensor are

$$\chi_{31} = -\kappa, \quad \chi_e = \sqrt{\frac{2}{3}}\kappa \tag{5.164}$$

From the displacement field, the stretching gradient can be obtained

$$\eta_{ijk}^{(1)} \eta_{ijk}^{(1)} = \frac{76}{75} \kappa^2 \tag{5.165}$$

Substituting the effective strain and effective strain gradient into the hardening law, equation (5.146), then

$$\dot{\Sigma}_e = \frac{3}{4} E_p \left[1 + \frac{\sqrt{38} l_1}{5(2x_2^2 + l_{cs}^2)^{1/2}} \right]^{1/2} \dot{E}_e \tag{5.166}$$

From Eq. (5.166), we find that the term reflecting the effect of strain gradient has no relation with the deformation history, so for the problem of ultra-thin beam bend, after integrating Eq. (5.166) one can obtain following equation

$$\Sigma_e = \left(\frac{\sqrt{3}}{2} \Sigma_0 + \frac{3}{4} E_p E_e \right) \left[1 + \frac{\sqrt{38} l_1}{5(2x_2^2 + l_{cs}^2)^{1/2}} \right]^{1/2} \tag{5.167}$$

Thus, it is reasonable and convenient to use Eq. (5.167) to solve the problem. Here the overall moments at the end faces are taken into account.

The non-vanishing stress components and couple stress components at the end faces are

$$\sigma_{11} = 2S_{11} = \frac{4\Sigma_e}{3E_e} \varepsilon_{11}'$$

$$= \left[\frac{\Sigma_0}{\sqrt{2}} (l_{cs}^2 + 2x_2^2)^{-\frac{1}{2}} + \kappa E_p \right] \left[1 + \frac{\sqrt{38} l_1}{5(2x_2^2 + l_{cs}^2)^{1/2}} \right]^{1/2} x_2$$

$$\tag{5.168}$$

$$m_{31} = \frac{2\Sigma_e}{3E_e} l_{cs}^2 \chi_{31}$$

$$= \left[\frac{-l_{cs}^2 \Sigma_0}{\sqrt{2}} (l_{cs}^2 + 2x_2^2)^{-\frac{1}{2}} - \frac{l_{cs}^2 \kappa}{2} E_p \right] \left[1 + \frac{\sqrt{38} l_1}{5(2x_2^2 + l_{cs}^2)^{1/2}} \right]^{1/2}$$

$$\tag{5.169}$$

Then the overall moments produced by the stresses and couple stresses at the end faces are

$$M = 2 \int_0^{h/2} \sigma_{11} b x_2 \, \mathrm{d} x_2 - 2 \int_0^{h/2} m_{31} b \, \mathrm{d} x_2 \qquad (5.170)$$

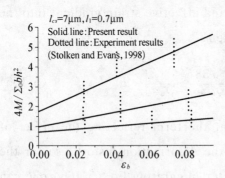

$l_{cs} = 7\mu\mathrm{m}, l_1 = 0.7\mu\mathrm{m}$
Solid line: Present result
Dotted line: Experiment results
(Stolken and Evans, 1998)

Figure 5.11   Comparisons between the experimental results (Stolken & Evans, 1998) and the theoretical predictions of C-W strain gradient theory.

The comparisons of Eq. (5.170) with the test results for Ni beam bend with different thickness (Stolken and Evans, (1998)) are shown in Figure 5.11, where $l_1 = 0.1 l_{cs}$ similar to Stolken and Evans (1998). From Figure 5.11 we can find that all curves predicted by Eq. (5.170) for different thickness are consistent well with the test results and here $l_{cs} = 7 \, \mu\mathrm{m}$.

5.6   Micro-indentation hardness

Chen et al. (2004) has analyzed the micro-indentation problem using C-W strain gradient plasticity theory combining finite element method.

5.6.1   Formula and model of finite element method

In this section, the finite element formulas are presented for the new strain gradient theory first. The principal of virtual work requires

$$\int_V (\sigma_{ij} \delta \varepsilon_{ij} + m_{ij} \delta \chi_{ij}) \mathrm{d} V = \int_S (t_k \delta u_k + q_k \delta \omega_k) \mathrm{d} S \qquad (5.171)$$

where V and S are the volume and surface of the material, respectively.

The virtual strains $\delta\varepsilon_{ij}$ are related to the virtual displacements δu_k and $\delta\chi_{ij}$ are related to the virtual rotation vector $\delta\omega_k$. t_k is surface stress traction and q_k is surface torque traction.

The displacement field can be interpolated by the element shape functions N_i and the nodal displacements. Similarly, the micro-rotation field can be obtained through interpolating the element shape functions N_i and the nodal rotation vectors. The strains and strain gradients can be obtained from $\varepsilon_{ij} = \dfrac{1}{2}(u_{i,j} + u_{j,i})$, $\eta_{ijk} = u_{k,ij}$, $\chi_{ij} = \omega_{i,j}$, $\varepsilon_e = \sqrt{\dfrac{2}{3}\varepsilon'_{ij}\varepsilon'_{ij}}$, $\chi_e = \sqrt{\dfrac{2}{3}\chi'_{ij}\chi'_{ij}}$, $\eta_1 = \sqrt{\eta_{ijk}^{(1)}\eta_{ijk}^{(1)}}$. The stresses are then obtained via the constitutive relations (5.148) and (5.149). The nodal displacements and rotation vectors have to be solved incrementally due to the new incremental hardening law. Therefore, the nodal displacements and the rotation vectors are solved for each loading step by rewriting the principle of virtual work Eq.(5.171) about the current solution as

$$\int_V (\Delta s_{ij}\delta\varepsilon'_{ij} + \Delta\sigma_m\delta\varepsilon_{kk} + \Delta m'_{ij}\delta\chi'_{ij} + \Delta m_m\delta\chi_{kk})dV$$

$$- \int_S (\Delta t_k\delta u_k + \Delta q_k\delta\omega_k)dS$$

$$= -\int_V (s_{ij}\delta\varepsilon'_{ij} + \sigma_m\delta\varepsilon_{kk} + m'_{ij}\delta\chi'_{ij}$$

$$+ m_m\delta\chi_{kk})dV + \int_S (t_k\delta u_k + q_k\delta\omega_k)dS \qquad (5.172)$$

where the superscript prime denotes the deviatoric quantities, Δ on the left-hand side stands for increments, whereas the right-hand side involves the current quantities.

a) The nodal degrees of freedom

It is convenient to express the field quantities in terms of the circular cylindrical coordinate system (r, θ, z) as shown in Figure 5.12. Both the geometry and loading are axis-symmetric and without loss of generality we consider the section $\theta = 0$. The indented solid is subjected to the displacement field

$$u_r = u_r(r, z) \quad u_\theta = 0 \quad u_z = u_z(r, z) \tag{5.173}$$

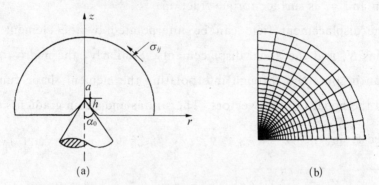

Figure 5. 12 Geometry of the axis-symmetric indentation model
(a) and finite element calculation model (b).

and the micro-rotation field

$$\omega_\theta = \omega_\theta(r, z) \quad \omega_r = \omega_z = 0 \tag{5.174}$$

Due to the independent parameter ω_i is introduced in addition to the displacement u_i in the present strain gradient theory, which is different from the theory proposed by Fleck and Hutchinson (1993), one node has three degrees of freedom, i. e. u_{ir}, u_{iz} and $\omega_{i\theta}$ for the axis-symmetric indentation case. The displacement field and the rotation vector field can be obtained through the shape function and the nodal displacement and nodal rotation vectors, i.e.

$$u_r = \sum_{i=1}^{n} N_i u_{ir} \tag{5.175}$$

$$u_z = \sum_{i=1}^{n} N_i u_{iz} \tag{5.176}$$

$$\omega_\theta = \sum_{i=1}^{n} N_i \omega_{i\theta} \tag{5.177}$$

b) The components of strain gradient

The components of stretch strain gradient terms can be obtained from the current nodal displacements through the shape functions. For the axis-symmetric case they can be written as

$$
\left\{
\begin{array}{ll}
\eta_{rrr} = \sum_{i=1}^{m} \dfrac{\partial^2 N_i}{\partial r^2} u_{ri} & \eta_{rrz} = \sum_{i=1}^{m} \dfrac{\partial^2 N_i}{\partial r^2} u_{zi} \\[4mm]
\eta_{r\theta\theta} = \eta_{\theta r\theta} = \eta_{\theta\theta r} = \dfrac{1}{r} \sum_{i=1}^{m} \dfrac{\partial N_i}{\partial r} u_{ri} - \dfrac{\sum_{i=1}^{m} N_i u_{ri}}{r^2} \\[4mm]
\eta_{rzr} = \eta_{zrr} = \sum_{i=1}^{m} \dfrac{\partial^2 N_i}{\partial r \partial z} u_{ri} & \eta_{zzz} = \sum_{i=1}^{m} \dfrac{\partial^2 N_i}{\partial z^2} u_{zi} \\[4mm]
\eta_{rzz} = \eta_{zrz} = \sum_{i=1}^{m} \dfrac{\partial^2 N_i}{\partial r \partial z} u_{zi} & \eta_{\theta\theta z} = \dfrac{1}{r} \sum_{i=1}^{m} \dfrac{\partial N_i}{\partial r} u_{zi} \\[4mm]
\eta_{\theta z\theta} = \eta_{z\theta\theta} = \dfrac{1}{r} \sum_{i=1}^{m} \dfrac{\partial N_i}{\partial z} u_{ri} & \eta_{zzr} = \sum_{i=1}^{m} \dfrac{\partial^2 N_i}{\partial z^2} u_{ri}
\end{array}
\right.
\tag{5.178}
$$

where N_i is the shape function and m is the node number of element; u_{ri} and u_{zi} are the ith nodal displacements in the directions of x axis and z axis, respectively.

c) Choice of element

Many researchers (Chen and Wang, 2002b; Shu and Fleck, 1998; Xia and Hutchinson, 1996; Wei and Hutchinson, 1997) have found that the choice of the element for gradient plasticity is complicated and in particular, quite sensitive to details of the constitutive relation. Xia and Hutchinson (1996) have discussed some choices of finite elements for strain gradient plasticity with the emphasis on plane strain cracks. Several elements have been developed for the phenomenological theory of strain gradient plasticity to investigate the crack tip field, microindentation experiments and stress concentrations around a hole.

In order to consider the strain gradient, the constant strain element is excluded since there is no strain gradient in this kind of element. For the two-dimensional case, such as the problem of plane strain and the axis-symmetry, second-order element can be used, such as the eight-node and nine-node elements. In the present case, nine-node element has been used to analyze the indentation problem. The displacement and rotation vectors in the element are interpolated through the shape function, whereas the strain and the rotation gradient tensors in the element are then obtained. This element is only suitable for solids with vanishing higher-order stress traction on the surface. For example, the element has worked very well in the fracture analysis of strain gradient plasticity (Wei and Hutchinson, 1997), where the higher-order stress tractions vanish on the crack face and on the remote boundary. This element also works well in the study of microindentation experiments (Huang et al., 2000) because the higher-order stress tractions are zero on the indented surface. Since the new strain gradient theory does not include higher-order stress and higher-order stress tractions, these kinds of elements will work well in the axis-symmetric indentation as discussed in the next section.

d) Assumptions in the numerical simulation

The assumptions made in the present calculation are (1) The indenter is assumed to be axis-symmetric, which greatly simplifies the finite element analysis. This assumption has been adopted by previous strain gradient plasticity analyses of micro-indentation experiments. Furthermore, we simulate a conical indenter shown in Figure 5.12. The half-angle of the indenter is taken to be $\alpha_0 = 72°$, corresponding to a Vickers indenter. The displacement at the tip of indentation is δ, whereas the contact radius of the indentation is a. (2) We assume that the indenter is frictionless such that there is no sticking between the indenter and the substrate.

e) Calculation model

The indentation calculation model is not the same as those in all other references. The elastic stress field corresponding to the indentation of classical elastic theory is loaded on the outer boundary as shown in Figure 5.12 and the tip of the indenter is assumed to be static. (r, θ, z) is the cylindrical coordinate and (R, θ, φ) is the spherical coordinate for the cross section as shown in Figure 5.12. The materials are compressed to slide up and down the face of the indenter by the outer stress field loaded on the external boundary of the materials. In Figure 5.12, there are the following relations:

$$R^2 = r^2 + z^2, \quad r = R\sin\varphi, \quad z = R\cos\varphi \qquad (5.179)$$

$$
\begin{cases}
\sigma_r = \dfrac{P}{2\pi R^2}\left(\dfrac{1-2\nu}{1+\cos\varphi} - 3\sin^2\varphi\cos\varphi\right) \\[3mm]
\sigma_z = \dfrac{-3P}{2\pi R^2}\cos^3\varphi \\[3mm]
\sigma_{rz} = \dfrac{-3P}{2\pi R^2}\sin\varphi\cos^2\varphi \\[3mm]
\sigma_\theta = \dfrac{(1-2\nu)P}{2\pi R^2}\left(\cos\varphi - \dfrac{1}{1+\cos\varphi}\right)
\end{cases}
\qquad (5.180)
$$

The outer elastic field σ_{ij} loaded on the outer boundary in Figure 5.12 denotes the stress components σ_{RR} and $\sigma_{\varphi R}$, which can be obtained from Eq. (5.180). The couple stresses loading on the outer boundary are

$$m_{RR} = 0, \quad m_{\varphi R} = 0, \quad m_{\theta R} = 0 \qquad (5.181)$$

Due to the vanishing couple stress on the outer boundary, the independent rotation vectors in this problem vanish, from where one can see that the rotation gradient has no effect on the indentation problem and the results will only be influenced by the stretch gradient. The value of the length scale l_{cs} will not be considered. Only the length scale relate with the stretch gradient, l_1, will be a parameter.

f) Boundary condition

Since the calculation model in the present paper is different from the other existing models, the boundary conditions are different from those. The displacement u_r is zero along the axis of symmetry, where (r, z) are cylindrical coordinates. The displacement u_z at the point of the indenter tip is zero also. Elastic stress field is loaded on the external boundary and couple stress field vanishes on the outer boundary. The contact boundary conditions are added to simulate the real indent process as follows.

The contact between the indenter and indented material is simulated by assuming a contact radius a of indentation, and iterating to find the proper outer elastic stress field in order to satisfy the normal stress

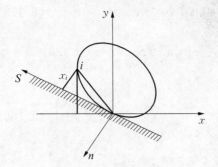

Figure 5. 13 Contact model for the calculation.

traction t_n at the periphery of contact vanish as shown in Figure 5. 13,

$$t_n |_{r<a} < 0, \ t_n |_{r \geq a} = 0$$

(5. 182)

where the subscript n denotes the normal of the contact face.

The contact boundary is assumed to be frictionless, i.e.,

$$t_s = 0 \qquad (5. 183)$$

where the subscript s denotes the tangent of the contact face.

On the contact boundary, the face torque vanishes too. The displacement u_r of the points on the contact boundary is not constrained in prior, which is different from all other existing calculation models, i.e. u_r of the contact points is the natural calculated outcome for the present model. The points on the contact boundary must be sure to stay on the contact face, i.e.,

$$u_z = - (r + u_r) \mathrm{ctg}\, \alpha_0 = - r^* \mathrm{ctg}\, \alpha_0 \qquad (5. 184)$$

where $r^* = r + u_r$, r is the coordinate of each node on the contact boundary before deformation and r^* is the corresponding coordinate after deformation.

If one point goes beyond the contact face, it must be drawback to the contact face as shown in Figure 5. 13 i.e. render $x_i \geq 0$.

It should be pointed out also that for both pile up and sink-in, the periphery of the contact between the indenter and the indented material is governed by Eq. (5. 184) and Eq. (5. 182). Therefore, pileup or sink-in is not imposed a priori, but a natural outcome of the indentation analysis.

The relation between the contact radius a and the plastic depth of indentation h is given by

$$h = \frac{a}{\tan \alpha_0} \tag{5.185}$$

where $\alpha_0 = 72°$ is a half angle of the indenter as shown in Figure 5.12.

The total force, P, exerted on the indenter is the sum of nodal forces in the z direction for those nodes in contact with the indenter (i.e. $r \leqslant a$). The indentation hardness H is defined as

$$H = \frac{P}{\pi a^2} \tag{5.186}$$

5.6.2 Numerical results for indentation

a) Deformation characteristics

The numerical results are shown in the following. First, the classical plasticity theory, i.e. the intrinsic length scales $l_1 = l_{cs} = 0$, is used to calculate the indentation, and the indented material is perfectly elastic-plastic material, we find that the hardness is almost 3 times the yield stress, which proves that the finite element program is correct.

For power-law hardening materials, the deformed surface under the indenter is shown in Figure 5.14 for different contact radius. In this

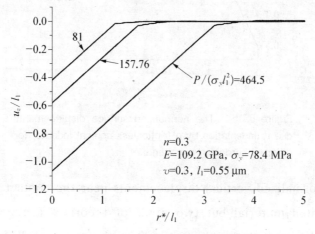

Figure 5.14 Deformed surface profiles for several indentation depths.

figure, the radius and vertical locations have been normalized by the material length scale l_1, which is assumed to be a material property. It must be noted that in Figure 5.14, the radius r^* for each point is the original coordinate r plus the displacement u_r of this point and in the following figures r^* has the same meaning. From Figure 5.14, we find that for the same hardening exponent, the larger the contact radius, the larger the external loading but the smaller the hardness.

In Figure 5.15, the normalized vertical displacements near the contact face are shown with the same contact radius and different hardening exponent n. From Figure 5.15 we could find that while the indented material tends to be an elasticity one, pileup will transfer to be sink-in, which denotes that stiff material tends to sink-in and soft material tends to pile up. It is consistent with all experiment observations.

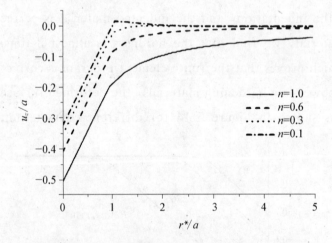

Figure 5.15 The normalized surface displacements due to indentation by a frictionless conical indenter for different hardening exponents.

The normalized vertical displacements near the contact face for the same indented material but two kinds of theories, i.e., the classical plasticity theory and the strain gradient theory, are shown in Figure 5.16. From Figure 5.16, we find that for the same contact radius, the hardness with strain gradient is larger than that without strain gradient and pileup transfers to be sink-in while the effect of strain gradient is considered, which means that the strain gradient considered will render the material stiffer. It is consistent well with the results in Begley and Hutchinson (1998).

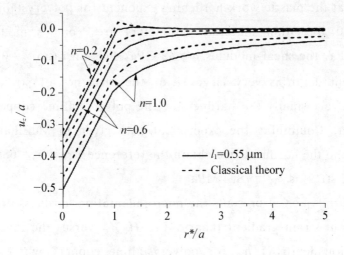

Figure 5. 16   Comparisons of the indented surface profiles for both strain gradient theory and the classical theory.

b) Comparison with experiment

The exponential hardening law is used for the poly-crystal copper and single-crystal copper when no strain gradient effects are considered. The conventional hardening law is as follows,

$$\sigma_e = E\varepsilon_e, \ \varepsilon_e < \varepsilon_0 \tag{5.187}$$

$$\sigma_e = \sigma_0 \varepsilon_e^n, \ \varepsilon_e \geqslant \varepsilon_0 \tag{5.188}$$

From above equations, we can obtain the yield stress σ_y,

$$\sigma_y = \left(\frac{\sigma_0}{E^n} \right)^{\frac{1}{1-n}}. \tag{5.189}$$

The indentation hardness calculated by the finite element method for the strain gradient theory and indentation model in the previous sections are presented as following. In particular, we focus on the comparisons between the experiment measured microindentation hardness data for polycrystalline copper and single crystal copper given by McElhaney et al. (1998) and the numerical calculation hardness data.

From the experiment data given in McElhaney et al. (1998), we know that the plastic work-hardening exponent for polycrystalline copper is $n = 0.3$. Other material parameters are Young's modulus $E = 109.2 \text{ GPa}$, the shear modulus $\mu = 42 \text{ GPa}$, Poisson ratio $\nu = 0.3$. While the indent depth is very large, i. e. the influence of strain gradient becomes very small, the hardness of the polycrystalline copper is $H_0 = 834 \text{ MPa}$. Combining the experiment data given in McElhaney et al. (1998) and the hardness, we obtain the reference stress $\sigma_0 = 688 \text{ MPa}$ and the yield stress is $\sigma_Y = 78.4 \text{ MPa}$.

Figure 5.17 (a) presents the microindentation hardness predicted by the present strain gradient theory, $(H/H_0)^2$, versus the inverse of the indentation depth, $1/h$, for polycrystalline copper, where H is the microindentation hardness, $H_0 = 834 \text{ MPa}$ is the indentation hardness without the strain gradient effect and h is the depth of indentation. Figure 5.17 (b) shows the relation between the normalized indentation hardness, H/H_0, versus the inverse of the square root of the indentation depth, $1/h^{1/2}$. The experiment data given by McElhaney et al. (1998) are also presented in Figure 5.17 (a) and (b) for comparison. It is clearly observed that the predicted hardness based on the C-W strain gradient theory agrees very well with the experimentally measured microindentation hardness data over a wide range of indentation depth, from 0.1 μm to several microns when $l_1 = 0.55 \ \mu$m. Furthermore, the numerical results based on the C-W strain gradient theory do give an approximate straight line in Figure 5.17 (a), which is consistent with the estimation by Nix and Gao (1998). While in Figure 5.17 (b), instead of linearity, a relatively complex function, approximately a parabolic relation, exists between H/H_0 and $1/h^{1/2}$, due to which, simple linear relation between $(H/H_0)^2$ and $1/h$ is used commonly for describing the size effects in microindentation.

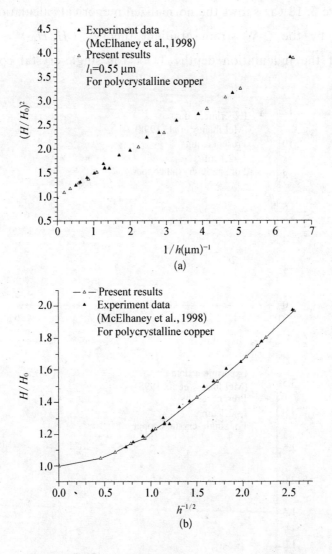

Figure 5.17   Comparisons of the indentation experimental results (McElhaney et al., 1998) for polycrystalline copper with the theoretical predictions of C-W strain gradient theory.

We also analyze the single-crystal copper. The reference stress is $\sigma_0 = 436$ MPa and the working hardening exponent $n = 0.3$, Poisson's ratio $\nu = 0.3$. The Young's modulus is $E = 109.2$ MPa. The yield stress is

$\sigma_y = 41$ MPa. The hardness in a large-scale test is $H_0 = 581$ MPa, i. e. , the hardness without strain gradient effects.

Figure 5. 18 (a) shows the normalized numerical calculation hardness predicted by the C-W strain gradient theory, $(H/H_0)^2$, versus the inverse of the indentation depth, $1/h$, for single-crystal copper. The

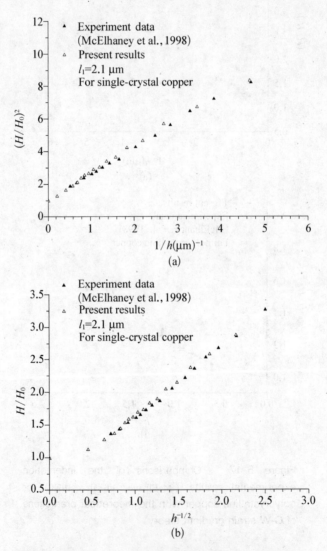

Figure 5. 18   Comparisons of the indentation experimental results (McElhaney et al. , 1998) for single-crystal copper with the theoretical predictions of C-W strain gradient theory.

relation between the normalized indentation hardness, H/H_0, versus the inverse of the square root of the indentation depth, $1/h^{1/2}$, is shown in Figure 5.18 (b). The experiment measured hardness data are also shown in Figure 5.18 (a) and (b) in order to compare with the numerical results. From Figure 5.18, one can see that the predicted hardness based on the C-W strain gradient theory agrees very well with the experimentally measured microindentation hardness data over a wide range of indentation depth, from 0.1 μm to several microns when $l_1 = 2.1 \mu$m. The relation between $(H/H_0)^2$ and $1/h$ is almost linear, which is also consistent well with the estimate by Nix and Gao (1998). Also, an approximately parabolic relation exists between H/H_0 and $1/h^{1/2}$ in Figure 5.18 (b).

Figure 5.19 (a) shows the relation between the square of the normalized indentation hardness, $(H/H_0)^2$, and the inverse of the square root of the contact area, $1/\sqrt{A}$, for polycrystalline copper. The relation between the normalized indentation hardness, H/H_0, and $A^{-1/4}$, is shown in Figure 5.19 (b). Experiment results with the corresponding relations for polycrystalline copper are also shown both in Figure 5.19 (a) and Figure 5.19 (b) for comparisons. From the two figures, one can see that a linear function describes the relation between $(H/H_0)^2$ and $1/\sqrt{A}$ and a nonlinear relation exists between H/H_0 and $A^{-1/4}$, which can be proved from the relation between $(H/H_0)^2$ and $1/h$ since $\sqrt{A}$ has the same dimension as h. The relation for single crystal copper between $(H/H_0)^2$ and $1/\sqrt{A}$ and that between H/H_0 and $A^{-1/4}$ are shown in Figure 5.20 (a) and Figure 5.20 (b), respectively. The corresponding relations existing between these two groups of variables are the same as those in Figure 5.19 (a) and Figure 5.19 (b).

Both the numerical analysis and the microindentation experiments show approximate linear dependences of the square of indentation hardness on the inverse of indentation depth, which is an important result obtained also by Nix and Gao (1998). However nonlinear relations exist between H/H_0 and $1/h^{1/2}$ or between H/H_0 and $A^{-1/4}$. The agreements between the numerically predicted results and the experiment results serve as a self-consistent check of the C-W strain gradient theory.

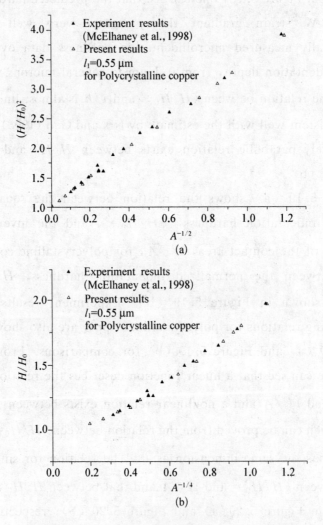

Figure 5. 19   Dependence of the normalized indentation hardness on the contact area for polycrystalline copper.

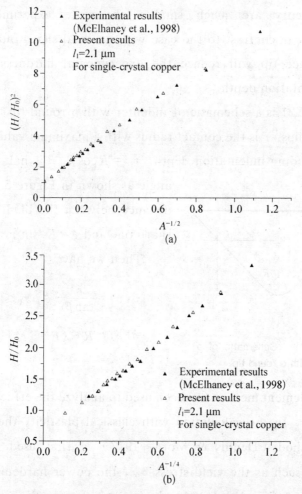

Figure 5.20　Dependence of the normalized indentation hardness on the contact area for single-crystal copper.

5.6.3　The effects of curvature of indenter tip

Tao et al. (2004) have analyzed the effect of indenter tip curvature. Both the classical plasticity and C-W strain gradient plasticity theories are adopted. The influence of indenter tip curvature on the measured hardness is considered. The results show that the strain gradient plasticity theory can describe the complex relation between the hardness and the indentation depth very well, but the results predicted by the classical plasticity theory are much smaller than the experimental data. Furthermore, in contrast to the case with an ideal sharp indenter tip, a round indenter tip will reduce the experimental hardness during the shallow indentation depth.

Figure 5.21 is a schematic of indenter with a round tip and R is the curvature radius. r is the contact radius with a maximum value a. $\delta(r)$ is the corresponding indentation depth. $r_0 = R\cos\beta$, β is half of the cone angle as shown in Figure 5.21. ξ is the distance between the blunt tip and the sharp one and $\xi = R/\sin\beta - R$.

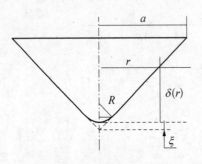

Figure 5.21　Schematic of a indenter with a round tip.

Then we have

$$\begin{cases} \delta(r) = \dfrac{r}{\tan\beta} - \xi & r_0 \leqslant r \leqslant a \\ \delta(r) = R - (R^2 - r^2)^{\frac{1}{2}} & r \leqslant r_0 \end{cases}$$

$$(5.190)$$

Finite element method has been used to analyze the effect of indenter tip curvature. In the calculation with classical plasticity theory, virtual Newton method (Dennis & Moré, 1977) is first used to calibrate parameters, such as the yield stress σ_Y, the power hardening exponent n. In the simulation with C-W strain gradient theory, the intrinsic length scale l_1, besides the yield stress and the power hardening exponent, is needed to be determined first according to the experiment results of indentation load as a function of indentation depth. Details are neglected and only the numerical results are shown in this section. The curvature radius of the indenter tip is assumed to be 100 nm in this study.

a) The effect of indenter tip curvature with classical plasticity theory

The parameters for single crystal silver used in the Ma and Clarke (1995) experiment are $\mu = 46$ GPa, $\nu = 0.2$ and $E = 100.4$ GPa. Fitting the load-depth curves with large indentation depth yields the other parameters: the power law hardening exponents is $n = 0.2$ and the yield stress σ_Y = 37.5 MPa. Figure 5.22 give the comparison between the experiment and simulation results, in which the classical plasticity theory is used and the curvature radius of the indenter tip takes R = 100 nm. For the large indentation depth, both results are consistent with each other; the calculating results are lower than the experiment one at small indentation depth, which has been amplified in Figure 5.23.

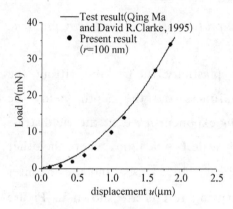

Figure 5.22   Comparison of the experimental results（Ma & Clarke, 1995）with the prediction of classical plasticity theory.

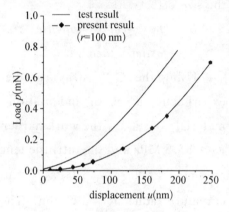

Figure 5.23   Amplification of the curves in figure 5.22 for shallow indentation depth.

Figure 5.24 give the comparison of the experiment results and the calculating results using classical J_2 plasticity theory and considering the indenter curvature. One can see that it is very obvious that the calculating results are much lower than the experimental ones. Furthermore, the indentation hardness decreases when the indentation depth decreases, a different trend for

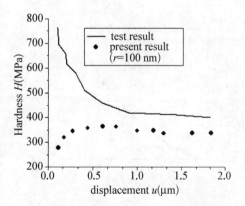

Figure 5.24   Comparison of the experimental results of hardness with the theoretical prediction of classical plasticity theory considering the tip curvature.

the calculating results from the experiment predictions. The calculating results are consistent with the trend of the Swadener et al. (2002) experiments, in which they studied the effects of different radius of spherical indenters. On the other hand, it can be concluded that the size effects in the micro-indentation experiments are not due to the effects of indenter curvature, on the contrary, the indenter curvature will reduce the size effects.

b) *The effect of indenter tip curvature with C-W strain gradient plasticity theory*

Using the C-W strain gradient plasticity theory and fitting the experiment curves of indentation hardness and the depth yields the material constants: the work hardening exponent $n = 0.2$, the yield stress $\sigma_Y = 37.5$ MPa and the intrinsic length scale $l_1 = 0.4$ μm, where the other parameters take $\mu = 46$ GPa, $\nu = 0.2$, $E = 100.4$ GPa and the indenter curvature radius $R = 100$ nm. The fitting results are shown in Figure 5.25, where the numerical results are consistent well with the experiment predictions (Ma and Clarke, 1995). The amplification picture is shown in Figure 5.26 for the shallow indentation depth, where both results agree well with each other.

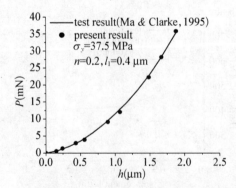

Figure 5.25 Fitting the experimental load-displacement curve using the strain gradient theory and a round indenter tip.

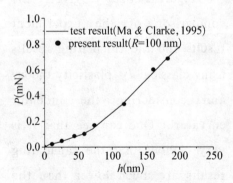

Figure 5.26 Amplification of the fitting curve in figure 5.25 for shallow indentation depth.

The calculating results of indentation hardness as a function of the indentation depth are shown in Figure 5. 27 using C-W strain gradient plasticity theory and considering the effects of indenter curvature. One can see that the numerical results are consistent with the experimental measurements. At the shallow indentation depth, the hardness decreases when the indentation depth decreases, which agree with the phenomenon found by Swadener et al. (2002). Generally, the numerical results of the strain gradient theory are much higher than those of the classical plasticity theory and can describe the experiment results.

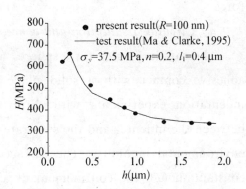

Figure 5. 27   Comparison of the experimental results with the theoretical prediction of C-W strain gradient plasticity considering a round indenter tip.

5.6.4   The effects of capillary force on indentation hardness

The influence of the indenter shapes and various parameters on the magnitude of the capillary force is studied on the basis of models describing the wet adhesion of indenters and substrates joined by liquid bridges. In the former, we consider several shapes, such as conical, spherical and truncated conical one with a spherical end. In the latter, the effects of the contact angle, the radius of the wetting circle, the volume of the liquid bridge, the environmental humidity, the gap between the indenter and the substrate, the conical angle, the radius of the spherical indenter, the opening angle of the spherical end in the truncated conical indenter are included. The meniscus of the bridge is described using a circular approximation, which is reasonable under some conditions. Different dependences of the capillary force on the indenter shapes and the geometric parameters are observed. The results can be applicable to the micro- and nano-indentation experiments. It shows that the measured hardness is underestimated due to the effect of the capillary force.

a) *Circular assumption and conception of relative humidity*

The capillary force for a sphere, a cone and a truncated cone in wet adhesive contact with a solid plane will be studied to simulate the indentation experiments with different indenter shapes. The liquid between the indenter and the substrate is assumed to be water due to the environmental humidity. The surface tension $\Delta\gamma$ is assumed to be a constant though the confinement of a liquid or even the presence of a solid surface may change the effective surface tension of the liquid at a nano-scale, i.e., $\Delta\gamma = 0.072$ N/m. The liquid bridge surface is curved because of an interaction of the liquid molecules with each other. We assume the meniscus of the bridge to be a circular arc according to Pakarinen et al. (2005) and Farshchi-Tabrizi et al. (2006). Thus the contact angles θ_1 and θ_2 of the liquid on the indenter and the substrate can be described as θ, i.e.,

$$\theta_1 = \theta_2 = \theta. \tag{5.191}$$

The environmental humidity is described by the relative vapor pressure P/P_0, where P is the actual vapor pressure and P_0 is the saturation vapor pressure of a reference planar liquid surface, which can be calculated using the Kelvin equation

$$\frac{P}{P_0} = \exp\left[-\frac{\Delta\gamma V_m}{R_G T}\left(\frac{1}{r} - \frac{1}{l}\right)\right] \tag{5.192}$$

in which $R_G = 8.268$ J/(K $\cdot$ mol) is the gas constant, $T = 298$ K is the temperature, $V_m = 18\times10^{-6}$ m^3/mol and $\Delta\gamma = 0.072$ N/m are the molar volume and surface tension of water, respectively. r and l describe two principal radii of curvature.

b) *Wet adhesion between a conical indenter and a solid plane*

Figure 5.28 shows a model for the analysis of wet adhesion between a conical indenter and a solid substrate, where b is the radius of the circle of the liquid bridge wetting the cones, α is half of the cone angle, $\theta_1 = \theta_2 = \theta$ is the contact angle, D is the gap between the indenter and the substrate, the curvature radii r and l of the liquid bridge are also shown in the figure.

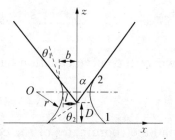

Figure 5.28 Schematic illustration of a cone in wet adhesion with a substrate, the gap between them is D.

The magnitude of the capillary force F_c depends on two components. The first one is determined by the surface tension of the liquid $\Delta\gamma$. The second one is owing to the pressure difference Δp inside and outside the meniscus. Since the effect of gravity is neglected, Δp is a constant within the meniscus.

b.1) For the case of $D \geqslant 0$, the capillary force is

$$F_c = -\pi b^2 \Delta p + 2\pi b \Delta\gamma \cos(\alpha - \theta) \tag{5.193}$$

and the pressure difference is described by the Laplace equation,

$$\Delta p = \Delta\gamma \left(\frac{1}{l} - \frac{1}{r} \right) \tag{5.194}$$

where the two principal radii of curvature can be obtained from geometric relations,

$$r = \frac{[b/\tan\alpha + D]}{\sin(\alpha - \theta) + \cos\theta} \quad l = b - r[1 - \cos(\alpha - \theta)] \tag{5.195}$$

Substituting equation (5.194) into (5.193) yields

$$F_c = \pi b \Delta\gamma \left[2\cos(\alpha - \theta) + b\left(\frac{1}{r} - \frac{1}{l} \right) \right] \tag{5.196}$$

The volume of the liquid bridge V_l can be obtained as the volume of the figure yielded by rotating a circular arc of radius r about the y axis minus the volumes of the indenter immersed in the liquid V_s, that is

$$V_l = \int_{z_1}^{z_2} \pi x^2 dz - V_s = \int_{z_1}^{z_2} \pi G^2(z)dz - V_s \qquad (5.197)$$

where the curve equation has the form

$$G(z) = r + l - \sqrt{r^2 - (z - r\cos\theta)^2} \qquad (5.198)$$

and the coordinates of the contact points 1 and 2 as shown in Figure 5.28 are

$$x_1 = r + l - r\sin\theta \quad x_2 = b \qquad (5.199)$$

and

$$z_1 = 0 \quad z_2 = \frac{b}{\tan\alpha} + D \qquad (5.200)$$

After derivation, the volume of the liquid bridge is written as

$$V_l = \pi(z_2 - z_1)[(r + l)^2 + r^2] - \frac{\pi}{3}[(z_2 - r\cos\theta)^3$$

$$- (z_1 - r\cos\theta)^3] - 2\pi(r + l)\left[\frac{z - r\cos\theta}{2}\sqrt{r^2 - (z - r\cos\theta)^2}\right.$$

$$\left. + \frac{r^2}{2}\arcsin\frac{z - r\cos\theta}{r}\right]\Big|_{z_1}^{z_2} - V_s$$

$$(5.201)$$

The volume of V_s in Figure 5.28 with $D \geqslant 0$ can be expressed as

$$V_s = \frac{\pi b^3}{3\tan\alpha} \qquad (5.202)$$

b.2) if $D < 0$, the capillary force can be written as

$$F_c = \pi\Delta\gamma\left(\frac{1}{r} - \frac{1}{l}\right)[b^2 - (D\tan\alpha)^2] + 2\pi b\Delta\gamma\cos(\alpha - \theta)$$

$$(5.203)$$

and the volume of the indenter immersed in the liquid is

$$V_s = \frac{\pi}{3}\left(\frac{b}{\tan\alpha} + D\right)[b^2 + (D\tan\alpha)^2 + b|D|\tan\alpha] \qquad (5.204)$$

The formula of curvature radii of the liquid bridge, the coordinates of the contact points 1 and 2 are identical to equations (5. 195), (5. 199) and (5. 200), except that D has different sign.

c) Wet adhesion between a spherical indenter and a solid plane

The analysis model of a spherical indenter in wet adhesive contact with a substrate is shown in Figure 5. 29, in which the distance between the substrate and the sphere is $D \geqslant 0$, ϕ is the filling angle, R is the radius of the sphere, b is the radius of the circle of the liquid bridge wetting the sphere, $\theta_1 = \theta_2 = \theta$ is the contact angle, r and l are the curvature radii of the liquid bridge.

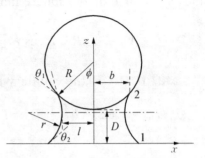

Figure 5. 29　Schematic illustration of a sphere in wet adhesion with a substrate, the gap between them is D.

The liquid pressure difference Δp inside and outside the meniscus is also expressed by the Young-Laplace equation (5. 194), where the curvature radii of the liquid bridge are written as

$$r = \frac{R(1 - \cos \phi) + D}{\cos(\theta + \phi) + \cos \theta} \tag{5.205}$$

and

$$l = r\sin(\theta + \phi) + R\sin \phi - r \tag{5.206}$$

c. 1) The capillary force F_c is the sum of the pressure difference and the axial component of the surface tension acting on the sphere. For the case of $D \geqslant 0$, the expression of the capillary force is

$$F_c = \pi R \sin \phi \Delta \gamma \left[2\sin(\theta + \phi) + R\sin \phi \left(\frac{1}{r} - \frac{1}{l} \right) \right] \tag{5.207}$$

The volume of the liquid bridge has the same form as that in equation (5. 197), but the coordinates of contact points 1 and 2 as shown in Figure 5. 29 are,

$$x_1 = r + l - r\sin\theta \quad x_2 = b = R\sin\phi \tag{5.208}$$

$$z_1 = 0 \quad z_2 = r\cos(\theta + \phi) + r\cos\theta \tag{5.209}$$

and the volume of the sphere immersed in the liquid is

$$V_s = \frac{\pi}{6}(R - R\cos\phi)[3(R\sin\phi)^2 + R^2(1 - \cos\phi)^2] \tag{5.210}$$

c.2) if $D < 0$, the capillary force F_c can be written as

$$F_c = -\pi\Delta p\{b^2 - [R^2 - (R+D)^2]\} + 2\pi b\Delta\gamma\sin(\theta + \phi) \tag{5.211}$$

and the volume of the sphere immersed in the liquid is

$$V_s = \frac{\pi}{6}(R - R\cos\phi + D)\{3b^2 + 3[R^2 - (R+D)^2] + (R - R\cos\phi + D)^2\} \tag{5.212}$$

The other formula are the same as those for $D \geqslant 0$.

d) *Wet adhesion between a truncated conical indenter and a solid plane*

In the micro- and nano-indentation experiments, the indenter tip is not actually ideal sharp due to the limitation of industry technology or tip wear after many times of experiments. The indenter tip is often represented by a spherical end. The capillary force between a truncated conical indenter and a substrate is studied in this section.

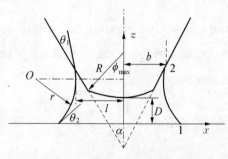

Figure 5.30   Schematic illustration of a truncated cone with a spherical end in wet adhesion with a substrate and D is gap between them.

The truncated conical indenter is shown in Figure 5.30, where R is the radius of the sphere, b is the radius of the circle of the liquid bridge wetting the truncated cone, ϕ_{max} is half of the opening angle of the spherical part, α is half of the cone angle and D is the distance between the indenter and the substrate.

The formula of the capillary force and the volume of the immersed indenter are different for different indentation depths.

d.1) First, we study the case of $D \geqslant 0$, i.e., the indenter does not penetrate into the substrate.

d.1a) If $b < R \sin \phi_{max}$, the contact point 2 lies on the sphere boundary, the liquid bridge forms between the spherical end and the substrate. All the formula are the same as those in section c) for $D \geqslant 0$.

d.1b) If $b \geqslant R \sin \phi_{max}$, the contact point 2 lies on the cone boundary. The curvature radii of the liquid bridge can be described as

$$r = \frac{\dfrac{b - R \sin \phi_{max}}{\tan \alpha} + D + R (1 - \cos \phi_{max})}{\sin (\alpha - \theta) + \cos \theta} \qquad (5.213)$$

$$l = r \cos (\alpha - \theta) + b - r \qquad (5.214)$$

and the coordinates of contact points 1 and 2 in z direction are

$$z_1 = 0 \qquad z_2 = r \sin (\alpha - \theta) + r \cos \theta \qquad (5.215)$$

The capillary force in this case can be written as

$$F_c = \pi b \Delta \gamma \left[2 \cos (\alpha - \theta) + b \left(\frac{1}{r} - \frac{1}{l} \right) \right] \qquad (5.216)$$

where the Young-Laplace equation has been used.

The volume of the capillary liquid is still obtained as equations (5.197) and (5.198), but the volume of the truncated conical indenter immersed in the liquid is

$$V_s = \frac{\pi}{3} R^3 (1 - \cos \phi_{max}) (1 + \sin^2 \phi_{max} - \cos \phi_{max})$$

$$+ \frac{\pi}{3} h [(R \sin \phi_{max})^2 + b^2 + b R \sin \phi_{max}] \qquad (5.217)$$

where

$$h = \frac{b - R \sin \phi_{max}}{\tan \alpha} \qquad (5.218)$$

d.2) For the case of $D < 0$, two models will be analyzed for $|D| \leqslant$

$R - R\cos\phi_{max}$ and $|D| > R - R\cos\phi_{max}$, respectively.

d.2a) $|D| \leqslant R - R\cos\phi_{max}$ and $b \leqslant R\sin\phi_{max}$. The liquid bridge forms between the spherical end and the substrate. All the formula describing the capillary force, the volume of the liquid bridge are the same as those in section c) for $D < 0$.

d.2b) $|D| \leqslant R - R\cos\phi_{max}$ and $b > R\sin\phi_{max}$. The contact point 2 lies on the cone boundary. The curvature radii of the liquid bridge can be written as

$$r = \frac{\dfrac{b - R\sin\phi_{max}}{\tan\alpha} + D + R(1 - \cos\phi_{max})}{\sin(\alpha - \theta) + \cos\theta} \tag{5.219}$$

$$l = r\cos(\alpha - \theta) + b - r \tag{5.220}$$

and the coordinates of contact point 1 and 2 in z direction are

$$z_1 = 0 \quad z_2 = r\sin(\alpha - \theta) + r\cos\theta \tag{5.221}$$

Combining the two components, i.e., the pressure difference and the liquid surface tension acting in axial direction yields the capillary force,

$$F_c = -\pi\Delta p[b^2 - R^2 + (R + D)^2] + 2\pi b\Delta\gamma\cos(\alpha - \theta) \tag{5.222}$$

where Δp is expressed by the Young-Laplace equation.

The volume of the liquid bridge can also be expressed by equation (5.201), but the volume of the indenter immersed in the liquid consists of includes two parts

$$V_s = \frac{\pi}{3}\frac{b - R\sin\phi_{max}}{\tan\alpha}[b^2 + (R\sin\phi_{max})^2 + bR\sin\phi_{max}]$$

$$+ \frac{\pi h}{6}\{3(R\sin\phi_{max})^2 + 3[R^2 - (R + D)^2] + h^2\} \tag{5.223}$$

where the parameter h is

$$h = z_2 - \frac{b - R\sin\phi_{max}}{\tan\alpha} \tag{5.224}$$

d.2c) $|D| > R - R\cos\phi_{max}$. In order to ensure the existence of the liquid bridge, $b > R\sin\phi_{max} + [|D| - R(1 - \cos\phi_{max})]\tan\alpha$ is required. In this case, the curvature radii of the liquid bridge are

$$r\sin(\alpha - \theta) + r\cos\theta = \frac{b - R\sin\phi_{max}}{\tan\alpha} + D + R(1 - \cos\phi_{max})$$

(5.225)

and

$$l = r\cos(\alpha - \theta) + b - r \qquad (5.226)$$

The coordinates of contact points 1 and 2 in z direction are

$$z_1 = 0 \qquad z_2 = r\sin(\alpha - \theta) + r\cos\theta \qquad (5.227)$$

The capillary force is

$$F_c = -\pi\Delta\gamma\left(\frac{1}{l} - \frac{1}{r}\right)\left[b^2 - \left(\frac{b}{\tan\alpha} - z_2\right)^2\tan^2\alpha\right] + 2\pi b\Delta\gamma\cos(\alpha - \theta)$$

(5.228)

and the volume of the liquid bridge can be described by equations (5.197) and (5.198), but the volume of the indenter immersed in the liquid is

$$V_s = \frac{\pi z_2}{3}\left[b^2 + \left(\frac{b}{\tan\alpha} - z_2\right)^2\tan^2\alpha + b\left(\frac{b}{\tan\alpha} - z_2\right)\tan\alpha\right] \qquad (5.229)$$

e) *Results and Discussions*

e.1) The case of a conical indenter and a substrate

From equation (5.195), one can see that for determined contact angle θ and cone angle 2α, if the radius of the circle of the liquid bridge wetting the cone b keeps unchanged, the curvature radius r will increase and l will decrease when the gap D between the cone and the substrate increases, then the capillary force F_c will decrease according to equation (5.196). If the gap D between the cone and the substrate keeps unchanged, then the capillary force will increase with an increasing radius of wetting circle b according to equations (5.195) and (5.196). An example is shown in Figure 5.31(a) In order to be continuous, the results for $D < 0$ according to equations (5.195) and (5.203) are also included in Figure 5.31(a), from which one can see that the capillary force will increase when the indentation depth increases. The corresponding volumes of the liquid bridge can be obtained from equations (5. 201), (5. 202) and (5. 204), which are shown in Figure 5. 31(b). Comparing Figure 5. 31(a) and 5. 31(b), one can see that if the contact angle, the cone angle and the radius of the wetting circle are fixed, the volume of the liquid bridge will decrease and the capillary force will increase when the indentation depth increases. This conclusion is only obtained from the mathematics point of view and has no physical meaning.

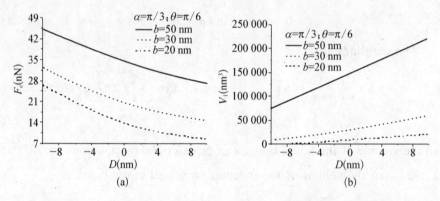

Figure 5. 31　(a) The capillary force F_c as a function of the gap D between the cone and the substrate for different values of b (the radius of the liquid bridge wetting the cones). (b) The volume of the liquid bridge as a function of the gap D between the cone and the substrate for different values of b (the radius of the liquid bridge wetting the cones).

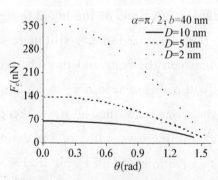

Figure 5. 32　The capillary force F_c as a function of the contact angle θ for different values of the gap D between the cone and the substrate.

The contact angle embodies the features of hydrophobicity and hydrophilicity of objects. Figure 5. 32 shows the capillary force as a function of the contact angle θ when the cone angle α, the radius of the wetting circle b and the gap D between the cone and the substrate are unchanged. From Figure 5. 32, one can see that the capillary force decreases when the contact angle increases, i. e. , the surfaces varying from hydrophilic to hydrophobic. With a fixed contact angle θ, the capillary force decreases when the gap between the cone and the substrate increases.

With regard to the model of wet adhesion between a cone and a substrate shown in Figure 5. 28 it is convenient to use the radius of wetting circle b as a parameter. When the parameter b is varied, the values of the curvature radii r and l can be obtained as well as the relative humidity according to equation (5. 192). Figure 5. 33(a) shows the capillary force as a function of the relative humidity, where one can see that the capillary force increases with humidity. The shape of the curve changes and the strength of the capillary force increases more quickly for a vanishing gap between the cone and substrate. For a fixed humidity, the

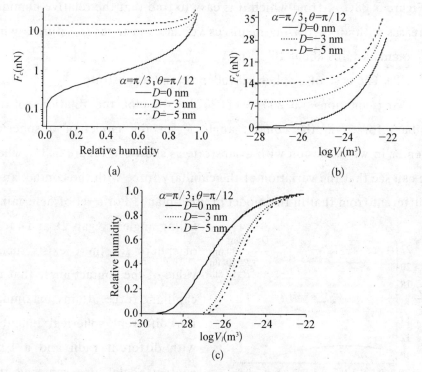

Figure 5. 33 (a) The capillary force F_c between a cone and a substrate versus humidity for different values of the gap D. (b) The dependence of the capillary force F_c on the volume of the liquid bridge for different values of gap D. (c) The dependence of the relative humidity on the meniscus volume for different values of gap D.

capillary force increases with an increasing indentation depth. The capillary force in Figure 5.33(a) is based on the Kelvin equation, which assumes a thermodynamic equilibrium of system. However, due to the speed of tip motion in small scale indenter, system with capillary condensed meniscus may not be governed by the Kelvin equation. In this case, constant meniscus volume has to be assumed. Figure 5.33(b) shows the dependences of the capillary force on the volume of the liquid bridge for different gaps between the cone and substrate. One can see that the capillary force increases with the volume of the liquid bridge. Furthermore, one can find that, for a constant meniscus volume, the capillary force increases with an increasing indentation depth. The relation between the relative humidity and the meniscus volume is plotted in Figure 5.33(c), from which it is easy to find that the relative humidity increases with an increasing meniscus volume and tends to saturate when the volume attains about 10^{-22} m^3.

e.2) The case of a spherical indenter and a substrate

Using equations (5.205)-(5.207), we plot the relations of the capillary force via the contact angle θ for the model of a spherical indenter in wet adhesion with a substrate as shown in Figure 5.34, where one can see that the variation of the capillary force with the contact angle is different from that in the model of cone-plane. For a set of determined filling angle ϕ, gap D and radius of sphere R, there exists such a value of the contact angle that the capillary force attains maximum. For different spherical indenters with different radii and a fixed contact angle, one can find that the capillary force increases with the radius of the spherical indenter.

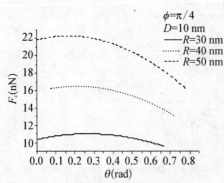

Figure 5.34   The capillary force F_c as a function of the contact angle θ for different radii of the spherical indenter.

Using the resultant equations in Section b), we can also determine the dependence of the capillary force on the volume of the liquid in the bridge. The variation of the capillary force via the volume of the liquid bridge is shown in Figure 5.35(a) for different values of the distance

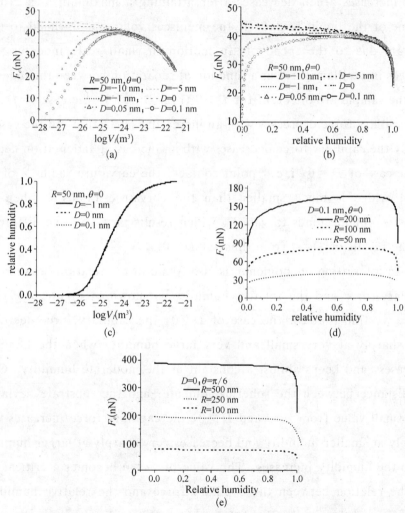

Figure 5.35   (a) The capillary force F_c as a function of the volume of the liquid bridge for different gaps D between the spherical indenter and the substrate. (b) The capillary force F_c as a function of the humidity for different gaps between the spherical indenter and the substrate. (c) The dependence of the relative humidity on the meniscus volume for different values of D. (d) The capillary force F_c as a function of the humidity for different radii of the sphere and the gap between the sphere and the substrate is $D = 0.1$ nm. (e) The capillary force F_c as a function of the humidity for different radii of the sphere and vanishing gap between the sphere and the substrate.

between the indenter and the substrate. From Figure 5.35(a), one can see that the shape of the curves for $D>0$ and $D\leqslant0$ has large difference. In the case of $D\leqslant0$, the capillary force is always decreasing with an increasing volume of the liquid bridge. In the case of $D>0$, the capillary force increases, then decreases after attaining a maximum at a critical volume of the liquid bridge. If the meniscus volume is assumed to be a constant due to the speed of tip motion in small scale indenter, the changes in capillary force as a function of separation between the indenter and the sample are different for $D>0$ from $D\leqslant0$. In the case of $D>0$, the capillary force decreases with an increasing separation. In the case of $D\leqslant0$, the capillary force decreases with an increasing indentation depth. In the case of $D=0$, i.e., point contact, the curvature radius r of the liquid bridge is much smaller than the curvature radius l when the meniscus volume tends to vanish, which results in qualitative difference for the results of $D=0$ from those of $D>0$.

An interesting phenomenon is also found in the relation between the capillary force and the relative humidity as shown in Figure 5.35(b), where we find that for the case of $D\leqslant0$, the capillary force decreases very sharply at very small and very large humidity when the humidity increases, and keeps almost a constant at the moderate humidity. Once the distance between the spherical indenter and the substrate deviate a very small value from zero and $D>0$, the capillary force increases very sharply at smaller humidity and decreases very sharply at larger humidity when the humidity increases. The value of $D=0$ becomes a critical one for the relation between the capillary force and the relative humidity. The effect of the van der Waals force at small humidity has been discussed by Farshchi-Tabrizi et al. (2006). The relation between the meniscus volume and the relative humidity is shown in Figure 5.35(c) in order to give a more clear understanding, from which one can see that the relative humidity increases when the meniscus volume increases, and at a critical value of the volume the relative humidity saturates.

Figures 5. 35(d) and 5. 35(e) show the relation between the capillary force and the relative humidity for the case of spherical indenter with different radii. The capillary force increases when the radius of the spherical indenter increases, which is consistent well with the numerical results in Pakarinen et al. (2005).

The effect of contact angle on the capillary force is shown in Figure 5. 36, where it is easy to find that the capillary force decreases with increasing contact angle, i. e., if the surfaces become hydrophobic from hydrophilic, the capillary force will decrease.

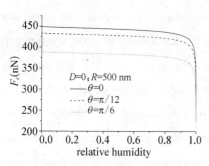

Figure 5. 36   Capillary force F_c between a sphere and a substrate versus humidity for different contact angles θ.

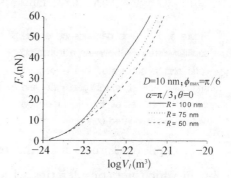

Figure 5. 37   The dependence of the capillary force F_c between a truncated cone and a substrate on the volume of the liquid bridge for different radii of the spherical end.

e. 3) The case of a truncated conical indenter and a substrate

Figure 5. 37 shows the relation between the capillary force and the volume of the liquid bridge for the model of a truncated cone with a spherical end in wet adhesion with a substrate, in which the gap D between the truncated cone and the substrate, the opening angle of the spherical end, the cone angle and the contact angle are fixed, except for the radius of the spherical end. One can see that for a determined radius of the spherical end, the capillary force increases with an increasing volume of the liquid bridge. If the volume of the liquid bridge keeps a small constant, the capillary force increases with a decreasing radius of the spherical end. For a large constant of the volume of the liquid bridge, the case is on the contrary.

The effect of the contact angle on the capillary force is shown in Figure

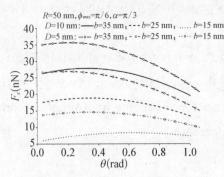

Figure 5. 38   The dependence of the capillary force F_c between a truncated cone and a substrate on the contact angles θ for different gaps D and different radii b of the liquid bridge wetting the truncated cone.

5. 38, where all the parameters are fixed except for the contact angle. One can see the capillary force increases at small contact angle, then decreases after a critical value of the contact angle, at which the capillary force attains maximum value. Figure 5. 38 also shows that the capillary force increases with a decreasing gap between the truncated end and the substrate if all the other parameters keep unchanged.

The capillary force versus the relative humidity is shown in Figure 5. 39, in which we consider tips with smooth ($\alpha + \phi_{max} = 90°$) and non-smooth ($\alpha + \phi_{max} \neq 90°$) transitions between the spherical and conical parts and two cases of $D = 0$ and $D \neq 0$. For the case of $D \neq 0$, one can see that the capillary force increases with the relative humidity up to a relatively high humidity for the case of a smooth transition, the spherical end dominates the capillary force. The conical part is only important at very high humidity. For the case of a non-smooth transition, the relation between the capillary force and the relative humidity consists of three regimes along with an increasing relative humidity: (i) the capillary force increases at the initial stage, (ii) decreases at certain value of the relative humidity, (iii) then increases once again. The three regimes correspond to the dominations of spherical end, intermediate transition and conical part, respectively. For the case of $D = 0$, the capillary force keeps almost a constant up to a relatively high humidity when the spherical end dominates the capillary force, the conical part is only important at very high humidity also.

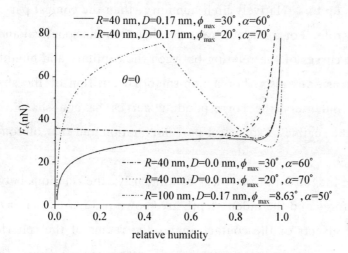

Figure 5. 39 The capillary force F_c between a truncated cone and a substrate as a function of the humidity for different sets of parameters.

When a truncated conical indenter penetrates a depth into the substrate, the relation between the capillary force and the relative humidity is shown in Figure 5. 40. The capillary force decreases up to a relatively high humidity, then increases, which means the spherical end

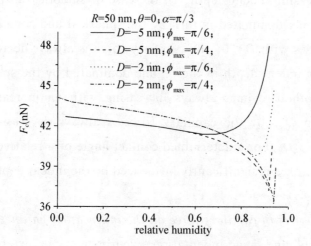

Figure 5. 40 The capillary force F_c between a truncated cone and a substrate as a function of the humidity for different gaps D and half of the opening angle ϕ_{max} of the spherical end.

dominates up to a relatively high humidity, then the conical part plays an important role. For a smooth transition between the spherical and conical parts, the curves of the relation between the capillary and humidity have smooth transitions also. For a non-smooth transition of the shape of a truncated indenter, the corresponding curves have a sharp transition between the regime of spherical part domination and that of conical part domination.

If the indent depth increases continuously, the relations between the capillary force and the indent depth are shown in Figure 5. 41 (a)–(c), in which the effects of the contact angle, the radius of the spherical end, the relative humidity are considered, respectively. From the three figures, one can see that the curves of the capillary force via the indenting depth consists of four regimes for the case of non-smooth transition between the spherical and conical parts of indenter, and three regimes for the case of smooth transition as shown in Figure 5. 42. In the case of non-smooth transition, when $D < 0$, the capillary is in turn dominated by the spherical part, intermediate transition part and the conical part along with an increasing indent depth. In the case of smooth transition, when $D < 0$, it is only dominated in turn by the spherical and conical parts. In these two cases with $D < 0$, the capillary force is always decreasing with an increasing indent depth in the regime dominated by the spherical part and in the other regimes always increasing with an increasing indent depth. When $D > 0$, the capillary force is always decreasing with an increasing gap D. For a determined contact angle or a relative humidity, the capillary force is significantly influenced by the indent depth as shown in Figures 5. 41(a) and 5. 41(c).

f) The effect of capillary force on the indentation hardness

In micro- and nano-indentation experiments, an external load is added on the indenter and normal to the indented surface which is compressed to form an indentation. We define the external force as F_n, which is measured by the indentation instrument spontaneously. If the

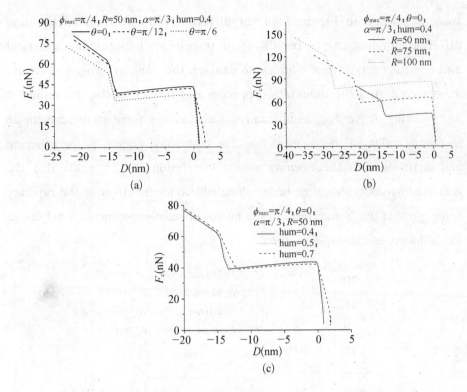

Figure 5.41 The capillary force F_c between a truncated cone and a substrate as a function of the gap D: (a) for different contact angles θ; (b) for different radii of the spherical end; (c) for different humidity.

capillary force F_c is attractive, the indented depth is amplified as well as the contact area A in the experiment, which is also measured by the indentation instrument automatically. The definition of the hardness

$$H = \frac{F_n}{A} \tag{5.230}$$

leads to an underestimation due to the overestimated contact area A. On the other hand, the measured hardness should be overestimated if the capillary force is repulsive.

For convenience, the commonly used Berkovich indenter in the indentation experiments is usually approximated to be a cone with half of the cone angle $\alpha = 70.3°$ in the FEM simulations. Due to the cone wear, the tip is rounded with a radius about $R = 50$ nm – 100 nm. The capillary force is plotted in Figure 5.42 for different radii of rounded tips and different opening angles for different transitions between the spherical and conical parts, from which one can see the capillary force is always attractive during the indentation process and influenced by the radius R and opening angle ϕ_{max} significantly. The capillary force increases with an increasing radius of the rounded tip. The dominated regime by the spherical end increases with the opening angle. Conclusion can be made that the measured hardness should be underestimated due to the effect of the capillary force, so that the "size effect" in the micro- or nano-experiments is not due to the influence of the capillary force.

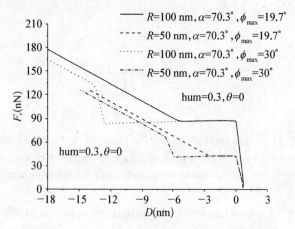

Figure 5.42 The dependence of the capillary F_c between a conical indenter with a rounded tip and a substrate on the gap D between the indenter and the substrate for different sets of radii R and half of the opening angle ϕ_{max} of the rounded tip.

5.7 Size effects in particle reinforced metal-matrix composites

In order to check the C-W strain gradient plasticity theory, Chen and

Wang (2002c) have used finite element method to analyze the size effects in particles reinforced metal-matrix composites and the results are compared with those of experiments. Two kinds of particles are considered, spheroid and cylinder. The simplified cell models are shown in Figure 5.43. For the axial-symmetrical condition, only the one fourth of the material region needs to be considered as shown in Figure 5.43. The normalized cell sizes for the spheroidal particles are

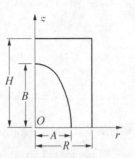

Figure 5.43 Cell model and the coordinate system.

$$A = \left(\frac{3\kappa}{4\pi}\right)^{1/3} \frac{V_p^{1/3}}{l_1}, \quad B = \frac{A}{\kappa}, \quad R = \left(\frac{\kappa}{2\pi f_p}\right)^{1/3} \frac{V_p^{1/3}}{l_1}, \quad H = \frac{R}{\kappa} \qquad (5.231)$$

where A, B, R and H are shown in Figure 5.43; V_p and f_p are the particle volume and volume fraction respectively and

$$\kappa = \frac{A}{B} = \frac{R}{H} \qquad (5.232)$$

is the particle and cell aspect ratios. Note that the cell volume can not take unity as usual because the reference length is l_1, instead of the usual cell size. The relation between the two material length scales is taken as $l_{cs} = l_1 = L$. Therefore, three independent parameters for the cell geometry description are needed, instead of only two independent parameters for the usual cell model description. From dimensional analysis, additional composite parameter, $V_p^{1/3}/l_1$, describing the cell size and the strain gradient effects, must appear in the analysis inevitably.

For the cylindrical particle case, we have

$$A = \left(\frac{\kappa}{\pi}\right)^{1/3} \frac{V_p^{1/3}}{l_1}, \quad B = \frac{A}{\kappa}, \quad R = \left(\frac{\kappa}{\pi f_p}\right)^{1/3} \frac{V_p^{1/3}}{l_1}, \quad H = \frac{R}{\kappa} \qquad (5.233)$$

The boundary conditions as shown in Figure 5.43 are described as

$$u_z = 0, \ \sigma_{rz} = 0, \ m_{\theta z} = 0 \quad \text{on } z = 0 \qquad (5.234)$$

$$u_z = \varepsilon_c H, \ \sigma_{rz} = 0, \ m_{\theta z} = 0 \quad \text{on } z = H \qquad (5.235)$$

$$u_r = C_0 \quad \sigma_{zr} = 0, \int_0^H \sigma_{rr} dz = 0, \ m_{\theta r} = 0 \quad \text{on} \quad r = R \qquad (5.236)$$

where C_0 is a constant to be determined by the third equation in Eq. (5.236).

The metal matrix is treated as an elastic-plastic material considering strain gradient. The particle is treated as an elastic material with Young's modulus E_p and Poisson's ratio ν_P.

The parameter dependence of the stress strain relations of the PMMC can be written as

$$\frac{\sigma_C}{\sigma_Y} = F\left(\varepsilon_C, \ \frac{E_p}{E}, \ f_p, \ \kappa, \ n, \ \frac{E}{\sigma_Y}, \ \nu, \ \nu_P, \ \frac{V_p^{1/3}}{l_1}\right) \qquad (5.237)$$

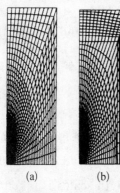

(a)   (b)

Figure 5.44   Mesh division of the calculation model of spherical particle (a) and cylindrical particle (b) reinforced metal-matrix composites.

where E, n, ν are the Young's modulus, the strain hardening exponent and Poisson ratio of the matrix material respectively.

Chen and Wang (2002c) take (E/σ_Y, ν, ν_P) = (300, 0.3, 0.3), where σ_Y is the yield stress of the matrix material. $V_p^{1/3}/l_1$ is a parameter. A large value of $V_p^{1/3}/l_1$ means a large particle size; Conversely a small value corresponds to a small particle.

The element form is shown in Figure 5.44. For comparison, meshes for the two kinds of particles, i. e. spheroidal and cylindrical particles are shown in Figure 5.44(a) and (b).

5.7.1   Results for spheroidal particle case

Composites reinforced by spheroidal particles are investigated with different particle volume fractions, different particle sizes, different

Young's modulus ratio of particle and matrix and the different aspect ratios (the ratio of width with height of particle). In all calculations Poisson's ratio is 0.3 for both the particle and the matrix material.

Figure 5.45 shows the stress strain curves of the composites for different particle volume fractions and different particle sizes when Young's modulus values of both particle and matrix are equal and the particle aspect ratio is 0.3. From Figure 5.45, one can find that both the particle volume fraction and particle size have strong effects on the composite strength. The larger the particle volume fraction, the larger the PMMC strength and the smaller the particle size, the larger the PMMC strength.

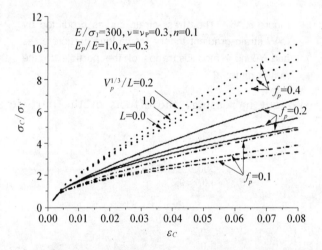

Figure 5.45   The stress-strain curves predicted by C-W strain gradient theory for various particle volume fractions and particle sizes.

Figure 5.46 depicts the dependence of the stress strain relations on the Young's modulus ratios for spherical particles. From Figure 5.46 one can find that the stress strain curves are not sensitive to the Young's ratio while the Young's ratio is near unit. But it is very sensitive to the particle sizes, with Young's modulus ratio increasing.

Figure 5.47 demonstrates that the stress strain curves also depend on the strain hardening exponent of the matrix material. Larger strain hardening exponent, larger the overall composite stress. While the strain

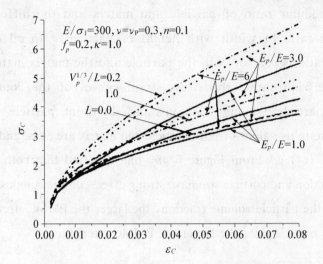

Figure 5. 46   The stress-strain curves predicted by
C-W strain gradient theory for various particle sizes
and Young's modulus ratios of the particle to the
matrix material.

hardening exponent increasing, the effects of the particle size become
stronger.

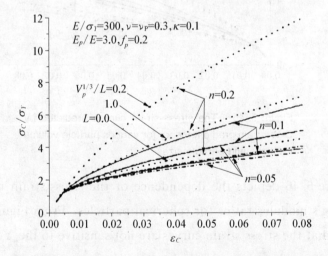

Figure 5. 47   The stress-strain curves predicted by C-
W strain gradient theory for various particle sizes and
strain hardening exponents.

The results in Figure 5. 48 include three cases of the aspect ratios:
$\kappa = 0.1, 1.0, 10$. $\kappa = 0.1$ means the particle shape is rather thin; $\kappa = 1.0$

corresponds the spherical shape and $\kappa = 10.0$ represents the flat particle shape. When the particle volume fraction is fixed, the composite strengthening is the smallest for the spherical particle case. When the aspect ratio is very large or very small, the composite stresses are almost the same. For the same aspect ratio, the stress is larger while the particle size is smaller, which tends to explain the phenomena found in the experiments (Lloyd, 1994; Ling, 2000).

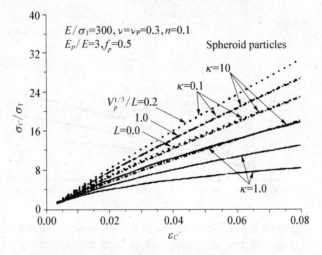

Figure 5. 48   The stress-strain curves predicted by C-W strain gradient theory for various particle sizes and particle aspect ratios.

5.7.2 Results for cylindrical particle case

Composites reinforced by cylindrical particles are investigated with different particle volume fractions, different particle sizes, different Young's modulus ratio of particle and matrix and the different aspect ratio (the ratio of width with height of particle). In all calculations, the results are similar to those for spheroidal particle and the composite strength also depend on the Particle size, the particle aspect ratio, Young's modulus ratio of the particle and matrix materials and particle volume fractions, as well as the strain hardening exponent of matrix material.

    Figure 5. 49 shows the comparison of the results of spheroidal particle
with those of cylindrical particle when all other parameters are fixed.
From Figure 5. 49, one can find that the flow stress for cylindrical
particle reinforced composite is larger than that for spheroidal particle
reinforced composite, which can be found in the conventional composite
calculations.

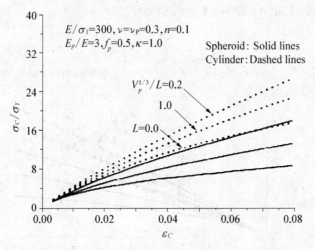

Figure 5. 49   Comparisons of the stress-strain curves
between the spherical particle and the cylindrical
particle reinforced composites.

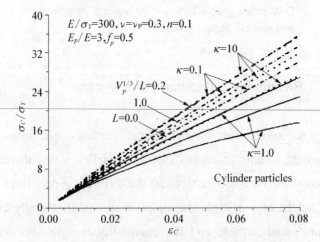

Figure 5. 50   The stress-strain curves predicted by
C-W strain gradient theory for cylindrical particle
reinforced composites with different particle sizes and
particle aspect ratios.

The dependence of stress strain relations on the particle aspect ratio is depicted in Figure 5.50. The following conclusions are readily obtained: (i) the composite strengthening is the smallest for $\kappa = 1.0$. (ii) When the particle ratio is very low or very high, the difference between two results with size effect considered disappears very quickly.

The influences on the composite strength of the other composite factors in the cylindrical particle reinforced metal-matrix composite are almost the same tendency with that in spheroidal particle reinforced metal-matrix composite. Here the results are omitted.

5.7.3 Comparison with experiments

In order to determine the internal material scales for a determined composite, the calculation results will be compared with the experimental results. The above method has been used and the results are compared with the experiment results given by Ling (2000).

A series of uniaxial compression tests of 17% volume fraction SiC_p/ 2124Al composites with different particle sizes were carried out by Ling (2000). According to Ling (2000), the material parameters are $E = 70$ GPa, $E_p = 420$ Gpa, $n = 0.1$, $\sigma_Y = 200$ MPa, $\kappa = 1.0$, $f_p = 0.17$ and $\nu = \nu_p = 0.3$. The dependence of the compressive stress strain curves on the particle sizes for this lower particle volume fraction from experimental result and calculation result is shown in Figure 5.51 for particle radii 3 μm and 37 μm. From Figure 5.51, one can find that the present calculation results with length scale $l_1 = 6$ μm agree with the experimental result by Ling (2000). The calculation has been done on a rectangular unit cell with spherical reinforcement, which is subject to uniformly prescribed boundary conditions, however in the real experimental sample, the reinforcements have irregular shapes and particle-particle interaction poses constraint far more complicated than the simple model we have used. Particles also tend to form clusters, rather than being uniformly distributed as assumed here. These factors may all contribute to the discrepancy remaining between calculation and experiment results.

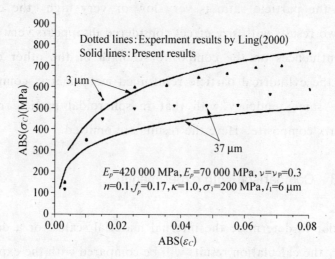

Figure 5.51   Comparison between the experimental results (Ling, 2000) and the theoretical prediction of C-W strain gradient theory.

References

Acharya, A. and Bassani, J. L., 1995. On non-local flow theories that preserve the classical structure of incremental boundary value problems. In Micromechanics of Plasticity and Damage of Multiphase Materials, IUTAM Symposium, Paris, Aug 29 – Sept 1.

Acharya, A. and Shawki, T. G., 1995. Thermodynamic restrictions on constitutive equations for second-deformation-gradient inelastic behavior. J. Mech. Phys. Solids 43, 1751 – 1772.

Aifantis, E. C., 1984. On the microstructural origin of certain inelastic models. Trans. ASME J. Eng. Mater. Technol. 106, 326 – 330.

Begley, M. R. and Hutchinson, J. W., 1998. The mechanics of size-dependent indentation. J. Mech. Phys. Solids 46, 2049 – 2068.

Chen, S. H. and Wang, T. C., 2000. A new hardening law for strain gradient plasticity. Acta Mater., 48(16), 3997 – 4005.

Chen, S. H. and Wang, T. C., 2002a. A new deformation theory for strain gradient effects. Int. J. Plasticity 18, 971 – 995.

Chen, S. H. and Wang, T. C., 2002b. Finite element solutions for plane strain mode I crack with strain gradient effects. Int. J. Solids Struct. 39, 1241 – 1257.

Chen, S. H. and Wang, T. C., 2002c. Size effects in the particle-reinforced metal-matrix composites. Acta Mech. 157, 113 – 127.

Chen, S. H., Tao, C. J., Wang, T. C., 2004. A study of micro-indentation with size effects. Acta Mech., 167(1 – 2), 57 – 71.

Dennis, J. E., Moré, J. J., 1977. Quasi-Newton methods, motivation and theory. SIAM Review 19(1), 46 – 89.

Farshchi-Tabrizi, M., Kappl, M., Cheng, Y., Gutmann, J., Butt, H., 2006. On the adhesion between fine particles and nanocontacts; an atomic force microscope study. Langmuir, 22, 2171 – 2184.

Fleck, N. A. and Hutchinson, J. W., 1993. A phenomenological theory for strain gradient effects in plasticity. J. Mech. Phys. Solids 41, 1825 – 1857.

Fleck, N. A. and Hutchinson, J. W., 1997. Strain Gradient Plasticity. Advances in Applied Mechanics ed. J. W. Hutchinson and T. Y. Wu, 33, 295 – 361 Academic Press, New York.

Fleck and Hutchinson, 2001. A reformulation of strain gradient plasticity. J. Mech. Phys. Solids 49, 2245 – 2271.

Fleck, N. A., Muller, G. M., Ashby, M. F. and Hutchinson, J. W., 1994. Strain gradient plasticity; theory and experiment. Acta Metal. et Mater. 42, 475 – 487.

Gao, H., Huang, Y., Nix, W. D. and Hutchinson, J. W., 1999. Mechanism-based strain gradient plasticity-I. theory. J. Mech. Phys. Solids 47, 1239 – 1263.

Green, A. E., Mcinnis, B. C. and Naghdi, P. M., 1968. Elastic-plastic continua with simple force dipole. Int. J. Engng Sci. 6, 373 – 394.

Gurtin, M. E., 1965a. Thermodynamics and the possibility of spatial interaction in rigid heat conductors. Arch. Ration. Mech. Anal. 18, 335 – 342.

Gurtin, M. E., 1965b. Thermodynamics and the possibility of spatial interaction in elastic materials. Arch. Ration. Mech. Anal. 19, 339 – 352.

Hill, R., 1950. Mathematical theory of plasticity. Oxford University Press, Oxford, England.

Huang, Y., Xue, Z., Gao, H., Nix, W. D., Xia, Z. C., 2000. A study of micro-indentation hardness tests by mechanism-based strain gradient plasticity. J. Mater. Res. 15, 1786 – 1796.

Kachanov, L. M., 1971. Foundations of the theory of plasticity. North-Holland Publication Company-Amsterdam, London.

Ling, Z., 2000. Deformation behavior and microstructure effect in 2124Al/SuCp composite. J. Comp. Mater. 34, 101 – 115.

Lloyd, D. J., 1994. Particle-reinforced aluminum and magnesium matrix composite. Int. Mater. Rev., 39, 1 – 23.

Ma, Q., Clarke, D. R., 1995. Size dependent hardness in silver single crystals. J. Mater. Res. 10, 853 – 863.

McElhaney, K. W., Vlassak, J. J., Nix, W. D., 1998. Determination of indenter tip geometry and indentation contact area for depth-sensing indentation experiments. J. Mater. Res. 13, 1300 – 1306.

Muhlhaus, H. B. And Aifantis, E. C., 1991. The influence of microstructure-induced gradients on the localization of deformation in viscoplastic materials. Acta Mech., 89, 217 – 231.

Nix, W. D., Gao, H., 1998. Indentation size effects in crystalline materials: a law for strain gradient plasticity. J. Mech. Phys. Solids 46, 411 – 425.

Pakarinen, O. H., Foster, A. S., Paajanen, M., et al., 2005. Towards an accurate description of the capillary force in nanoparticle-surface interactions. Modelling Simul. Mater. Sci. Eng., 13, 1175 – 1186.

Shu, J. Y., Fleck, N. A., 1998. The prediction of a size effect in microindentation. Int. J. Solids Struct. 35, 1363 – 1383.

Smyshlyaev, V. P. and Fleck, N. A., 1996. The role of strain gradients in the grain size effect for polycrystals. J. Mech. Phys. Solids 44, 465 – 495.

Spencer, A. J. M., 1971. Theory of invariants, Continuum physics, ed. by C. Eringen. Academic press, 239 – 353.

Stolken, J. S. and Evans, A. G., 1998. A microbend test method for measuring the plasticity length scale. Acta Mater. 46, 5109 – 1515.

Swadener, J. G., George, E. P., Pharr, G. M., 2002. The correlation of the indentation size effect measured with indenters of various shapes. J. Mech. Phys. Solids, 50, 681 – 694.

Tao, C. J., Wang, T. C., Chen, S. H., 2004. Analysis of micro-indentation considering the indenter tip curvature and strain gradient effects. Acta Mech. Sinica, 36(6) 680 – 687 (in Chinese).

Wei, Y. and Hutchinson, J. W., 1997. Steady-state crack growth and work of fracture for solids characterized by strain gradient plasticity. J. Mech. Phys. Solids 45, 1253 – 1273.

Xia, Z. C. and Hutchinson, J. W., 1996. Crack tip fields in strain gradient plasticity. J.

Mech. Phys. Solids 44, 1621 – 1648.

Zbib, H. and Aifantis, E. C., 1989. On the localization and postlocalization behavior of plastic deformation. Part Ⅰ. On the initiation of shear bands; Part Ⅱ. On the evolution and thickness of shear bands; Part Ⅲ. On the structure and velocity of Portevin-Le Chatelier bands. Res. Mech., 261 – 277, 279 – 292, and 293 – 305.

Zbib, H. and Aifantis, E. C., 1992. On the gradient-dependent theory of plasticity and shear banding. Acta Mech., 92, 209 – 225.

6 Strain curl theory

6.1 The continuum theory of dislocation

a) Geometry of dislocation

Consider an open smooth surface S bounded by a close loop c in body

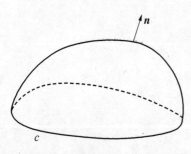

Figure 6.1 Schematic of the normal vector direction of a surface.

V as shown in Figure 6.1. Assume the body contains defects and the displacement u no long satisfies the compatibility law. Define the Bugers vector b of the dislocations as the sum of the infinitesimal vectors of du alone the Bugers loop c

$$b = \oint_c du \qquad (6.1)$$

In order to establish the basic field equation of the dislocation theory, we consider the continuous distribution of dislocations instead of single dislocation. With the help of Stokes' theorem, the equation (6.1) can be expressed as

$$b = \iint_S \text{curl } \boldsymbol{\beta} \cdot n \, dS \qquad (6.2)$$

where n is the unit out normal of surface S. The positive direction of Burgers loop c is chosen anti-clockwise when sighting from positive side of normal n as shown in Figure 6.1.

β is the distortion tensor. If the deformation is compatible, β is the gradient of the displacement u

$$\left.\begin{array}{c} \beta = \mathrm{grad}\, u \\[2mm] \beta_{ij} = \partial_i u_j \end{array}\right\} \tag{6.3}$$

The exact definition of the distortion tensor β for general incompatible deformation is given in differential form by

$$\left.\begin{array}{c} \mathrm{d}u_j = \beta_{ij}\,\mathrm{d}x_i \\[2mm] \mathrm{d}u = \mathrm{d}x \cdot \beta \end{array}\right\} \tag{6.4}$$

Introduce the dislocation density tensor α

$$\alpha = \mathrm{curl}\,\beta \tag{6.5}$$

The equation (6.2) can be rewritten as

$$b = \iint_S \alpha \cdot n\,\mathrm{d}S \tag{6.6}$$

For the continuum theory of dislocation, the distortion tensor β and dislocation density tensor α are more important than the displacement tensor u since the u may not be a single-value function and the definition (6.3) may be non sense. In other words, one can assume that both the distortion tensor β and the dislocation density tensor α do exist, but the global displacement field may not exist.

b) *Elastic theory of dislocation*

Consider an elastic body, containing defects of dislocations. If the dislocation density tensor α is given, then the fundamental field equations of the boundary-value problem of linear elastic theory of dislocations consist of following equations:

Equilibrium equation

$$\sigma_{ij,\,i} = 0 \quad \text{in} \ V \tag{6.7}$$

Hook's law

$$\sigma_{ij} = L_{ijkl}\varepsilon_{kl} \quad \text{in} \ V \tag{6.8a}$$

$$\varepsilon_{ij} = \frac{1}{2}(\beta_{ij} + \beta_{ji}) \quad \text{in} \ V \tag{6.8b}$$

Incompatibility equation

$$\boldsymbol{\alpha} = \text{curl}\boldsymbol{\beta} \tag{6.9}$$

Boundary condition

$$p_i = \sigma_{ij}n_j = \overline{p}_i \quad \text{on} \quad S \tag{6.10}$$

where surface S is the boundary of V, $\overline{p}_i$ is the prescribed traction on the surface S.

Since the dislocation density tensor $\boldsymbol{\alpha}$ satisfies automatically the following identity

$$\text{div}\boldsymbol{\alpha} = 0 \quad \text{in} \quad V \tag{6.11}$$

Hence the equation (6.9) only consists of 6 scalar independent equations.

The field equations (6.7)–(6.9) constitute a system of 15 scalar equations with 15 unknowns: 6 components of stress tensor and 9 components of the distortion tensor $\boldsymbol{\beta}$. Solving above boundary-value problem, one can get the stress tensor $\boldsymbol{\sigma}$ and distortion tensor $\boldsymbol{\beta}$.

c) *Plastic theory of dislocation*

For the plastic media, the plastic deformation is important besides the elastic deformation.

The total distortion tensor $\boldsymbol{\beta}^t$ can be decomposed into the elastic distortion tensor $\boldsymbol{\beta}$ and the plastic distortion tensor $\boldsymbol{\beta}^p$ so that

$$\boldsymbol{\beta}^t = \boldsymbol{\beta} + \boldsymbol{\beta}^p \tag{6.12}$$

The superscript, p, denotes the quantity related to the plastic deformation, while the elastic distortion tensor $\boldsymbol{\beta}$ is denoted without superscript. We know that the elastic distortion tensor $\boldsymbol{\beta}$ is incompatible, which satisfies the incompatibility equation (6.9).

Kröner (1981) argued that the cohesive forces in the body are strong enough to prevent its breaking into small pieces. It means that the total distortion tensor $\boldsymbol{\beta}^t$ satisfies the compatibility law. We have the following equation

$$\text{curl } \boldsymbol{\beta}^t = 0 \tag{6.13}$$

It is well known that the plastic deformation is induced due to the movements of numeral dislocations. Figure 6.2 shows the glides of great number dislocations out of the single crystal, which results in large plastic deformation. The most important contribution for the plastic deformation comes from the dislocations which move out the single crystal. The incompatible elastic deformation is induced due to the dislocations remained inside the body, which is much smaller than the plastic strain. One can image that, the incompatible

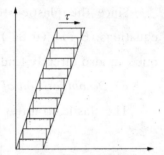

Figure 6.2　Schematic of dislocation gliding out of a single crystal.

plastic strain is also much smaller than the compatible plastic strain. Therefore modifying the incompatible plastic strain in order to satisfy the Eq. (6.13) does not change the essential feature of the plastic strain.

From Eqs. (6.9) and (6.13), one obtains

$$\boldsymbol{\alpha} = \text{curl } \boldsymbol{\beta} = -\text{curl } \boldsymbol{\beta}^p \tag{6.14}$$

It means that the dislocation density $\boldsymbol{\alpha}$ is produced from the intermediate configuration to current configuration, while the dislocation density induced from the natural (initial) configuration to the intermediate configuration is equal to $-\boldsymbol{\alpha}$. Hence the deformation from the nature (initial) configuration to current configuration is compatible.

In the plastic theory of dislocations proposed by Kröner(1981), the plastic distortion tensor $\boldsymbol{\beta}^p$ is assumed to be a known quantity. The dislocation density $\boldsymbol{\alpha}$ is obtained from the Eq. (6. 14). Then the elastic distortion tensor $\boldsymbol{\beta}$ can be determined from the fundamental field equations (6. 7)–(6. 10).

The total displacement $\boldsymbol{u}^t$ can be determined from following equation

$$\partial_i u_j^t = \beta_{ij}^t \tag{6.15}$$

The equation (6. 8a) can be rewritten as

$$\sigma_{ij} = L_{ijkl}(\varepsilon_{kl}^t - \varepsilon_{kl}^p) \tag{6.8a'}$$

Since the plastic strain ε_{ij}^p is also a known quantity, using the equations (6. 7), (6. 8a′) and (6. 15) with certain boundary conditions, one can also directly find the total displacement $\boldsymbol{u}^t$.

c) *Decomposition of the dislocation density tensor α*

The elastic strain ε_{ij} can be expressed as

$$\varepsilon_{ij} = \frac{1}{2}(\beta_{ij} + \beta_{ji}) \tag{6.16}$$

Introduce an elastic rotation tensor W_{ij}

$$W_{ij} = \frac{1}{2}(\beta_{ij} - \beta_{ji}) \tag{6.17}$$

The elastic distortion tensor $\boldsymbol{\beta}$ takes the form

$$\beta_{ij} = \varepsilon_{ij} + W_{ij} \tag{6.18}$$

Since W_{ij} is an anti-symmetric tensor, it is convenient replacing it by the elastic rotation vector θ_i

$$\theta_i = \frac{1}{2}e_{ijk}W_{jk}$$
$$W_{ij} = e_{ijk}\theta_k \tag{6.19}$$

The equation (6. 5) can be rewritten as

$$\alpha_{ij} = e_{ikl}\partial_k\varepsilon_{lj} + e_{ikl}\partial_k W_{lj} \tag{6.20}$$

The second term of right side of above equation becomes

$$e_{ikl} \partial_k W_{lj} = e_{ikl} e_{ljm} \partial_k \theta_m = (\delta_{ij}\delta_{km} - \delta_{im}\delta_{kj})\partial_k \theta_m = \partial_k \theta_k \delta_{ij} - \partial_j \theta_i$$

$$(6.21)$$

Now we have

$$\alpha_{ij} = e_{ikl} \partial_k \varepsilon_{lj} + \partial_k \theta_k \delta_{ij} - \partial_j \theta_i \tag{6.22}$$

Eq. (6.22) can be rewritten as

$$\alpha_{ij} = e_{ikl} \partial_k \varepsilon_{lj} + \tilde{\chi}_{kk}\delta_{ij} - \tilde{\chi}_{ji} \tag{6.23}$$

where $\tilde{\chi}_{ji}$ is the elastic curvature tensor

$$\tilde{\chi}_{ji} = \partial_j \theta_i \tag{6.24}$$

The distortion density tensor $\boldsymbol{\alpha}$ can be also expressed in terms of the plastic strain and plastic curvature tensor

$$-\alpha_{ij} = e_{ikl} \partial_k \varepsilon_{lj}^P + \tilde{\chi}_{kk}^P \delta_{ij} - \tilde{\chi}_{ji}^P \tag{6.25}$$

where the plastic curvature tensor $\tilde{\chi}_{ji}^P$ takes the form

$$\tilde{\chi}_{ji}^P = \partial_j \theta_i^P \tag{6.26}$$

The plastic rotation vector θ_i^P is given by

$$\left.\begin{array}{l} \theta_i^P = \dfrac{1}{2} e_{ijk} W_{jk}^P \\[2mm] W_{ij}^P = \dfrac{1}{2}(\beta_{ij}^P - \beta_{ji}^P) \end{array}\right\} \tag{6.27}$$

6.2   Plastic strain curl theory

In this section and the following sections 6.3 – 6.4, the superscript, t, for the total quantities is omitted for simplicity of writing and the superscript, e, will be used for the elastic quantities so that the elastic strain will be expressed as ε_{ij}^e.

The main mechanisms for the hardening of metal materials are the multiplication, accumulation and interaction of dislocations. The dislocation density tensor can be decomposed into two parts: one is plastic strain curl tensor and the other is plastic curvature tensor. The influence of the plastic curvature on the plastic stress state and stress level can be characterized by introducing the couple stress. The plastic strain curl is supposed to play the most important role for the stress level. Three rotational degrees of freedom ω_i, named as micro rotation, are introduced besides the displacement components u_i. Micro rotations ω_i have no direct dependence upon u_i while material rotation $\theta = \nabla \times u / 2$. The generalized normal law is used to describe the constitutive relations of the Cauchy's stresses versus strains and couple stresses versus curvatures. Plastic strain curl is incorporated into the instantaneously tangent modulus. In this way, the generalized equivalent stress is no longer a single-variable function of the generalized equivalent strain. The plastic strain energy density is no longer determined by the generalized equivalent strain solely either.

The working hardening of metallic materials is caused by the storage of dislocations. According to Taylor's hardening law, the flow stress of the material is related to the dislocation density in the material as following formula:

$$\sigma = CGb\sqrt{\rho} \tag{6.28}$$

where C is a constant coefficient, G is the shear modulus and b is the magnitude of Burger's vector b. The dislocations are stored as two types: the statistically stored dislocations and the geometrically necessary dislocations (Ashby, 1970; Nix and Gao, 1998). Then the flow stress is

$$\sigma = CGb\sqrt{\rho_S + \rho_G} = CGb\sqrt{\rho_S}\sqrt{1 + \frac{\rho_G}{\rho_S}} \tag{6.29}$$

where ρ_S is the statistically stored dislocation density and ρ_G is the geometrically necessary dislocation density.

If the geometrically necessary dislocation density is negligibly small, the flow stress can be expressed as

$$\sigma = CGb\sqrt{\rho_S} \qquad (6.30)$$

On the other hand, the uniaxial stress-strain law of the classical theory of plasticity can be written as

$$\sigma = \sigma_0 A(\varepsilon) \qquad (6.31a)$$

or

$$\sigma_e = \sigma_0 A(\varepsilon_{ep}) \qquad (6.31b)$$

where σ_0 is the yield stress, A is work hardening function, σ_e is the equivalent stress and ε_{ep} is the equivalent plastic strain. From Eqs. (6.30), (6.31a) and (6.31b), one can see that the statistically stored dislocation density is the function of equivalent plastic strain and the effect of the statistically stored dislocations density on the effective stress can be characterized the effective plastic strain.

In the conventional theories of plasticity, only the influence of statistically stored dislocations is considered. Comparing with the statistically stored dislocation density, the geometrically necessary dislocation density is negligible at macro scales. That is why the conventional theories of plasticity are successfully used at those scales.

The geometrically necessary dislocation density is related to the inhomogeneous plastic strain (Ashby, 1970). Once the size of the inhomogeneous plastic deformation zone is of a few microns or less, the plastic strains vary sharply in a small zone and then the geometrically necessary dislocation density cannot be neglected anymore. Therefore, the local stress level may be much higher than the calculated results using a conventional plasticity model.

A plastic strain curl theory (Xia and Wang, 2004) is presented in this section. The initial idea of the new theory comes from the continuum theory of dislocation (Kröner, 1981). The dislocation density tensor can be written as

$$\boldsymbol{\alpha} = -\operatorname{curl} \boldsymbol{\beta}^p = -\operatorname{curl} \boldsymbol{\varepsilon}^p - (\operatorname{tr} \tilde{\boldsymbol{\chi}}^p) \boldsymbol{I} + (\tilde{\boldsymbol{\chi}}^p)^T \qquad (6.32)$$

where $\boldsymbol{\varepsilon}^p$ is the plastic strain tensor, $\tilde{\boldsymbol{\chi}}^p$ is the plastic curvature tensor, I is the unit tensor. Eq. (6.32) shows clearly that the uniform plastic distortion has no contribution to the dislocation density tensor $\boldsymbol{\alpha}$. On the other hand, at the micro scale, the statistically stored dislocations rapidly accumulate by trapping one another in a random distribution way and introduce no incompatibility into the material element of continuum mechanics. Only the geometrically necessary dislocations are required for the incompatible deformation in the material element of continuum mechanics.

Hence, the dislocation density tensor calculated in conformity to Eq. (6.32) can only be the geometrically necessary dislocation density tensor, i. e.

$$\boldsymbol{\alpha}_G = -\operatorname{curl} \boldsymbol{\beta}^p = -\operatorname{curl} \boldsymbol{\varepsilon}^p - (\operatorname{tr} \tilde{\boldsymbol{\chi}}^p) \boldsymbol{I} + (\tilde{\boldsymbol{\chi}}^p)^T \qquad (6.33)$$

It is evident that the geometrically necessary dislocation density tensor $\boldsymbol{\alpha}_G$ can be decomposed into two parts: one is plastic strain curl tensor and another is related to the plastic curvature tensor. One can image that the work conjugate of the curvature tensor is the couple stress. Hence, the effect of the plastic curvature tensor on the plastic deformation can be described by introducing the couple stress. Thus, the plastic strain curl will play the key role in the new theory.

Plastic strain curl theory is constructed based on general couple stress theory in chapter Ⅲ. Micro rotations ω_i are introduced. Micro curvatures χ are the gradients of micro rotations $\boldsymbol{\omega}$. The constitutive relations of Cauchy's stresses versus strains and couple stresses versus micro curvatures are deduced from the generalized normal law.

All materials consist of jillion discrete micro particles (e. g. atoms, molecules, ions, etc.). The location changes of all the particle centers form a displacement field, denoted by u. Material rotation θ is dependent on the displacement, i.e. $\theta = \nabla \times u/2$. The micro rotation ω has no direct dependence upon the displacement u. It is the angular displacement of a particle. In fact, micro rotation ω is the sum of material rotation θ and relative rotation φ. The relation between micro rotation ω and material rotation θ is illustrated in Figure 6.3.

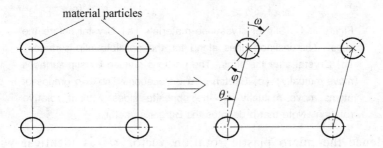

Figure 6.3　Relation between micro rotation ω and material rotation θ.

The plastic curvature tensor $\tilde{\chi}_{ij}^{P}$ in continuum theory of dislocations is defined in the form that

$$d\theta_j^P = \tilde{\chi}_{ij}^P dx_i \qquad (6.34)$$

where θ_i^P is the plastic material rotation. In the plastic strain curl theory, however, the micro curvature tensor χ is defined as the gradient of micro rotation ω, i.e.

$$\chi_{ij} = \partial_i \omega_j \qquad (6.35)$$

Let us consider the plastic curvature tensor. As shown in Figure 6.4, during the plastic deformation, the two groups of micro particles will move mutually on the opposite sides of a slip plane without relative rotation. Therefore plastic relative rotation $\varphi^P = 0$. Thus it is evident that

$$\omega_i^P = \theta_i^P, \quad \chi_{ij}^P = \tilde{\chi}_{ij}^P \qquad (6.36)$$

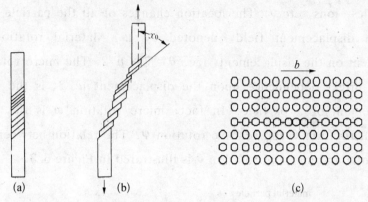

Figure 6.4   Slip of crystalline materials (a) Crystal before the slips. The inclined lines stand for the possible slip surfaces; (b) Crystal after the slips. The portions divided by slip surfaces move mutually; (c) Sketch of a dislocation. The two groups of atoms move mutually on the opposite sides without relative rotation. Note that b denotes the Burger's vector.

Hence the micro plastic rotation vector $\boldsymbol{\omega}^p$ is identical with the plastic material rotation vector $\boldsymbol{\theta}^p$, and the micro plastic curvature tensor χ_{ij}^P is identical with the plastic curvature tensor $\tilde{\chi}_{ij}^P$ in the present plastic strain curl theory.

In the present theory, only the symmetric part of Cauchy's stress $\boldsymbol{\sigma}$ and couple stress $\boldsymbol{m}$ are considered. The antisymmetric part of Cauchy's stress is supposed to be zero. If body forces and body couples are negligible, the equilibrium relation within body V gives:

$$\sigma_{ij,\,j} = 0, \ l_{cs}^{-1} m_{ij,\,j} = 0 \tag{6.37}$$

Traction equilibrium on the surface S of body V implies:

$$\sigma_{ij} n_j = t_i, \ m_{ij} n_j = q_i \tag{6.38}$$

where n_i is the outer normal of surface S, t_i and q_i are surface tractions and surface torque per unit area, respectively.

The constitutive equations of plastic strain curl theory can be obtained through an analogy with the conventional theory of plasticity. According to the normal law in conventional J_2 deformation theory, plastic strains can be written as

$$\varepsilon_{ij}^{p} = \frac{3\varepsilon_{ep}}{2\sigma_{e}}s_{ij} \tag{6.39}$$

where s_{ij} is deviatoric stress, σ_{e} is equivalent stress and ε_{ep} is equivalent plastic strain. Eq. (6.39) can be easily rewritten as

$$s_{ij} = \frac{2\sigma_{e}}{3\varepsilon_{ep}}\varepsilon_{ij}^{p} \tag{6.40}$$

In another hand, the relation between mean stress and volume strain is

$$\frac{\sigma_{kk}}{3} = K\varepsilon_{kk} \tag{6.41}$$

where σ_{ij} is stress, ε_{ij} is strain and K is volume modulus. Combining Eq. (6.40) and (6.41), the constitutive equations in the conventional J_2 deformation theory are written as

$$\sigma_{ij} = \frac{2\sigma_{e}}{3\varepsilon_{ep}}\varepsilon_{ij}^{p} + \delta_{ij}K\varepsilon_{kk} \quad (\sigma_{e} \geqslant \sigma_{0}) \tag{6.42}$$

In a similar way, the constitutive equations in plastic curl theory can be obtained, i.e.

$$\begin{cases} \sigma_{ij} = \dfrac{2\Sigma_{e}}{3E_{ep}}\varepsilon_{ij}^{p} + \delta_{ij}K\varepsilon_{kk} \\[4mm] l_{cs}^{-1}m_{ij} = \dfrac{2\Sigma_{e}}{3E_{ep}}l_{cs}\chi_{ij}^{p} + \delta_{ij}K_{1}l_{cs}\chi_{kk} \end{cases} \quad (\Sigma_{e} > \sigma_{0}) \tag{6.43}$$

where l_{cs} is a material length and K_1 is the volume modulus of curvature tensor. A generalized normal law has been employed here. Generalized equivalent stress Σ_{e} and generalized equivalent plastic strain E_{ep} have substituted the equivalent stress σ_{e} and equivalent plastic strain ε_{ep} in Eq. (6.43), respectively. The expressions of generalized stress Σ_{e} and generalized plastic strain E_{ep} are

$$\Sigma_{e}^{2} = \sigma_{e}^{2} + l_{cs}^{-2}m_{e}^{2} \quad E_{ep}^{2} = \varepsilon_{ep}^{2} + l_{cs}^{2}\chi_{ep}^{2} \tag{6.44}$$

where $m_{e} = (3m'_{ij}m'_{ij}/2)^{1/2}$ is equivalent couple stress, $\chi_{ep} = (2\chi_{ij}^{p}\chi_{ij}^{p}/3)^{1/2}$

is equivalent plastic curvature and m'_{ij} is deviatoric couple stress.

The incremental version of Eq. (6. 43) is

$$
\begin{cases}
\dot{\sigma}_{ij} = \dfrac{2\Sigma_e}{3E_{ep}}\dot{\varepsilon}^P_{ij} + \dfrac{2\dot{\Sigma}_e}{3E_{ep}}\varepsilon^P_{ij} - \dfrac{2\Sigma_e}{3E^2_{ep}}\dot{E}_{ep}\varepsilon^P_{ij} + \delta_{ij}K\dot{\varepsilon}_{kk} \\[4mm]
l^{-1}_{cs}\dot{m}_{ij} = \dfrac{2\Sigma_e}{3E_{ep}}l_{cs}\dot{\chi}^P_{ij} + \dfrac{2\dot{\Sigma}_e}{3E_{ep}}l_{cs}\chi^P_{ij} - \dfrac{2\Sigma_e}{3E^2_{ep}}\dot{E}_{ep}l_{cs}\chi^P_{ij} + \delta_{ij}K_1 l_{cs}\dot{\chi}_{kk}
\end{cases}
$$

$$(\Sigma_e > \sigma_0)\ (6.45)$$

Eq. (6. 42) and (6. 45) are similar to the constitutive equations of general couple stress theory. However, the plastic curl theory is distinguished from general couple stress theory by its formulation of instantaneously tangent modulus.

The hardening law in the theory of conventional plasticity is

$$\sigma_e = \sigma_0 A(\varepsilon_{ep}) \quad \text{or} \quad \dot{\sigma}_e = \sigma_0 A'(\varepsilon_{ep})\dot{\varepsilon}_{ep} \tag{6.46}$$

where $\sigma_0 A'(E_{ep})$ is the instantaneously tangent modulus in the theory of conventional plasticity. Similarly, the hardening law in general couple stress theory is

$$\Sigma_e = \sigma_0 A'(E_{ep}) \quad \text{or} \quad \dot{\Sigma}_e = \sigma_0 A'(E_{ep})\dot{E}_{ep} \tag{6.47}$$

where $\sigma_0 A'(E_{ep})$ is the instantaneously tangent modulus in general couple stress theory.

The incremental version of hardening law in plastic strain curl theory is different from Eq. (5. 47), i.e.

$$\dot{\Sigma}_e = \sigma_0 H(E_{ep}, l_1\eta_{ep})\dot{E}_{ep} = \sigma_0 A'(E_{ep})R(E_{ep}, l_1\eta_{ep})\dot{E}_{ep}$$

$$(6.48)$$

where $\sigma_0 H(E_{ep}, l_1\eta_{ep})$ is the instantaneously tangent modulus in plastic strain curl theory. Since the plastic strain curl take a negligible effect at the macro scale, the value of $R(E_{ep}, l_1\eta_{ep})$ should be 1 when the characterized scale of plastic deformation zone is far greater than l_1. Hinted by the proposal of Chen and Wang (2000, 2001 and 2002), the expression of coefficient $R(E_{ep}, l_1\eta_{ep})$ is

$$R(E_{ep}, l_1\eta_{ep}) = \sqrt{1 + \frac{l_1\eta_{ep}}{E_{ep}}} \qquad (6.49)$$

where η_{ep} is a measure of both the plastic strain curl and the plastic curvature tensor, i.e.

$$\eta_{ep} = \eta_{ep}(\xi_{ij}^P \xi_{ij}^P, \; \xi_{ij}^P \xi_{ji}^P, \; \chi_{ij}^P \chi_{ij}^P, \; \chi_{ij}^P \chi_{ji}^P, \; \chi_{kk}^P) \qquad (6.50a)$$

where $\xi^P = \text{rot } \varepsilon^P$ is the plastic strain curl tensor. Since the effect of plastic curvature tensor can be described by introducing the couple stress, η_{ep} can be rewritten as a function of plastic strain curl only, i.e.

$$\eta_{ep} = \sqrt{\xi_{ij}^P \xi_{ij}^P + c\,\xi_{ij}^P \xi_{ji}^P} \qquad (6.50b)$$

where c is a dimensionless constant.

It is clear that coefficient $R(E_{ep}, l_1\eta_{ep})$ manifests the influence of plastic strain curl (or, in other words, the dislocation density) on the instantaneously tangent modulus. This is one of the key characters of plastic strain curl theory. As another important character, since the existence of coefficient $R(E_{ep}, l_1\eta_{ep})$, generalized equivalent stress Σ_e is no longer a single-variable function of generalized equivalent plastic strain E_{ep} and strain energy density w is no longer determined by strain $\boldsymbol{\varepsilon}$ and curvature tensor $\boldsymbol{\chi}$ only. Both the generalized equivalent stress Σ_e and the strain energy density w depend on the loading history.

An exponent law of hardening is employed in the present work. The expression of work hardening function $A(\varepsilon_{ep})$ is

$$A(\varepsilon_{ep}) = \left(1 + \frac{\varepsilon_{ep}}{\varepsilon_0}\right)^n \qquad (6.51)$$

where n is hardening exponent, ε_0 is a reference strain and it is taken as the equivalent strain at which the material yields, i.e.

$$\varepsilon_0 = \frac{\sigma_0}{3\mu} \qquad (6.52)$$

After a laborious deduction, Eq. (6. 45) can be rewritten as another form. Then the complete constitutive equations of plastic strain curl theory, with both the elastic and plastic ranges, can be written as

$$
\begin{cases}
\dot{\sigma}_{ij} = \left[2\mu\delta_{ik}\delta_{jl} + \left(K - \frac{2\mu}{3} \right)\delta_{ij}\delta_{kl} \right]\dot{\epsilon}_{kl} \\
l_{cs}^{-1}\dot{m}_{ij} = \left[2\mu\delta_{ik}\delta_{jl} + \left(K_1 - \frac{2\mu}{3} \right)\delta_{ij}\delta_{kl} \right]l_{cs}\dot{\chi}_{kl} \quad (\Sigma_e < \sigma_0)
\end{cases}
$$

(6. 53a)

$$
\begin{cases}
\dot{\sigma}_{ij} = D^{(1)}_{ijkl}\dot{\epsilon}_{kl} + D^{(2)}_{ijkl}l_{cs}\dot{\chi}_{kl} \\
l_{cs}^{-1}\dot{m}_{ij} = D^{(2)}_{klij}\dot{\epsilon}_{kl} + D^{(3)}_{ijkl}l_{cs}\dot{\chi}_{kl}
\end{cases}
\quad (\Sigma_e \geqslant \sigma_0) \qquad (6. 53b)
$$

where

$$
D^{(1)}_{ijkl} = C_1\delta_{ik}\delta_{jl} + \left(K - \frac{C_1}{3} \right)\delta_{ij}\delta_{kl} + C_2\frac{\epsilon^P_{ij}\epsilon^P_{kl}}{E^2_{ep}} \qquad (6. 54a)
$$

$$
D^{(2)}_{ijkl} = C_2\frac{l_{cs}\epsilon^P_{ij}\chi^P_{kl}}{E^2_{ep}} \qquad (6. 54b)
$$

$$
D^{(3)}_{ijkl} = C_1\delta_{ik}\delta_{jl} + \left(K_1 - \frac{C_1}{3} \right)\delta_{ij}\delta_{kl} + C_2\frac{l^2_{cs}\chi^P_{ij}\chi^P_{kl}}{E^2_{ep}} \qquad (6. 54c)
$$

$$
C_1 = \frac{2\mu B_1}{2\mu + B_1} \qquad (6. 55a)
$$

$$
C_2 \doteq \frac{4\mu^2 B_2 E^2_{ep}}{(2\mu + B_1)(2\mu + B^*)} \qquad (6. 55b)
$$

$$
B^* = B_1 + B_2(I_1 + I_2) \qquad (6. 56)
$$

$$
B_1 = \frac{2\Sigma_e}{3E_{ep}} \qquad (6. 57a)
$$

$$
B_2 = \frac{4}{9E^2_{ep}}\left[\sigma_0 H(E_{ep}, l_1\eta_{ep}) - \frac{\Sigma_e}{E_{ep}} \right] \qquad (6. 57b)
$$

$$
I_1 = \epsilon^P_{ij}\epsilon^P_{ij}, \quad I_2 = l^2_{cs}\chi^P_{ij}\chi^P_{ij} \qquad (6. 58)
$$

Furthermore, based on the generalized normal law, one can obtain

$$\frac{\varepsilon^P_{ij}}{E_{ep}} = \frac{3s_{ij}}{2\Sigma_e} \qquad \frac{l_{cs}\chi^P_{ij}}{E_{ep}} = \frac{3l^{-1}_{cs}m'_{ij}}{2\Sigma_e} \tag{6.59}$$

Therefore,

$$\frac{\varepsilon^P_{ij}\varepsilon^P_{kl}}{E^2_{ep}} = \frac{9s_{ij}s_{kl}}{4\Sigma^2_e} \qquad \frac{l_{cs}\varepsilon^P_{ij}\chi^P_{kl}}{E^2_{ep}} = \frac{9l^{-1}_{cs}s_{ij}m'_{kl}}{4\Sigma^2_e} \qquad \frac{l^2_{cs}\chi^P_{ij}\chi^P_{kl}}{E^2_{ep}} = \frac{9l^{-2}_{cs}m'_{ij}m'_{kl}}{4\Sigma^2_e}$$

Using above equations, the Eq. (6.54) can be rewritten as

$$D^{(1)}_{ijkl} = C_1\delta_{ik}\delta_{jl} + \left(K - \frac{C_1}{3}\right)\delta_{ij}\delta_{kl} + C_2\frac{9s_{ij}s_{kl}}{4\Sigma^2_e} \tag{6.60a}$$

$$D^{(2)}_{ijkl} = C_2\frac{9l^{-1}_{cs}s_{ij}m'_{kl}}{4\Sigma^2_e} \tag{6.60b}$$

$$D^{(3)}_{ijkl} = C_1\delta_{ik}\delta_{jl} + \left(K_1 - \frac{C_1}{3}\right)\delta_{ij}\delta_{kl} + C_2\frac{9l^{-2}_{cs}m'_{ij}m'_{kl}}{4\Sigma^2_e} \tag{6.60c}$$

It should be emphasized that the stiffness coefficients introduced in Eq. (6.54) will not take the value of infinity when generalized equivalent plastic strain E_{ep} approaches to zero. In fact, substitute Eq. (6.57a) into Eq. (6.55a), the expression of coefficient C_1 takes the form

$$C_1 = \frac{2\mu\dfrac{2\Sigma_e}{3E_{ep}}}{2\mu + \dfrac{2\Sigma_e}{3E_{ep}}} = \frac{2\mu\Sigma_e}{3\mu E_{ep} + \Sigma_e} \tag{6.61}$$

It is evident that the value of C_1 will be 2μ when generalized equivalent plastic strain E_{ep} equals zero. Then substitute Eqs. (6.56) – (6.58) into Eq. (6.55b), one gets

$$C_2 = \frac{4\mu^2\dfrac{4}{9}\left(\sigma_0 A'(E_{ep})R(E_{ep},\ l_1\eta_{ep}) - \dfrac{\Sigma_e}{E_{ep}}\right)}{\left(2\mu + \dfrac{2\Sigma_e}{3E_{ep}}\right)\left[2\mu + \dfrac{2\Sigma_e}{3E_{ep}} + \dfrac{2}{3}\left(\sigma_0 A'(E_{ep})R(E_{ep},\ l_1\eta_{ep}) - \dfrac{\Sigma_e}{E_{ep}}\right)\right]} \tag{6.62}$$

Furthermore the coefficient C_2 can be rewritten as

$$C_2 = \frac{4\mu^2 \left[\sigma_0 A'(E_{ep}) E_{ep} - \dfrac{\Sigma_e}{R(E_{ep}, l_1 \eta_{ep})} \right]}{(3\mu E_{ep} + \Sigma_e) \left[\dfrac{3\mu}{R(E_{ep}, l_1 \eta_{ep})} + \sigma_0 A'(E_{ep}) \right]} \quad (6.63)$$

When E_{ep} equals zero, it can be seen from Eq. (6.49) and (6.51) that $A'(E_{ep}) = n/\varepsilon_0$ and $1/R(E_{ep}, l_1 \eta_{ep}) = 0$, hence the value of C_2 will be zero.

6.3　Finite element simulation of micro-indentation tests

The principle of virtual work is

$$\int_V (\sigma_{ij}\delta\varepsilon_{ij} + m_{ij}\delta\chi_{ij}) dV - \int_S (t_i\delta u_i + q_i\delta\omega_i) dS = 0 \quad (6.64)$$

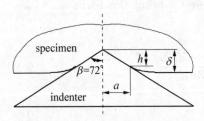

Figure 6.5　Calculation model for microindentation test.

A stiff conical indenter is employed in the calculation so the simulation of microindentation can be simplified as an axisymmetric problem, as shown in Figure 6.5. Then the non-vanishing displacement and micro rotation components are

$$u_r = u_r(r, z), \ u_z = u_z(r, z), \ \omega_\theta = \omega_\theta(r, z) \quad (6.65)$$

The indenter is supposed to be frictionless and the nodes in the contact region are constrained to fall on the indenter, with freedom to slide up and down the face of indenter. Therefore, for small strain theory and shallow indenter considered here, only u_z is prescribed and no restriction is assigned to u_r (Begley and Hutchinson, 1998). Hence, the following boundary conditions in the contact region are imposed

$$u_z(r) = \delta - \frac{r}{\tan \beta} \text{ and no restriction on } u_r \qquad (6.66)$$

where δ is the penetrating depth of the indenter and β is the half-angle of the indenter.

A nine-noded isoparametric element is chosen and each node has three degrees of freedom. The indented solid in Figure 6.5 is divided into 600 elements with 2601 nodes in total.

During the calculation, the z-displacement of indenter tip δ is prescribed in each loading increment and then $u_z(r)$, the z-displacements of nodes in contact region, are calculated. If $u_z(r)$ of a certain node on the surface of the solid is greater than the value described in Eq. (6.66), the calculation will enter the next increment. If it is equal to that value, the z-displacement of that node will be prescribed in the next increment. If it is smaller, the incremental value of δ will be reduced and the calculation will be restarted from the previous increment.

First two samples of Copper investigated by McElhaney et al. (1998) are chosen. One sample was strain-hardened and another had been annealed. The strain-hardened sample was polycrystalline with a grain size that was large compared to the size of the indentation depth. The annealed sample was a single crystal Copper with the (111) orientation. The material parameters are Young's modulus $E = 109.2$ GPa, Poisson's ratio $\nu = 0.3$, work hardening exponent $n = 0.3$ (Fleck et al., 1994), dimensionless constant c is taken to be zero. Yield stress $\sigma_0 = 73.8$ MPa and macroscopic hardness $H_0 = 834$ MPa for polycrystalline copper while $\sigma_0 = 38.5$ MPa and $H_0 = 581$ MPa for single crystal copper (McElhaney et al., 1998). The simulation results are shown in Figures 6.6 and 6.7, respectively. The FEM results based on the plastic strain curl theory simulate the experimental data successfully. A linear law is shown between the squared hardness H^2 and the inverse of indentation depth $1/h$. When the indentation depth h is large enough, the value of hardness

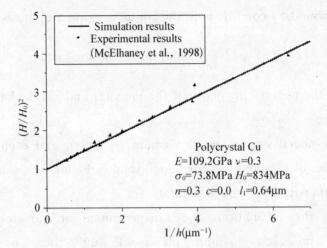

Figure 6.6　Simulation of the microindentation test on polycrystalline copper.

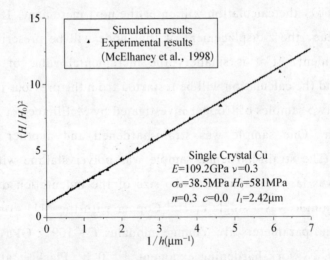

Figure 6.7　Simulation of the microindentation test on single crystal copper.

H approaches the macroscopic hardness H_0. The hardness increases as the indentation depth decreases. The slope of the polycrystalline Copper curve is about 7.36 while the other is about 6.86, i.e. the former is only slightly higher than the latter. However, the fitting value of material length l_1 is 0.64 μm for polycrystalline copper while 2.42 μm for single crystal copper. The obvious difference of the fitting values of material length l_1 may be caused by the different microstructures of the two types of material. The grain boundaries divided the polycrystalline body into a large amount of grains. The plastic deformations in the grains introduce a great deal of geometrically necessary dislocation accumulated near the grain boundaries. This means that the geometrically necessary dislocations are easier to be stored in the polycrystalline materials than in the single crystal materials. Therefore, a relatively smaller material length l_1 is needed for the polycrystalline materials to get the same effect of stress elevation as the single crystal materials. In another hand, the characteristic scale of a polycrystalline material is its grain size, i.e. about several μm. When the size of the nonuniform plastic deformation zone is of the order or smaller than the grain size, the material shows strong size effect. When the size of the non-uniform plastic deformation zone is much larger than the grain size, the size effect is not so evident. For the single crystal materials, however, such a characteristic size should be larger, although its physical background is still not so clear. It should be emphasized that when the total elements in the finite element simulation are doubled, the fitting values are the same. Therefore, we may draw a conclusion that our calculation results are available, which are independent of mesh chosen.

Second, the microindentation test of single crystal tungsten (Stelmashenko et al., 1993) is simulated. The material parameters are $E = 410$ GPa, $\nu = 0.278$, $\sigma_0 = 410$ MPa, $H_0 = 3\,160$ MPa (Stelmashenko et al., 1993), $n = 0.245$ and $c = 0$. The value of hardening exponent n is obtained by fitting the value of H_0. The results are shown in Figures 6.8 – 6.10. The numbers in parentheses represent the orientation of crystallographic plane onto which the indenter is pressed. The numbers in brackets represent the diagonal orientation of the Vickers' indenter. It can be seen that the fitting values of the length scales are quite different in case of different crystalline orientations, which show the anisotropy of single crystal. The FEM results based on the plastic strain curl theory simulate the experimental data successfully. The similar linear laws as the Copper samples are shown between the squared hardness H^2 and the inverse of the contacting depth $1/h$. It can be seen that the line slopes in Figures 6. 8 – 6. 10 are about 0. 269, 0. 263 and 0. 287, respectively, i. e. the values are very close to each other. The observation of line slope

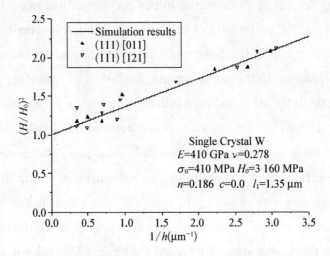

Figure 6. 8   Simulation of the microindentation test on single crystal tungsten, (111) plane is indented.

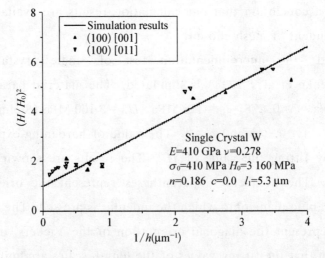

Figure 6. 9   Simulation of the microindentation test on single crystal tungsten, (100) plane is indented.

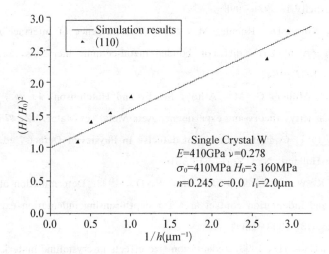

Figure 6. 10   Simulation of the microindentation test
on single crystal tungsten, (110) plane is indented.

seems to imply that the relation between the squared hardness H^2 and the
inverse of the contacting depth $1/h$ has no dependence on the factors such
as the grain size, the crystalline orientation, and so on. The fitting values
of the length scales are quite different in case of different crystalline
orientations. This phenomenon shows the anisotropy of a single crystal.
Hence, a more accurate study should be based on a theory of anisotropy
plasticity.

References

Ashby, M. F., 1970. The deformation of plastically non-homogeneous alloys.
Philosophical Magazine 21, 399.

Begley, M. R., Hutchinson, J. W., 1998. The mechanics of size-dependent indentation.
J. Mech. Phys. Solids 46, 2049 – 2068.

Chen, S. H., Wang, T. C., 2000. A new hardening law for strain gradient plasticity.
Acta Mater. 48, 3997 – 4005.

Chen, S. H., Wang, T. C., 2001. Strain gradient theory with couple-stress for
crystalline solids. Eur. J. Mech. A / Solids 20, 739 – 756.

Chen, S. H., Wang, T. C., 2002. A new deformation theory for strain gradient effects.

Int. J. Plasticity 18, 971 – 995.

Elssner, G. , Korn, D. , Ruehle, M. , 1994. The influence of interface impurities on fracture energy of UHV diffusion bonded metal-ceramic bicrystals, Scripta Metall. Mater. 31, 1037 – 1042.

Fleck, N. A. , Muller, G. M. , Ashby, M. F. and Hutchinson, J. W. , 1994. Strain gradient plasticity: theory and experiment. Acta Metal. et Mater. 42, 475 – 487.

Kröner, E. , 1981. Continuum theory of defects. In Physics of Defects, ed. Balian R et al. , North-Holland, New York: 219 – 316.

McElhaney, K. W. , Vlassak, J. J. , Nix, W. D. , 1998. Determination of indenter tip geometry and indentation contact area for depth-sensing indentation experiments. J. Mater. Res. 13, 1300 – 1306.

Nix, W. D. , Gao, H. , 1998. Indentation size effects in crystalline materials: a law for strain gradient plasticity. J. Mech. Phys. Solids 46, 411 – 425.

Stelmashenko, N. A. , Walls, M. G. , Brown, L. M. , Milman, Y. V. , 1993. Microindentation on W and Mo oriented single crystals: an STM study. Acta Metall. Mater. 41, 2855 – 2865.

Xia, S. , Wang, T. C. , 2004. Plastic strain curl theory. Acta Mech. , 172, 46 – 63.

7 Strain gradient theory based on energy non-local model

The classical elasticity and plasticity theories follow a local assumption that the stress at a given material point is determined only by the strain, the history of deformation and temperature at that point. The first gradient of the displacement field and Cauchy stress tensor are treated as the constitutive variables. However, in practice, both the nature materials and man-made materials have complicated internal structures and the size ranges over many orders of magnitude. When the macroscopic characteristic length of the material is much larger than the internal characteristic length, the material can be treated as a simple material and the classical theories are adequate to describe the mechanics properties. Otherwise, the model needs to be enriched so as to capture the real processes more adequately and it is often more effective to use various forms of generalized continuum formulations (non-local models), dealing with materials that are non-simple or polar, or both. Many attempts on this subject have been done, which can be classified into three families according to Bazant and Jirasek (2002): The first one is the micropolar continuum model proposed first by Cosserat and Cosserat (1909), which is developed by many researchers into couple-stress theory, theory of elasticity with micro-structure, micropolar theory et al.

(for examples, Mindlin and Tiersten, 1962; Toupin, 1962; Koiter, 1964; Mindlin, 1964; Eringen 1964); The second one is the gradient theories, in which the displacement field is the only independent kinematic field, but the gradients of strain are incorporated into the constitutive equations (For examples, Fleck and Hutchinson, 1993, 1997; Gao et al., 1999; Chen and Wang, 2000, 2002; Hwang et al., 2002); The third one consists of non-local models of the integral type, which is also called strongly non-local model (Geers et al., 2001).

Recent years, many experiments have shown that materials display strong size effects when the characteristic length scale associated with non-uniform plastic deformation is on the order of microns. The classical plasticity theories can not predict this size dependence of material behavior at the micron scale because their constitutive models possess no internal length scale.

In order to explain the size effect, developing a non-local generalized continuum theory for micron level is needed. According to the classification in Bažant and Jirasek (2002), the non-local theories can be categorized into strongly non-local theories and weakly non-local theories. In the weakly non-local theories, the strain gradient and intrinsic length are introduced in the constitutive relations, such as the theories proposed by Fleck and Hutchinson (1993, 1997), Gao et al. (1999), Chen and Wang (2000, 2002) and Hwang et al. (2002) among others.

Generally speaking, the strongly non-local integral approach is constructed in the basis of replying a certain variable by its non-local counterpart obtained by weighted averaging over a spatial neighborhood of each point under consideration. If $f(x)$ is some local field in a solid body occupying a domain V, the corresponding non-local field, labeled by an overbar, is defined by

$$\bar{f}(x) = \int_V \alpha(x, x')f(x')dx' \tag{7.1}$$

where $\alpha(x, x')$ is a non-local weight function, which depends usually on the distance between points x and x', $\alpha(x, x') = \alpha(|x' - x|)$.

7.1   Classical non-local theory of elasticity

Non-local elasticity theory were proposed and refined by Rogua (1965), Eringen (1966), Kroner (1966), Edelen (1969) among others. A simplified non-local theory of elasticity, which can be used for the practical application contains only the non-local constitutive equation, while the equilibrium and kinematical equations and the corresponding boundary condition retain their standard forms:

Equilibrium equation

$$\sigma_{ij,i} = 0 \quad \text{in } V \tag{7.2}$$

Kinematic equation

$$\varepsilon_{ij} = \frac{1}{2}(\partial_i u_j + \partial_j u_i) \quad \text{in } V \tag{7.3}$$

Boundary condition

$$p_i = \sigma_{ij} n_j = \overline{p}_i \quad \text{on} \quad S \tag{7.4}$$

The non-local constitutive equation for linear, homogenous and isotropic elastic solids is given by an integral formula

$$\sigma_{ij}(x) = \int_V \alpha(|x' - x|)\{\lambda\varepsilon_{kk}(x')\delta_{ij} + 2\mu\varepsilon_{ij}(x')\}dx' \tag{7.5}$$

where V is the volume occupied by the body, α is an attenuation function. Then the stress σ_{ij} at the point x depends on the strains $\varepsilon_{kl}(x')$ at all points x' in the volume V. Hence the stress σ_{ij} is a non-local quantity. Eq.(7.5) can be rewritten as

$$\sigma_{ij}(\boldsymbol{x}) = \int_V \alpha(\boldsymbol{x}' - \boldsymbol{x}) t_{ij} \mathrm{d}\boldsymbol{x}'$$

$$t_{ij}(\boldsymbol{x}') = \lambda \varepsilon_{kk}(\boldsymbol{x}') \delta_{ij} + 2\mu\varepsilon_{ij}(\boldsymbol{x}') \tag{7.6}$$

where t_{ij} is the conventional local stress.

For the infinite body, the attenuation function α satisfies the normalizing condition

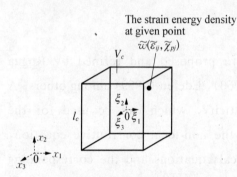

The strain energy density at given point $\widetilde{w}(\widetilde{\varepsilon}_{ij}, \widetilde{\chi}_{pij})$

$$\int_V \alpha(|\xi|) \mathrm{d}\xi = 1 \tag{7.7}$$

Figure 7.1 The representative volume element.

For a finite cubic body V_c and homogeneous material as shown in Figure 7.1, we can take the weight function $\alpha(|\boldsymbol{x}' - \boldsymbol{x}|) = 1/V_c$ and assume $\widetilde{\varepsilon}_{ij} = \varepsilon_{ij} + \varepsilon_{ij,k}\xi_k$, then we can find that the first order gradient of strain tensor, $\varepsilon_{ij,k}$, has no contributions to the stress tensor and as a result, the strain gradient theory can not be derived from the non-local model of this type. On the other hand, the non-local model of this type (as shown in the Eq. (7.5) for the non-local elasticity) provides only the stress tensor and does not provide any formula for the high order stress tensor.

7.2 A new framework of non-local theory

In order to derive the strain gradient theory primitively from a non-local model, Yi, Wang and Chen(2008)proposed a new non-local theory. The global strain energy density of the representative volume element is taken as a non-local variable as shown in Figure 7.1, i.e.,

$$w = \frac{1}{V_c} \int_{V_c} \tilde{w}(\mathbf{x} + \xi) dV_c \qquad (7.8)$$

where V_c is the volume of a representative cubic element with each boundary length l_c, ξ is the local coordinate as shown in Figure 7.1, with the original point at the center of cubic volume. $\mathbf{x}$ is the global coordinate, w is the global strain energy density and $\tilde{w}(\mathbf{x} + \xi)$ is the local one. The integral in the Eq. (7.8) is carried out for the local coordinate ξ.

7.2.1 Constitutive equation of a new non-local theory

Constructing the constitutive equation for a composite or a heterogeneous material in the mesoscale, one should consider a cell model for a representative volume element of the materials, which can capture the essential features of the internal structures of the materials. If the length scale of the cell model is much smaller than the characteristic scale of the macroscopic material, the conventional continuum description is adequate and the effect of microstructure details on the macroscopic constitutive equation could be neglected since the macroscopic material element contains numerous cells with different internal structures of the materials and the statistical average will give a unified (equilibrium state) macroscopic constitutive equation.

Figure 7.2 shows an axisymmetric cell model for a two phase composite. The cylindrical cell models for an elastic-plastic matrix reinforced by an elastic spherical particle or cylindrical fiber are depicted in Figure 7.2 (a) and Figure 7.2 (b), respectively. Both the matrix and particles or fibers are assumed to be isotropic, but the cell model of the materials is anisotropic.

The energy density for a two phase composite can be expressed as

$$w = \frac{1}{V_c} \int_{V_c} \tilde{w}(\mathbf{x} + \xi) dV = \frac{1}{V_c} \int_{V_M} \tilde{w}_M(\mathbf{x} + \xi) dV + \frac{1}{V_c} \int_{V_r} \tilde{w}_r(\mathbf{x} + \xi) dV$$

$$(7.9)$$

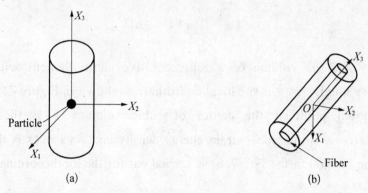

(a)   (b)

Figure 7.2 (a) the cylindrical cell model for an elastic plastic
matrix reinforced by an elastic spherical particle. (b) the
cylindrical cell model for an elastic plastic matrix reinforced by a
cylindrical fiber.

where $\tilde{w}_M$ is the local energy density for matrix phase, and $\tilde{w}_r$ is the local
energy density for reinforcement phase. For the elastic reinforcement
phase $\tilde{w}_r$ is given by

$$\tilde{w}_r = \frac{1}{2} k \, \tilde{\varepsilon}_v^2 + \mu \, \tilde{\varepsilon}_{eq}^2 \qquad (7.10)$$

where the volume strain $\tilde{\varepsilon}_v = \tilde{\varepsilon}_{11} + \tilde{\varepsilon}_{22} + \tilde{\varepsilon}_{33}$ and $\tilde{\varepsilon}_{eq}$ is effective strain

$$\tilde{\varepsilon}_{eq} = \left(\frac{2}{3} \tilde{\varepsilon}_d : \tilde{\varepsilon}_d \right)^{\frac{1}{2}} \qquad (7.11)$$

here $\tilde{\varepsilon}_d$ is the deviatoric strain.

For an elastic-plastic power law hardening matrix, $\tilde{w}_M$ takes
the form

$$\tilde{w}_M = \frac{\sigma_0 \varepsilon_0}{n+1} \left(\frac{\tilde{\varepsilon}_{eq}}{\varepsilon_0} \right)^{n+1} + \frac{1}{2} K \tilde{\varepsilon}_v^2 \quad (7.12)$$

where ε_0 denotes a reference strain and n is the
strain hardening exponent.

Figure 7.3 is a sketch of a cell model for
multiphase composite or general heterogeneous
material such as granule material and geophysical
material among others. The energy density w has

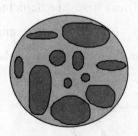

Figure 7.3   The
cell model for multi-
phase composite.

shown in Eq. (7.8). General speaking, the distribution of the material constituents in the volume V_c is random, hence one need to choose enough samples of different representative volumes to describe statistically the constitutive behaviors of the material in the mesoscale.

Since the plastic deformation of the matrix around the particles or fibers is non-uniform for the composite, the effect of rotation gradient on the constitutive behavior is quite strong, hence the local energy density in the matrix should takes account the effect of the rotation gradient.

Instead of Eq. (7.12), one need use the following equation

$$\tilde{w}_M = \frac{\sigma_Y \varepsilon_Y}{1+n} \left(\frac{\tilde{E}_e}{\varepsilon_Y}\right)^{n+1} + \frac{1}{2} K \tilde{\varepsilon}_v^2 \tag{7.13}$$

where $K = \dfrac{E}{3(1-2v)}$, $\tilde{E}_e$ is the local generalized effective strain and

$$\tilde{E}_e^2 = \frac{2}{3} \tilde{\varepsilon}'_{ij} \tilde{\varepsilon}'_{ij} + l_{cs}^2 \tilde{\chi}_e^2 \quad \tilde{\chi}_e^2 = \frac{2}{3} \tilde{\chi}_{ij} \tilde{\chi}_{ij} \tag{7.14}$$

here E is Young's module, v is Poisson ratio, l_{cs} is the intrinsic length for rotation gradient, $\tilde{\varepsilon}'_{ij}$ is the deviatoric strain. The equations (7.13) and (7.14) are also used for the heterogeneous material.

Eq. (7.8) shows clearly that the energy density w is a non-local variable. The first variation of the global strain energy density w can be written as

$$\delta w = \frac{1}{V_c} \int_{V_c} \delta \tilde{w}(x, \xi) dV_c$$

$$= \frac{1}{V_c} \int_{V_c} [\tilde{\sigma}_{ij}(x + \xi) \delta \tilde{\varepsilon}_{ij}(x + \xi) + \tilde{m}_{ij}(x + \xi) \delta \tilde{\chi}_{ij}(x + \xi)] dV_c$$

$$\tag{7.15}$$

where $\tilde{\varepsilon}_{ij}$ is the local strain, $\tilde{\chi}_{ij}$ is the local rotation gradient, $\tilde{\sigma}_{ij}$ is the local stress tensor, $\tilde{m}_{ji}$ is the local couple stress.

For homogeneous materials, it is reasonable to take the value of l_c in a range of sub-micrometers to micro-meters. For composites, l_c should be the length scale of a representative volume cell, which is often used to describe the characters of composites in composite mechanics. For a proper value of l_c, we have

$$\tilde{\varepsilon}_{ij} = \varepsilon_{ij} + \varepsilon_{ij,k}\,\xi_k, \quad \tilde{\chi}_{pj} = \chi_{pj} = e_{pki}\varepsilon_{ij,k} \tag{7.16}$$

where ε_{ij} and $\varepsilon_{ij,k}$ are the global strain and the global strain gradient respectively.

Substituting Eq. (7.16) into Eq. (7.15) yields

$$\delta w = \frac{1}{V_c}\int_{V_c}\tilde{\sigma}_{ij}(x+\xi)\delta\varepsilon_{ij}(x)\mathrm{d}V_c + \frac{1}{V_c}\int_{V_c}\tilde{\sigma}_{ij}(x+\xi)\delta\varepsilon_{ij,k}(x)\xi_k\,\mathrm{d}V_c$$

$$+ \frac{1}{V_c}\int_{V_c}\tilde{m}_{pj}(x+\xi)e_{pki}\delta\varepsilon_{ij,k}(x)\mathrm{d}V_c = \sigma_{ij}\delta\varepsilon_{ij} + \hat{\tau}_{ijk}\delta\varepsilon_{ij,k}$$

$$\tag{7.17}$$

where σ_{ij} and $\hat{\tau}_{ijk}$ are stresses and high order stresses, respectively,

$$\sigma_{ij} = \frac{\partial w}{\partial\varepsilon_{ij}}, \quad \hat{\tau}_{ijk} = \frac{\partial w}{\partial\varepsilon_{ij,k}} \tag{7.18}$$

$\hat{\tau}_{ijk}$ consists of a symmetric part τ_{ijk} and an asymmetric one τ_{ijk}^A,

$$\tau_{ijk} = \frac{1}{2}\left(\frac{\partial w}{\partial\varepsilon_{ij,k}} + \frac{\partial w}{\partial\varepsilon_{ji,k}}\right), \quad \tau_{ijk}^A = \frac{1}{2}\left(\frac{\partial w}{\partial\varepsilon_{ij,k}} - \frac{\partial w}{\partial\varepsilon_{ji,k}}\right) \tag{7.19}$$

Noting $\tau_{ijk}^A\delta\varepsilon_{ij,k} = 0$, Eq. (7.17) can be written as

$$\delta w = \sigma_{ij}\delta\varepsilon_{ij} + \hat{\tau}_{ijk}\delta\varepsilon_{ij,k} = \sigma_{ij}\delta\varepsilon_{ij} + \tau_{ijk}\delta\varepsilon_{ij,k} \tag{7.20}$$

Then, the stress σ_{ij} and high order stress τ_{ijk} can be expressed as

$$\sigma_{ij} = \frac{\partial w}{\partial\varepsilon_{ij}} = \frac{1}{V_c}\int_{V_c}\tilde{\sigma}_{ij}(x+\xi)\mathrm{d}V_c \tag{7.21}$$

$$\tau_{ijk} = \frac{1}{2}\left(\frac{\partial w}{\partial\varepsilon_{ij,k}} + \frac{\partial w}{\partial\varepsilon_{ji,k}}\right)$$

$$= \frac{1}{V_c}\int_{V_c}\left\{\tilde{\sigma}_{ij}(x+\xi)\xi_k + \frac{1}{2}\left[\tilde{m}_{pj}(x+\xi)e_{pki} + \tilde{m}_{pi}(x+\xi)e_{pkj}\right]\right\}\mathrm{d}V_c$$

$$\tag{7.22}$$

7.2.2 Equilibrium equations and boundary conditions

Total potential energy Π can be written as

$$\Pi = \int_V w \, \mathrm{d}V - \int_V f_i u_i \, \mathrm{d}V - \int_S \overline{p}_i u_i \, \mathrm{d}S - \int_S \overline{r}_i \mathrm{D} u_i \, \mathrm{d}S \qquad (7.23)$$

where V is the volume occupied by the body, S is the boundary of V, f_i is the force per unit volume, u_i is the displacement, D is defined in the following Eq. (7.27), $\overline{p}_i$ is the surface traction and $\overline{r}_i$ is the high order surface traction.

The variation of the total potential energy is

$$\delta\Pi = \int_V \delta w \, \mathrm{d}V - \int_V f_i \delta u_i \, \mathrm{d}V - \int_S \overline{p}_i \delta u_i \, \mathrm{d}S - \int_S \overline{r}_i \mathrm{D}\delta u_i \, \mathrm{d}S$$

$$= \int_V (\sigma_{ij} \delta\varepsilon_{ij} + \tau_{ijk} \delta\varepsilon_{ij,k}) \mathrm{d}V - \int_V f_i \delta u_i \, \mathrm{d}V - \int_S \overline{p}_i \delta u_i \, \mathrm{d}S - \int_S \overline{r}_i \mathrm{D}\delta u_i \, \mathrm{d}S$$

$$= \int_V (\sigma_{ij} \delta\varepsilon_{ij} - \tau_{ijk,k} \delta\varepsilon_{ij} + (\tau_{ijk} \delta\varepsilon_{ij})_{,k}) \mathrm{d}V - \int_V f_i \delta u_i \, \mathrm{d}V$$

$$- \int_S \overline{p}_i \delta u_i \, \mathrm{d}S - \int_S \overline{r}_i \mathrm{D}\delta u_i \, \mathrm{d}S \qquad (7.24)$$

According to divergence theorem, Eq. (7.24) can be written as

$$\delta\Pi = - \int_V (\sigma_{ij} - \tau_{ijk,k})_{,j} \delta u_i \, \mathrm{d}V + \int_S (\sigma_{ij} - \tau_{ijk,k}) n_j \delta u_i \, \mathrm{d}S$$

$$+ \int_S \tau_{ijk} n_k \delta\varepsilon_{ij} \, \mathrm{d}S - \int_V f_i \delta u_i \, \mathrm{d}V - \int_{S_{\sigma}} \overline{p}_i \delta u_i \, \mathrm{d}S - \int_{S_{\tau}} \overline{r}_i \mathrm{D}\delta u_i \, \mathrm{d}S$$

$$(7.25)$$

The spatial gradient operator $\nabla = \{\partial_i\}$ at the boundary surface S can be decomposed into its tangential and normal components, that is

$$\left. \begin{array}{l} \nabla = \overline{\nabla} + n\mathrm{D} \\[2mm] \partial_i = \overline{\partial}_i + n_i \mathrm{D} \end{array} \right\} \qquad (7.26)$$

$$\left. \begin{array}{l} \overline{\nabla} = (I - nn) \cdot \nabla, \quad \mathrm{D} = n \cdot \nabla \\[2mm] \overline{\partial}_i = (\delta_{ij} - n_i n_j)\partial_j, \quad \mathrm{D} = n_m \partial_m \end{array} \right\} \qquad (7.27)$$

where I is the unit dyadic, n is the unit outward normal to S.

Thus we have

$$\left. \begin{array}{l} \Phi : \nabla u = \Phi : \bar{\nabla} u + n \cdot \Phi \cdot Du \\ \phi_{ij} \partial_i u_j = \phi_{ij} \bar{\partial}_i u_j + n_i \phi_{ij} Du_j \end{array} \right\} \tag{7.28}$$

where Φ is a dyadic.

Furthermore, Eq. (7.28) can be written as

$$\left. \begin{array}{l} \Phi : \nabla u = \bar{\nabla} \cdot (\Phi \cdot u) - (\bar{\nabla} \cdot \Phi) \cdot u + n \cdot \Phi \cdot Du \\ \phi_{ij} \partial_i u_j = \bar{\partial}_i (\phi_{ij} u_j) - (\bar{\partial}_i \phi_{ij}) u_j + n_i \phi_{ij} Du_j \end{array} \right\} \tag{7.29}$$

Using the surface divergence theorem (Brand, 1947) for a smooth and closed surface,

$$\left. \begin{array}{l} \displaystyle\int_S \bar{\nabla} \cdot (\Phi \cdot u) dS = \int_S (\bar{\nabla} \cdot n) n \cdot \Phi \cdot u dS \\ \displaystyle\int_S \bar{\partial}_i (\phi_{ij} u_j) dS = \int_S (\bar{\partial}_k n_k) n_i \phi_{ij} u_j dS \end{array} \right\} \tag{7.30}$$

leads to

$$\int_S \Phi : \nabla u dS = \int_S (\bar{\nabla} \cdot n) n \cdot \Phi \cdot u dS - \int_S (\bar{\nabla} \cdot \Phi) \cdot u dS$$

$$+ \int_S n \cdot \Phi \cdot Du dS$$

$$\int_S \phi_{ij} \partial_i u_j dS = \int_S (\bar{\partial}_p n_p) n_i \phi_{ij} u_j dS - \int_S (\bar{\partial}_i \phi_{ij}) u_j dS + \int_S n_i \phi_{ij} Du_j dS$$

$$\tag{7.31}$$

If $\phi_{ij} = \tau_{ijk} n_k$, then

$$\int_S \tau_{ijk} n_k \delta \varepsilon_{ij} dS = \int_S \tau_{ijk} n_k \partial_i \delta u_j dS$$

$$= \int_S (\bar{\partial}_p n_p) n_i \tau_{ijk} n_k \delta u_j dS - \int_S (\bar{\partial}_i \tau_{ijk} n_k) \delta u_j dS$$

$$+ \int_S n_i \tau_{ijk} n_k D\delta u_j dS \tag{7.32}$$

Substituting Eq. (7.32) into the third term on the right-hand of Eq. (7.25), and noting $\delta \Pi = 0$, one can obtain equilibrium equation

$$(\sigma_{ij} - \tau_{ijk,k})_{,j} + f_i = 0 \quad \text{in} \quad V \tag{7.33}$$

In addition, the traction and displacement boundary conditions can be written as

$$[\sigma_{ij} - \tau_{ijk,k} + (\overline{\partial}_p n_p) \tau_{ijk} n_k] n_j - \overline{\partial}_j \tau_{ijk} n_k - \overline{P}_i = 0$$
$$\text{on} \quad S_\sigma \tag{7.34}$$

$$n_j n_k \tau_{ijk} = \overline{r}_i \quad \text{on} \quad S_\tau \tag{7.35}$$

$$u_i = \overline{u}_i \quad \text{on} \quad S_u \tag{7.36}$$

$$D u_i = D \overline{u}_i \quad \text{on} \quad S_{Du} \tag{7.37}$$

7.3 Constitutive equations of strain gradient theory

According to Fleck and Hutchinson (1993) and Chen and Wang (2000), the local strain energy-density is assumed to be the function of a local generalized effective strain, $\tilde{E}_e$, and the local volume strain $\tilde{\varepsilon}_v$, which is equal to the volume strain at point x.

$$\tilde{w} = \int_0^{\tilde{E}_e} \Sigma_e \, d\tilde{E}_e + \frac{1}{2} K \tilde{\varepsilon}_v^2 = \int_0^{\tilde{E}_e} \sigma_Y \left(\frac{\tilde{E}_e}{\varepsilon_Y}\right)^n d\tilde{E}_e + \frac{1}{2} K \tilde{\varepsilon}_v^2$$

$$= \frac{\sigma_Y \varepsilon_Y}{1+n} \left(\frac{\tilde{E}_e}{\varepsilon_Y}\right)^{1+n} + \frac{1}{2} K \tilde{\varepsilon}_v^2 \tag{7.38}$$

The local strain energy density $\tilde{w}$ can be approximately expressed as

$$\tilde{w} = w^0 + w^0_{,k} \xi_k + \frac{w^0_{,kl}}{2} \xi_k \xi_l \quad \text{on} \quad V_c \tag{7.39}$$

where

$$w^0 = (\widetilde{w})_{\xi=0} = \frac{\sigma_Y \varepsilon_Y}{1+n} \left(\frac{E_e}{\varepsilon_Y} \right)^{1+n} + \frac{1}{2} K \varepsilon_v^2 \tag{7.40}$$

$$w^0_{,kl} = (\widetilde{w}_{,kl})_{\xi=0} = \frac{2\sigma_Y}{3(\varepsilon_Y)^n} \left[(n-1)(E_e)^{n-2} \varepsilon'_{mn} \varepsilon'_{mn,k} E_{e,l} \right.$$

$$\left. + (E_e)^{n-1} \varepsilon'_{ij,l} \varepsilon'_{ij,k} \right] + K \varepsilon_{v,l} \varepsilon_{v,k}$$

$$= \frac{2\sigma_Y}{3(\varepsilon_Y)^n} \left[\frac{2(n-1)(E_e)^{n-3} \varepsilon'_{mn} \varepsilon'_{mn,k} \varepsilon'_{ij} \varepsilon'_{ij,l}}{3} \right.$$

$$\left. + (E_e)^{n-1} \varepsilon'_{ij,l} \varepsilon'_{ij,k} \right] + K \varepsilon_{v,l} \varepsilon_{v,k} \tag{7.41}$$

Substituting Eq. (7.39) into Eq. (7.38) yields

$$w = \frac{1}{V_c} \int_{V_c} \left(w^0 + w^0_{,k} \xi_k + \frac{w^0_{,kl}}{2} \xi_k \xi_l \right) dV_c = w^0 + A_k w^0_{,k} + B_{kl} w^0_{,kl} \tag{7.42}$$

where

$$A_k = \frac{1}{V_c} \int_{V_c} \xi_k dV_c \qquad B_{kl} = \frac{1}{2V_c} \int_{V_c} \xi_k \xi_l dV_c \tag{7.43}$$

ξ_k is an anti-symmetric function in V_c about center of cubic region, then

$$A_k = 0 \qquad B_{kl} = B\delta_{kl} = \frac{1}{2V_c} \int_{V_c} (\xi_1)^2 dV_c \delta_{kl} = \frac{l_c^2}{24} \delta_{kl} \tag{7.44}$$

$$w = w^0 + B_{kl} w^0_{,kl} \tag{7.45}$$

The global stress σ_{ij} and high order stress τ_{ijk} can be written as

$$\sigma_{ij} = \frac{\partial w}{\partial \varepsilon_{ij}} = \frac{2\sigma_Y}{3(\varepsilon_Y)^n} (E_e)^{n-1} \varepsilon'_{ij} + K\varepsilon_v \delta_{ij} + \frac{2\sigma_Y}{3(\varepsilon_Y)^n} \frac{2(n-1)B}{3}$$

$$\left[\frac{2(n-3)(E_e)^{n-5} \varepsilon'_{mn} \varepsilon'_{mn,k} \varepsilon'_{pq} \varepsilon'_{pq,k}}{3} + (E_e)^{n-3} \varepsilon'_{mn,k} \varepsilon'_{mn,k} \right] \varepsilon'_{ij}$$

$$+ \frac{2\sigma_Y}{3(\varepsilon_Y)^n} \frac{2(n-1)B}{3} 2(E_e)^{n-3} \varepsilon'_{mn} \varepsilon'_{mn,k} \varepsilon'_{ij,k} \tag{7.46}$$

$$\tau_{ijk} = \frac{1}{2}\left(\frac{\partial w}{\partial \varepsilon_{ij,k}} + \frac{\partial w}{\partial \varepsilon_{ji,k}}\right) = \frac{4\sigma_Y B(E_e)^{n-1}}{3(\varepsilon_Y)^n}\varepsilon'_{ij,k}$$

$$+ \left(\frac{l_{cs}^2 \sigma_Y E_e^{n-1}}{3(\varepsilon_Y)^n} + \frac{4\sigma_Y B(n-1)(n-3)l_{cs}^2(E_e)^{n-5}\varepsilon'_{mn}\varepsilon'_{mn,k}\varepsilon'_{st}\varepsilon'_{st,k}}{27(\varepsilon_Y)^n}\right.$$

$$+ \left.\frac{2\sigma_Y B(n-1)(E_e)^{n-3}l_{cs}^2\varepsilon'_{mn,\,l}\varepsilon'_{mn,l}}{9(\varepsilon_Y)^n}\right)(e_{pki}\chi_{pj} + e_{pkj}\chi_{pi})$$

$$+ \frac{8\sigma_Y B(n-1)(\varepsilon_e)^{n-3}\varepsilon'_{ij}\varepsilon'_{mn}\varepsilon'_{mn,k}}{9(\varepsilon_Y)^n} + 2BK\varepsilon_{v,k}\delta_{ij} \qquad (7.47)$$

From above, one can see that the formula for the stresses and high order stresses in the constitutive relations of the new strain gradient theory are derived strictly from the new framework of the non-local model. The present strain gradient theory possesses obvious physical significance. Two length scales are involved, one is the length scale l_c of the representative volume element and the other is the intrinsic length scale l_{cs} related with the rotation gradient.

7.4   Thin wire torsion and ultra-thin beam bend

a) Thin wire torsion

The size effects emerging in the experiment of thin-wire torsion (Fleck et al., 1994) is analyzed using the new strain gradient theory. A Cartesian coordinate system (x_1, x_2, x_3) and a cylindrical polar coordinate system (r, θ, x_3) are introduced as shown in Figure 7.4. The radius of the wire denotes as α. κ is the twist per unit length of the wire.

The displacement fields

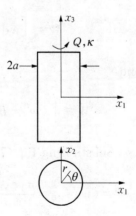

Figure   7.4
Coordinate systems
for thin wires.

$$u_1 = -\kappa x_2 x_3, \quad u_2 = \kappa x_1 x_3, \quad u_3 = 0 \qquad (7.48)$$

Lead to the non-vanishing strain components, strain gradient and rotation gradient components as

$$\varepsilon_{13} = \varepsilon_{31} = -\frac{1}{2}\kappa x_2, \quad \varepsilon_{23} = \varepsilon_{32} = \frac{1}{2}\kappa x_1 \qquad (7.49)$$

$$\varepsilon_{13,2} = \varepsilon_{31,2} = -\frac{1}{2}\kappa, \quad \varepsilon_{23,1} = \varepsilon_{32,1} = \frac{1}{2}\kappa \qquad (7.50)$$

$$\chi_{11} = \chi_{22} = -\frac{1}{2}\kappa, \quad \chi_{33} = \kappa \qquad (7.51)$$

According to Eqs. (7.49)–(7.51), we have

$$(\tilde{E}_e)_{\xi=0} = E_e = \kappa\sqrt{\frac{r^2 + 3l_{cs}^2}{3}} \qquad (7.52)$$

$$\varepsilon_{mn}\varepsilon_{mn,k} = 2\varepsilon_{13}\varepsilon_{13,k} + 2\varepsilon_{23}\varepsilon_{23,k} = \kappa(\varepsilon_{23,k}x_1 - \varepsilon_{13,k}x_2) \qquad (7.53)$$

$$\varepsilon'_{mn}\varepsilon'_{mn,k}\varepsilon'_{ij}\varepsilon'_{ij,l} = \kappa^2(\varepsilon_{23,k}x_1 - \varepsilon_{13,k}x_2)(\varepsilon_{23,l}x_1 - \varepsilon_{13,l}x_2) \qquad (7.54)$$

$$\varepsilon_{ij,l}\varepsilon_{ij,k} = 2\varepsilon_{13,l}\varepsilon_{13,k} + 2\varepsilon_{23,l}\varepsilon_{23,k} \qquad (7.55)$$

The total strain energy for a unit length of the bar is given by

$$W = \int_V w\,dV = \int_V (w^0 + B_{kl}w^0_{,kl})\,dV = \int_0^\kappa Q(\kappa)\,d\kappa \qquad (7.56)$$

and

$$W = \int_V (w^0 + B_{kl}w^0_{,kl})\,dV = \int_0^{2\pi} d\theta \int_0^a (w^0 + B_{kl}w^0_{,kl})\,r\,dr \qquad (7.57)$$

Substituting Eq. (7.52) into Eq. (7.40) yields

$$w^0 = (\tilde{w})_{\xi=0} = \frac{\sigma_Y \varepsilon_Y}{1+n}\left(\frac{E_e}{\varepsilon_Y}\right)^{1+n} = \frac{\sigma_Y}{(1+n)\varepsilon_Y^n}\left(\frac{1}{3}\right)^{\frac{1+n}{2}}\kappa^{1+n}(r^2 + 3l_{cs}^2)^{\frac{1+n}{2}}$$

$$(7.58)$$

Substituting Eqs. (7.52)–(7.55) into Eq. (7.41), we have

$$B_{kl}w^0_{,kl} = B\delta_{kl}w^0_{,kl}$$

$$= \frac{2B\sigma_Y}{3(\varepsilon_Y)^n}\left[\frac{2(n-1)(E_e)^{n-3}\varepsilon'_{mn}\varepsilon'_{mn,k}\varepsilon'_{ij}\varepsilon'_{ij,k}}{3}\right.$$

$$\left. + (E_e)^{n-1}\varepsilon'_{ij,k}\varepsilon'_{ij,k}\right]$$

$$= \frac{2B\sigma_Y}{3(\varepsilon_Y)^n}\left\{\frac{2(n-1)\left[\frac{1}{3}\kappa^2(r^2+3l_c^2)\right]^{\frac{n-3}{2}}\left(\frac{\kappa^4 r^2}{4}\right)}{3}\right.$$

$$\left. + \left[\frac{1}{3}\kappa^2(r^2+3l_c^2)\right]^{\frac{n-1}{2}}\kappa^2\right\} \tag{7.59}$$

then, it follows

$$W = \int_V (w^0 + B_{kl}w^0_{,kl})dV = \int_0^{2\pi}d\theta\int_0^a (w^0 + B_{kl}w^0_{,kl})r\,dr$$

$$= \frac{2\pi\sigma_Y}{(1+n)(3+n)\varepsilon_Y^n}\left(\frac{1}{3}\right)^{\frac{1+n}{2}}\kappa^{1+n}\left[(a^2+3l_{cs}^2)^{\frac{n+3}{2}} - (3l_{cs}^2)^{\frac{n+3}{2}}\right]$$

$$+ \frac{4\pi B\sigma_Y\kappa^{n+1}}{3^{\frac{n+1}{2}}(\varepsilon_Y)^n}\left[\frac{(a^2+3l_{cs}^2)^{\frac{n+1}{2}}}{2} - \frac{3l_{cs}^2}{2}(a^2+3l_{cs}^2)^{\frac{n-1}{2}}\right] \tag{7.60}$$

Let $\beta = \dfrac{3l_{cs}^2}{a^2}$, equation (7.60) can be rewritten as

$$W = \frac{2\pi\sigma_Y\kappa^{n+1}a^{n+3}}{3^{\frac{n+1}{2}}(1+n)(3+n)(\varepsilon_Y)^n}$$

$$\left\{\left[(1+\beta)^{\frac{n+3}{2}} - \beta^{\frac{n+3}{2}}\right] + \frac{B(1+n)(3+n)}{a^2}\left[(1+\beta)^{\frac{n+1}{2}} - \beta(1+\beta)^{\frac{n-1}{2}}\right]\right\} \tag{7.61}$$

The torque Q can be written as

$$Q = \frac{dW}{d\kappa} = \frac{(1+n)W}{\kappa} \tag{7.62}$$

Combining Eqs. (7.61) and (7.62) leads to

$$Q = \frac{2\pi\sigma_Y\kappa^n a^{n+3}}{(3+n)\varepsilon_Y^n 3^{\frac{1+n}{2}}}\left\{\left[(1+\beta)^{\frac{n+3}{2}} - \beta^{\frac{n+3}{2}}\right] + \frac{B(1+n)(3+n)}{a^2}(1+\beta)^{\frac{n-1}{2}}\right\} \tag{7.63}$$

If $l_c/a \ll 1$, hence $\beta \ll 1$, Eq. (7.63) can be simplified as

$$Q = \frac{2\pi\sigma_Y \kappa^n a^{n+3}}{(3+n)\varepsilon_Y^n 3^{\frac{1+n}{2}}} \left[(1+\beta)^{\frac{n+3}{2}} - \beta^{\frac{n+3}{2}} \right] \qquad (7.64)$$

One can interestingly see that Eq. (7.64) is identical with the result in Fleck et al. (1994). Furthermore, Eq. (7.64) can be re-written as

$$\frac{Q}{a^3} = \frac{(1+n)W}{\kappa} = \frac{2\pi\sigma_Y}{(3+n)\varepsilon_Y^n} (\kappa a)^n \left(\frac{1}{3}\right)^{\frac{1+n}{2}} \qquad (7.65)$$

Since the intrinsic lengths l_{cs} and l_c are much smaller than 170 μm, we choose the torque experiment results of the thin-wire with diameter $2a = 170 \ \mu$m as a calibration curve and obtain $\dfrac{2\pi\sigma_Y}{(3+n)\varepsilon_Y^n} \left(\dfrac{1}{3}\right)^{\frac{1+n}{2}} =$ 232.7 MPa, $n = 0.21$, which is in surprise close to the tensile experimental result given by Fleck et al. (1994), $n = 0.22$.

If we take $l_c = 0.1 \ \mu$m as suggested by Gao et al. (1999) and $l_{cs} = 3.7 \ \mu$m given by Fleck et al. (1994), the comparison of the theoretical results with the experiment ones is shown in Figure 7.5. One can clearly

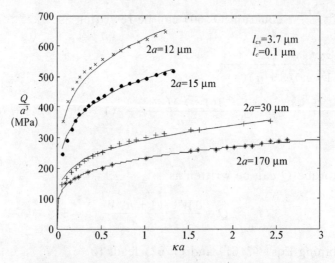

Figure 7.5   Plots of torque against the surface strain for copper wires with different diameters. The solid lines denote the theoretical calculation results (Yi, Wang and Chen, 2008) and the dotted data denote the experimental data (Fleck et al., 1994).

see that the two results are well consistent.

b) *Ultra-thin beam bend*

Now, we study the problem of Ultra-thin beam bending with different micro-meters thickness using the present strain gradient theory. The model is shown in Figure 7.6, in which (x_1, x_2, x_3) is a Cartesian coordinate system, h is the thickness of beams, b is the width and κ is the curvature.

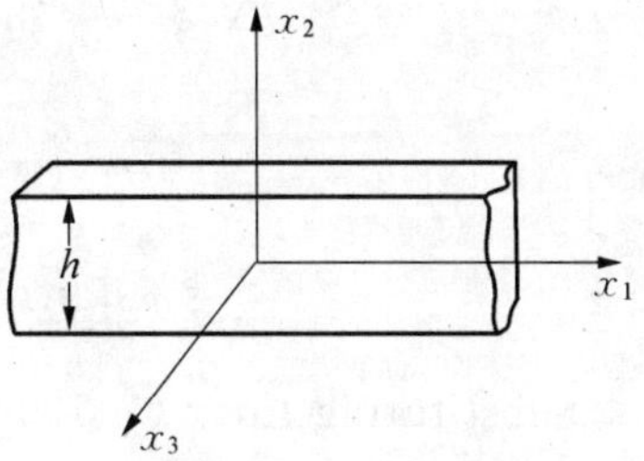

The displacement fields

$$u_1 = \kappa x_1 x_2, \quad u_2 = \kappa \frac{(x_1^2 + x_2^2)}{2}, \quad u_3 = 0 \tag{7.66}$$

Figure 7.6 Coordinate systems (x_1, x_2, x_3) on an ultra-thin beam.

Leads to the non-vanishing strain components, strain gradient and rotation gradient components as follows,

$$\varepsilon_{11} = -\varepsilon_{22} = \kappa x_2, \quad \varepsilon_{11,2} = -\varepsilon_{22,2} = \kappa, \quad \chi_{31} = -\kappa \tag{7.67}$$

Following Stölken and Evans (1998), neglecting the elastic deformation, the relation between the local generalized effective stress and the local generalized effective strain can be expressed as

$$\tilde{\Sigma}_e = \frac{\sqrt{3}}{2}\Sigma_0 + \frac{3}{4}E_p\tilde{E}_e \tag{7.68}$$

where Σ_0 is the yield strength, E_p is the hardening coefficient.

The total strain energy per unit length is given by

$$W = \int_V (w^0 + B_{kl}w^0_{,kl})\,\mathrm{d}V \tag{7.69}$$

where

$$w^0 = (\tilde{w})_{\xi=0} = \left[\int_0^{\tilde{E}_e} \tilde{\Sigma}_e\,\mathrm{d}(\tilde{E}_e)\right]_{\xi=0} = \frac{\sqrt{3}}{2}\Sigma_0 E_e + \frac{3}{8}E_pE_e^2 \tag{7.70}$$

$$B_{kl}w^0_{,kl} = B_{kl}\frac{\sqrt{3}\Sigma_0}{3}\left[-\frac{2}{3}(E_e)^{-3}\varepsilon'_{mn}\varepsilon'_{mn,k}\varepsilon'_{ij}\varepsilon'_{ij,l}\right.$$

$$+ (E_e)^{-1} \epsilon'_{ij,l} \epsilon'_{ij,k} \Big] + \frac{1}{2} E_p \epsilon'_{mn,l} \epsilon'_{mn,k} \qquad (7.71)$$

According to Eq. (7.67), we have

$$E_e = \sqrt{\frac{2}{3} \epsilon'_{ij} \epsilon'_{ij} + \frac{2}{3} l^2_{cs} \chi_{ij} \chi_{ij}} = \kappa \sqrt{\frac{2}{3} (2 x^2_2 + l^2_{cs})} \qquad (7.72)$$

$$\epsilon'_{mn} \epsilon'_{mn,k} = \kappa x_2 (\epsilon_{11,k} - \epsilon_{22,k}) \qquad (7.73)$$

$$\epsilon_{ij,l} \epsilon_{ij,k} = \epsilon_{11,l} \epsilon_{11,k} + \epsilon_{22,l} \epsilon_{22,k} \qquad (7.74)$$

Substituting Eqs. (7.72)–(7.74) into Eqs. (7.70, 7.71) yields

$$w^0 = \kappa \Sigma_0 \sqrt{x^2_2 + \frac{l^2_{cs}}{2}} + \frac{1}{4} E_p \kappa^2 (2 x^2_2 + l^2_{cs}) \qquad (7.75)$$

$$B_{kl} w^0_{,kl} = B \delta_{kl} w^0_{,kl} = \frac{4 \sqrt{3} B \Sigma_0 (E_e)^{-3} \kappa^4 l^2_{cs}}{9} + B E_p \kappa^2 \qquad (7.76)$$

The total strain energy for a unit length of the beam can be obtained by means of Eqs. (7.75), (7.76) and (7.69) as

$$W = 2b \int_0^{\frac{h}{2}} \left[\kappa \Sigma_0 \sqrt{x^2_2 + \frac{l^2_{cs}}{2}} + \frac{1}{2} E_p \kappa^2 \left(x^2_2 + \frac{l^2_{cs}}{2} \right) \right. $$
$$\left. + \frac{4 \sqrt{3} B \Sigma_0 (E_e)^{-3} \kappa^4 l^2_{cs}}{9} + B E_p \kappa^2 \right] dx_2$$

$$= 2 b \kappa \Sigma_0 \left[\frac{h}{4} \sqrt{\frac{h^2}{4} + \frac{l^2_{cs}}{2}} + \frac{l^2_{cs}}{4} \ln \left(\frac{h}{\sqrt{2} l_{cs}} + \sqrt{\frac{h^2}{2 l^2_{cs}} + 1} \right) \right]$$

$$+ 2 b \left(\frac{1}{48} E_p \kappa^2 h^3 + \frac{B \Sigma_0 \kappa h}{\sqrt{h^2 + 2 l^2_{cs}}} + B E_p \kappa^2 \frac{h}{2} + E_p \kappa^2 \frac{l^2_{cs}}{8} h \right) \qquad (7.77)$$

Substituting Eq. (7.77) into

$$M = \frac{dW}{d\kappa} \qquad (7.78)$$

yields the non-dimensional bending moment

$$\frac{4M\Sigma_0}{bh^2} = \sqrt{1 + \frac{2l_{cs}^2}{h^2}} + \frac{2l_{cs}^2}{h^2}\ln\left(\frac{h}{\sqrt{2}\,l_{cs}} + \sqrt{\frac{h^2}{2l_{cs}^2} + 1}\right) + \frac{8B}{h^2\sqrt{1 + \frac{2l_{cs}^2}{h^2}}}$$

$$+ \frac{2}{3\Sigma_0}E_p\varepsilon_b + \frac{16BE_p\varepsilon_b}{h^2\Sigma_0} + \frac{2E_pl_{cs}^2\varepsilon_b}{h^2\Sigma_0} \tag{7.79}$$

where $\varepsilon_b = h\kappa/2$ is surface plastic strain.

The yield strength Σ_0 and the hardening coefficient E_p for beam bending with different thicknesses were measured by Stölken and Evans (1998) and listed in Table 7.1. We take $l_c = 0.1$ μm and use Eq. (7.79) to fit the experiment results given by Stölken and Evans (1998). We find the intrinsic length scale $l_{cs} = 5.8$ μm. The comparison between the theoretical results and the experiment data is shown in Figure 7.7. One can see that the theoretical results are in reasonable agreement with the experiment results.

Table 7.1   The relation between h, Σ_0 and E_p(Stölken and Evans, 1998)

$h(\mu m)$	$\Sigma_0(MPa)$	$E_p(GPa)$
12.5	56	1.15
25	75	1.30
50	103	1.05

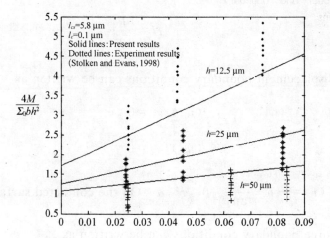

Figure 7.7   Plots of bending moment against the surface strain for three beams with different thickness.

7.5 Analysis of micro-indentation

7.5.1 Indentation model

As shown in Figure 7.8, the indenter is assumed to be axisymmetric and conical. The half-angle of the indenter, $\beta = 72°$. The indenter is

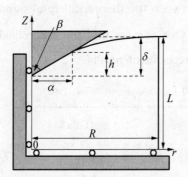

assumed to be frictionless. The film thickness is $t = 2\,\mu\text{m}$, and the depth of indentation is δ. The contact radius of indentation is a and the contact depth $h = a/\tan\beta$. The total force, P, exerted on the indenter is the sum of nodal forces in the z direction for those nodes in contact with the indenter. The indentation hardness is defined as

Figure 7.8 Geometry of axisymmetric micro-indentation model and boundary conditions.

$$H = \frac{|P|}{\pi a^2} \tag{7.80}$$

The displacement boundary conditions can be written as

$$(u_r)_{r=0} = 0 \tag{7.81}$$

$$(u_z)_{z=0} = 0 \tag{7.82}$$

$$u_z(r) = -\delta + \frac{r}{\tan\beta} \quad 0 \leqslant r \leqslant a \quad \text{On the contacted surface} \tag{7.83}$$

The force boundary conditions can be written as

$$\overline{p}_z = 0, \ r > a \tag{7.84}$$

$$\overline{p}_r = 0, \quad r > 0 \tag{7.85}$$

$$\overline{r}_z = \overline{r}_r = 0, \quad r \geqslant 0 \tag{7.86}$$

where $\overline{p}$ is the surface traction, and $\overline{r}$ is the higher order surface traction.

7.5.2 Calculation results

a) Simulation results for micro indentation of polycrystalline copper

Referring to Qiu (2001), the elastic modulus, Poisson's ratio, reference stress and the plastic hardening exponent of the polycrystalline copper are $E = 109.2$ GPa, $v = 0.3$, $\sigma_{ref} = 688$ Mpa, and $n = 0.3$ respectively. The half-angle of the indenter, $\beta = 72°$. According to Fleck et al. (1994), the intrinsic length of copper for rotation gradient is in the range $2.7 \sim 5.1$ μm. We take the intrinsic length $l_{cs} = 2.6$ μm.

The stress-strain law of copper in uniaxial tension is shown as

$$\sigma = \begin{cases} E\varepsilon_x, & \varepsilon \leqslant \sigma_Y/E \\ \sigma_{ref} \, \varepsilon_x^n, & \varepsilon > \sigma_Y/E \end{cases} \tag{7.87}$$

Figure 7.9 shows the calculation results of the new theory with $l_c = 0.1$ μm. The calculation result predicts an indentation hardness of $H = 810.3$ MPa for large indentation depth (larger than 2 μm), which agrees well with the experimental data of $H_0 = 834$ MPa (McElhaney et al., 1998). The calculation results of the new theory are in reasonable agreement with the experiment results.

From Figure 7.9, one can observe that the indentation hardness of polycrystalline copper depends on the depth of indentation when the depth of indentation is in the range $0.1 - 2$ μm. From Figure 7.10, one can clearly see that the linear relation between the square of indentation hardness, H^2, and the inverse of indentation depth, $1/\delta$, do exist when the indentation depth δ is less than 1 μm.

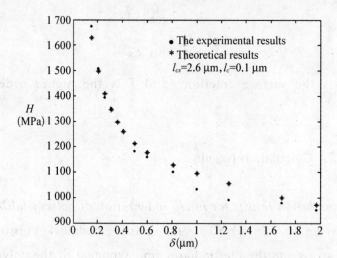

Figure 7.9 Comparison of the theoretical results (Yi and Wang, 2008) with the experiment data by McElhaney et al. (1998) for microindentation hardness H on polycrystalline copper.

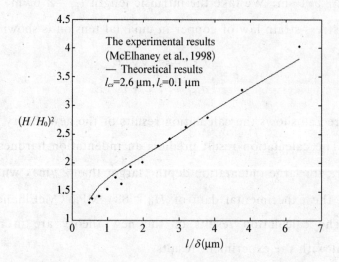

Figure 7.10 Plots of $(H/H_0)^2$ against the inverse of indentation depth, $1/\delta$.

  b) *Simulation results for micro indentation of a soft film on a hard substrate*

Nano-indentation experiments of a soft metal film on a hard substrate have been carried out by Saha et al. (2001) and Chen et al. (2004), as shown in Figure 7.11. In the experiments, by indenting a soft film (Al) on a hard substrate (glass), two kinds of phenomena have been observed. When the indentation depth is much smaller than the film thickness, the hardness of the thin film-substrate system significantly increases with decrease of the depth of indenter. The second phenomenon is that when the indenter tip approaches the hard substrate, the hardness of the thin film-substrate

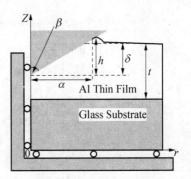

Figure 7.11 A schematic diagram of the micro-indentation model of a soft film on a hard substrate.

system increases with increase of the depth of indenter. The phenomenon at shallow indentation is usually associated with strain gradient effect; meanwhile the phenomenon at deep indentation is due to the effect of hard substrate.

The glass substrate is assumed to be an elastic body in the present simulation. According to Saha et al. (2001), the elastic modulus and Poisson's ratio of the glass are $E^{glass} = 73$ GPa; $\nu^{glass} = 0.24$. The elastic modulus, Poisson's ratio, yield stress for thickness $t = 2$ μm and the plastic hardening exponent of the aluminum are $E^{Al} = 70$ GPa, $\nu^{Al} = 0.33$, $\sigma_Y^{Al} = 129$ MPa and $n = 0.05$ respectively.

The calculation results for the micro-indentation hardness H versus the depth of indentation δ for a 2 μm Al film on a glass substrate are shown in Figure 7.12. Form Figure 7.12 One can find that:

(i) When the indentation depth δ is much smaller than the film thickness t, the micro-indentation hardness increases with decrease of the indentation depth. The size effect is similar to bulk metallic materials.

(ii) When the depth of indenter δ is comparable to the film thickness, the hardness of the thin film-substrate system increases with increase of the depth of indenter due to substrate effect.

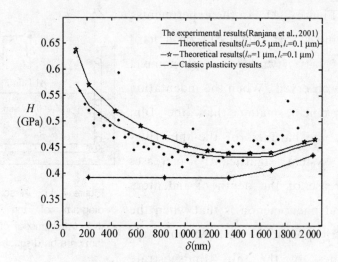

Figure 7. 12　Micro-indentation hardness H versus the depth of indentation δ for a 2 μm Al film on a glass substrate.

(iii) The results of the new theory agree well with the experimental results (Saha et al., 2001), and the classic plasticity results are remarkable lower than the experimental results.

References

Bažant, Z. P. and Jirasek, M. , 2002. Non-local integral formulations of plasticity and damage: survey of progress. J. Engng. Mech. , 1119 – 1149.

Brand, I. , 1947. Vector and tensor analysis. John Wiley & Sons.

Chen, S. H. , Wang, T. C. , 2000. A new hardening law for strain gradient plasticity. Acta Mater. , 48, 3997 – 4005.

Chen, S. H. , Wang, T. C. , 2002. A new deformation theory for strain gradient effects. Int. J. Plasticity 18, 971 – 995.

Chen S. H. , Liu L. and Wang T. C. , 2004. Size dependent nanoindentation of a soft film on a hard substrate. Acta Mater. , 52: 1089 – 1095.

Cosserat, E. , Cosserat, F. , 1909. Theorie des corps deformables. Herrman, Paris.

Edelen, D. G. B. , 1969. Protoelastic bodies with large deformation. Arch. Ration. Mech. Anal. , 34, 283 – 300.

Eringen, A. C. , 1964. Simple microfluids. Int. J. Eng. Sci. , 2, 205 – 217.

Eringen, A. C. , 1966. A unified theory of thermomechanical materials. Int. J. Engng. Sci. , 4: 179 – 202.

Fleck, N.A. , Hutchinson, J.W. , 1993. A phenomenological theory for strain gradient effects in plasticity. J. Mech. Phys. Solids 41: 1825 – 1857.

Fleck, N.A. , Muller, G.M. , Ashby, M. F, Hutchinson, J.W. , 1994. Strain gradient plasticity: theory and experiment. Acta Metal. Mater. 42: 475 – 487.

Fleck, N. A. , Hutchinson, J. W. , 1997, in: Hutchinson, J. W. , Wu, T. Y. (Eds.). Strain Gradient Plasticity. Advances in Applied Mechanics, Vol. 33. Academic Press, New York, pp.295 – 361.

Gao, H. , Huang, Y. , Nix, W. D. , Hutchinson, J. W. , 1999. Mechanism-based strain gradient plasticity – I. Theory. J. Mech. Phys. Solids 47: 1239 – 1263.

Geers, M. G. D. , Engelen, R. A. B. , and Ubachs, R. J. M. , 2001. On the numerical modeling of ductile damage with an implicit gradientenhanced formulation. Rev. Euro. Elements finis, 10, 173 – 191.

Hwang, K.C. , Jiang, H. , Huang, Y. , Gao, H. , Hu, N. , 2002. A finite deformation theory of strain gradient plasticity. J. Mech. Phys. Solids 50, 81 – 99.

Koiter, W. T. , 1964. Couple stresses in the theory of elasticity. Proc. K. Ned. Akad. Wet. , Ser. B: Phys. Sci. 67, 17 – 44.

Kroner, E. , 1966. Continuum mechanics and range of atomic cohesion forces. Proc. , 1st Int. Conf. on Fracture, T. Yokobori, T. Kawasaki, and J. Swedlow, eds. , Japanese Society for Strength and Fracture of Materials, Sendai, Japan, 27.

McElhaney, K. W. , Vlassak, J. J. , Nix, W. D. , 1998. Determination of indenter tip geometry and indentation contact area for depth-sening indentation experiments. J. Mater. Res. 13, 1300 – 1306.

Mindlin, R. D. , and Tiersten, H. F. , 1962. Effects of couple stresses in linear elasticity. Arch. Ration. Mech. Anal. , 11, 415 – 448.

Mindlin, R.D. , 1964. Microstructure in linear elasticity. Arch. Rational Mech. Anal. 16: 51 – 78.

Qiu X. , Development and applications of mechanism based strain gradient plasticity. [Doctor thesis]. Beijing: Tsinghua University, 2001.

Saha. R. , Xue. Z. , Huang. Y. , Nix, W. D. , 2001. Indentation of a soft metal film on a hard substrate: strain gradient hardening effects. J. Mech. Phys. Solids 49, 1997 – 2014.

Rogula, D. , 1965. Influence of spatial acoustic dispersion on dynamical properties of dislocations. I Bull. Acad. Pol. Sci. , Ser. Sci. Tech. , 13, 337 – 343.

Stölken, J.S. , Evans, A.G. , 1998. A microbend test method for measuring the plasticity length scale. Acta Mater., 46, 5109 – 5115.

Toupin, R., 1962. Elastic materials with couple-stresses. Arch. Rational Mech. Anal., 11, 385 – 414.

Yi, D. K., Wang, T. C., Chen, S. H., 2009. New strain gradient theory and analysis. Acta Mechanica Solida Sinica, 22, 45 – 52.

Yi, D. K., Wang, T. C., 2009. Energy non-local model and new strain gradient theory, Acta Mech. Sinica (in Chinese), 41, 60 – 66.

8 Cleavage fracture near crack tip

Motivation for exploring the effect of plastic strain gradients on crack tip tractions derives from deficiencies based on conventional plasticity theory, coupled with recent developments in the strain gradient theory suggesting that more realistic predictions may be enabled by the theory. The deficiencies concern the maximum stress levels attainable ahead of a growing sharp crack surrounded by a plastic strain cracks in mode I, the maximum normal stress that can be attained ahead of the tip is about 2.6 times the initial tensile yield stress σ_Y, if the material is elastic perfectly plastic (Drugan et al. , 1982). Strain hardening gives rise to a stress singularity, but numerical studies for growing cracks in conventional elastic-plastic solids indicate that this singularity must be exceptionally weak. For relevant distances ahead of the tip, the maximum normal stress never exceeds about 4, or at most 5, times σ_Y, depending on N. Maximum crack tip tractions present a paradox for fracture occurring by cleavage or decohesion at the atomic scale (Bagchi and Evans, 1996). Atomic separation requires traction levels on the order of the theoretical lattice strength, which for most metals is more typically on the order of $10\sigma_Y$ or more. Thus, conventional plasticity theory predictions would appear to rule out a fracture mechanism based on atomic separation whenever a well developed plastic zone surrounds the crack tip. The paradox pertains as well to crack propagation along strong metal-ceramic interfaces where similarly low normal interface tractions within the plastic zone are predicted.

Several proposals have been put forward to justify higher crack tip stresses. When the crack velocity is sufficiently high and material rate effects are taken into account, a robust elastic singularity within the plastic zone re-emerges, and traction levels required for lattice separation arise (Freund and Hutchinson, 1985). This description only applies to cracks running at high speeds. It does not explain how cracks are able to propagate quasi-statically when atomic separation is the fracture mechanism. Experiments on metal-ceramic interfaces (Elssner et al., 1994) have provided detailed evidence of quasi-static propagation of interface decohesion cracks in the presence of substantial plasticity in the metal. Another approach, pursued by Suo et al. (1993) and Beltz et al. (1996), employs a model which excludes plasticity within some distance D from the crack tip. In this way, an elastic stress singularity exists at the tip, enabling the normal traction to attain levels necessary for lattice separation at distances on the order of an atomic spacing from the tip. A difficulty with this type of model, which will be more evident shortly, is the retention of conventional plasticity to describe material deformation outside the elastic exclusionary zone. Strain gradient plasticity theories may be helpful to explain the high stress tractions at the crack tip.

8.1 Steady-state crack growth and work of fracture for solids characterized by strain gradient plasticity

Wei and Hutchinson (1997) have analyzed mode I steady-state crack growth under plane strain conditions in small scale yielding. The elastic-plastic solid is characterized by a generalization of J_2 flow theory which accounts for the influence of the gradients of plastic strains on hardening. The constitutive model involves one new parameter, a material length l, specifying the scale of nonuniform deformation at which hardening elevation owing to strain gradients becomes important. Gradients of plastic strain at a sharp crack tip result in a substantial increase in tractions ahead of the tip. This has important consequences for crack growth in materials that fail by decohesion or cleavage at the atomic scale. The new constitutive law is used in conjunction with a model which represents the fracture process by an embedded traction-separation relation applied on the plane ahead of the crack tip. The ratio of the parameters characterizing the fracture process and the solid, with particular emphasis on the role of l.

8.1.1　Flow theory of F-H strain gradient plasticity

The deformation theory of F-H strain gradient plasticity has been given in chapter 3. Here we introduce the flow theory, which has been used by Wei and Hutchinson (1997).

Let $\sigma'_{ij} = \sigma_{ij} - \dfrac{1}{3}\delta_{ij}\sigma_{pp}$ be the stress deviator, $\tau^{(4)}_{ijk} = \tau^H_{ijk} = \dfrac{1}{4}(\delta_{ik}\tau_{jpp} + \delta_{jk}\tau_{ipp})$ be the hydrostatic part of τ, with $\tau' = \tau - \tau^H$ as the deviator. Decompose τ into the four mutually orthogonal tensors $\tau^{(I)}$.

The elastic strain energy density of the solid is taken to be

$$W^e = E\left[\frac{1}{2(1+\nu)}\varepsilon_{ij}\varepsilon_{ij} + \frac{\nu}{2(1+\nu)(1-2\nu)}\varepsilon^2_{jj}\right] + El^2_e\left[\sum_{I=1}^{4}\kappa^{(I)^2}_e\eta^{(I)}_{ijk}\eta^{(I)}_{ijk}\right]$$

(8.1)

The length scales $l_e\kappa^{(I)}_e$ characterizing the strain gradient energy contribution in the elastic range are adopted to ensure a positive definite energy density. They are not presented on the basis of any physical grounds at the scales of interest for plastic strain gradient phenomena.

These length scales must be chosen sufficiently small such that they have essentially no influence on any solution for which plastic strain gradients dominate elastic strain gradients for elastic deformations, it follows

$$\sigma_{ij} = L_{ijkl}\varepsilon_{kl} , \quad \tau_{ijk} = J_{ijklmn}\eta_{lmn} \tag{8.2}$$

where

$$L_{ijkl} = \frac{E}{2(1+\nu)}\left[\delta_{ik}\delta_{jl} + \delta_{il}\delta_{jk} + \frac{2\nu}{(1-2\nu)}\delta_{ij}\delta_{kl}\right] \tag{8.3}$$

and

$$J_{ijklmn} = 2El_e^2 \sum_{I=1}^{4} \kappa_e^{(I)^2} T_{ijklmn}^{(I)} \tag{8.4}$$

The isotropic projection tensors $T^{(I)}$ share the indicial symmetries:
$T_{ijklmn}^{(I)} = T_{jiklmn}^{(I)} = T_{ijkmln}^{(I)} = T_{lmnijk}^{(I)}$ and are expressed as

$$T_{ijkpqr}^{(1)} = \frac{1}{6}\{(\delta_{ip}\delta_{jq} + \delta_{iq}\delta_{jp})\delta_{kr} + (\delta_{jp}\delta_{kq} + \delta_{jq}\delta_{kp})\delta_{ir}$$

$$+ (\delta_{ip}\delta_{kq} + \delta_{iq}\delta_{kp})\delta_{jr}\} - \frac{1}{15}\{(\delta_{ij}\delta_{kr} + \delta_{jk}\delta_{ir} + \delta_{ki}\delta_{jr})\delta_{pq}$$

$$+ (\delta_{ij}\delta_{kp} + \delta_{jk}\delta_{ip} + \delta_{ki}\delta_{jp})\delta_{qr} + (\delta_{ij}\delta_{kq} + \delta_{jk}\delta_{iq}$$

$$+ \delta_{ki}\delta_{jq})\delta_{rp}\} \tag{8.5}$$

$$T_{ijkpqr}^{(2)} = \frac{1}{12}\{e_{ikq}e_{jpr} + e_{jkq}e_{ipr} + e_{ikp}e_{jqr} + e_{jkp}e_{iqr}\}$$

$$+ \frac{1}{12}\{2(\delta_{ip}\delta_{jq} + \delta_{iq}\delta_{jp})\delta_{kr} - (\delta_{jp}\delta_{kq} + \delta_{jq}\delta_{kp})\delta_{ir}$$

$$- (\delta_{kp}\delta_{iq} + \delta_{kq}\delta_{ip})\delta_{jr}\} \tag{8.6}$$

$$T_{ijkpqr}^{(3)} = \frac{1}{12}\{-e_{ikq}e_{jpr} - e_{jkq}e_{ipr} - e_{ikp}e_{jqr} - e_{jkp}e_{iqr}\} - \frac{1}{8}\{(\delta_{ip}\delta_{jk}$$

$$+ \delta_{jp}\delta_{ik})\delta_{qr} + (\delta_{iq}\delta_{jk} + \delta_{jq}\delta_{ik})\delta_{pr}\} + \frac{1}{12}\{2(\delta_{ip}\delta_{jq}$$

$$+ \delta_{iq}\delta_{jp})\delta_{kr} - (\delta_{jp}\delta_{kq} + \delta_{jq}\delta_{kp})\delta_{ir} - (\delta_{kp}\delta_{iq} + \delta_{kq}\delta_{ip})\delta_{jr}\}$$

$$+ \frac{1}{15}\{(\delta_{ij}\delta_{kr} + \delta_{jk}\delta_{ir} + \delta_{ki}\delta_{jr})\delta_{pq} + (\delta_{ij}\delta_{kp} + \delta_{jk}\delta_{ip}$$

$$+ \delta_{ki}\delta_{jp})\delta_{qr} + (\delta_{ij}\delta_{kq} + \delta_{jk}\delta_{iq} + \delta_{ki}\delta_{jq})\delta_{rp}\} \tag{8.7}$$

$$T^{(4)}_{ijkpqr} = \frac{1}{8}\{(\delta_{ik}\delta_{jp} + \delta_{jk}\delta_{ip})\delta_{qr} + (\delta_{ik}\delta_{jq} + \delta_{jk}\delta_{iq})\delta_{pr}\} \quad (8.8)$$

The inverse elastic relations are

$$\varepsilon_{ij} = M_{ijkl}\sigma_{kl}, \quad \eta_{ijk} = K_{ijklmn}\tau_{lmn} \quad (8.9)$$

where

$$\left. \begin{array}{l} M_{ijkl} = \dfrac{1}{E}\left[\dfrac{1+\nu}{2}(\delta_{ik}\delta_{jl} + \delta_{il}\delta_{jk}) - \nu\delta_{ij}\delta_{kl}\right] \\[2em] K_{ijklmn} = \dfrac{1}{2El_e^2}\sum_{I=1}^{4} \kappa_e^{(I)^{-2}} T^{(I)}_{ijklmn} \end{array} \right\} \quad (8.10)$$

An effective stress quantity Σ_e generalizing the von Mises stress σ_e is defined in terms of the deviator stress quantities as

$$\Sigma_e^2 = \frac{3}{2}\sigma'_{ij}\sigma'_{ij} + l^{-2}\sum_{I=1}^{3} \kappa^{(I)^{-2}} \tau^{(I)}_{ijk}\tau^{(I)}_{ijk} \quad (8.11)$$

where $l\kappa^{(I)} = l_I (I = 1, 3)$ are the length quantities associated with the plastic strain gradients introduced in the deformation theory. Take l to be the largest of the l_I, all of which are assumed to be nonzero.

The yield surface in this generalization of J2 flow theory is

$$\Phi(\Sigma_e, Y) = \Sigma_e - Y \quad (8.12)$$

where Y is the current effective tensile flow stress.

Plastic loading requires $\Sigma_e = Y$ and $\dot{\Sigma}_e > 0$. Normality of plastic flow for any plastic loading increment requires

$$(\dot{\varepsilon}^P_{ij}, \dot{\eta}^P_{ijk}) = \frac{\dot{\Sigma}_e}{h(\Sigma_e)}\left(\frac{\partial\Phi}{\partial\sigma'_{ij}}, \frac{\partial\Phi}{\partial\tau'_{ijk}}\right) \quad (8.13)$$

The hardening rate $h(\Sigma_e)$ is defined by data from a uniaxial tension test, which for the above reduces to $\dot{\varepsilon}^P_e = \dot{\sigma}_e/h(\sigma_e)$. Thus, the dependence of h on Σ_e is identical to its dependence on σ_e in conventional J_2 flow theory. The plastic work rate is $\sigma_{ij}\dot{\varepsilon}^P_{ij} + \tau_{ijk}\dot{\eta}^P_{ijk} =$

$\Sigma_e \dot{\Sigma}_e / h(\Sigma_e)$, and an effective plastic strain rate can be defined which is equal to $\dot{\Sigma}_e / h(\Sigma_e)$.

The incremental constitutive relation summing elastic contributions and plastic contributions are expressed as

$$\dot{\sigma}_{ij} = \left[L_{ijkl} - \frac{9\mu}{(2+H)\sigma_e^2} \sigma'_{ij}\sigma'_{kl} \right] \dot{\epsilon}_{kl} + \left[-\frac{6E(l_e/l)^2}{(3+H)\sigma_e^2} \sigma'_{ij} \sum_{I=1}^{3} \left(\frac{\kappa_e^{(I)}}{\kappa^{(I)}} \right)^2 \tau_{klm}^{(I)} \right] \dot{\eta}_{klm}$$

$$(8.14)$$

$$\dot{\tau}_{ijk} = \left[-\frac{6E(l_e/l)^2}{(3+H)\sigma_e^2} \sigma'_{mn} \sum_{I=1}^{3} \left(\frac{\kappa_e^{(I)}}{\kappa^{(I)}} \right)^2 \tau_{ijk}^{(I)} \right] \dot{\epsilon}_{mn}$$

$$+ \left[J_{ijklmn} - \frac{8(1+\nu)E(l_e/l)^4}{(3+H)\sigma_e^2} \sum_{I=1}^{3} \left(\frac{\kappa_e^{(I)}}{\kappa^{(I)}} \right)^2 \tau_{ijk}^{(I)} \sum_{J=1}^{3} \left(\frac{\kappa_e^{(J)}}{\kappa^{(J)}} \right)^2 \tau_{lmn}^{(I)} \right] \dot{\eta}_{lmn}$$

$$(8.15)$$

where μ is the shear modulus and

$$H = \left(\frac{\Sigma_e}{\sigma_e} \right)^2 \left[1 + \frac{2El_e^2}{h\Sigma_e^2 l^4} \sum_{I=1}^{3} \frac{\kappa_e^{(I)^2}}{\kappa^{(I)^4}} \tau_{ijk}^{(I)} \tau_{ijk}^{(I)} \right] \frac{h}{\mu} \qquad (8.16)$$

A piecewise-power law tensile stress-strain curve will be used to characterize the solid in the crack growth problems such that

$$\epsilon_e = \begin{cases} \sigma_e/E & \text{for} \quad \sigma \leqslant \sigma_Y \\ (\sigma_Y/E)(\sigma_e/\sigma_Y)^{1/N} & \text{for} \quad \sigma > \sigma_Y \end{cases} \qquad (8.17)$$

The corresponding hardening rate function is

$$\frac{1}{h} = \begin{cases} 0 & \text{for} \quad \Sigma_e \leqslant \sigma_Y \\ \frac{1}{E} \left[\frac{1}{N} \left(\frac{\Sigma_e}{\sigma_Y} \right)^{(1-N)/N} - 1 \right] & \text{for} \quad \Sigma_e > \sigma_Y \end{cases} \qquad (8.18)$$

8.1.2　Traction and opening displacement in steady-state growth

The normal traction t_2 acting on the plane ahead of the crack tip in the small scale yielding, steady-state problem in Figure 8.1 has the form

$$\frac{t_2}{\sigma_Y} = \bar{t}_2\left(\frac{x_1}{R_p}, \frac{l}{R_p}, \frac{l_e}{l}, N, \frac{\sigma_Y}{E}, \nu\right)$$

(8.19)

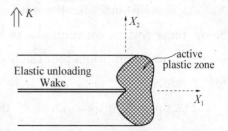

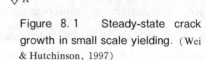

Figure 8.1　Steady-state crack growth in small scale yielding. (Wei & Hutchinson, 1997)

where $\bar{t}_2$ is a dimensionless function of the arguments displayed. The dependence on l_e/l is explicitly listed, although its important is secondary. The quantity R_p is the half-height of the plastic zone, which can be defined in terms of the remote stress intensity factor K as $R_p = K^2/(3\pi\sigma_Y^2)$. Results for t_2/σ_Y as a function of x_1/R_p for the SG solid are plotted in Figure 8.2 for a solid with $l_e/l = 0.5$, $E/\sigma_Y = 300$, $\nu = 0.3$ and $N = 0.1$ [Figure 8.2(a)] and $N = 0.2$ [Figure 8.2(b)]. In each of the two figures, the curve for $l/R_p = 0$ corresponds to the conventional J_2 flow theory solid. The curves for the nonzero values of l/R_p apply to the SG solid. The strong influence of strain gradients as measured by l/R_p in elevating the tractions within a distance of about $R_p/10$ from the crack tip is evident.

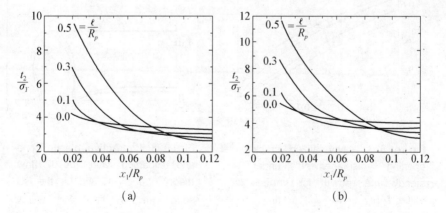

(a)　　　　　　　　　　　　　　(b)

Figure 8.2　Traction on the plane ahead of the crack tip in the region where the strain gradients have strong influence. (a) $N = 0.1$ and (b) $N = 0.2$. (Wei & Hutchinson, 1997)

Note that at distances further out from the tip, the tractions drop slightly below those for the conventional solid, consistent with the requirement of overall force equilibrium that the higher tractions near the tip be offset by lower values.

The opening displacement of the crack faces behind the crack tip, $\delta = u_2(x_1, 0^+) - u_2(x_1, 0^-)$, for the case with $N = 0.2$ is plotted in Figure 8.3. Strain gradient hardening reduces the opening near the tip, creating a significantly sharper crack tip. It is recalled that the crack tip of a growing crack in the conventional J_2 flow theory solid is already quite sharp (Drugan, et al., 1982). Boundaries of plastic zones are displayed in Figure 8.4 for $l/R_p = 0.3$ along with the boundary for the conventional theory ($l/R_p = 0$). Strain gradient hardening has only a minor effect on the size and shape of the plastic zone. This is not surprising because strain gradients become important only in a small region near the tip, well inside the plastic zone. For $N = 0.2$, the half-height of the steady-state plastic zone is approximately 20% greater than the reference quantity R_p. The thin region just above the crack face along the negative x_1 axis is a zone of plastic reloading.

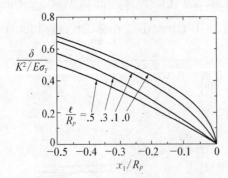

Figure 8.3   Normalized crack opening displacement under steady-state growth for various value l/R_p. (Wei & Hutchinson, 1997)

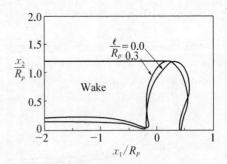

Figure 8.4   Active plastic zone and unloading wake for J2 flow theory ($l/R_p = 0$) and for the SG solid with $l/R_p = 0.3$. (Wei & Hutchinson, 1997)

All the results in Figures 8.2 – 8.4 were computed with l_e/l fixed at 0.5.

The elastic strain gradient contributions were introduced in (2) to ensure a positive energy density and an invertible constitutive law. They are not considered to have any physical significance for strain gradient plasticity. The relatively minor influence of l_e/l on the traction ahead of the crack tip can be seen in Figure 8.5 for the case $N = 0.2$, $E/\sigma_Y = 300$ and $\nu = 0.3$.

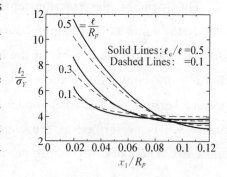

Figure 8.5　The effect of l_e/l on traction ahead of the crack tip for several values of l/R_p. (Wei & Hutchinson, 1997)

8.1.3　The influence of l on steady-state fracture toughness

In this section, the SG solid is taken as the description of the elastic-plastic solid in the embedded fracture process zone model (EPZ model) of Needleman (1987) and Tvergaard and Hutchinson (1992). In this model, the traction-separation law characterizing the fracture process as a boundary condition along the plane ahead of the crack tip, as depicted in Figure 8.6. The continuum description of the elastic-plastic solid holds everywhere off the extended fracture plane.

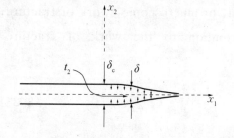
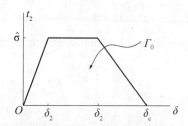

Figure 8.6　Embedded process zone model for determination of steady-state toughness. The traction-separation relation characterizing the fracture process is applied along the plane ahead of the tip and is specified by the work of separation Γ_0, the peak traction $\hat{\sigma}$ and the two shape factors $\lambda_1 = \delta_1/\delta_c$ and $\lambda_2 = \delta_2/\delta_c$. (Wei & Hutchinson, 1997)

The form of the traction-separation law shown in Figure 8.6 is exactly the same as that employed in Tvergaard and Hutchinson (1992). However, within the context of the higher order theory, it is t_2, not σ_{22}, that is work conjugate to the crack opening separation δ. Thus, in the present version of the EPZ model, the relation between t_2 and δ in Figure 8.6 is prescribed as the condition along the plane ahead of the crack tip. The work of fracture per unit area, Γ_0, is related to σ and δ by

$$\Gamma_0 = \int_0^{\delta_c} t_2 \mathrm{d}\delta = \frac{1}{2}\hat{\sigma}\delta_c (1 + \lambda_2 - \lambda_1) \qquad (8.20)$$

where $\lambda_1 = \delta_1/\delta_c$ and $\lambda_2 = \delta_2/\delta_c$.

The iteration scheme must satisfy the traction-separation relation ahead of the tip and must adjust the level of the remote stress intensity K such that the propagation condition at the tip is met, i.e.

$$\delta = \delta_c \quad \text{at} \quad x_1 = 0 \qquad (8.21)$$

The outcome of the calculation is the relation between K_{ss} and the parameters specifying the fracture process and the SG solid. The results will be presented using the equivalent energetic measure of steady-state toughness

$$\Gamma_{ss} = \frac{1 - \nu^2}{E} K_{ss}^2 \qquad (8.22)$$

This quantity measures the total, or macroscopic, work of fracture; $\Gamma_{ss} - \Gamma_0$ is the plasticity contribution to the work of fracture. Dimensional considerations now give

$$\frac{\Gamma_{ss}}{\Gamma_0} = F\left(\frac{l}{R_0}, N, \frac{\hat{\sigma}}{\sigma_Y}, \frac{\sigma_Y}{E}, \frac{l_e}{l}, \nu, \lambda_1, \lambda_2\right) \qquad (8.23)$$

where R_0 is the same reference length used by Tvergaard and Hutchinson (1992)

$$R_0 = \frac{1}{3\pi(1 - \nu^2)} \frac{E\Gamma_0}{\sigma_Y^2} \qquad (8.24)$$

Other than l and l_e, R_0 is the only length quantity in the model. It can be interpreted as an estimate of the half-height of the plastic zone in the limit that Γ_{ss} is only slightly greater than Γ_0. Equivalently, it can be thought of as the estimate of the half-height of the plastic zone when $K = \sqrt{E\Gamma_0/(1-\nu^2)}$ is applied remotely. Note that R_p is precisely (Γ_{ss}/Γ_0) R_0. The nondimensional parameter which have the greatest effect on Γ_{ss}/Γ_0 are l/R_0, N and $\hat{\sigma}/\sigma_Y$. The shape factors for the traction-separation law, λ_1 and λ_2, have been shown from the earlier study to the relatively unimportant. From the expression of Γ_0, it can be noted that the critical separation δ_c is determined when Γ_0, $\hat{\sigma}$ and the shape factors have been specified.

The role of strain gradient hardening in determining toughness is seen in Figure 8.7 for the case of a solid with moderately high strain hardening $N = 0.2$, $E/\sigma_Y = 300$, $\nu = 0.3$, $\lambda_1 = 0.15$, $\lambda_2 = 0.5$, $l_e/l = 0.5$ and various values of l/R_0. The limiting curve for $l/R_0 = 0$ is that for the conventional J2 flow theory solid, which is in agreement with the result obtained by Tvergaard and Hutchinson (1992) for the same model. The effect of replacing the conventional solid by the SG solid in the model

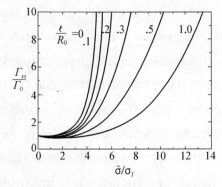

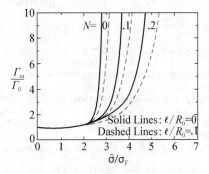

Figure 8.7 Influence of strain gradient effects on steady-state toughness. Curves of Γ_{ss}/Γ_0 as a function of the normalized peak separation traction $\hat{\sigma}/\sigma_Y$.

Figure 8.8 Influence of a small value of l/R_0 on the relation of Γ_{ss}/Γ_0 to $\hat{\sigma}/\sigma_Y$ for several levels of strain hardening N. (Wei & Hutchinson, 1997)

is profound. Strain gradient hardening elevates the traction ahead of the crack tip, thereby allowing higher peak separation stresses to be overcome. The trends displayed in Figure 8.7 are seen all levels of strain hardening. Figure 8.8 shows the effect of a relatively small value of l/R_0 on the steady-state toughness for three levels of strain hardening and $E/\sigma_Y = 300$, $\nu = 0.3$, $\lambda_1 = 0.15$, $\lambda_2 = 0.5$, $l_e/l = 0.5$. The effect is greatest at the highest level of strain hardening, but it persists even for the case with $N = 0$.

8.2　Fracture in MSG plasticity

Fracture in MSG plasticity has been studied by Jiang et al. (2001) via the finite element method in order to explain the observed cleavage fracture in ductile materials (Elssner et al., 1994). The results show the transition from the remotely imposed elastic K field through a plastic zone to the crack tip field in MSG plasticity.

The finite element method for MSG plasticity is based on the principle of virtual work. Wei and Hutchinson (1997) developed a higher-order element to investigate steady-state crack propagation in strain gradient plasticity. Huang et al. (2000b) used these elements to study micro-indentation experiments, and found the hardness predicted by MSG plasticity agrees very well with experimental data of McElhaney et al. (1998). They also showed that the numerical results from these elements agree well with all the existing analytic solutions in strain gradient plasticity.

Jiang et al. (2001) adopt these finite elements to study the full-field solution of mode-I fracture in MSG plasticity. They take a circular domain of radius $10^3 l$ centered at the crack tip in their plane-strain finite element analysis, where l is the internal material length in MSG plasticity. Very fine mesh is used near the crack tip, around which the size of the smallest element is less than $10^{-3}l$.

The crack faces remain traction-free. The classical mode-I elastic K field is imposed on the outer boundary of the finite element domain (of radius $10^3 l$). The elastic stress intensity factor, K_I, of the remotely applied field increases monotonically such that there is no unloading. In order to better characterize plastic yielding, the following elastic-plastic stress-strain relation in uniaxial tension is used,

$$\sigma_e = E\varepsilon_e, \quad \varepsilon_e < \frac{\sigma_Y}{E} \tag{8.25}$$

$$\sigma_e = \sigma_{ref}\varepsilon_e^N, \quad \varepsilon_e \geqslant \frac{\sigma_Y}{E} \tag{8.26}$$

where E is the elastic modulus, σ_Y the yield stress in uniaxial tension, N is the plastic work hardening exponent $(0 \leqslant N < 1)$, and the reference stress σ_{ref} is given by $\sigma_{ref} = \sigma_Y(E/\sigma_Y)^N$.

In the following, stresses σ_{ij} are normalized by the yield stress σ_Y in uniaxial tension, while the distance r to the crack tip is normalized by the internal material length l in MSG plasticity. The normalized, remotely applied stress intensity factor is $K_I/\sigma_Y l^{1/2}$. The stress distribution then depends on the following nondimensional parameters: the plastic work hardening exponent N; the ratio of yield stress to elastic modulus, σ_Y/E; the Poisson's ratio ν; and nondimensional stress intensity factor $K_I/\sigma_Y l^{1/2}$. It should be pointed out that the internal material length l has been used to normalize r and K_I, and does not appear explicitly in the nondimensional stress distributions. Accordingly, the normalized stress distributions do not depend on the Taylor coefficient α. Unless otherwise specialed, the numerical results presented in this section are for the following set of nondimensional material properties:

$$N = 0.2, \quad \sigma_Y/E = 0.2\%, \quad \nu = 0.3 \tag{8.27}$$

Figure 8.9 shows that normalized effective stress, σ_e/σ_Y, versus the nondimensional distance to the crack tip, r/l, ahead of the crack tip (at polar angle $(\theta = 1.014°)$ predicted by MSG plasticity, where $\sigma_e = (3\sigma'_{ij}\sigma'_{ij}/2)^{1/2}$ is the effective stress. The remotely applied stress intensity factor is $K_I/\sigma_Y l^{1/2} = 20$, while the nondimensional material properties are given in (8.27). The plastic zone size is a bit more than $10l$, as seen from the interception of MSG plasticity curve with the horizontal line of $\sigma_e/\sigma_Y = 1$ (representing plastic yielding). The corresponding stress distribution in classical plasticity (without strain gradient effects) is also shown in Figure 8.9. It is observed that, outside the plastic zone (as determined by $\sigma_e/\sigma_Y \leqslant 1$), both MSG and classical plasticity theories give the same straight line of slope $-1/2$, corresponding to the elastic K_I field. The predictions of MSG and classical plasticity theories are also the same within the plastic zone at a distance larger than $0.3l$ to the crack tip. For a typical estimate of $l = 4$ μm for copper (Fleck et al., 1994; Gao et al., 1999a), the above result indicates that the strain gradient effects are significant within a zone of approximately 1 μm in copper. This agrees with the Xia and Hutchinson's (1996) estimate of the size of dominance zone for the asymptotic crack tip field in strain gradient plasticity. It is not unreasonable that the local dislocation density reaches $10^{14}/m^2$ near a crack tip in metallic materials, which gives an average dislocation spacing of 0.1 μm. Therefore, this zone of 1 μm size is much larger than the average dislocation spacing so that continuum plasticity is still applicable. Once the distance to the crack tip is less than $0.3l$, the effective stress predicted by MSG plasticity increases much quicker than its counterpart in classical plasticity. At a distance of $0.1l$ to the crack tip, which is approximately 0.4 μm for copper and is within the intended range of applications of MSG plasticity (Gao et al., 1999b; Huang et al., 2000a), the effective stress given by MSG plasticity is more than twice that in classical plasticity. Moreover, for small distance to the crack tip (e. g., $r/l \leqslant 0.3$), classical plasticity gives a straight line in Figure 8.9, and the slope of the straight line is $- N/(N + 1)$, corresponding to the HRR field (Hutchinson, 1968; Rice and Rosengren, 1968) in classical plasticity. For $r/l \leqslant 0.3$, MSG plasticity gives a curve in Figure 8.9, and the absolute value of the slope at each point on the curve not only is much larger than that for the HRR field ($|\text{slope}| = N/(N + 1)$), but also exceeds or equals to that for elastic K_I field ($|\text{slope}| = 1/2$). This indicates that stresses around a crack tip in MSG plasticity are more singular than the HRR field, and the order of stress singularity exceeds or equals to the square-root singularity.

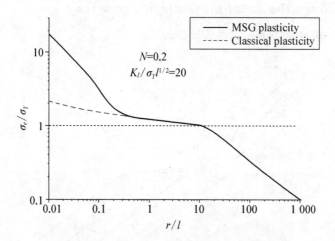

Figure 8.9   The normalized effective stress versus the normalized distance to the crack tip ahead of the crack tip (polar angle $\theta = 1.014°$). (Jiang et al., 2001)

Figure 8.10 shows the normalized effective stress, σ_e/σ_Y, versus the normalized distance to the crack tip, r/l, ahead of the crack tip (polar angle $\theta = 1.014°$) for four levels of applied stress intensity factor, $K_I/\sigma_Y l^{1/2} = 2, 5, 10$ and 20. The material properties are given in (8.27). The interception of each curve with the horizontal line $\sigma_e/\sigma_Y = 1$ separates the plastic yielding from elastic deformation. The deformation outside the plastic zone is essentially the elastic K_I field, as evidenced by the straight line with the slope of $-1/2$ for large r. At a small distance r to the crack tip, all curves approach to another set of straight lines, with the absolute value of the slope larger or equal to $1/2$. This confirms that the crack tip field in MSG plasticity is more singular than the HRR field in classical plasticity; the order of stress singularity exceeds or equals to the square-root singularity in the elastic K_I field. It is also observed from Figure 8. 10 that the plastic zone size increases rapidly with the applied loading. The plastic zone size for $K_I/\sigma_Y l^{1/2} = 20$ is approximately 100 times that for $K_I/\sigma_Y l^{1/2} = 2$. However, the size of the dominance zone of the crack tip field in MSG plasticity increases relatively slow with the applied loading; the size of the dominance zone for $K_I/\sigma_Y l^{1/2} = 20$ is less than twice of that for $K_I/\sigma_Y l^{1/2} = 2$.

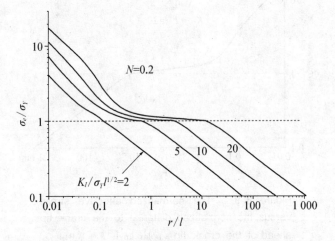

Figure 8. 10   The distribution of effective stress σ_e ahead of the crack tip (polar angle $\theta = 1.014°$) for different remotely applied elastic stress intensity factors. (Jiang et al. , 2001)

Figure 8. 11 shows the effect of plastic work hardening on the effective stress distribution ahead of the crack tip (polar angle $\theta = 1.014°$). The applied stress intensity factor is $K_I/\sigma_Y l^{1/2} = 10$, and the plastic work hardening exponent are $N = 0.2, 0.33, 0.5$. One interesting observation is that, at small distance r to the crack tip, all curves approach straight lines that have the same slope. This means the crack tip singularity in MSG plasticity is essentially independent of the plastic work hardening exponent. It is, in fact, consistent with the asymptotic analysis of the crack tip field in MSG plasticity (Shi et al., 2000). Shi et al. (2000) showed that, near a crack tip in MSG plasticity, the strain gradient term $l\eta$ is more singular than the strain term, $\sigma_{ref}^2 f^2(\varepsilon_e)$. Therefore, the strain gradient term dominates such that the crack tip field is essentially independent of the uniaxial strain-stress relation $\sigma_{ref} f(\varepsilon_e)$ and therefore does not depend on the plastic work hardening exponent N. The numerical results in the present study confirm this prediction. In terms of dislocation terminologies, this means that the density of geometrically necessary dislocations is much higher than that of statistically stored dislocations near a crack tip, and therefore dominates the flow stress from the Taylor model.

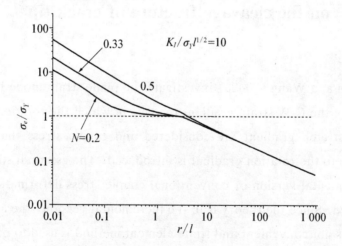

Figure 8.11　The distribution of effective stress σ_e ahead of the crack tip (polar angle $\theta = 1.014°$) for different plastic work hardening exponent N. (Jiang et al., 2001)

The above observations, in conjunction with the SSV model (Suo et al., 1993; Beltz et al., 1996), provide the following multiscale view of cleavage fracture in ductile materials: (i) At the scale as small as the dislocation spacing, the SSV model governs the crack tip behavior, i.e. , there exists a core free of dislocations around the crack tip. (ii) At a larger scale that is at least one order of magnitude larger than dislocation spacing and is comparable to the internal material length l, geometrically necessary dislocations begin to dominate, and MSG plasticity governs the crack tip behavior. (iii) At a distance much larger than the internal material length l, MSG plasticity degenerates to classical plasticity, and statistically stored dislocations play a dominating role in the plastic work hardening of materials. This multiscale view of fracture provides a reasonable picture for cleavage fracture in ductile materials.

8.3   Application of C-W strain gradient plasticity on the cleavage fracture of crack tip

Chen and Wang (2002a) investigate the plane strain mode I crack tip field using the C-W strain gradient theory, in which the rotation gradient and the stretch gradient are considered and couple stress that is work conjugate to the rotation gradient is introduced. The essential structure of the incremental version of conventional couple stress deformation theory is retained. Since the theory is in the incremental version, the asymptotic analysis is not convenient and finite element method is used to provide the near-tip stress and strain distributions for mode I crack tip field.

8.3.1   Brief review of the C-W strain gradient plasticity theory

In fact, the present new strain gradient theory is the combination of the strain gradient theory proposed by Chen and Wang (2002b) and the hardening law given by Chen and Wang (2000a). It preserves the essential structure of the incremental version of conventional couple stress deformation theory and no extra boundary value conditions beyond the conventional ones, are required. No higher-order stress or higher-order strain rates are introduced either. The key features of the new theory are that the rotation gradient influences the material character through the interaction between the Cauchy stresses and the couple stresses; the stretch gradient measures explicitly enter the constitutive relations only through the instantaneous tangent modulus and the boundary value problem of incremental equilibrium is the same as in the conventional theories. The tangent hardening modulus is influenced by not only the generalized effective strain but also the effective stretch gradient.

The strain gradient theory proposed by Chen and Wang (2001, 2002b) is briefly reviewed here. It preserves the basic structure of the general couple stress theory and involves no higher-order stress or higher-order strain rates. Its key features are that the rotation gradient influences the material behavior through the interaction between Cauchy stresses and couple stresses, while the stretch gradient explicitly enters the constitutive relations through the instantaneous tangent modulus. The tangent hardening modulus is influenced by not only the generalized effective strain but also the effective stretch gradient.

In a Cartesian reference frame x_i, the strain tensor ε_{ij} and the stretch gradient tensor η_{ijk} (Smyshlyaev and Fleck, 1996) are related to the displacement u_i by

$$\varepsilon_{ij} = \frac{1}{2}(u_{i,j} + u_{j,i}), \quad \eta_{ijk} = u_{k,ij} \tag{8.28}$$

The rotation gradient is related with the independent micro-rotation vectors ω_i

$$\chi_{ij} = \omega_{i,j} \tag{8.29}$$

The effective strain, effective rotation gradient and effective stretch gradient are defined as

$$\varepsilon_e = \sqrt{\frac{2}{3}\varepsilon'_{ij}\varepsilon'_{ij}}, \quad \chi_e = \sqrt{\frac{2}{3}\chi'_{ij}\chi'_{ij}}, \quad \eta_1 = \sqrt{\eta^{(1)}_{ijk}\eta^{(1)}_{ijk}} \qquad (8.30)$$

where ε'_{ij}, χ'_{ij} are the deviatoric part of the counterparts and the definition of $\eta^{(1)}_{ijk}$ can be found in (Smyshlyaev and Fleck, 1996).

The constitutive relation are as follows

$$\sigma_{ij} = \frac{2\Sigma_e}{3E_e}\varepsilon'_{ij} + K\varepsilon_m\delta_{ij}, \quad m_{ij} = \frac{2\Sigma_e}{3E_e}l^2_{cs}\chi'_{ij} + K_1 l^2_{cs}\chi_m\delta_{ij} \qquad (8.31)$$

$$\begin{cases} E^2_e = \varepsilon^2_e + l^2_{cs}\chi^2_e, \quad \Sigma_e = (\sigma^2_e + l^{-2}_{cs}m^2_e)^{1/2} \\[2mm] \sigma^2_e = \frac{3}{2}s_{ij}s_{ij}, \quad m^2_e = \frac{3}{2}m'_{ij}m'_{ij} \end{cases} \qquad (8.32)$$

E_e is called the effective generalized strain and Σ_e is the work conjugate of E_e; l_{cs} is an intrinsic material length, which reflects the effects of rotation gradient on the material behaviors; K is the volumetric modulus and K_1 is the bend-torsion volumetric modulus.

In order to consider the influence of stretch gradient, the new hardening law (Chen and Wang, 2000) is introduced

$$\begin{cases} \dot{\Sigma}_e = A'(E_e)\left(1 + \frac{l_1\eta_1}{E_e}\right)^{\frac{1}{2}}\dot{E}_e = B(E_e, l_1\eta_1)\dot{E}_e, \quad \Sigma_e \geqslant \sigma_Y \\[3mm] \dot{\Sigma}_e = 3\mu\dot{E}_e, \quad \Sigma_e < \sigma_Y \end{cases} \qquad (8.33)$$

where $B(E_e, l_1\eta_1)$ is the hardening function; l_1 is the second intrinsic material length associated with the stretch gradient, σ_Y is the yield stress and μ the shear modulus.

The equilibrium relations in V are

$$\sigma_{ij,j} = 0, \quad m_{ij,j} = 0 \qquad (8.34)$$

The traction boundary conditions for force and moment are

$$\sigma_{ij}n_j = T^0_i \quad \text{on } S_T, \quad m_{ij}n_j = q^0_i \quad \text{on } S_q \qquad (8.35)$$

The additional boundary conditions are

$$u_i = u_i^0, \text{ on } S_u, \ \omega_i = \omega_i^0 \text{ on } S_\omega \qquad (8.36)$$

According to Eqs. (8.31), the constitutive relations of the C-W deformation theory in incremental form are

$$\begin{cases} \dot\sigma_{ij} = 2\mu\,\dot\varepsilon'_{ij} + K\dot\varepsilon_m\delta_{ij} \\ \dot m_{ij} = 2\mu l_{cs}^2\dot\chi'_{ij} + K_1 l_{cs}^2\dot\chi_m\delta_{ij} \end{cases}, \ \Sigma_e < \sigma_Y \qquad (8.37)$$

$$\begin{cases} \dot\sigma_{ij} = \dfrac{2\Sigma_e}{3E_e}\dot\varepsilon'_{ij} + \dfrac{2\dot\Sigma_e}{3E_e}\varepsilon'_{ij} - \dfrac{2\Sigma_e}{3E_e^2}\varepsilon'_{ij}\dot E_e + K\dot\varepsilon_m\delta_{ij} \\[3mm] \dot m_{ij} = \dfrac{2\Sigma_e}{3E_e}l_{cs}^2\dot\chi'_{ij} + \dfrac{2\dot\Sigma_e}{3E_e}l_{cs}^2\dot\chi'_{ij} - \dfrac{2\Sigma_e}{3E_e^2}l_{cs}^2\chi'_{ij}\dot E_e + K_1 l_{cs}^2\dot\chi_m\delta_{ij} \end{cases}, \ \Sigma_e \geqslant \sigma_Y$$

$$(8.38)$$

8.3.2   Numerical formulation with strain gradient effects

a) The nodal degrees of freedom

Due to the independent parameter ω_i is introduced in addition to the displacement u_i in the present strain gradient theory, which is different from the theory proposed by Fleck and Hutchinson (1993), one node has six degrees of freedom. For a 2D plane case there are three degrees of freedom, i.e. u_{ix}, u_{iy} and ω_i. The displacement field and the rotation vector field can be obtained through the shape function and the nodal displacement and nodal rotation vectors, i.e.

$$u_x = \sum_{i=1}^n N_i u_{ix}, \ u_y = \sum_{i=1}^n N_i u_{iy}, \ \omega = \sum_{i=1}^n N_i\omega_i \qquad (8.39)$$

b) The stiffness matrix D

It is noted that this kind of strain gradient theory belongs to the non-linear elastic problem. While the current flow stress Σ_e is less than the yield stress σ_Y, i.e. the material is in the linear elastic state, the elastic D matrix is the same as the classical one. While the current flow stress Σ_e is larger than the yield stress σ_Y, D matrix is

$$\left\{ \begin{array}{l} D_{11} = K + \dfrac{4\Sigma_e}{9E_e} + \dfrac{4}{81E_e^2}(2\varepsilon_{xx} - \varepsilon_{yy})^2 \left[A'(E_e)\left(1 + \dfrac{l_1\eta_1}{E_e}\right)^{1/2} - \dfrac{\Sigma_e}{E_e} \right] \\[3mm] D_{12} = K - \dfrac{2\Sigma_e}{9E_e} + \dfrac{4}{81E_e^2}(2\varepsilon_{xx} - \varepsilon_{yy})(2\varepsilon_{yy} - \varepsilon_{xx}) \left[A'(E_e)\left(1 + \dfrac{l_1\eta_1}{E_e}\right)^{1/2} - \dfrac{\Sigma_e}{E_e} \right] \\[3mm] D_{13} = \dfrac{2}{27E_e^2}(2\varepsilon_{xx} - \varepsilon_{yy})\gamma_{xy} \left[A'(E_e)\left(1 + \dfrac{l_1\eta_1}{E_e}\right)^{1/2} - \dfrac{\Sigma_e}{E_e} \right] \\[3mm] D_{14} = \dfrac{4l^2}{27E_e^2}(2\varepsilon_{xx} - \varepsilon_{yy})\chi_{zx} \left[A'(E_e)\left(1 + \dfrac{l_1\eta_1}{E_e}\right)^{1/2} - \dfrac{\Sigma_e}{E_e} \right] \\[3mm] D_{15} = \dfrac{4l^2}{27E_e^2}(2\varepsilon_{xx} - \varepsilon_{yy})\chi_{zy} \left[A'(E_e)\left(1 + \dfrac{l_1\eta_1}{E_e}\right)^{1/2} - \dfrac{\Sigma_e}{E_e} \right] \end{array} \right. \tag{8.40}$$

$$\left\{ \begin{array}{l} D_{22} = K + \dfrac{4\Sigma_e}{9E_e} + \dfrac{4}{81E_e^2}(2\varepsilon_{yy} - \varepsilon_{xx})^2 \left[A'(E_e)\left(1 + \dfrac{l_1\eta_1}{E_e}\right)^{1/2} - \dfrac{\Sigma_e}{E_e} \right] \\[3mm] D_{23} = \dfrac{2}{27E_e^2}(2\varepsilon_{yy} - \varepsilon_{xx})\gamma_{xy} \left[A'(E_e)\left(1 + \dfrac{l_1\eta_1}{E_e}\right)^{1/2} - \dfrac{\Sigma_e}{E_e} \right] \\[3mm] D_{24} = \dfrac{4l^2}{27E_e^2}(2\varepsilon_{yy} - \varepsilon_{xx})\chi_{zx} \left[A'(E_e)\left(1 + \dfrac{l_1\eta_1}{E_e}\right)^{1/2} - \dfrac{\Sigma_e}{E_e} \right] \\[3mm] D_{25} = \dfrac{4l^2}{27E_e^2}(2\varepsilon_{yy} - \varepsilon_{xx})\chi_{zy} \left[A'(E_e)\left(1 + \dfrac{l_1\eta_1}{E_e}\right)^{1/2} - \dfrac{\Sigma_e}{E_e} \right] \end{array} \right. \tag{8.41}$$

$$\left\{ \begin{array}{l} D_{33} = \dfrac{\Sigma_e}{3E_e} + \dfrac{\gamma_{xy}^2}{9E_e^2} \left[A'(E_e)\left(1 + \dfrac{l_1\eta_1}{E_e}\right)^{1/2} - \dfrac{\Sigma_e}{E_e} \right] \\[3mm] D_{34} = \dfrac{2l^2}{9E_e^2}\gamma_{xy}\chi_{zx} \left[A'(E_e)\left(1 + \dfrac{l_1\eta_1}{E_e}\right)^{1/2} - \dfrac{\Sigma_e}{E_e} \right] \\[3mm] D_{35} = \dfrac{2l^2}{9E_e^2}\gamma_{xy}\chi_{zy} \left[A'(E_e)\left(1 + \dfrac{l_1\eta_1}{E_e}\right)^{1/2} - \dfrac{\Sigma_e}{E_e} \right] \end{array} \right. \tag{8.42}$$

$$\left\{ \begin{array}{l} D_{44} = \dfrac{2l^2\Sigma_e}{3E_e} + \dfrac{4l^4}{9E_e^2}\chi_{zx}^2 \left[A'(E_e)\left(1 + \dfrac{l_1\eta_1}{E_e}\right)^{1/2} - \dfrac{\Sigma_e}{E_e} \right] \\[3mm] D_{45} = \dfrac{4l^4}{9E_e^2}\gamma_{zx}\chi_{zy} \left[A'(E_e)\left(1 + \dfrac{l_1\eta_1}{E_e}\right)^{1/2} - \dfrac{\Sigma_e}{E_e} \right] \\[3mm] D_{55} = \dfrac{2l^2\Sigma_e}{3E_e} + \dfrac{4l^4}{9E_e^2}\chi_{zy}^2 \left[A'(E_e)\left(1 + \dfrac{l_1\eta_1}{E_e}\right)^{1/2} - \dfrac{\Sigma_e}{E_e} \right] \end{array} \right. \tag{8.43}$$

8.3.3 Finite element computation for crack tip in homogeneous materials

a) Choice of elements

Many researchers have found that the choice of element for gradient plasticity is complicated and in particular, quite sensitive to details of the constitutive relation. Xia and Hutchinson (1996) have discussed some choices of finite elements for strain gradient plasticity with the emphasis on plane strain cracks. Several elements have been developed for the phenomenological theory of strain gradient plasticity to investigate the crack tip field, microindentation experiments and stress concentrations around a hole. A review of these elements can be found in the paper by Shu, King and Fleck (1999).

In order to consider the strain gradient, the constant strain element is excluded since there is no strain gradient in this kind of element. For the two-dimensional case, such as the problem of plane strain and the axis-symmetry, second-order element can be used, such as the eight-node and nine-node elements.

Two kinds of elements have been used in Chen and Wang (2002) to study the plane strain crack tip fields. One is the eight-node isoparametric element and the other is the nine-node isoparametric element. Results for these two kind of elements are almost the same so only the results for 9-node element are given below. The displacement and rotation vectors in the element are interpolated through the shape function, whereas the strain and the rotation gradient tensors in the element are then obtained via Eq. (8.28)–Eq. (8.30). This element is only suitable for solids with vanishing higher-order stress traction on the surface. For example, the element has worked very well in the fracture analysis of strain gradient plasticity (Wei and Hutchinson, 1997; Chen, Wei et al., 1999), where the higher-order stress tractions vanish on the crack face and on the remote boundary. This element also works well in the study of microindentation experiments (Huang, et al. , 2000b) because the higher-order stress tractions are zero on the indented surface. Since the C-W strain gradient theory does not include higher-order stress and higher-order stress tractions, these kind of elements will work well in the study of plane strain crack tip field as discussed in the next section.

b) *Computation model*

The plane strain crack tip field is studied and the domain for the finite element analysis is a circle, whose central point is at the crack tip and the radius is $R = 1000 l_{cs}$ as shown in Figure 8.12, in which we

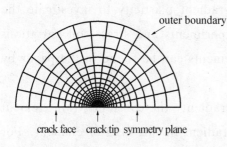

take $R = 3000 \ \mu m$ as the circle radius, i.e. the reference material parameter $l_{cs} = 3.0 \ \mu m$. It should be pointed out that the internal material length l_{cs} has been used to normalize r and K_I in the following text and does not appear explicitly in the non-dimensional stress distributions. Here $l_{cs} =$

Figure 8.12   Finite element mesh for crack tip problem using nine-node iso-parametric element with $R = 1000 l_{cs}$.

$3.0 \ \mu m$ is only a length related with the computation domain. The classical K fields are imposed on the outer boundary. For the small scale yielding configuration, only the upper half geometry is made discrete by the symmetry of the problem. A fine mesh is used near the crack tip, around which the smallest element size is on the order of $10^{-3} l_{cs}$, and effort is made to ensure elements having aspect ratio close to 1. The computation model is shown in Figure 8.12. Several kinds of size ratios of neighboring element are computed and it is found that the ratio has little influence on the calculating results. In the next section all the results are calculated adopting 1.2 of the neighboring element size ratio.

c) *Boundary conditions*

In the above section it is mentioned that the classical K field is imposed on the outer boundary and the detail normal and tangent stress tractions are as follows,

$$
\begin{cases}
\sigma_{rr} = \dfrac{K_I}{\sqrt{2\pi r}} \cos \dfrac{\theta}{2} \left(1 + \sin^2 \dfrac{\theta}{2} \right) \\[4mm]
\sigma_{r\theta} = \dfrac{K_I}{2\sqrt{2\pi r}} \cos \dfrac{\theta}{2} \sin \theta
\end{cases}
\tag{8.44}
$$

where K_I is the stress intensity factor of mode I crack tip field. (r, θ) is the polar coordinate that the origin point is located at the crack tip.

The couple stress tractions on the outer boundary are taken as

$$
m_{rr} = m_{\theta r} = 0 \tag{8.45}
$$

On the boundary of the symmetric axis $(x > 0, y = 0)$, the displacement u_y, the micro-rotation ω_z and shear stress τ_{xy} are vanish.

On the crack surface, the stress tractions and the couple stress tractions are all vanish.

d) Numerical results

Numerical solutions obtained using the finite element methods are presented in this section. The 9-noded isoparametric element with three freedoms for each node is used and the mesh is shown in Figure 8.12. The results presented below were computed with $\sigma_Y/E = 0.2\%$, $\nu = 0.3$, $R = 1\,000 l_{cs}$, although calculations were also carried out for other values of these parameters.

If the internal lengths l_{cs} and l_1 are zero, the strain gradient theory degenerates to be the classical theory. Figure 8.13 shows the normalized effective stresses, σ_e/σ_Y, at polar angle $\theta = 0°$ versus the normalized distance r/l_{cs} ahead of the crack tip for the classical plasticity deformation theory (without strain gradient effects) and the plastic hardening exponent takes $n = 0.2$. Theoretical results of classical HRR solution and K field solution are shown in Figure 8.13 also. The remotely applied stress intensity is $K_I/(\sigma_Y l_{cs}^{1/2}) = 20$. Here, it must be noted that during the finite element calculation we take $l_{cs} = l_1 = 0$ which means that no strain gradient effects are considered, l_{cs} in the normalized distance r/l_{cs} is not zero but the same as that used in the computation model, i.e. $l_{cs} = 3$ μm. While the curves of the theoretical results are drawn $l_{cs} = 3$ μm is also used to normalize the distance. From Figure 8.13 we can find that the slope of near tip field is almost $-n/(n+1)$, which is consistent with the theoretical HRR field. Remote from the crack tip, the field tends to be K field with the slope to be $-1/2$. The calculation results are consistent with the theoretical results, which proves that the present calculation result (without strain gradient effects) is right.

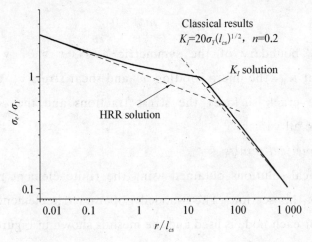

Figure 8.13　Distributions of normalized effective stresses σ_e/σ_Y ahead of the crack tip at polar angle $\theta = 0°$ versus the normalized distance r/l_{cs} for the conventional plasticity deformation theory with external loading $K_I/(\sigma_Y l_{cs}^{1/2}) = 20$.

In order to compare the results with those in Jiang et al. (2001), Chen and Wang (2002) first take the relation between the internal material lengths as $l_1 = l_{cs}$.

Figure 8.14 shows the normalized effective stresses, σ_e/σ_Y at polar angle $\theta = 0°$ versus the normalized distance r/l_{cs} for the C-W strain gradient theory with the plastic hardening exponent $n = 0.2$ and $l_1 = l_{cs}$. The remotely applied stress intensity factor is $K_I/(\sigma_Y l_{cs}^{1/2}) = 20$. The

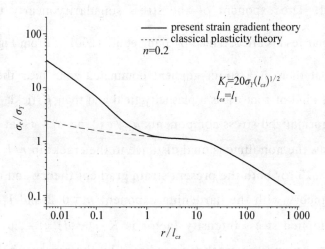

Figure 8. 14   Distributions of normalized effective stresses σ_e/σ_Y ahead of the crack tip at polar angle $\theta = 0°$ versus the normalized distance r/l_{cs} with the external loading $K_1/(\sigma_Y l_{cs}^{1/2}) = 20$ for C-W strain gradient theory and the classical plasticity deformation theory.

plastic zone size is a bit more than $10 l_{cs}$, which is almost the same as that in Jiang et al. (2001) with the same stress intensity factor. The corresponding stress distribution in classical plasticity (without strain gradient effects) is also shown in Figure 8. 14. It is observed that, outside the plastic zone, both the present strain gradient theory and the classical plasticity theory give the same straight line with slope $-1/2$, which corresponds to the elastic K field. The predictions of the present strain gradient theory and the classical plasticity theory are almost the same within the plastic zone at a distance larger than $0.3 l_{cs}$ to the crack tip, which also agrees with the estimates in Jiang et al. (2001) and Xia and Hutchinson (1996). The physical reasonability can be found in Jiang et al. (2001). At a distance of $0.1 l_{cs}$ to the crack tip, the effective stress given by the C-W strain gradient theory is much higher than that in classical plasticity and the absolute value of the slope is larger than that for the HRR field, which means that the stress singularity around the crack tip in the C-W strain gradient theory is stronger than that of the

HRR field. The exponent of the stress singularity nearly tends to be $-\frac{1}{2}$. Similar results are obtained by Jiang et al. (2001). From Figure 8.14, it is found that there is a strain gradient dominated zone near the crack tip, outside this kind of zone, it is a plasticity field and then K field.

The normalized stress components σ_{rr}/σ_Y and $\sigma_{\theta\theta}/\sigma_Y$ at polar angle $\theta = 0°$ versus the non-dimensional distance to the crack tip r/l_{cs} are shown in Figure 8.15 for both the present strain gradient theory and the classical plasticity theory with the hardening exponent $n = 0.2$ and $l_1 = l_{cs}$. The remotely applied stress intensity factor is $K_I/(\sigma_Y l_{cs}^{1/2}) = 20$. The stress components around the crack tip predicted by the present theory and the classical plasticity theory are different within a distance of $0.1 l_{cs}$ and the former is larger than the latter. From Figure 8.15 we can find that the transition is clearly observed from the remote elastic K field to a plasticity field, then to the strain gradient dominated field.

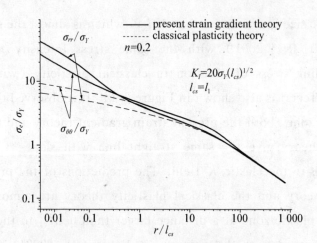

Figure 8.15   Normalized stress components σ_{rr}/σ_Y, $\sigma_{\theta\theta}/\sigma_Y$ distributions versus the normalized distance r/l_{cs} for C-W strain gradient theory and the classical plasticity theory.

According to Begley and Hutchinson (1998) and Stolken and Evans (1998), the relation between the intrinsic material lengths l_{cs} and l_1

basically is $l_1 \approx 0.1 l_{cs}$.

Figure 8.16 shows the normalized effective stresses, σ_e / σ_Y, at polar angle $\theta = 0°$ versus the normalized distance r / l_{cs} for the present strain gradient theory with the plastic hardening exponent $n = 0.2$ and $l_1 = 0.1 l_{cs}$. The remotely applied stress intensity factor in Figure 8.16 is $K_I / (\sigma_Y l_{cs}^{1/2}) = 20$. It must be noted that the relation between the intrinsic lengths l_1 and l_{cs} is different from that in Figure 8.14. The plastic zone size is a bit more than $10 l_{cs}$. The corresponding stress distribution in classical plasticity (without strain gradient effects) is also shown in Figure 8.16. Outside the plastic zone, it is observed that both the present C-W strain gradient theory and the classical plasticity theory give the same straight line with slope $-1/2$, which corresponds to the elastic K field. The predictions of the present strain gradient theory and the classical plasticity theory are almost the same within the plastic zone at a distance larger than $0.06 l_{cs}$ to the crack tip. At a distance of $0.03 l_{cs}$ to

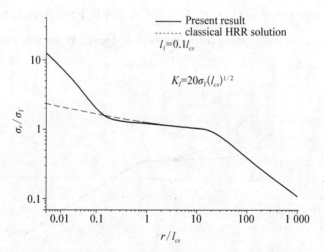

Figure 8.16   Distributions of normalized effective stresses σ_e / σ_Y ahead of the crack tip at polar angle $\theta = 0°$ versus the normalized distance r / l_{cs} with the external loading $K_I / (\sigma_Y l_{cs}^{1/2}) = 20$ and $n = 0.2$, $l_1 = 0.1 l_{cs}$ for C-W strain gradient theory and the classical plasticity deformation theory.

the crack tip, the effective stress given by the C-W strain gradient theory is much higher than that in classical plasticity and the absolute value of the slope is larger than that for the HRR field, which means that the stresses around the crack tip in the C-W strain gradient theory are more singular than the HRR field. The order of the stress singularity nearly tends to be $-1/2$. From Figure 8.16 one can also find that there is a strain gradient dominated zone near the crack tip, remote from the crack tip, it is a plasticity field and then K field dominates the outer field.

In Figure 8.17, materials with various hardening exponents are calculated and the effects of the hardening exponents on the effective stress distribution ahead of the crack tip are shown in Figure 8.17. The remotely applied stress intensity factor is $K_I/(\sigma_Y l_{cs}^{1/2}) = 10$ also and $l_1 = 0.1 l_{cs}$. The hardening exponents are $n = 0.1, 0.2, 0.33$. One can find from Figure 8.17 that near the crack tip there is a domain dominated by the strain gradient, the slope is hardly related to the hardening exponents and nearly the same as that of classical K field. Remotely from the crack tip, there are a plastic field and classical K field. With the same remotely

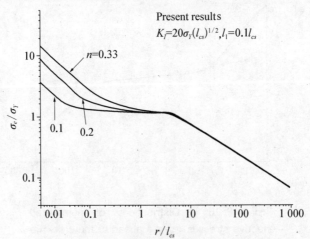

Figure 8.17 Normalized effective stresses σ_e/σ_Y distributions versus the normalized distance r/l_{cs} for various hardening exponents with the external field $K_I/(\sigma_Y l_{cs}^{1/2}) = 10$ and $l_1 = 0.1 l_{cs}$ for the present C-W strain gradient theory.

stress intensity factor and different hardening exponents, the plastic domain size is almost the same but with different slope, the classical K fields are the same and have no relation to the hardening exponents. The larger the hardening exponents, the higher the effective stress near the crack tip in the strain gradient dominated domain with the same external stress field.

Figure 8.18 shows the normalized effective stress σ_e/σ_Y at polar angle $\theta = 0°$, versus the non-dimensional distance to the crack tip r/l_{cs} for three levels of remotely applied stress intensity factor, $K_I/(\sigma_Y l_{cs}^{1/2})$ $= 5$, 10, 20 and the other parameters are identical. From Figure 8.18, one can find that the size of the plastic zone increases quickly while the remotely applied stress intensity factor is increasing but the scale increase of near tip strain gradient dominated zone is not obvious and very slow, which shows that the strain gradient dominated zone is not sensitive to the outer K field and almost in the order of the intrinsic material length. From Figure 8.18 it is easy to find that all curves approach to another set of straight lines, at the small distance to the crack tip, and the slope of

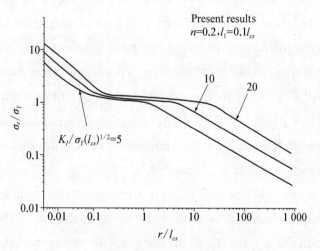

Figure 8.18　Distribution of normalized effective stress σ_e/σ_Y versus the normalized distance r/l_{cs} with different loading $K_I/(\sigma_Y l_{cs}^{1/2}) = 5$, 10, 20 for the present C-W strain gradient theory.

the set of straight lines tends to be the same as that of classical K field. All these phenomena can be found also in Jiang et al. (2001), which analyzed the crack tip field with MSG theory (Gao, et al., 1999b).

Above calculation results seem to be consistent with the SSV model of Suo et al. (1993). The SSV model assumes that there is an elastic zone of height D above the interface in the metal film rightly near the interface crack tip. The size of height D is the same as the dislocation spacing. Plastic deformation occurs outside the elastic zone. The SSV model provides a reasonable picture for cleavage fracture in interface between a ductile metal film and thick oxide substrate.

The present calculation results confirm that the exponent of the stress singularity nearly tends to be $-1/2$, in despite of different plastic hardening exponents were simulated. It means that immediately near the crack tip, there is an elastic dominated zone.

e) Discussion

Under remotely imposed classical K fields, plane strain mode I crack tip field at microscale based on the C-W strain gradient theory is studied, the full field solutions are obtained numerically for elastic-plastic materials with strain gradient effects. It is found that the stresses near the crack tip are significant influenced by strain gradient effects. For mode I fracture under small scale yielding condition, transition from the remote classical K field to the near tip strain gradient dominated zone goes through a plasticity field. The singularity exponent in the strain gradient dominated domain is independent of the material plastic hardening exponents and is almost $-1/2$.

At a distance that is much larger than the dislocation spacing such that continuum plasticity is expected to be applicable. The near tip stresses predicted by the C-W strain gradient theory are significantly higher than that in HRR field. The increase in the near tip stress level provides an explanation to the experimental observation of cleavage fracture in ductile materials (Elssner et al., 1994).

While the relation of the two length scales is $l_1 = l_{cs}$, the numerical results are almost the same as that in Jiang et al. (2001), which proves that the C-W strain gradient seems to be capable of bridging the gap between the macroscopic cracking and atomic fracture also.

8.3.4 Finite element computation for interface crack tip

The finite element method with C-W strain gradient theory is also used to analyze the interface crack tip field (Chen and Wang, 2002c). Several kinds of interface cracks are considered such as interface crack in bimaterial between an elastic-plastic solid and a rigid substrate, interface crack in bimaterial of two different elastic-plastic solids.

a) Comparison with Shih and Asaro (1988)

In order to verify the finite element program, the strain gradient is not considered first, i. e., $l_1 = l_{cs} = 0$ and the results will be compared with those in Shih and Asaro (1988). The calculation model is similar to that used in Shih and Asaro (1988). A large plate is loaded by remote uniform stresses, in which the upper material is elastic-plastic solid and the lower material is rigid substrate and a center crack exists on the interface. Only the right half of the deformable medium need to be considered in the finite element analysis since the problem possesses reflective symmetry with respect to the vertical plane bisecting the crack. The half-crack length is a, and the half-width and height of the deformable slab is $100a$. The finite-element model is constructed using 9-node quadrilateral Lagrangian elements and 3×3 Gauss points are used. The remote loading is expressed by σ_{22}^{∞} and σ_{11}^{∞}. We take the following loading as that used in Shih and Asaro (1988),

$$\sigma_{11}^{\infty} = \frac{\nu_1}{1 - \nu_1} \sigma_{22}^{\infty} \tag{8.46}$$

where ν_1 is the Poisson ratio and we take $\nu_1 = 0.3$ in the calculation.

The calculation results agree very well with those in Shih and Asaro

(1988). When the external loading is very small, $\sigma_{22}^{\infty}/\sigma_Y = 2.0 \times 10^{-5}$, the plastic zone is confined to a distance of about $10^{-11} a$, the small strain asymptotic field for an interface crack is characterized by oscillatory stresses and the oscillate can be significant fractions of the crack length, which has been obtained by Shih and Asaro (1988). The stress is negative within the plastic zone, the slope of the curve becomes positive for $r/a <$ 10^{-14}. At a higher load level, $\sigma_{22}^{\infty}/\sigma_Y = 6.0 \times 10^{-3}$, the hoop stress increases monotonically over the entire distance under discussion, i. e., there is no trace of an oscillatory field.

   b) *Interface crack in a bimaterial between an elastic-plastic solid and a rigid substrate*

   The interface crack with a rigid substrate is often found in engineering problems and here this special kind of case is calculated and the strain gradient is considered. A finite square plate subject to uniform tensile is considered and the calculation model is shown in Figure 8. 19, in which only the right half of the deformable medium is considered. The half of the crack length is a and the width of the calculated model is $10a$. On the boundary of $y = 0$, all the nodes are fixed in x and y direction. On the boundary of $y = 10a$, only normal stress σ_{22}^{∞} is imposed. On the left boundary, all the nodes are fixed in x direction for symmetry. Traction for both the force and moment is free on the right boundary. During the calculation the parameters of the upper material are $\sigma_y/E = 0.2\%$, $\nu = 0.3$, $n = 0.2$.

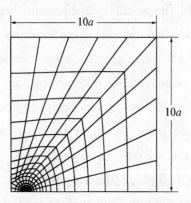

Figure 8. 19   Finite element mesh for an interface crack between a deformable material and a rigid substrate and only half of the deformable material is needed.

   In all the calculation, we take $l_{cs} = 1$ μm and stresses σ_{ij} are normalized by the yield stress σ_Y in uniaxial tension, while the distance r

to the crack tip is normalized by the internal material length l_{cs} in the C-W strain gradient theory proposed. The normalized remotely applied stress is $\sigma_{22}^{\infty}/\sigma_Y$.

Figure 8.20 shows the normalized effective stresses, σ_e/σ_Y, versus the non-dimensional distance to the crack tip, r/l_{cs}, ahead of the crack tip (at polar angle $\theta = 3.15°$) predicted by the C-W strain gradient theory. The remotely applied stress is $\sigma_{22}^{\infty}/\sigma_Y = 1/6$. There are four kinds of cases in Figure 8.20, in which three results are corresponding to different relations of l_{cs} and l_1, the other one is for the classical theory. Since the material length l_{cs} is taken prior, the value of l_1 for each case is known also. The horizontal line $\sigma_e/\sigma_Y = 1$ separates the elastic and plastic zones for each curve. Outside the plastic zone and $r/l_{cs} < 5$, both the present strain gradient theory and the classical plasticity theory give the same straight line with slope $-1/2$, which corresponds to the elastic K field. As $r/l_{cs} > 5$, there is an elastic field, which is influenced by the outer boundary. From Figure 8.20, one can find the interface crack tip field is significantly influenced the material length l_1 when $l_1 \geqslant 0.01 \ \mu m$. When $l_1 > 0.1 \ \mu m$, the HRR type field seems to vanish, there is no HRR type field, which is different from the results for crack tip field in homogeneous material (Jiang et al., 2001; Chen and Wang, 2002a). We call the plasticity zone in this kind of interface crack tip as the generalized plasticity zone. This interesting phenomenon may be due to the intrinsic properties of the interface crack between an elastic-plastic solid and a rigid substrate. Since the lower material is rigid substrate, the material points along interface in both directions are fixed, which results in the greater strain gradient along y direction near the interface. Hence the strain gradient could be larger than that in the homogeneous material. From Figure 8.20, one can see that the length scale l_1 has no effect on the size of the plastic zone size while the applied stress is the same. Since there is hardly classical plasticity zone existing for the strain gradient theory, the generalized plastic domain like the classical plasticity zone will increase accompany with the increasing external load. When the value of material length l_1 decrease, the result tends to the classical solution, which reflects that the length scale l_1 plays an important role in crack tip field.

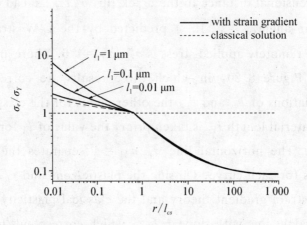

Figure 8. 20   Plots of the normalized effective stresses, σ_e / σ_Y, near the polar angle of $\theta =$ 3. 15° versus the normalized distance r/l_{cs} with different material length l_1.

Figure 8. 21 shows the normalized effective stress σ_e / σ_Y at polar angle $\theta = 3.15°$, versus the non-dimensional distance to the crack tip r/l_{cs} for three levels of remotely applied stress, $\sigma_{22} / \sigma_Y = 1/12$, 1/6 and 1/3. The relation $l_1 = l_{cs}$ is taken and the other parameters are the same as that in Figure 8. 20. The deformation outside the plastic zone is essentially the elastic K field, as evidenced by the straight line with the slope of $-1/2$ for large r, then it tends to be the zone influenced by the out limit boundary. At a small distance r to the crack tip, all curves approach to another set of straight lines, with the absolute value of the slope larger or equal to $1/2$. This confirms that the singularity of the crack tip stress field in C-W strain gradient theory is stronger than the classical field. It is also observed from Figure 8. 21 that the plastic zone size increases rapidly with the applied loading and there is no classical HRR type field, it is different from that in Jiang et al. (2001) and Chen and Wang (2002a) for the crack tip field in homogeneous material and in which the strain gradient dominated zone increases relatively slow with the applied loading, while the whole plastic zone size increases rapidly with the applied loading.

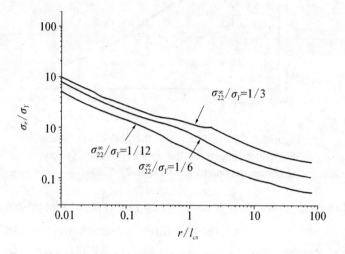

Figure 8.21　Plots of the normalized effective stress σ_e/σ_Y at $\theta = 3.15°$ versus the distance to the crack tip r/l_{cs} for three levels of applied stress, $\sigma_{22}^{\infty}/\sigma_Y = 1/12$, 1/6 and 1/3.

Figure 8.22 shows the normalized effective stresses versus the non-dimensional distance to the crack tip r/l_{cs} with different hardening exponents $n = 0.1, 0.2$, and 0.3 respectively. The remotely applied stress is the same as that in Figure 8.20 and $l_1 = l_{cs}$. One can find the effect of plastic work hardening on the effective stress distribution ahead of the crack tip (polar angle $\theta = 3.15°$). One interesting observation is that, at small distance r to the crack tip, all curves approach straight lines that have the same slope. This means the interface crack tip singularity in C-W strain gradient theory is essentially independent of the plastic work hardening exponent, which is the same as that in Jiang et al. (2001) and Chen and Wang (2002a). Furthermore, the larger the hardening exponents, the higher the effective stress near the crack tip in the strain gradient dominated domain with the same external loading.

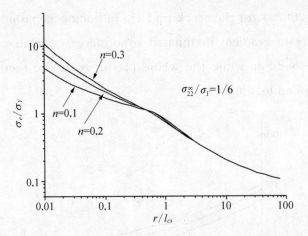

Figure 8.22   Plots of the effective stress distribution ahead of the crack tip with various hardening exponents $n = 0.1, 0.2, 0.333$.

c) Interface crack in a bimaterial of two general elastic-plastic solids

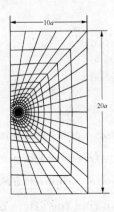

Figure 8.23   Finite element mesh of an interface crack in finite width plate and only half of the deformable medium is needed.

Here, the interface crack tip field in a bimaterial of two elastic-plastic solids is investigated. Also, we take a finite width plate as the calculation model, which is shown in Figure 8.23 and half of the crack length is a. Only half of the deformable medium needs to be considered in the finite element analysis due to the possesses reflective symmetry. The lower material is designated as material 1 and the upper material is designated as material 2. The mesh division is the same as that in Figure 8.19 except the lower deformable part is meshed.

We assume that both materials have the same elastic properties but different plastic properties. The parameters are taken as follows: $\sigma_y / E = 0.2\%$, $\nu = 0.3$, $n_1 = 0.3$, $n_2 = 0.1$, $l_1 = l_{cs}$. The applied load is $\sigma_{22}^\infty = \sigma_Y/6$, the traction for moment vanishes along the whole outside boundary.

Figure 8.24 and Figure 8.25 show the normalized effective stresses,

σ_e/σ_Y, along the polar angle of $\theta = -3.15°$ and $\theta = 3.15°$ versus the normalized distance r/l_{cs} for the lower material 1 and upper material 2, respectively. The corresponding stress distribution in classical plasticity (without strain gradient effects) is also shown in Figure 8.24 and Figure 8.25. It is observed that, outside the plastic zone (as determined by $\sigma_e/\sigma_Y \leqslant 1$), both the gradient theory and classical plasticity theory give the same straight line slope $-1/2$, corresponding to elastic K field. But it is also different from the solution to crack tip field in homogeneous materials that there is no HRR type field within the plastic zone. Once the plasticity is produced the effects of strain gradient are very large, which is due to the stiffness difference between the upper and lower material. The generalized plastic zone size can not be predicted because it changes as the external loading changes. Comparing Figure 8.24 with Figure 8.25, one can find that though the singularity in the strain gradient dominated domain is hardly related with the hardening exponents, the value of the effective stress is influenced by the hardening exponents and the larger the hardening exponents, the larger the effective stress in the strain gradient dominated domain for the interface crack tip field will be.

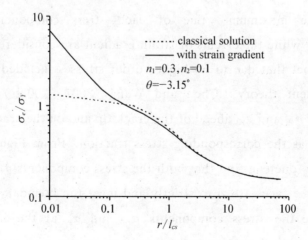

Figure 8.24　Plots of the normalized effective stress σ_e/σ_Y at $\theta = -3.15°$ versus the distance to the crack tip r/l_{cs} in the lower deformable material.

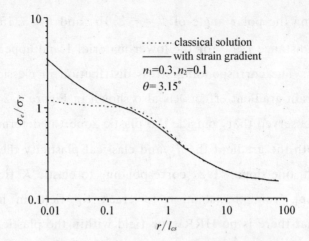

Figure 8. 25   Plots of the normalized effective stress σ_e/σ_Y at $\theta = 3.15°$ versus the distance to the crack tip r/l_{cs} in the upper deformable material.

To develop a better understanding of the interface crack tip field with strain gradient, the angular distribution is given at some distance from the crack tip and within the generalized plastic zone. Figure 8. 26 and Figure 8. 27 show the stress component distributions versus the polar angle without and with strain gradient effects, respectively, and the stress distributions in these two figures lie on the same radius. One can find that the absolute maximum value of each stress components increase significantly while the effects of strain gradient are considered. It should be pointed out that due to no higher order stresses included in the C-W strain gradient theory (Chen and Wang, 2001, 2002b), the stress components $\sigma_{\theta\theta}$ and $\sigma_{r\theta}$ ahead of the crack tip and on the crack free faces is the same as the corresponding stress traction. From Figure 8. 26 and Figure 8. 27, one can find that both the stress components $\sigma_{\theta\theta}$ and $\sigma_{r\theta}$ on the crack free faces are zero strictly and meet the boundary conditions. Furthermore the stress components σ_{rr} and σ_e at the interface are discontinuous but the other stress components are continuous. Comparing these two figures, one can also find that the discontinuity of the stress components for the C-W strain gradient theory are larger than that for classical plasticity theory, which denotes that the influences of the strain gradient effects on the stresses for materials with different hardening exponents are stronger than the influences of different hardening exponents on stresses.

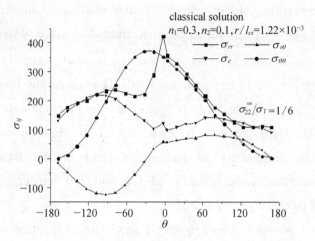

Figure 8.26　Plots of the stress components of classical plasticity solution at some distance from the crack tip versus the angle.

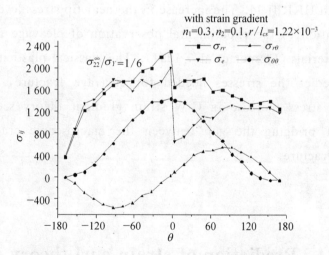

Figure 8.27　Plots of the stress components with strain gradient effects at some distance from the crack tip versus the angle.

d) Conclusions

For remotely imposed tension loading, several kinds of full field solutions are obtained numerically for different interface cracks, such as interface crack between two different deformable materials and interface crack between a deformable material and a rigid material.

It is found that the stresses near an interface crack tip are significant influenced by strain gradient effects. Under small scale yielding condition and $l_1 > 0.1$ μm, the remote classical K field goes directly to the near tip strain gradient dominated zone without a classical plasticity field. The material length scale l_1 has an important influence on the interface crack tip field and once the plasticity is produced, the effects of strain gradient dominate the field, which is different from that in homogeneous material. The singularity of the stress field in the strain gradient dominated domain is independent of the material hardening exponents and is equal to or larger than $r^{-1/2}$.

At a distance that is much larger than the dislocation spacing such that continuum plasticity is expected to be applicable. The near tip stresses predicted by the strain gradient theory are significantly higher than that in HRR field. The increase in the near tip stress level provides an explanation to the experimental observation of cleavage fracture in ductile materials (Elssner et al., 1994). The classical plasticity theories fail to predict the stresses needed for cleavage fracture, while the significant stress increase in C-W strain gradient theory seems to be capable of bridging the gap between the macroscopic cracking and atomistic fracture.

8.4 Prediction of strain-curl theory on plane-strain crack tip field

In this section, the strain curl theory proposed by Xia and Wang

(2004) in Chapter 6 is used to predict the plain strain crack tip field.

For the FEM formulation of a plane-strain problem, suppose that the z-axis is parallel to the crack front, the y-axis perpendicular to the crack surface and the positive half of the x-axis lying ahead of the crack, as shown in Figure 8. 28.

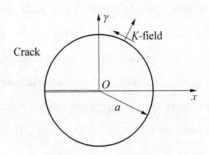

Figure 8. 28   The calculated domain. The crack tip field is induced by a linear elastic mode- I K-field.

The non-vanishing displacement and micro rotation components in a plane-strain problem are

$$u_x = u_x(x, y), \ u_y = u_y(x, y), \ \omega_z = \omega_z(x, y) \qquad (8.47)$$

The J-integral of a plane-strain mode- I crack is

$$J_1 = \int_{\Gamma} (wn_1 - n_{\alpha}\sigma_{\alpha\beta}u_{\beta, 1})d\Gamma \qquad (8.48)$$

where Γ is a contour starting from the lower surface of the crack and ending at the upper one; n_{α} is the normal of Γ; $\alpha, \beta = 1, 2$; w is the strain energy density and

$$w = \int \sigma_{ij}d\varepsilon_{ij} + \int m_{ij}d\chi_{ij} \qquad (8.49)$$

The calculated domain was a circular domain centered at the crack tip as shown in Figure 8. 28. The radius of the circular domain was a. The classical mode- I K-field was imposed on the outer boundary of this domain. The crack surface was supposed to be traction-free and the elastic stress intensity factor, K_I, of the remotely applied field increased monotonically.

An eight-noded isoparametric element was chosen and each node had three degrees of freedom. The value of l_1/a was about 10^{-7} to 10^{-3} and the size of the smallest elements was less than $10^{-3}l_1$. Efforts were paid to make the ratio of the length to the width of the elements approximate to unit. Only the upper half of the domain was calculated due to the symmetric condition. The half domain was divided circumferentially into 12 portions and radially into N_r portions, respectively. In order to investigate the influence of the mesh, the value of N_r was taken as 50 and 100 respectively. The calculated results are shown in Figure 8.29. It is evident that results when $N_r = 50$ and 100 are almost identical, so N_r is taken as 50 in the following calculations.

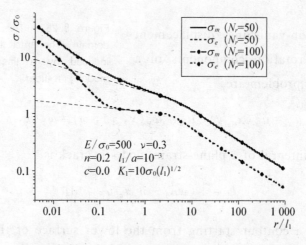

Figure 8.29   Calculated equivalent stress σ_e and mean stress σ_m with different mesh density.

In order to verify the reliability of the finite element program, the case of conventional plasticity was investigated first. Taking the material length scale l_1 as zero, the comparison was made with the result of Chen and Wang (2002a). Both the two results are plotted in Figure 8.30. The parameters are chosen as same as Chen and Wang (2002a) did, i.e. the reference length scale $l_0 = 10^{-3} a$, the ratio of yield strength to Young's modulus $\sigma_0/E = 0.2\%$, Poisson's ratio $\nu = 0.3$, hardening exponent $n = 0.2$ and stress intensity factor $K_I = 20 l_0^{1/2}$. In addition, the dimensionless constant c is taken as zero. The two results are almost identical.

Then the calculation was performed in the case of $l_1/a = 10^{-3}$, $\sigma_0/E = 0.2\%$, $\nu = 0.3$, $n = 0.2$, $K_I = 10\sigma_0 l_1^{1/2}$ and $c = 0$.

The calculated stresses ahead of crack tip (at polar angle $\theta = 3.18°$)

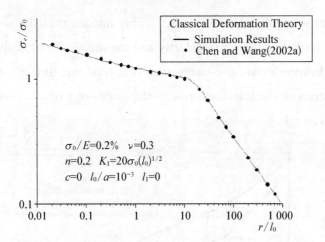

Figure 8.30 Comparison with the result by Chen and Wang (2002a).

are plotted in Figures 8.31 and 8.32. Figure 8.31 shows the distribution of normalized mean stress σ_m/σ_0 and equivalent stress σ_e/σ_0 versus normalized distance r/l_1 from the crack tip. Figure 8.32 shows the distribution of normalized stress components σ_{rr}/σ_0 and $\sigma_{\theta\theta}/\sigma_0$ versus r/l_1. It can be seen that the size of plastic zone (the range in which $\sigma_e/\sigma_0 \geqslant 1$) is a bit larger than $5l_1$. Elastic K-field exists beyond the plastic zone. The curves are all straight lines with a slope of $-1/2$ in the elastic zone. As the distance from crack tip r decreases, the curves are transited into the more even straight lines. This zone, ranging from about $0.2l_1$ to $5l_1$, is the range of HRR type field. The calculated results of plastic strain curl theory and conventional theory are identical in both elastic zone and HRR zone, which means that the effect of geometrically necessary dislocation density (or, in other words, plastic strain curl) is negligible in these two ranges. When $r < 0.2l_1$, geometrically necessary dislocation density (plastic strain curl) play an evident role. Therefore, the calculated results with plastic strain curl effect are much higher than the results with conventional plasticity in that range. This means that the calculated stress level at crack tip will be elevated greatly by the effect of plastic strain curl. By the way, the slope of mean stress curve is about $-1/2$ near the crack tip while the

equivalent stress curve is more inclined. This implies that the singularity of
mean stress is the square root singularity and the singularity of equivalent stress
is higher. However, since the mean stress is at least one time greater than the
equivalent stress in the calculated range, the slopes of stress component curves
are still nearly $-1/2$.

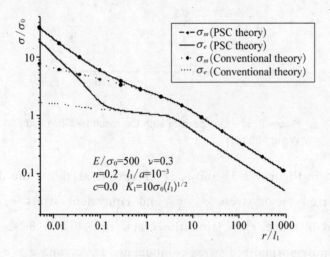

Figure 8.31   Normalized mean stress σ_m/σ_0 and
effective stress σ_e/σ_0 versus normalized distance r/l_1
from the crack tip.

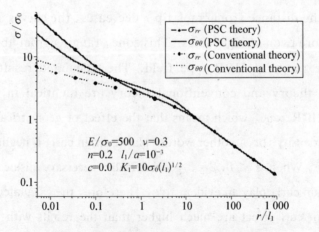

Figure 8.32   Normalized stress components σ_{rr}/σ_0
and $\sigma_{\theta\theta}/\sigma_0$ versus normalized distance r/l_1 from the
crack tip.

Figure 8.33 is the plot of normalized J-integral $JE/[(1-\nu^2)K_I^2]$ versus normalized distance r/l_1 from the crack tip. The calculated contours are 100 circles centered at the crack tip with different radii. It can be clearly observed that J-integral is path independent in the range of $r/l_1 \geqslant 0.1$.

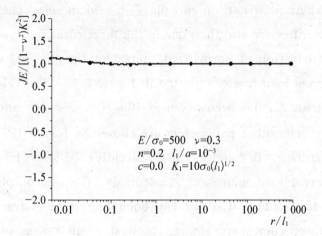

Figure 8.33   Normalized J-integral $JE/[(1-\nu^2)K_I^2]$
versus normalized distance r/l_1 from the crack tip.

The influence of exponent n is shown in Figure 8.34. The value of n has been taken to be 0.1, 0.2 and 0.3, respectively. The other parameters are chosen as $l_1/a = 10^{-3}$, $\sigma_0/E = 0.2\%$, $\nu = 0.3$, $K_I = 10\sigma_0$

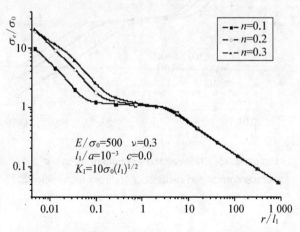

Figure 8.34   Normalized equivalent stress σ_e/σ_0
versus normalized distance r/l_1 from the crack tip.

$l_1^{1/2}$ and $c = 0$. It can be seen that the greater the value of hardening exponent n is, the higher the stress level in the plastic zone will be. In the range of HRR type field, the greater value of n leads to the steeper inclination of the curve. In fact, the stress singularity of HRR type field is $r^{-n/(n+1)}$. The slopes of three curves are approximately the same in the range where plastic strain curl plays an evident role. Therefore, the stress singularities are also the same in the three cases.

The distribution of normalized equivalent stress σ_e/σ_0 versus r/l_1 under different load levels is plotted in Figure 8.35. The value of stress intensity factor K_I has been taken as $10\sigma_0 l_1^{1/2}$, $20\sigma_0 l_1^{1/2}$ and $30\sigma_0 l_1^{1/2}$, respectively. The other parameters are chosen as $l_1/a = 10^{-3}$, $\sigma_0/E = 0.2\%$, $\nu = 0.3$, $n = 0.2$ and $c = 0$. Apparently, the stress level increases as the external load increases. Accordingly, the size of plastic zone, HRR type zone and plastic-strain-curl-dominating zone increase also. The slopes of three curves are almost identical in all ranges of calculated domain. It seems that stress singularity is independent on the load level.

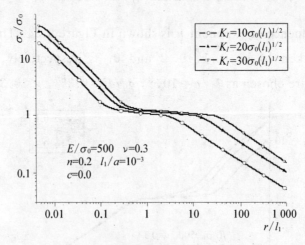

Figure 8.35 Normalized equivalent stress σ_e/σ_0 versus normalized distance r/l_1 from the crack tip.

References

Bagchi, A., and Evans, A. G., 1996. The mechanics and physics of thin film decohesion and its measurement. Interface Sci. 3, 169 – 193.

Beltz, G. E. , Rice, J. R. , Shih, C. F. and Xia, L. , 1996. A self-consistent model for cleavage in the presence of the plastic flow. Acta Mater. 44, 3943 – 3954.

Chen, J. Y. , Wei, Y. , Huang, Y. , Hutchinson, J. W. , Hwang, K. C. , 1999. The crack tip fields in strain gradient plasticity: the asymptotic and numerical analysis. Eng. Fracture Mech. 64, 2049 – 2068.

Chen, S. H. , Wang, T. C. , 2000. A new hardening law for strain gradient plasticity. Acta Mater. 48, 3997 – 4005.

Chen, S. H. , Wang, T. C. , 2001. Strain gradient theory with couple-stress for crystalline solids. Eur. J. Mech. A / Solids 20: 739 – 756.

Chen, S. H. and Wang, T. C. , 2002a. Finite element solutions for plane strain mode I crack with strain gradient effects. Int. J. Solids Struct. 39, 1241 – 1257.

Chen, S. H. , Wang, T. C. , 2002b. A new deformation theory for strain gradient effects. Int. J. Plasticity, 18, 971 – 995.

Chen, S. H. and Wang, T. C. , 2002c. Interface crack problem with strain gradient effects. Int. J. Fract. , 117, 25 – 37.

Drugan, W. J. , Rice, J. R. , and Sham, T. - L. , 1982. Asymptotic analysis of growing plane strain tensile cracks in elastic-ideally plastic solids. J. Mech. Phys. Solids 30, 447 – 473.

Elssner, G. , Korn, D. , Ruehle, M. , 1994. The influence of interface impurities on fracture energy of UHV diffusion bonded metal-ceramic bicrystals. Scripta Metall. Mater. 31, 1037 – 1042.

Fleck, N. A. , Hutchinson, J. W. , 1993. A phenomenological theory for strain gradient effects in plasticity. J. Mech. Phys. Solids 41, 1825 – 1857.

Fleck, N. A. , Muller, G. M. , Ashby, M. F. , Hutchinson, J. W. , 1994. Strain gradient plasticity: theory and experiment. Acta Metal. et Mater. 42, 475 – 487.

Freund, L. B. and Hutchinson, J. W. , 1985. High strain-rate crack growth in rate-dependent plastic solids. J. Mech. Phys. Solids 33, 169 – 191.

Gao, H. , Huang, Y. and Nix, W. D. , 1999a. Modeling plasticity at the micrometer scale. Naturwissenschaftler 86, 507 – 515.

Gao, H. , Huang, Y. , Nix, W. D. , Hutchinson, J. W. , 1999b. Mechanism-based strain gradient plasticity-I. theory. J. Mech. Phys. Solids 47, 1239 – 1263.

Huang, Y. , Gao, H. , Nix, W. D. , Hutchinson, J. W. , 2000a. Mechanism-based strain gradient plasticity-II. Analysis. J. Mech. Phys. Solids 48, 99 – 128.

Huang, Y. , Xue, Z. , Gao, H. , Nix, W. D. , Xia, Z. C. , 2000b. A study of microindentation hardness tests by mechanism-based strain gradient plasticity. J. Mater. Res. 15, 1786 – 1796.

Huang, Y., Zhang, L., Guo, T. F., Hwang, K. C., 1997. Mixed mode near-tip fields for cracks in materials with strain gradient effects. J. Mech. Phys. Solids 45, 439 – 465.

Hutchinson, J. W., 1968. Singular behavior at the end of a tensile crack in a hardening material. J. Mech. Phys. Solids 16, 13 – 31.

Jiang, H., Huang, Y., Zhuang, Z., Hwang, K. C., 2001. Fracture in mechanism-based strain gradient plasticity. J. Mech. Phys. Solids 49, 979 – 993.

McElhaney, K. W., Vlassak, J. J., Nix, W. D., 1998. Determination of indenter tip geometry and indentation contact area for depth-sensing indentation experiments. J. Mater. Res. 13, 1300 – 1306.

Needleman, A., 1987. A continuum model for void nucleation by inclusion debonding. J. Appl. Mech. 64, 525 – 531.

Rice, J. R. and Rosengren, G. F., 1968. Plane strain deformation near a crack tip in a power law hardening material. J. Mech. Phys. Solids 16, 1 – 12.

Shih, C. F., Asaro, R. J., 1988. Elastic-plastic analysis of cracks on bimaterial interfaces: Part I-small scale yielding. J. Appl. Mech., 55, 299 – 316.

Shi, M. X., Huang, Y., Gao, H., Hwang, K. C., 2000. Non-existence of separable crack tip field in mechanism-based strain gradient plasticity. Int. J. Solids Struct. 37, 5995 – 6010.

Shu, J. Y., King, W. E., Fleck, N. A., 1999. Finite elements for materials with strain gradient effects. Int. J. Numer. Methods Eng. 44, 373 – 391.

Smyshlyaev, V. P., Fleck, N. A., 1996. The role of strain gradients in the grain size effect for polycrystals. J. Mech. Phys. Solids 44, 465 – 495.

Stolken, J. S., Evans, A. G., 1998. A microbend test method for measuring the plasticity length scale. Acta Mater. 46, 5109 – 5115.

Suo, Z., Shih, C. F., Varias, A. G., 1993. A theory for cleavage cracking in the presence of plastic flow. Acta Metall. Mater. 41, 1551 – 1557.

Tvergarrd, V. and Hutchinson, J. W., 1992. The relation between crack growth resistance and fracture process parameters in elastic-plastic solids. J. Mech. Phys. Solids 40, 1377 – 1397.

Wei, Y., Hutchinson, J. W., 1997. Steady-state crack growth and work of fracture for solids characterized by strain gradient plasticity. J. Mech. Phys. Solids 45, 1253 – 1273.

Xia, Z. C., Hutchinson, J. W., 1996. Crack tip fields in strain gradient plasticity. J. Mech. Phys. Solids 44, 1621 – 1648.